The Personal History and Experience of David Copperfield the Younger

BY

CHARLES DICKENS

Abridged by Edith Freelove Smith
Illustrated by Harriet Savage Smith

New York
THE MACMILLAN COMPANY
1925

Set up and electrotyped.
Published September, 1925.

PRINTED IN THE UNITED STATES OF AMERICA BY
THE CORNWALL PRESS

CONTENTS

ILLUSTRATIONS

THE AUTHOR AND HIS BOOK

When an author is as genuinely beloved through his books as is Charles Dickens, we become interested in the man himself, his faults and his virtues, his failures and his successes. Formal biographies may give us facts about his life, histories tell of the great occurrences and social factors that form the background against which the events of his life move, and his friends relate incidents of which they know, giving us their estimate of the man and his achievements. But something is lacking—the man's own outlook upon life. We turn to his books and interpret the man through his words as the author, and his life by the incidents he has recorded. How valuable it is, then, to find a book built upon the facts of the author's life! What a wealth of autobiographical material exists for us who love Dickens can be appreciated only when we dip into the pages of *David Copperfield!*

Charles Dickens was born in a suburb of Portsmouth on the seventh of February, 1812. His father was a clerk in the navy pay-office. When Charles was four, his father was transferred to Chatham; there the family lived in comfortable circumstances. Charles learned to read, and, finding books in the attic, allowed his mind to imagine a local setting for all their events. Here were the stories of Fielding, Smollett, Goldsmith, and De Foe which David meets in Chapter IV. And as Charles retold the stories for his own enjoyment, so did David recount the tales of Robinson Crusoe, Peregrine Pickle, and Tom Jones for his playmates at Salem House (Chapter VII). In this county of Kent, Charles Dickens laid some of his happiest scenes, not only in *David Copperfield,* but also in the *Pickwick Papers* and *Great Expectations.*

This life continued until Charles was nine. Then, the family's fortunes changed. The father moved to London, where the circumstances of the family sank lower and lower. John Dickens, the original of Mr. Micawber, went deeper and deeper into debt until he finally was sent to The Marshalsea, the debtors' prison. As we read David's account of his visits to Mr. Micawber (Chapter XI) we can see how Charles suffered in his secret agony of stealthy visits to his father. In this period David, the little drudge, after his mother's second marriage, can be seen in Charles, the pitiful youngster employed in a blacking warehouse. Very possibly this experience was good training for his talents, but the bitterness always remained.

When Charles was twelve years old, the family's affairs improved. He was sent to a school which supplied many of the features of Salem House. Here he stayed for two years. Then he became an office boy for a lawyer. We can see how these years aided him and how he used the experiences gathered here. Imagine *David Copperfield* without Mr. Wickfield, Messrs. Spenlow and Jorkins, and Uriah Heep! The law episodes are the faithful recordings of an accurate observer of court scenes.

Young Dickens decided to become a reporter. He became, after self-mastery of shorthand (Chapter XXXVIII), "the best and most rapid reporter ever known." From journalism to literature is a natural step, and soon Charles, like David, began to write articles and sketches. *A Dinner at Poplar Walk,* later published in *The Sketches,* by Boz, was his first article. The first drafts of some of Dickens' best characters are to be found in these early writings.

From now on, Dickens' interests were entirely literary, and he rose to popularity with great rapidity. The stream of writings continued but the source was ever the same—the author's observations and experiences in life, rather than books. *Oliver Twist* contains some very powerful scenes of criminal life, for which Dickens must have secured the material when he lived as a child of ten in the London slums. *The Old Curiosity Shop* and *Barnaby Rudge* added to his fame. In *Nicholas Nickelby* Dickens exposed the type of boys' school in Dotheboys Hall where boys were abused, as he had in a less vivid fashion in *David Copperfield*. Mrs. Nickleby is drawn in part from Dickens' own mother, Elizabeth Dickens. Other works appeared in rapid succession—his marriage, his travels to the Continent and to America, interrupting his literary labors for but short intervals. And of all the vast amount he produced, Dickens loved *David Copperfield* best. It embodied himself together with the best of his humour, his joy in life, his sadnesses, and his gladnesses.

In *David Copperfield* we learn to love and pity Dora, we admire Agnes, we feel that Mr. Micawber, Miss Betsey, Peggotty, and the others are really alive. And when we come to realize that the reason every one loved Dickens is because all his characters are real live people, then we appreciate him. He has his faults, 'tis true, but they are the faults of some one we love. It is easy to understand how every one mourned when the man, Charles Dickens, died on the ninth of June, **1870**.

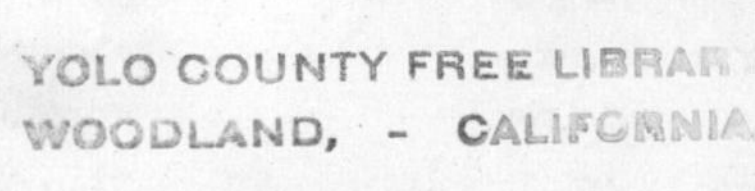

THE PERSONAL HISTORY AND EXPERIENCE OF DAVID COPPERFIELD THE YOUNGER

CHAPTER I

I AM BORN

WHETHER I shall turn out to be the hero of my own life, or whether that station will be held by anybody else, these pages must show. To begin with the beginning of my life, I record that I was born (as I have been informed and believe) on a Friday, at twelve o'clock at night. It was remarked that the clock began to strike, and I began to cry, simultaneously.

I was born at Blunderstone, in Suffolk, or "thereby," as they say in Scotland. My father's eyes had closed upon the light of this world six months, when mine opened on it. There is something strange to me, even now, in the reflection that he never saw me; and something stranger yet in the shadowy remembrance that I have of my first childish associations with his white grave-stone in the churchyard, and of the indefinable compassion I used to feel for it lying out alone there in the dark night, when our little parlour was warm and bright with fire and candle, and the doors of our house were—almost cruelly, it seemed to me sometimes—bolted and locked against it.

An aunt of my father's, consequently a great-aunt of mine, of whom I shall have more to relate by and by, was the principal magnate of our family. Miss Trotwood, or Miss Betsey, as my poor mother always called her, had been married to a husband younger than herself, who was very handsome, except in the sense of the homely adage, "handsome is, that handsome does"—for he was strongly suspected of having beaten Miss Betsey, and even of having once made some hasty but determined arrangements to throw her out of a two pair of stairs' window. These evidences of an incompatibility of temper induced Miss Betsey to effect a separation by mutual consent. He went to India, and there, according to a wild legend in our family, he was once seen riding on an elephant, in company with a baboon; but I think it must have been a baboo—or a begum. Anyhow, from India tidings of his death reached home, within ten years. How they affected my aunt, nobody knew; for immediately upon the separation she took her maiden name again, bought a cottage in a hamlet on the sea-coast a long way off, established herself there as a single woman with one servant, and was understood to live secluded ever afterwards, in an inflexible retirement.

My father had once been a favourite of hers, I believe; but she was mortally affronted by his marriage, on the ground that my mother was "a wax doll." She had never seen my mother, but she knew her to be not yet twenty. My father and Miss Betsey never met again. He was double my mother's age when he married, and of but a delicate constitution. He died a year afterwards, and, as I have said, six months before I came into the world.

This was the state of matters on the afternoon of, what *I* may be excused for calling, that eventful and important Friday. My mother was sitting by the fire, that bright, windy March afternoon, very timid and very sad, when lifting her eyes to the window opposite, she saw a strange lady coming up the garden.

My mother had a sure foreboding at the second glance that it was Miss Betsey; and when the strange lady reached the house, she gave proof of her identity. My father had often hinted that she seldom conducted herself like any ordinary Christian; and now, instead of ringing the bell, she came and looked in at that identical window, pressing the end of her nose against the glass to that extent that my poor dear mother used to say it became perfectly flat and white in a moment.

My mother had left her chair in her agitation, and gone behind it in the corner. Miss Betsey, looking round the room, slowly and inquiringly, carried her eyes on until they reached my mother. Then she made a frown and a gesture to my mother, like one who was accustomed to be obeyed, to come and open the door. My mother went.

"Mrs. David Copperfield, I *think*," said Miss Betsey.

"Yes," said my mother, faintly.

"Miss Trotwood," said the visitor. "You have heard of her, I dare say? Now you see her."

They went into the parlour my mother had come from, and when they were both seated, and Miss Betsey said nothing, my mother, after vainly trying to restrain herself, began to cry.

"Oh, tut, tut, tut!" said Miss Betsey, in a hurry. "Don't do that! Come, come!"

My mother couldn't help it notwithstanding, so she cried until she had had her cry out.

"Take off your cap, child," said Miss Betsey, "and let me see you."

My mother was too much afraid of her to refuse, therefore she did as she was told, and did it with such nervous hands that her hair (which was luxuriant and beautiful) fell all about her face.

"Why, bless my heart!" exclaimed Miss Betsey. "You are a very baby!"

My mother was, no doubt, unusually youthful in appearance even for her years; she hung her head, as if it were her fault, poor thing, and said, sobbing, that indeed she was afraid she was but a childish widow, and would be but a childish mother if she lived. In a short pause which ensued, she had a fancy that she felt Miss Betsey touch her hair, and that with no ungentle hand; but, looking at her, in her timid hope, she found that lady sitting with the skirt of her dress tucked up, her hands folded on her knee, and her feet upon the fender, frowning at the fire.

"In the name of Heaven," said Miss Betsey, suddenly, "why Rookery?"

"Do you mean the house, ma'am?" asked my mother.

"Why Rookery?" said Miss Betsey. "Cookery would have been more to the purpose, if you had had any practical ideas of life, either of you."

"The name was Mr. Copperfield's choice," returned my mother. "When he bought the house, he liked to think that there were rooks about it. We thought—Mr. Copperfield thought—it was quite a large rookery; but the nests were very old ones, and the birds have deserted them a long while."

"David Copperfield all over!" cried Miss Betsey. "David Copperfield from head to foot! Calls a house a rookery when there's not a rook near it, and takes the birds on trust, because he sees the nests!"

"Mr. Copperfield," returned my mother, "is dead, and if you dare to speak unkindly of him to me——"

My poor dear mother, I suppose, had some momentary intention of committing an assault and battery upon my aunt. But it passed with the action of rising from her chair; and she sat down again very meekly, and fainted.

When she came to herself, she found Miss Betsey standing at the window.

"I am all in a tremble," faltered my mother. "I don't know what's the matter. I shall die, I am sure!"

"No, no, no," said Miss Betsey. "Have some tea."

"Oh, dear me, dear me, do you think it will do me any good?" cried my mother in a helpless manner.

"Of course it will," said Miss Betsey. "What do you call your girl?"

"I don't know that it will be a girl, yet, ma'am," said my mother innocently.

"Bless the baby!" exclaimed Miss Betsey. "I don't mean that, I mean your servant."

"Peggotty," said my mother.

"Peggotty," repeated Miss Betsey, with some indignation. "Do you mean to say, child, that any human being has gone into a Christian church, and got herself named Peggotty?"

"It's her surname," said my mother, faintly. "Mr. Copperfield called her by it, because her Christian name was the same as mine."

"Here, Peggotty!" cried Miss Betsey, opening the parlour-door. "Tea. Your mistress is a little unwell. Don't dawdle."

Having issued this mandate as if she had been a recognised authority in the house ever since it had been a house, and having looked out to confront the amazed Peggotty coming along the passage with a candle at the sound of a strange voice, Miss Betsey shut the door again, and sat down as before: with her feet on the fender, the skirt of her dress tucked up, and her hands folded on one knee.

"You were speaking about its being a girl," said Miss Betsey. "I have no doubt it will be a girl. Now, child, from the moment of the birth of this girl——"

"Perhaps boy," my mother took the liberty of putting in.

"I tell you I have a presentiment that it must be a girl," returned Miss Betsey. "Don't contradict. From the moment of this girl's birth, child, I intend to be her friend. I intend to be her godmother, and I beg you'll call her Betsey Trotwood Copperfield. There must be no mistakes in life with *this* Betsey Trotwood. There must be no trifling with *her* affections, poor dear. I must make that *my* care."

There was a twitch of Miss Betsey's head, after each of these sentences, as if her own old wrongs were working within her.

"And was David good to you, child?" asked Miss Betsey, when she had been silent for a little while. "Were you comfortable together?"

"We were very happy," said my mother. "Mr. Copperfield was only too good to me."

"What, he spoilt you, I suppose?" returned Miss Betsey.

"I fear he did indeed," sobbed my mother.

"Well! Don't cry!" said Miss Betsey. "You were an orphan, weren't you?"

"Yes."

"And a governess?"

"I was nursery-governess in a family where Mr. Copperfield came to visit. Mr. Copperfield was very kind to me, and at last proposed to me. And I accepted him. And so we were married," said my mother simply.

"Ha! Poor baby!" mused Miss Betsey, with her frown still bent upon the fire. "Do you know anything?"

"I beg your pardon, ma'am," faltered my mother.

"About keeping house, for instance," said Miss Betsey.

"Not much, I fear," returned my mother. "But Mr. Copperfield was teaching me——"

("Much he knew about it himself!") said Miss Betsey in a parenthesis.

—"I kept my housekeeping-book regularly, and balanced it with Mr. Copperfield every night," cried my mother, breaking down again. —"And I am sure we never had a word of difference respecting it, except when Mr. Copperfield objected to my threes and fives being too much like each other, or to my putting curly tails to my sevens and nines."

"David had bought an annuity for himself with his money, I know," said Miss Betsey, by and by. "What did he do for you?"

"Mr. Copperfield," said my mother, answering with some difficulty, "was so considerate and good as to secure the reversion of a part of it to me."

"How much?" asked Miss Betsey.

"A hundred and five pounds a year," said my mother.

"He might have done worse," said my aunt.

The word was appropriate to the moment. My mother was so much worse that Peggotty, coming in with the tea-board and candles, and seeing at a glance how ill she was, conveyed her up-stairs to her own room with all speed; and immediately despatched Ham Peggotty, her nephew, who had been for some days past secreted in the

Mr. Chillip was fluttered again by the extreme severity of my aunt's manner.

house as a special messenger, to fetch the nurse and doctor.

Those allied powers were considerably astonished, when they arrived, to find an unknown lady of portentous appearance sitting before the fire, with her bonnet tied over her left arm.

The doctor was the meekest of his sex, the mildest of little men. He sidled in and out of a room, to take up the less space. He carried his head on one side, partly in modest depreciation of himself, partly in modest propitiation of everybody else.

Mr. Chillip was called up-stairs. After some quarter of an hour's absence, he returned.

"Well?" said my aunt.

"Well, ma'am," returned Mr. Chillip, "we are—we are progressing slowly, ma'am."

"Ba—a—ah!" said my aunt, with a perfect shake on the contemptuous interjection.

Mr. Chillip absolutely could not bear it. He preferred to go and sit upon the stairs, in the dark and a strong draught, until he was again sent for.

But the mild Mr. Chillip could not possibly bear malice at such a time, if at any time. He sidled into the parlour as soon as he was at liberty, and said to my aunt in his meekest manner:

"Well, ma'am, I am happy to congratulate you."

"What upon?" said my aunt, sharply.

Mr. Chillip was fluttered again by the extreme severity of my aunt's manner; so he made her a little bow, and gave her a little smile, to mollify her.

"Mercy on the man, what's he doing!" cried my aunt. impatiently. "Can't he speak?"

"Well, ma'am," resumed Mr. Chillip, as soon as he had courage, "I am happy to congratulate you. All is now over, ma'am, and well over."

"How is she?" said my aunt, folding her arms with her bonnet still tied on one of them.

"Well, ma'am, she will soon be quite comfortable, I hope," returned Mr. Chillip.

"And *she*—— How is *she?*" said my aunt, sharply.

Mr. Chillip laid his head a little more on one side, and looked at my aunt like an amiable bird.

"The baby," said my aunt. "How is she?"

"Ma'am," returned Mr. Chillip, "I apprehended you had known. It's a boy."

My aunt said never a word, but took her bonnet by the strings, in the manner of a sling, aimed a blow at Mr. Chillip's head with it, put it on bent, walked out, and never came back.

She vanished like a discontented fairy, and never came back any more.

CHAPTER II

I OBSERVE

THE first objects that assume a distinct presence before me are my mother with her pretty hair and youthful shape, and Peggotty, with no shape at all, cheeks and arms so hard and red that I wondered the birds didn't pick at her in preference to apples.

I believe I can remember these two at a little distance apart, and I going unsteadily from the one to the other. I have an impression of the touch of Peggotty's forefinger as she used to hold it out to me, and of its being roughened by needlework, like a pocket nutmeg-grater.

What else do I remember? Let me see.

There comes out of the cloud, our house—not new to me, but quite familiar, in its earliest remembrance. On the ground-floor is Peggotty's kitchen, opening into a back yard; with a pigeon-house on a pole, in the centre, without any pigeons in it; a great dog-kennel in a corner, without any dog; and a quantity of fowls. Then there are the two parlours: the parlour in which we sit of an evening, my mother and I and Peggotty—for Peggotty is quite our companion, when her work is done and we are alone—and the best parlour where we sit on Sunday; grandly, but not so comfortably.

And now I see the outside of our house, with the latticed bedroom windows standing open to let in the sweet-smelling air, and the ragged old rooks'-nests still dangling in the elm trees. Now I am in the garden at the back where my mother gathers gooseberries in a basket. A great wind rises, and the summer is gone in a moment. We are playing in the winter twilight, dancing about the parlour. When my mother is out of breath and rests herself in an elbow-chair, I watch her winding her bright curls round her fingers, and straightening her waist, and nobody knows better than I do that she likes to look so well, and is proud of being so pretty.

That is among my very earliest impressions. That, and a sense that we were both a little afraid of Peggotty, and submitted ourselves in most things to her direction.

Peggotty and I were sitting one night by the parlour fire, alone. I had been reading to Peggotty about crocodiles. (I remember she had a cloudy impression, after I had done, that they were a sort of vegetable.) I was tired of reading, and dead sleepy; but having leave, as a high treat, to sit up until my mother came home from spending the evening at a neighbor's, I would rather have died upon my post (of course) than have gone to bed.

"Peggotty," says I, suddenly, "were you ever married?"

"Lord, Master Davy," replied Peggotty, "what's put marriage in your head?"

She answered with such a start, that it quite awoke me. And then she stopped in her work, and looked at me, with her needle drawn out to its thread's length.

"But *were* you ever married, Peggotty?" says I. "You are a very handsome woman, an't you?"

"Me handsome, Davy!" said Peggotty. "Lawk, no, my dear! But what put marriage in your head?"

"I don't know!—You mustn't marry more than one person at a time, may you, Peggotty?"

"Certainly not," says Peggotty, with the promptest decision.

"But if you marry a person, and the person dies, why then you may marry another person, mayn't you, Peggotty?"

"You *may*," says Peggotty, "if you choose, my dear. That's a matter of opinion."

"But what is your opinion, Peggotty?" said I.

"My opinion is," said Peggotty, "that I never was married myself, Master Davy, and that I can't expect to be."

I remember going unsteadily from one to the other.

"You an't cross, I suppose, Peggotty, are you?" said I, after sitting quiet for a minute.

I really thought she was, but I was quite mistaken; for she laid aside her work and opening her arms wide, took my curly head within them, and gave it a good squeeze. I know it was a good squeeze, because, being very plump, whenever she made a little exertion after she was dressed, some of the buttons on the back of her gown flew off. And I recollect two bursting to the opposite side of the parlour, while she was hugging me.

"Now let me hear some more about the Crorkindills," said Peggotty, who was not quite right in the name yet, "for I an't heard half enough."

We had exhausted the crocodiles, and begun with the alligators, when the garden-bell rang. We went out to the door; and there was my mother, looking unusually pretty, I thought, and with her a gentleman with beautiful black hair and whiskers, who had walked home with us from church last Sunday.

He patted me on the head; but somehow, I didn't like him or his deep voice, and I was jealous that his hand should touch my mother's in touching me—which it did. I put it away as well as I could.

"Oh, Davy!" remonstrated my mother.

"Dear boy!" said the gentleman. "I cannot wonder at his devotion!"

I never saw such a beautiful colour on my mother's face before. She gently chid me for being rude; and, keeping me close to her shawl, turned to thank the gentleman for taking so much trouble as to bring her home. She put out her hand to him as she spoke, and, as he met it with his own, she glanced, I thought, at me.

"Let us say 'good night,' my fine boy," said the gentleman, when he had bent his head—I saw him!—over my mother's little glove.

"Good night!" said I.

"Come! Let us be the best friends in the world!" said the gentleman, laughing. "Shake hands!"

My right hand was in my mother's left, so I gave him the other.

"Why, that's the wrong hand, Davy!" laughed the gentleman.

My mother drew my right hand forward, but I was resolved, for my former reason, not to give it him, and I did not. I gave him the other, and he shook it heartily, and said I was a brave fellow, and went away.

Peggotty, who had not said a word or moved a finger, secured the fastenings instantly, and we all went into the parlour.

—"Hope you have had a pleasant evening, ma'am," said Peggotty, standing as stiff as a barrel, in the middle of the room, candle in hand.

"Much obliged to you, Peggotty," returned my mother in a cheerful voice. "I have had a *very* pleasant evening."

Peggotty continued to stand motionless in the middle of the room. I fell asleep, though I was not so sound asleep but that I could hear voices, without hearing what they said. When I half awoke from this uncomfortable doze, I found Peggotty and my mother both in tears, and both talking.

"Not such a one as this, Mr. Copperfield wouldn't have liked," said Peggotty. "That I say, and that I swear!"

"How can you have the heart to say such things to me?" cried my mother. "And my dear boy! Is it to be hinted that I am wanting in affection?"

"Nobody never went and hinted no such a thing," said Peggotty.

"You did, Peggotty! You know you did." Then turning affectionately to me, "Am I a naughty mamma? Say 'yes' and Peggotty will love you."

At this we all fell a-crying together, and I am afraid that I called Peggotty a "beast." She was in deep affliction and must have become quite buttonless, when, after having made it up with my mother, she kneeled down and made it up with me.

Whether it was the following Sunday when I saw the

gentleman again, or whether there was any greater lapse of time I cannot recall. But there he was, in church, and he walked home with us afterwards. He came in, too, to look at a famous geranium we had, in the parlour-window. It did not appear to me that he took much notice of it, but before he went he asked my mother to give him a bit of the blossom. He said he would never, never, part with it any more; and I thought he must be quite a fool not to know that it would fall to pieces in a day or two.

One autumn morning I was with my mother in the front garden, when Mr. Murdstone—I knew him by that name now—came by, on horseback. He reined up his horse to salute my mother, and merrily proposed to take me on the saddle before him if I would like the ride.

The air was so clear and pleasant, and the horse seemed to like the idea of the ride so much himself, as he stood snorting and pawing at the garden gate, that I had a great desire to go. So I was sent upstairs to Peggotty to be made spruce; and, in the meantime, Mr. Murdstone dismounted, and, with his horse's bridle drawn over his arm, walked slowly up and down on the outer side of the sweetbriar fence, while my mother walked slowly up and down on the inner, to keep him company. I recollect Peggotty and I peeping out at them from my little window; I recollect how closely they seemed to be examining the sweetbriar between them, as they strolled along; and how, from being in a perfectly angelic temper, Peggotty turned cross in a moment, and brushed my hair the wrong way, excessively hard.

Mr. Murdstone and I were soon off, and trotting along on the green turf by the side of the road. He held me quite easily with one arm, but I could not make up my mind to sit in front of him without turning my head sometimes, and looking up in his face. His hair and whiskers were blacker and thicker, looked at so near, than even I had given them credit for being. This, his regular eyebrows, and the rich white, and black, and brown, of his complexion—confound his complexion, and his memory!—made me think him a very handsome man. I have no doubt that my poor dear mother thought him so too.

It seems to me, at this distance of time, as if it were the next day when Peggotty broached the striking and adventurous proposition I am about to mention; but it was probably about two months afterwards.

We were sitting as before, one evening (when my mother was out as before), in company with the crocodile book, when Peggotty, after looking at me several times, and opening her mouth as if she were going to speak, without doing it—said coaxingly:

"Master Davy, how should you like to go along with me and spend a fortnight at my brother's at Yarmouth? Wouldn't *that* be a treat?"

"Is your brother an agreeable man, Peggotty?" I inquired, provisionally.

"Oh, what an agreeable man he is!" cried Peggotty, holding up her hands. "Then there's the sea; and the boats and ships; and the fishermen; and the beach; and Am to play with——"

Peggotty meant her nephew Ham, mentioned in my first chapter; but she spoke of him as a morsel of English Grammar.

I was flushed by her summary of delights, and replied that it would indeed be a treat, but what would my mother say?

"Why then I'll be as good as bet a guinea," said Peggotty, intent upon my face, "that she'll let us go. I'll ask her, if you like, as soon as ever she comes home. There now!"

"But what's she to do while we are away?" said I, putting my small elbows on the table to argue the point. "She can't live by herself, you know."

"Oh, bless you!" said Peggotty, "Don't you know? She's going to stay for a fortnight with Mrs. Grayper. Mrs. Grayper's going to have a lot of company."

Oh! If that was it, I was quite ready to go. I waited, in the utmost impatience, until my mother came home from

Mrs. Grayper's (for it was that identical neighbour), to ascertain if we could get leave to carry out this great idea. Without being nearly so much surprised as I expected, my mother entered into it readily; and it was all arranged that night, and my board and lodging during the visit were to be paid for.

The day soon came for our going. We were to go in a carrier's cart, which departed in the morning after breakfast. I would have given any money to have been allowed to wrap myself up overnight, and sleep in my hat and boots.

It touches me now, although I tell it lightly, to recollect how eager I was to leave my happy home; to think how little I suspected what I did leave forever.

I am glad to recollect that when the carrier began to move, my mother ran out at the gate, and called to him to stop, that she might kiss me once more. I am glad to dwell upon the earnestness and love with which she lifted up her face to mine, and did so.

CHAPTER III

I HAVE A CHANGE

The carrier's horse was the laziest horse in the world, I should hope, and shuffled along, with his head down, as if he liked to keep people waiting to whom the packages vere directed. I fancied, indeed, that he sometimes chuckled audibly over this reflection, but the carrier said he was only troubled with a cough.

The carrier had a way of keeping his head down, like his horse, and of drooping sleepily forward as he drove, with one of his arms on each of his knees. I say "drove," but it struck me that the cart would have gone to Yarmouth quite as well without him, for the horse did all that; and as to conversation, he had no idea of it but whistling.

We made so many deviations up and down lanes, and were such a long time delivering a bedstead at a public house, and calling at other places, that I was quite tired, and very glad, when we saw Yarmouth. It looked rather spongy and soppy, I thought, but Peggotty said, with greater emphasis than usual, that we must take things as we found them, and that, for her part, she was proud to call herself a Yarmouth Bloater.

When we got into the street (which was a strange enough one to me), and smelt the fish, and pitch, and oakum, and tar, and saw the sailors walking about, and the carts jingling up and down over the stones, I felt that I had done so busy a place an injustice; and said as much to Peggotty, who told me it was well known that Yarmouth was, upon the whole, the finest place in the universe.

"Here's my Am!" screamed Peggotty, "growed out of knowledge!"

He was waiting for us, in fact, at the public-house; and asked me how I found myself, like an old acquaintance. I did not feel, at first, that I knew him as well as he knew me, because he had never come to our house since the night I was born. But our intimacy was much advanced by his taking me on his back to carry me home. He was, now, a huge, strong fellow of six feet high, broad in proportion, and round-shouldered; but with a simpering boy's face and curly light hair that gave him quite a sheepish look.

Ham carrying me on his back and a small box of ours under his arm, and Peggotty carrying another small box of ours, we turned down lanes bestrewn with bits of chips and little hillocks of sand, and went past boat-builders' yards, caulkers' yards, riggers' lofts, smiths' forges, and a great litter of such places, until we came out upon the dull waste I had already seen at a distance; when Ham said:

"Yon's our house, Mas'r Davy!"

I looked in all directions, as far as I could stare over the wilderness, and away at the sea, and away at the river, but no house could *I* make out. There was a black barge, or some other kind of superannuated boat, not far off, high and dry on the ground, with an iron funnel sticking out of it for a chimney and smoking very cosily; but nothing else in the way of a habitation that was visible to *me*.

"That's not it?" said I. "That ship-looking thing?"

"That's it, Mas'r Davy," returned Ham.

If it had been Aladdin's palace, roc's egg and all, I suppose I could not have been more charmed with the romantic idea of living in it. There was a delightful door cut in the side, and it was roofed in, and there were little windows in it; but the wonderful charm of it was, that it was a real boat which had no doubt been upon the water hundreds of times, and which had never been intended to be lived in, on dry land.

It was beautifully clean inside, and as tidy as possible.

There was a table, and a Dutch clock, and a chest of drawers, and on the chest of drawers there was a tea-tray with a painting on it. The tray was kept from tumbling down by a Bible; and the tray, if it had tumbled down, would have smashed a quantity of cups and saucers and a teapot that were grouped around the book. Over the little mantel-shelf was a picture of the *Sarah Jane* lugger, with a real little wooden stern stuck on to it. There were some hooks in the beams of the ceiling, the use of which I did not divine then; and some lockers and boxes and conveniences of that sort, which served for seats and eked out the chairs.

All this I saw, and then Peggotty opened a little door and showed me my bedroom. It was the completest and most desirable bedroom ever seen—in the stern of the vessel; with a little window, where the rudder used to go through; a little looking-glass, just the right height for me, and framed with oyster-shells; a little bed, which there was just room enough to get into; and a nosegay of sea-weed in a blue mug on the table. One thing I particularly noticed in this delightful house, was the smell of fish; which was so searching, that when I took out my pocket-handkerchief I found it smelt exactly as if it had wrapped up a lobster. On my imparting this discovery to Peggotty, she informed me that her brother dealt in lobsters, crabs, and crawfish; and I afterwards found that a heap of these creatures, in a state of wonderful conglomeration with one another, and never leaving off pinching whatever they laid hold of, were usually to be found in a little wooden outhouse where the pots and kettles were kept.

We were welcomed by a very civil woman in a white apron, whom I had seen curtseying at the door when I was on Ham's back, about a quarter of a mile off. Likewise by a most beautiful little girl (or I thought her so), with a necklace of blue beads on, who wouldn't let me kiss her when I offered to, but ran away and hid herself. By and by, when we had dined in a sumptuous manner off boiled dabs, melted butter, and potatoes, with a chop

Ham carried me on his back and a small box of ours under his arm

for me, a hairy man with a very good-natured face came home. As he called Peggotty, "Lass," and gave her a hearty smack on the cheek, I had no doubt that he was her brother; and so he turned out—being presently introduced to me as Mr. Peggoty, the master of the house.

"Glad to see you, Sir," said Mr. Peggotty. "You'll find us rough, Sir, but you'll find us ready."

I thanked him, and replied that I was sure I should be happy in such a delightful place.

"How's your Ma, Sir?" said Mr. Peggotty. "Did you leave her pretty jolly?"

I gave Mr. Peggotty to understand that she was as jolly as I could wish, and that she desired her compliments—which was a polite fiction on my part.

"I'm much obleeged to her, I'm sure," said Mr. Peggotty. "Well, Sir, if you can make our here, for a fortnut, 'long wi' her," nodding at his sister, "and Ham, and little Em'ly, we shall be proud of your company."

After tea, when the door was shut and all was made snug, it seemed to me the most delicious retreat that the imagination of man could conceive. To hear the wind getting up out at sea, to know that the fog was creeping over the desolate flat outside, and to look at the fire and think that there was no house near but this one, and this one a boat, was like enchantment. Little Em'ly was sitting by my side upon the lowest and least of the lockers, and Mrs. Peggotty, with the white apron, was knitting on the opposite side of the fire. Mr. Peggotty was smoking his pipe. I felt it was a time for conversation and confidence.

"Mr. Peggotty!" says I.

"Sir," says he.

"Did you give your son the name of Ham, because you lived in a sort of ark?"

Mr. Peggotty seemed to think it a deep idea, but answered:

"No, Sir. I never giv him no name."

"Who gave him that name, then?" said I, putting question number two of the catechism to Mr. Peggotty.

"Why, sir, his father giv it him," said Mr. Peggotty.

"I thought you were his father!"

"My brother Joe was *his* father," said Mr. Peggotty.

"Dead, Mr. Peggotty?" I hinted, after a respectful pause.

"Drowndead," said Mr. Peggotty.

I was very much surprised that Mr. Peggotty was not Ham's father, and began to wonder whether I was mistaken about his relationship to anybody else there.

"Little Em'ly," I said, glancing at her. "She is your daughter, isn't she, Mr. Peggotty?"

"No, Sir. My brother-in-law, Tom, was *her* father."

"—Dead, Mr. Peggotty?" I hinted, after another respectful silence.

"Drowndead," said Mr. Peggotty.

I felt the difficulty of resuming the subject, but must get to the bottom somehow. So I said:

"Haven't you *any* children, Mr. Peggotty?"

"No, Master," he answered, with a short laugh. "I'm a bacheldore."

"A bachelor!" I said, astonished. "Why, who's that, Mr. Peggotty?" pointing to the person in the apron who was knitting.

"That's Missis Gummidge," said Mr. Peggotty.

"Gummidge, Mr. Peggotty?"

But at this point Peggotty—I mean my own peculiar Peggotty—made such impressive motions to me not to ask any more questions, that I could only sit and look at all the silent company, until it was time to go to bed. Then, in the privacy of my own little cabin, she informed me that Mrs. Gummidge was the widow of his partner in a boat, who had died very poor. He was but a poor man himself, said Peggotty, but as good as gold and as true as steel—those were her similes. The only subject, she informed me, on which he ever showed a violent temper or swore an oath, was this generosity of his; and if it were ever referred to, by any one of them, he struck the table a heavy blow with his right hand (had split it on one such occasion), and swore a dreadful oath that he would be "Gormed" if he didn't cut and run for good, if it was ever mentioned again.

I was very sensible of my entertainer's goodness, and listened to the women's going to bed at the opposite end of the boat, and to him and Ham hanging up two hammocks for themselves on the hooks I had noticed in the roof, in a very luxurious state of mind, enhanced by my being sleepy.

Almost as soon as morning shone upon the oyster-shell frame of my mirror I was out of bed, and out with little Em'ly, picking up stones upon the beach.

"You're quite a sailor, I suppose?" I said to Em'ly.

"No," replied Em'ly, shaking her head, "I'm afraid of the sea."

"Afraid!" I said, with a becoming air of boldness, and looking very big at the mighty ocean. "*I* an't!"

"Ah! but it's cruel," said Em'ly. "I have seen it very cruel to some of our men. I have seen it tear a boat as big as our house all to pieces."

"I hope it wasn't the boat that——"

"That father was drowned in?" said Em'ly. "No. Not that one. I never see that boat."

"Nor him?" I asked her.

Little Em'ly shook her head. "Not to remember!"

Here was a coincidence! But there were some differences between Em'ly's orphanhood and mine, it appeared. She had lost her mother before her father, and where her father's grave was no one knew, except that it was somewhere in the depths of the sea.

"Besides," said Em'ly, "your father was a gentleman and your mother is a lady; and my father was a fisherman and my mother was a fisherman's daughter, and my uncle Dan is a fisherman."

"Dan is Mr. Peggotty, is he?" said I.

"Uncle Dan—yonder," answer Em'ly, nodding at the boat-house. "Yes, I mean him."

"He must be very good, I should think?"

"Good?" said Em'ly. "If I was ever to be a lady, I'd give him a sky-blue coat with diamond buttons, nankeen trousers, a red velvet waistcoat, a cocked hat, a large gold watch, a silver pipe, and a box of money."

Of course I was in love with little Em'ly. We used to walk about that dim old flat at Yarmouth in a loving manner, hours and hours. I told Em'ly I adored her, and that unless she confessed she adored me I should be reduced to the necessity of killing myself with a sword. She said she did, and I have no doubt she did.

I soon found out that Mrs. Gummidge's was rather a fretful disposition, and she whimpered more sometimes than was comfortable for other parties in so small an establishment. I was very sorry for her; but there were moments when it would have been more agreeable, I thought, if Mrs. Gummidge had had a convenient apartment of her own to retire to, and had stopped there until her spirits revived.

Mr. Peggotty went occasionally to a public-house called The Willing Mind. I discovered this, by his being out on the second or third evening of our visit, and by Mrs. Gummidge's saying he was there, and that, what was more, she had known in the morning he would go there.

Mrs. Gummidge had been in a low state all day, and had burst into tears in the forenoon, when the fire smoked. "I am a lone lorn creetur'," were Mrs. Gummidge's words, "and everythink goes contrairy with me."

"Oh, it'll soon leave off," said Peggotty—I again mean our Peggotty—"and besides, you know, it's not more disagreeable to you than to us."

So at dinner, the fish were small and bony, and the potatoes were a little burnt. We all felt this something of a disappointment; but Mrs. Gummidge said she felt it more than we did, and shed tears again.

Accordingly, when Mr. Peggotty came home about nine o'clock, Mrs. Gummidge was knitting in her corner, in a very wretched and miserable condition. Peggotty had been working cheerfully. Ham had been patching up a great pair of waterboots; and I, with little Em'ly by my side, had been reading to them.

"Well, mates," said Mr. Peggotty, taking his seat, "and how are you?"

We all said something, or looked something, to welcome him, except Mrs. Gummidge.

"What's amiss?" said Mr. Peggotty.

Mrs. Gummidge did not appear to be able to cheer up.

"What's amiss?" said Mr. Peggotty. "Cheer up, old mawther!" (Mr. Peggotty meant old girl.)

"Nothing," returned Mrs. Gummidge. "You've come from The Willing Mind, Dan'l?"

"Why yes," said Mr. Peggotty.

"I'm sorry I should drive you there," said Mrs. Gummidge.

"Drive! I don't want no driving," returned Mr. Peggotty with an honest laugh. "I only go too ready."

"Very ready," said Mrs. Gummidge, shaking her head, and wiping her eyes. "I am sorry it should be along of me that you're so ready. I an't what I could wish myself to be. I am far from it. I know what I am. If I must go contrairy myself, let me go contrairy in my parish. Dan'l, I'd better go into the house, and die and be a riddance!"

Mrs. Gummidge retired with these words, and betook herself to bed. When she was gone, Mr. Peggotty, who had not exhibited a trace of any feeling but the profoundest sympathy, looked round upon us and said in a whisper:

"She's been thinking of the old 'un!"

I did not understand, until Peggotty, on seeing me to bed, explained that it was the late Mr. Gummidge; and that her brother always took that for truth on such occasions, and that it always had a moving effect upon him. And whenever Mrs. Gummidge was overcome in a similar manner during the remainder of our stay (which happened some few times), he always said the same thing, and always with the tenderest commiseration.

The fortnight slipped away and at last the day came for going home. My agony of mind at leaving little Em'ly was piercing. We went arm-in-arm to the public-house where the carrier put up, and I promised, on the road, to write to her.

Now, all the time I had been on my visit, I had thought little or nothing about my home. But I was no sooner turned towards it, than I felt it was my nest, and that my mother was my comforter and friend.

This gained upon me as we went along; so that the nearer we drew, and the more familiar the objects became that we passed, the more excited I was to get there, and to run into her arms. But Peggotty, instead of sharing in these transports, tried to check them (though very kindly), and looked confused and out of sorts.

Blunderston Rookery would come, however, in spite of her, when the carrier's horse pleased—and did.

The door opened, and I looked, half laughing and half crying for my mother. It was not she, but a strange servant.

"Why, Peggotty!" I said, ruefully. "Isn't she come home?"

"Yes, yes, Master Davy," said Peggotty. "She's come home. Wait a bit, Master Davy, and I'll—I'll tell you something."

She took me by the hand; led me, wondering, into the kitchen; and shut the door.

"Peggotty!" said I, quite frightened. "What's the matter?"

"Nothing's the matter, bless you, Master Davy dear!" she answered, assuming an air of sprightliness.

"Why hasn't mama come out to the gate, and what have we come in here for?" My eyes were full, and I felt as if I were going to tumble down.

"Bless the precious boy!" cried Peggotty. taking hold of me.

"Not dead, too! Oh, she's not dead, Peggotty?"

Peggotty cried out "No!" and then sat down, and began to pant.

I gave her a hug and then stood before her, looking at her in anxious inquiry.

"You see, dear, I should have told you before now," said Peggotty, "but I hadn't an opportunity. I ought to have made it, perhaps, but I couldn't azackly——"

"Go on, Peggotty," said I, more frightened than before.

"Master Davy," said Peggotty, "what do you think? You have got a Pa!"

I trembled, and turned white. Something—connected with the grave in the churchyard seemed to strike me like an unwholesome wind.

"A new one," said Peggotty.

"A new one?" I repeated.

"Come and see him."

"I don't want to see him."

"——and your mama," said Peggotty.

I ceased to draw back, and we went straight to the best parlour, where she left me. On one side of the fire sat my mother; on the other, Mr. Murdstone. My mother dropped her work and arose hurriedly, but timidly I thought.

"Now, Clara my dear," said Mr. Murdstone. "Recollect! Control yourself, always control yourself! Davy boy, how do you do?"

I gave him my hand. After a moment of suspense, I went and kissed my mother; she kissed me, patted me gently on the shoulder, and sat down again to her work. I could not look at her, I could not look at him, I knew quite well that he was looking at us both.

As soon as I could creep away, I crept up-stairs. My old dear bedroom was changed, and I was to lie a long way off. I rambled down-stairs to find anything that was like itself, and roamed into the yard. I very soon started back from there, for the empty dog-kennel was filled up with a great dog—deep-mouthed and black-haired like Him—and he was very angry at the sight of me, and sprang out to get at me.

CHAPTER IV

I FALL INTO DISGRACE

If the room to which my bed was removed could give evidence, I might appeal to it to bear witness for me what a heavy heart I carried to it. I went up there and sat down with my small hands crossed, and thought.

I was crying all the time, but I am sure I never thought why I cried. I began to consider that I was dreadfully in love with little Em'ly, and had been torn away from her to come here where no one seemed to want me, or to care about me. This made such a very miserable piece of business of it, that I rolled myself up in the counterpane, and cried myself to sleep.

I was awakened by somebody saying, "Here he is!" and uncovering my hot head. My mother and Peggotty had come to look for me.

"Davy," said my mother. "What's the matter?"

I thought it was very strange that she should ask me, and answered, "Nothing." I turned over on my face, I recollect, to hide my trembling lip, which answered her with greater truth.

"Davy," said my mother. "Davy, my child!"

I dare say no words she could have uttered would have affected me so much, then, as her calling me her child. I hid my tears in the bedclothes, and pressed her from me with my hand, when she would have raised me up.

I felt the touch of a hand that I knew was neither hers nor Peggotty's, and slipped to my feet at the bedside. It was Mr. Murdstone's hand, and he kept it on my arm as he said:

"What's this? Clara, my love, have you forgotten?—Firmness, my dear!"

"I am very sorry, Edward," said my mother.

"Go you below, my love," said Mr. Murdstone. "David and I will come down, together."

He watched my mother out, and Peggotty, with some uneasy glances at me, curtseyed herself out of the room.

When we two were left alone, he shut the door, and sitting on a chair, and holding me standing before him, looked steadily into my eyes. I felt my own attracted, no less steadily, to his. As I recall our being opposed thus, face to face, I seem again to hear my heart beat fast and high.

"David," he said, making his lips thin, "if I have an obstinate horse or dog to deal with, what do you think I do?"

"I don't know."

"I beat him."

I had answered in a kind of breathless whisper, but I felt, in my silence, that my breath was shorter now.

"I say to myself, 'I'll conquer that fellow.' What is that upon your face?"

"Dirt," I said.

He knew it was the mark of tears as well as I. But if he had asked the question twenty times, each time with twenty blows, I believe my baby heart would have burst before I would have told him so.

"You have a good deal of intelligence for a little fellow," he said, with a grave smile that belonged to him, "and you understood me very well, I see. Wash that face, Sir, and come down with me."

I had little doubt then, and I have less doubt now, that he would have knocked me down without the least compunction, if I had hesitated.

"Clara, my dear," he said, when I had done his bidding, and he walked me into the parlour with his hand still on my arm, "we shall soon improve our youthful humours."

God help me, I might have been improved for my whole life by a kind word at that season. A word of encouragement and explanation, of welcome home might have made me respect instead of hate him. I thought my mother was sorry to see me so scared and strange—but the word was not spoken, and the time for it was gone.

We dined alone, we three together. He seemed to be very fond of my mother—I am afraid I liked him none the better for that—and she was very fond of him. I gathered from what they said, that an elder sister of his was expected that evening.

After dinner, when we were sitting by the fire, a coach drove up to the garden-gate, and he went out to receive the visitor. My mother followed him. I was timidly following her, when she turned round at the parlour-door, in the dusk, and taking me in her embrace as she had been used to do, whispered me to love my new father and be obedient to him. She did this hurriedly and secretly, as if it were wrong, but tenderly; and, putting out her hand behind her, held mine in it, until we came near to where he was standing in the garden, where she let mine go, and drew hers through his arm.

It was Miss Murdstone who was arrived, and a gloomy-looking lady she was. She brought with her two uncompromising hard black boxes, with her initials on the lids in hard brass nails. When she paid the coachman she took her money out of a hard steel purse, and she kept the purse in a bag which hung upon her arm by a heavy chain, and shut up like a bite.

She was brought into the parlour with many tokens of welcome, and there formally recognized my mother as a new and near relation. Then she looked at me, and said:

"Is that your boy, sister-in-law?"

My mother acknowledged me.

"Generally speaking," said Miss Murdstone, "I don't like boys. How d'ye do, boy?"

Under these encouraging circumstances, I replied that I was very well, and that I hoped she was the same; with such an indifferent grace, that Miss Murdstone disposed of me in two words:

"Wants manner!"

Having uttered which with great distinctness, she begged

the favour of being shown to her room, which became to me from that time forth a place of awe and dread.

On the very first morning after her arrival she was up and ringing her bell at cock-crow. When my mother came down to breakfast and was going to make the tea, Miss Murdstone gave her a kind of peck on the cheek, which was her nearest approach to a kiss, and said:

"Now, Clara, my dear, I am come here, you know, to relieve you of all the trouble I can. You're much too pretty and thoughtless"—my mother blushed but laughed—"to have any duties that can be undertaken by me. If you'll be so good as give me your keys, my dear, I'll attend to all this sort of thing in future."

From that time, Miss Murdstone kept the keys, and my mother had no more to do with them than I had.

My mother did not suffer her authority to pass from her without a shadow of protest. One night when Miss Murdstone had been developing certain household plans to her brother, my mother suddenly began to cry, and said she thought she might have been consulted.

"Clara!" said Mr. Murdstone sternly. "Clara! I wonder at you."

"Oh, it's very well to say you wonder, Edward!" cried my mother, "and it's very well for you to talk about firmness, but you wouldn't like it yourself."

"Edward," said Miss Murdstone, "let there be an end of this. I go to-morrow."

"Jane Murdstone," said her brother, "be silent!"

"I am sure," my poor mother went on with many tears, "I don't want anybody to go. I only want to be consulted sometimes. I thought you were pleased, once, with my being a little inexperienced and girlish, Edward—I am sure you said so—but you seem to hate me for it now, you are so severe."

"Edward," said Miss Murdstone, again, "let there be an end of this. I go to-morrow."

"Jane Murdstone," thundered Mr. Murdstone. "Will you be silent? How dare you?"

"Clara," he continued, looking at my mother, "you surprise me! You astound me! When Jane Murdstone is kind enough to come and to assume, for my sake, a condition something like a housekeeper's, and when she meets with a base return——"

"Oh, pray, pray, Edward," cried my mother, "don't accuse me of being ungrateful. Oh, don't, my dear!"

"When Jane Murdstone meets, I say," he went on, after waiting until my mother was silent, "with a base return——"

"Don't, my love, say that!" implored my mother very piteously. "Oh, don't, Edward! Pray let us be friends. I am sorry. Jane, I don't object to anything. I should be quite broken-hearted if you thought of leaving——" My mother was too much overcome to go on.

"Jane Murdstone," said Mr. Murdstone to his sister, "any harsh words between us are, I hope, uncommon. It is not my fault tonight. I was betrayed into it by another. Nor is it your fault. You were betrayed into it by another. Let us both try to forget it."

Going down next morning rather earlier than usual, I paused outside the parlour-door, on hearing my mother's voice. She was very earnestly and humbly entreating Miss Murdstone's pardon. I never knew my mother afterwards to give an opinion on any matter, without first appealing to Miss Murdstone, and I never saw Miss Murdstone move her hand towards her bag as if she were going to take out the keys and resign them to my mother, without seeing that my mother was in a terrible fright.

There had been some talk on occasions of my going to boarding-school. Mr. and Miss Murdstone had originated it, and my mother had of course agreed with them. Nothing, however, was concluded on the subject yet. In the meantime I learnt lessons at home.

Shall I ever forget those lessons! They were presided over nominally by my mother, but really by Mr. Murdstone and his sister. I had been apt enough to learn, and willing enough, when my mother and I had lived alone

I trip over a word

together. But these solemn lessons I remember as daily drudgery and misery. They were very long, very numerous, very hard—and I was generally as much bewildered by them as I believe my poor mother was herself.

Let me remember how it used to be, and bring one morning back again.

I come into the second-best parlour after breakfast, with my books, and an exercise-book, and a slate. My mother is ready for me at her writing-desk, but not half so ready as Mr. Murdstone in his easy-chair by the window (though he pretends to be reading a book), or as Miss Murdstone, sitting near my mother stringing steel beads. The very sight of these two has such an influence over me, that I begin to feel the words I have been at infinite pains to get into my head, all sliding away, and going I don't know where. I wonder where they *do* go, by the by?

I hand the first book to my mother. Perhaps it is a grammar, perhaps a history, or geography. I take a last drowning look at the page as I give it into her hand, and start off aloud at a racing pace while I have got it fresh. I trip over a word. Mr. Murdstone looks up. I trip over another word. Miss Murdstone looks up. I redden, tumble over half-a-dozen words, and stop. I think my mother would show me the book if she dared, but she does not dare, and she says softly:

"Oh, Davy, Davy!"

"Now, Clara," says Mr. Murdstone, "be firm with the boy. Don't say, 'Oh, Davy, Davy!' That's childish. He knows his lesson, or he does not know it."

"He does *not* know it," Miss Murdstone interposes awfully.

"I am really afraid he does not," says my mother.

"Then you see, Clara," returns Miss Murdstone, "you should just give him the book back, and make him know it."

"Yes, certainly," says my mother; "that is what I intend to do, my dear Jane. Now, Davy, try once more, and don't be stupid."

I obey the first clause of the injunction by trying once more, but I am not so successful with the second, for I am very stupid. I tumble down before I get to the old place, at a point where I was all right before, and stop to think. But I can't think about the lesson. I think of the number of yards of net in Miss Murdstone's cap, or of the price of Mr. Murdstone's dressing-gown, or any such ridiculous problem that I have no business with, and don't want to have anything at all to do with. Mr. Murdstone makes a movement of impatience which I have been expecting for a long time. Miss Murdstone does the same. My mother glances submissively at them, shuts the book, and lays it by as an arrear to be worked out when my other tasks are done.

There is a pile of these arrears very soon, and it swells like a rolling snowball. The bigger it gets, the more stupid *I* get. The despairing way in which my mother and I look at each other, as I blunder on, is truly melancholy. But the greatest effect in these miserable lessons is when my mother (thinking nobody is observing her) tries to give me the cue by the motion of her lips. At that instant, Miss Murdstone says in a deep warning voice:

"Clara!"

My mother starts, colours, and smiles faintly. Mr. Murdstone comes out of his chair, takes the book, throws it at me or boxes my ears with it, and turns me out of the room by the shoulders.

Even when the lessons are done, the worst is yet to happen, in the shape of an appalling sum. This is invented for me by Mr. Murdstone, and begins, "If I go into a cheesemonger's shop, and buy five thousand double-Gloucester cheeses at fourpence-halfpenny each, present payment——" I pore over these cheeses without any result or enlightenment until dinner-time, when I have a slice of bread to help me out, and am in disgrace for the rest of the evening.

The natural result of this treatment, continued, I suppose, for some six months or more, was to make me sullen, dull, and dogged. I believe I should have been almost stupefied but for one circumstance.

It was this. My father had left a small collection of books in a little room up-stairs, to which I had access (for it adjoined my own) and which nobody else in our house ever troubled. From that blessed little room, Roderick Random, Peregrine Pickle, Humphrey Clinker, Tom Jones, the Vicar of Wakefield, Don Quixote, Gil Blas, and Robinson Crusoe came out, a glorious host, to keep me company. They kept alive my fancy, and my hope of something beyond that place and time—they, and the *Arabian Nights*, and the *Tales of the Genii*—— It is astonishing to me now how I found time, in the midst of my porings and blunderings over heavier themes, to read those books as I did. It is curious to me how I could ever have consoled myself by impersonating my favourite characters in them—as I did—and by putting Mr. and Miss Murdstone into all the bad ones—which I did, too.

One morning when I went into the parlour with my books, I found my mother looking anxious, Miss Murdstone looking firm, and Mr. Murdstone binding something round the bottom of a cane—a lithe and limber cane, which he left off binding when I came in, and poised and switched in the air.

"I tell you, Clara," said Mr. Murdstone, "I have been often flogged myself."

"To be sure, of course," said Miss Murdstone.

"Certainly, my dear Jane," faltered my mother, meekly.

I felt apprehensive that I was personally interested in this dialogue, and sought Mr. Murdstone's eye as it lighted on mine.

"Now, David," he said, "you must be far more careful to-day than usual." He gave the cane another poise, and another switch; and laid it down beside him, with an impressive look.

We began badly, and went on worse. I had come in conceiving that I was very well prepared; but it turned out to be quite a mistake. Book after book was added to the heap of failures. And when we came at last to the five thousand cheeses (canes he made it that day, I remember), my mother burst out crying.

"Clara!" said Miss Murdstone, in her warning voice.

I saw him wink, solemnly, at his sister, as he rose and said, taking up the cane:

"Why, Jane, we can hardly expect Clara to bear, with perfect firmness, the worry and torment that David has occasioned her to-day. David, you and I will go up-stairs, boy."

As he took me out at the door, my mother ran towards us. Miss Murdstone said, "Clara! are you a perfect fool?" and interfered. I saw my mother stop her ears then, and I heard her crying.

He walked me up to my room slowly and gravely—I am certain he had a delight in that formal parade of executing justice—and when we got there, suddenly twisted my head under his arm.

"Mr. Murdstone! Sir!" I cried to him. "Don't! Pray don't beat me! I have tried to learn, Sir, but I can't learn while you and Miss Murdstone are by. I can't indeed!"

"Can't you, indeed, David?" he said. "We'll try that."

He had my head as in a vise, but I twined round him somehow, and stopped him for a moment, entreating him not to beat me. It was only for a moment that I stopped him, for he cut me heavily an instant afterwards, and in the same instant I caught the hand with which he held me in my mouth, between my teeth, and bit it through. It sets my teeth on edge to think of it.

He beat me then, as if he would have beaten me to death. Above all the noise we made, I heard them running up the stairs, and crying out—I heard my mother crying out—and Peggotty. Then he was gone; and the door was locked outside; and I was lying, fevered and hot, and torn, and sore, and raging in my puny way, upon the floor.

How well I recollect, when I became quiet, what an unnatural stillness seemed to reign through the whole house!

How well I remember, when my smart and passion began to cool, how wicked I began to feel!

I sat listening for a long while, but there was not a sound. I crawled up from the floor, and saw my face in the glass, so swollen, red, and ugly that it almost frightened me. My stripes were sore and stiff, and made me cry afresh, when I moved; but they were nothing to the guilt I felt.

It had begun to grow dark, and I had shut the window (I had been lying, for the most part, with my head upon the sill), when the key was turned, and Miss Murdstone came in with some bread and meat, and milk. These she put down upon the table without a word and then retired, locking the door after her.

I never shall forget the waking next morning; the being cheerful and fresh for the first moment, and then the being weighed down by remembrance. Miss Murdstone reappeared before I was out of bed; told me, in so many words, that I was free to walk in the garden for half an hour and no longer; and retired.

I did so, and did so every morning of my imprisonment, which lasted five days. If I could have seen my mother alone, I should have gone down on my knees to her and besought her forgiveness; but I saw no one, Miss Murdstone excepted, during the whole time—except at evening prayers in the parlour, where I was stationed all alone by myself near the door.

On the last night of my restraint, I was awakened by hearing my own name spoken in a whisper. I started up in bed, and putting out my arms in the dark, said:

"Is that you, Peggotty?"

There was no immediate answer, but presently I heard my name again, a tone so very mysterious and awful, that I think I should have gone into a fit if it had not occurred to me that it must have come through the keyhole.

I groped my way to the door, and putting my own lips to the keyhole, whispered:

"Is that you, Peggotty dear?"

"Yes, my own precious Davy," she replied. "Be as soft as a mouse, or the Cat'll hear us."

I understood this to mean Miss Murdstone, and was sensible of the urgency of the case, her room being close by.

"How's mama, dear Peggotty? Is she very angry with me?"

"No. Not very."

"What is going to be done with me, Peggotty dear? Do you know?"

"School. Near London," was Peggotty's answer.

"When, Peggotty?"

"To-morrow."

"Shan't I see mama?"

"Yes," said Peggotty. "Morning."

Then Peggotty fitted her mouth close to the keyhole, and delivered these words through it with much feeling and earnestness:

"Davy, dear. If I ain't been azackly as intimate with you. Lately, as I used to be. It ain't because I don't love you. It's because I thought it better. Davy, my darling, are you listening? Can you hear?"

"Ye—ye—ye—yes, Peggotty!" I sobbed.

"My own!" said Peggotty, with infinite compassion. "What I want to say is. That you must never forget me. For I'll never forget you. And I'll take as much care of your mama, Davy. As ever I took of you. And I'll write to you, my dear. Though I ain't no scholar . And I'll—I'll——" Peggotty fell to kissing the keyhole, as she couldn't kiss me.

"Thank you, dear Peggotty!" said I. "Oh, thank you! Thank you! Will you promise me one thing, Peggotty? Will you write and tell Mr. Peggotty and little Em'ly, and Mrs. Gummidge and Ham, that I am not so bad as they might suppose, and that I sent 'em all my love—especially to little Em'ly? Will you, if you please, Peggotty?"

The kind soul promised, and we both of us kissed the keyhole with the greatest affection—I patted it with my hand, I recollect, as if it had been her honest face—and parted.

In the morning Miss Murdstone appeared as usual, and told me I was going to school. She also informed me that I was to come down-stairs into the parlour, and have my breakfast. There I found my mother, very pale and with red eyes; into whose arms I ran, and begged her pardon from my suffering soul.

"Oh, Davy!" she said. "That you could hurt any one I love! Try to be better, pray to be better! I forgive you; but I am so grieved, Davy, that you should have such bad passions in your heart."

They had persuaded her that I was a wicked fellow, and she was more sorry for that, than for my going away. I felt it sorely. I tried to eat my parting breakfast, but my tears dropped upon my bread-and-butter, and trickled into my tea. I saw my mother look at me sometimes, and then glance at the watchful Miss Murdstone, and then look down, or look away.

"Master Copperfield's box there!" said Miss Murdstone, when wheels were heard at the gate.

I looked for Peggotty, but it was not she; neither she nor Mr. Murdstone appeared. My former acquaintance, the carrier, was at the door; the box was taken out to his cart, and lifted in.

"Clara!" said Miss Murdstone, in her warning note.

"Ready, my dear Jane," returned my mother. "Good-bye, Davy. You are going for your own good. Good-bye, my child. You will come home in the holidays, and be a better boy."

"Clara!" Miss Murdstone repeated.

"Certainly, my dear Jane," replied my mother, who was holding me. "I forgive you, my dear boy. God bless you!"

"Clara!" Miss Murdstone repeated.

Miss Murdstone was good enough to take me out to the cart, and to say on the way that she hoped I would repent, before I came to a bad end; and then I got into the cart, and the lazy horse walked off with it.

CHAPTER V

I AM SENT AWAY FROM HOME

WE might have gone about half a mile, and my pocket-handkerchief was quite wet through, when the carrier stopped short.

Looking out, I saw, to my amazement, Peggotty burst from a hedge and climb into the cart. She took me in both her arms, and squeezed me to her stays until the pressure on my nose was extremely painful, though I never thought of that till afterwards when I found it very tender. Not a single word did Peggotty speak. Releasing one of her arms, she put it down in her pocket to the elbow, and brought out some paper bags of cakes which she crammed into my pockets, and a purse which she put into my hand, but not one word did she speak. After another and a final squeeze with both arms, she got down from the cart and ran away; and my belief is, and has always been, without a solitary button on her gown. I picked up one, of several that were rolling about, and treasured it as a keepsake for a long time.

The carrier looked at me, as if to inquire if she were not coming back. I shook my head, and said I thought not. "Then, come up," said the carrier to the lazy horse; who came up accordingly.

Having by this time cried as much as I possibly could, I began to think it was of no use crying any more. The carrier, seeing me in this resolution, proposed that my pocket-handkerchief should be spread upon the horse's back to dry. I thanked him, and assented; and particularly small it looked.

I had now leisure to examine the purse. It was a stiff

leather purse, with a snap, and had three bright shillings in it, which Peggotty had evidently polished up with whitening, for my greater delight. But its most precious contents were two half-crowns folded together in a bit of paper, on which was written, in my mother's hand, "For Davy, with my love." I was so overcome by this, that I asked the carrier to be so good as to reach me my pocket-handkerchief again; but he said he thought I had better do without it, and I thought I really had, so I wiped my eyes on my sleeve and stopped myself.

For good, too; though I was still occasionally seized with a stormy sob. After we had jogged on for some little time, I asked the carrier if he was going all the way.

"All the way where?" inquired the carrier.

"There," I said.

"Where's there?" inquired the carrier.

"Near London," I said.

"Why that horse," said the carrier, jerking the rein to point him out, "would be deader than pork afore he got over half the ground."

"Are you only going to Yarmouth, then?" I asked.

"That's about it," said the carrier. "And there I shall take you to the stage-cutch, and the stage-cutch that'll take you to—wherever it is."

As this was a great deal for the carrier (whose name was Mr. Barkis) to say, I offered him a cake as a mark of attention, which he ate at one gulp.

"Did *she* make 'em, now?" said Mr. Barkis, leaning forward, in his slouching way.

"Peggotty, do you mean, Sir?"

"Ah!" said Mr. Barkis. "Her."

"Yes. She makes all our pastry and does all our cooking."

"Do she though?" said Mr. Barkis.

He made up his mouth as if to whistle, but he didn't whistle. He sat looking at the horse's ears, as if he saw something new there; and sat so for a considerable time. By-and-by, he said:

"No sweethearts, I b'lieve?"

"Sweetmeats did you say, Mr. Barkis?" For I thought he wanted something else to eat, and had pointedly alluded to that description of refreshment.

"Hearts," said Mr. Barkis. "Sweethearts; no person walks with her?"

"With Peggotty?"

"Ah!" he said. "Her."

"Oh, no. She never had a sweetheart."

"Didn't she, though?" said Mr. Barkis.

Again he made up his mouth to whistle, and again he didn't whistle, but sat looking at the horse's ears.

"So she makes," said Mr. Barkis, after a long interval of reflection, "all the apple parsties, and does all the cooking, do she?"

I replied that such was the fact.

"Well. I'll tell you what," said Mr. Barkis. "P'raps you might be writin' to her?"

"I shall certainly write to her," I rejoined.

"Ah!" he said, slowly turning his eyes towards me. "Well! If you was writin' to her, p'raps you'd recollect to say that Barkis was willin'; would you?"

"That Barkis was willing," I repeated, innocently. "Is that all the message?"

"Ye—es," he said, considering. "Ye—es. Barkis is willin'."

While I was waiting for the coach in the hotel at Yarmouth that very afternoon, I procured a sheet of paper and an inkstand and wrote a note to Peggotty, which ran thus: "My dear Peggotty. I have come here safe. Barkis is willing. My love to mama. Yours affectionately. P. S. He says he particularly wants you to know—*Barkis is willing.*"

When I had taken this commission on myself prospectively, Mr. Barkis relapsed into perfect silence; and I, feeling quite worn out by all that had happened lately, lay down on a sack in the cart and fell asleep. I slept soundly until we got to Yarmouth; which was so entirely new and strange to me in the inn-yard to which we drove, that I at once abandoned a latent hope I had had of meeting with some of Mr. Peggotty's family there, perhaps even with little Em'ly herself.

The coach was in the yard, shining very much all over, but without any horses to it as yet. I was wondering what would ultimately become of my box, which Mr. Barkis had put down on the yard-pavement by the pole, and also what would ultimately become of me, when a lady looked out of a bow-window where some fowls and joints of meat were hanging up, and said:

"Is that the little gentleman from Blunderstone?"

"Yes, ma'am," I said.

"What name?" inquired the lady.

"Copperfield, ma'am," I said.

"That won't do," returned the lady. "Nobody's dinner is paid for here, in that name."

"Is it Murdstone, ma'am?" I said.

"If you're Master Murdstone," said the lady, "why do you go and give another name, first?"

I explained to the lady how it was, who then rang a bell, and called out, "William! show the coffee-room!" and upon which a waiter came running out of a kitchen on the opposite side of the yard to show it, and seemed a good deal surprised when he found he was only to show it to me.

It was a large long room, and when the waiter laid a cloth on purpose for me, and put a set of casters on it, I think I must have turned red all over with modesty.

He brought me some chops, and vegetables, and took the covers off in such a bouncing manner that I was afraid I must have given him some offence. But he greatly relieved my mind by putting a chair for me at the table, and saying very affably, "Now, six-foot! come on!"

I thanked him, and took my seat; but found it extremely difficult to handle my knife and fork or to avoid splashing myself with the gravy, while he was standing opposite, staring so hard. After watching me into the second chop, he said:

"There's half a pint of ale for you. Will you have it now?"

I thanked him and said, "Yes." Upon which he poured it into a large tumbler.

"My eye!" he said. "It seems a good deal, don't it?"

"It does seem a good deal," I answered with a smile.

"There was a gentleman here yesterday," he said—"a stout gentleman, by the name of Topsawyer—perhaps you know him?"

"No," I said bashfully, "I haven't the pleasure——"

"He came in here," said the waiter, "ordered a glass of this ale—*would* order it—I told him not—drank it, and fell dead."

I was very much shocked, and said I thought I had better have some water.

"Why you see," said the waiter, "our people don't like things being ordered and left. But *I'll* drink it, if you like. I don't think it'll hurt me, if I throw my head back, and take it off quick. Shall I?"

I replied that he would much oblige me by drinking it, if he thought he could do it safely. When he did throw his head back, and take it off quick, I had a horrible fear, of seeing him meet the fate of Mr. Topsawyer. But it didn't hurt him. On the contrary, I thought he seemed the fresher for it.

"What have we got here?" he said, putting a fork into my dish. "Not chops?"

"Chops," I said.

"Lord bless my soul!" he exclaimed. "I didn't know they were chops. Why, a chop's the very thing to take off the bad effects of that beer! Ain't it lucky?"

So he took a chop by the bone in one hand, and a potato in the other, and ate away with a very good appetite, to my extreme satisfaction. He afterwards took another chop, and another potato; and after that another chop and another potato. When he had done, he brought me a pudding, and set it before me.

"How's the pie?" he said.

A lady looked out from a bow window.

"It's a pudding," I made answer.

"Pudding!" he exclaimed. "You don't mean to say it's a batter-pudding?"

"Yes, it is indeed."

"Why, a batter-pudding," he said, taking up a table-spoon, "is my favourite pudding! Come on, little 'un, and let's see who'll get most."

The waiter certainly got most. I never saw any one enjoy a pudding so much, I think; and he laughed, when it was all gone, as if his enjoyment of it lasted still.

Finding him so very friendly and companionable, it was then that I asked for the pen and ink and paper to write to Peggotty. When I had finished, he asked me where I was going to school.

I said, "Near London," which was all I knew.

"Oh! my eye!" he said, looking very low-spirited, "I am sorry for that."

"Why?" I asked him.

"Oh, Lord!" he said, shaking his head, "that's the school where they broke the boy's ribs—two ribs—a little boy he was. I should say he was—let me see—how old are you, about?"

I told him between eight and nine.

"That's just his age," he said. "He was eight years and six months old when they broke his first rib; eight years and eight months old when they broke his second, and did for him."

I could not disguise from myself, or from the waiter, that this was an uncomfortable coincidence, and inquired how it was done. His answer was not cheering to my spirits, for it consisted of two dismal words, "With whopping."

It was a little disconcerting to me, to find, when I was being helped up behind the coach, that I was supposed to have eaten all the dinner without any assistance. I discovered this, from overhearing the lady in the bow-window say to the guard, "Take care of that child, George, or he'll burst!" and from observing that the women-servants who were about the place came out to look and giggle at me as a young phenomenon.

We had started from Yarmouth at three o'clock in the afternoon, and we were due in London about eight next morning. It was midsummer weather, and the evening was very pleasant. When we passed through a village, I pictured to myself what the insides of the houses were like; and when boys came running after us, and got up behind and swung there for a little way, I wondered whether their fathers were alive, and whether they were happy at home.

The night was not so pleasant as the evening, for it got chilly; and being put between two gentlemen to prevent my tumbling off the coach, I was nearly smothered. They squeezed me so hard sometimes, that I could not help crying out, "Oh, if you please!"—which they didn't like at all, because it woke them. Opposite me was an elderly lady in a great fur cloak. This lady had a basket with her, and she hadn't known what to do with it, until she found that, on account of my legs being short, it could go underneath me. It cramped and hurt me so, that it made me perfectly miserable; but if I moved in the least, and made a glass that was in the basket rattle, she gave me the cruellest poke and said, "Come, don't *you* fidget. *Your* bones are young enough, *I'm* sure!"

At last the sun rose, and we approached London by degrees, and got, in due time, to the inn in the Whitechapel district, for which we were bound.

The guard's eye lighted on me as he was getting down, and he said at the booking-office door:

"Is there anybody here for a yoongster, booked in the name Murdstone, from Bloonderstone, Sooffolk, to be left till called for?"

Nobody answered.

"Try Copperfield, if you please, Sir," said I, looking helplessly down.

"Is there anybody here for a yoongster, booked in the name of Murdstone, from Bloonderstone, Sooffolk, but owning to the name of Copperfield, to be left till called for?" said the guard. "Come! *Is* there anybody?"

No. There was nobody.

More solitary than Robinson Crusoe, who had nobody to look at him and see that he was solitary, I went into the booking-office, and, by invitation of the clerk on duty, passed behind the counter, and sat down on the scale at which they weighed the luggage. Here, as I sat looking at the parcels, a procession of most tremendous considerations began to march through my mind. Supposing nobody should ever fetch me, how long would they consent to keep me there? Supposing Mr. Murdstone had devised this plan to get rid of me, what should I do? If I started off at once, and tried to walk back home, how could I ever hope to walk so far, how could I make sure of any one but Peggotty, even if I got back? These thoughts, and a hundred other such thoughts, turned me burning hot, and made me giddy with apprehension and dismay. I was in the height of my fever when a man entered and whispered to the clerk, who presently pushed me over to him.

As I went out of the office, hand in hand with this new acquaintance, I stole a look at him. He was a gaunt, sallow young man, with hollow cheeks.

"You're the new boy?" he said.

"Yes, Sir," I said.

I supposed I was. I didn't know.

"I'm one of the Masters at Salem House," *he* said.

I made him a bow and felt very much overawed.

"If you please, Sir," I said, "is it far?"

"It's a good step," he said. "We shall go by the stage-coach. It's about six miles."

I was so faint and tired, that the idea of holding out for six miles more was too much for me. I took heart to tell him that I had had nothing all night, and that if he would allow me to buy something to eat, I should be very much obliged to him. He appeared surprised at this—and after considering for a few moments, said he wanted to call on an old person who lived not far off, and that the best way would be for me to buy some bread and make my breakfast at her house, where we could get some milk.

Accordingly, we decided in favour of a nice little loaf of brown bread, which cost me threepence. Then, at a grocer's shop, we bought an egg and a slice of streaky bacon; which still left what I thought a good deal of change, out of the second of the bright shillings, and made me consider London a very cheap place. These provisions laid in, we went on through a great noise and uproar and over a bridge which, no doubt, was London Bridge, until we came to the poor person's house.

The Master at Salem House lifted the latch, and we went into the little house. On seeing the Master enter, an old woman said something that I thought sounded like "My Charley!" but on seeing me come in too, she got up, and rubbing her hands made a confused sort of half curtsey.

"Can you cook this young gentleman's breakfast for him, if you please?" said the Master at Salem House.

"Can I?" said the old woman. "Yes can I, sure!"

I sat down to my brown loaf, my egg, and my rasher of bacon, with a basin of milk besides, and made a most delicious meal. While I was yet in the full enjoyment of it, the old woman said to the Master:

"Have you got your flute with you?"

"Yes," he returned.

"Have a blow at it," said the old woman, coaxingly. "Do!"

The Master, upon this, put his hand underneath the skirts of his coat and brought out his flute in three pieces, which he screwed together, and began immediately to play. My impression is, that there never can have been anybody in the world who played worse. I don't know what the tunes were, but the influence was to make me so sleepy that I couldn't keep my eyes open.

When I seemed to have been dozing for a long while, the Master at Salem House unscrewed his flute into the three pieces, put them up as before, and took me away. We found the coach very near at hand, but I was so dead sleepy, that I slept profoundly, until I found the coach going at a footpace up a steep hill among green leaves. Presently it stopped.

A short walk brought us—I mean the Master and me—to Salem House, which was enclosed with a high brick wall, and looked very dull. Over a door in this wall was a board with SALEM HOUSE upon it; and through a grating we were surveyed, when we rang the bell, by a surly face, which belonged to a stout man with a wooden leg.

"The new boy," said the Master.

The man with the wooden leg eyed me all over—it didn't take long, for there was not much of me—and locked the gate behind us, and took out the key.

Salem House was a square brick building with wings, of a bare and unfurnished appearance. All about it was so very quiet, that I said to Mr. Mell I supposed the boys were out; but he seemed surprised at my not knowing that it was holiday-time. That all the boys were at their several homes. That Mr. Creakle, the proprietor, was down by the sea-side with Mrs. and Miss Creakle. And that I was sent in holiday-time as a punishment for my misdoing. All of which he explained to me as we went along.

I gazed upon the schoolroom into which he took me, as the most forlorn and desolate place I had ever seen. I see it now. A long room, with three long rows of desks, and six of forms, and bristling all around with pegs for hats and slates. Scraps of old copy-books and exercises litter the dirty floor.

Mr. Mell having left me, I went softly to the upper end of the room. Suddenly I came upon a pasteboard placard, beautifully written, which was lying on the desk, and bore these words: "Take care of him. He bites."

I got upon the desk immediately, apprehensive of at least a great dog underneath. But, though I looked all round with anxious eyes, I could see nothing of him. I was still engaged in peering about, when Mr. Mell came back, and asked me what I did up there?

"I beg your pardon, Sir," says I, "if you please, I'm looking for the dog."

"Dog?" says he. "What dog?"

"Isn't it a dog, sir?"

"Isn't what a dog?"

"That's to be taken care of, Sir; that bites?"

"No, Copperfield," says he, gravely, "that's not a dog. That's a boy. My instructions are, Copperfield, to put this placard on your back. I am sorry to make such a beginning with you, but I must do it."

With that he took me down, and tied the placard, which was neatly constructed for the purpose, on my shoulders like a knapsack; and wherever I went, afterwards, I had the consolation of carrying it.

What I suffered from that placard nobody can imagine. Whether it was possible for people to see me or not, I always fancied that somebody was reading it. I recollect that I positively began to have a dread of myself, as a kind of wild boy who did bite.

In the monotony of my life, and in my constant apprehension of the reopening of the school, it was an insupportable affliction! I had long tasks every day to do with Mr. Mell; but I did them, there being no Mr. and Miss Murdstone here, and got through them without disgrace. Before, and after them, I walked about—supervised by the man with the wooden leg. At one we dined, Mr. Mell and I, at the upper end of a long bare dining-room, full of deal tables, and smelling of fat. Then, we had more tasks until tea, which Mr. Mell drank out of a blue teacup, and I out of a tin pot. All day long, and until seven or eight in the evening, Mr. Mell, at his own detached desk in the schoolroom, worked hard with pen, ink, ruler, books, and writing paper, making out the bills (as I found) for last half-year. When he had put up his things for the night, he took out his flute, and blew at it.

I picture my small self in the dimly-lighted rooms, sitting with my head upon my hand, listening to the doleful performance of Mr. Mell, and conning to-morrow's lessons. I picture myself with my books shut up, still listening to the doleful performance of Mr. Mell, and listening through it to what used to be at home, and to the blowing of the wind on Yarmouth flats, and feeling very sad and solitary. I picture myself going to bed, among the unused rooms, and sitting on my bedside crying for a comfortable word from Peggotty. I picture myself coming down-stairs in the morning, looking at the school-bell hanging on the top of an outhouse with a weathercock above it; and dreading the time when it shall ring; and when the man with the wooden leg shall unlock the rusty gate to give admission to the awful Mr. Creakle.

CHAPTER VI

I ENLARGE MY CIRCLE OF ACQUAINTANCE

I HAD led this life about a month, when the man with the wooden leg began to stump about with a mop and a bucket of water, from which I inferred that preparations were making to receive Mr. Creakle and the boys. I was not mistaken.

One day I was informed by Mr. Mell, that Mr. Creakle would be home that evening. In the evening, after tea, I heard that he was come. Before bed-time, I was fetched by the man with the wooden leg to appear before him.

Mr. Creakle's presence so abashed me that I hardly saw Mrs. Creakle or Miss Creakle (who were both there, in the parlour), or anything but Mr. Creakle, a stout gentleman with a bunch of watch-chain and seals, in an arm-chair, with a tumbler and bottle beside him.

"So!" said Mr. Creakle. "This is the young gentleman whose teeth are to be filed! Turn him round."

The wooden-legged man turned me about so as to exhibit the placard; and having afforded time for a full survey of it, turned me about again, with my face to Mr. Creakle, and posted himself at Mr. Creakle's side. Mr. Creakle's face was fiery, and his eyes were small, and deep in his head; he had thick veins in his forehead, a little nose and a large chin. But the circumstance about him which impressed me most was that he had no voice, but spoke in a whisper. The exertion this cost him made his angry face much more angry, and his thick veins much thicker.

"Now," said Mr. Creakle, "what's the report of this boy?"

"There's nothing against him yet," returned the man with the wooden leg. "There has been no opportunity."

I thought Mr. Creakle was disappointed. I thought Mrs. and Miss Creakle (at whom I now glanced for the first time, and who were, both, thin and quiet) were not disappointed.

"Come here, Sir!" said Mr. Creakle, beckoning to me.

"Come here!" said the man with the wooden leg, repeating the gesture.

"I have the happiness of knowing your father-in-law," whispered Mr. Creakle, taking me by the ear; "and a worthy man he is, and a man of strong character. He knows me, and I know him. Do *you* know me? Hey?" said Mr. Creakle, pinching my ear with ferocious playfulness.

"Not yet, Sir," I said, flinching with the pain.

"Not yet? Hey?" reported Mr. Creakle. "But you will soon. Hey?"

"You [illegible]ill soon. Hey?" repeated the man with the wo[illegible]. I afterwards found that he generally acted, wi[illegible] his strong voice, as Mr. Creakle's interpreter to the boys.

I was very much frightened, and said I hoped so, if he pleased. I felt, all this while, as if my ear were blazing; he pinched it so hard.

"I'll tell you what I am," whispered Mr. Creakle, letting it go at last, with a screw at parting that brought the water into my eyes. "I'm a Tartar."

"A Tartar," said the man with the wooden leg.

"I am a determined character," said Mr. Creakle. "That's what I am. I do my duty. That's what *I* do. Now you have begun to know me, my young friend, and you may go. Take him away."

I was very glad to be ordered away, but I had a petition on my mind which concerned me so nearly, that I couldn't help saying, though I wondered at my own courage:

"If you please, Sir——"

Mr. Creakle whispered, "Hah! What's this?" and bent his eyes upon me, as if he would have burnt me up with them.

"If you please, Sir," I faltered, "if I might be allowed (I am very sorry indeed, Sir, for what I did) to take this writing off, before the boys come back——"

Whether Mr. Creakle was in earnest, or whether he only did it to frighten me, I don't know, but he made a burst out of his chair, before which I precipitately retreated and never once stopped until I reached my own bedroom, where, finding I was not pursued, I went to bed and lay quaking, for a couple of hours.

Next morning Mr. Sharp came back. Mr. Sharp was the first master, and superior to Mr. Mell. Mr. Mell took his meals with the boys, but Mr. Sharp dined and supped at Mr. Creakle's table. His hair was very smooth and wavy; but I was informed by the very first boy who came back that it was a wig (a second-hand one *he* said), and that Mr. Sharp went out every Saturday afternoon to get it curled.

It was a happy circumstance for me that T[illegible]dles came back first. He enjoyed my placard so m[illegible], that he saved me from the embarrassment of either disclosure or concealment, by presenting me to every other boy who came back, great or small, immediately on his arrival, in this form of introduction, "Look here! Here's a game!" Happily, too, the greater part of the boys came back low-spirited, and were not so boisterous at my expense as I had expected.

I was not considered as being formally received into the school, however, until J. Steerforth arrived. Before this boy, who was reputed to be a great scholar, and was very good-looking, and at least half-a-dozen years my senior, I was carried as before a magistrate. He inquired into the particulars of my punishment, and was pleased to express his opinion that it was "a jolly shame"; for which I became bound to him for ever afterwards.

"What money have you got, Copperfield?" he said, walking aside with me when he had disposed of my affair in these terms.

I told him seven shillings.

Tommy Traddles enjoyed my placard so much that he presented me to every other boy.

"You had better give it to me to take care of," he said. "At least, you can if you like. You needn't if you don't like."

I hastened to comply with his friendly suggestion, and opening Peggotty's purse, turned it upside down into his hand.

"Do you want to spend anything now?" he asked me.

"No, thank you," I replied.

"You can, if you like, you know," said Steerforth. "Say the word."

"No thank you, Sir," I repeated.

"Perhaps you'd like to spend a couple of shillings or so, in a bottle of currant wine by-and-by, up in the bedroom?" said Steerforth. "You belong to my bedroom, I find?"

It certainly had not occurred to me before, but I said, "Yes, I should like that."

"Very good," said Steerforth. "You'll be glad to spend another shilling or so, in almond cakes, I dare say?"

I said, "Yes, I should like that, too."

"And another shilling or so in biscuits, and another in fruit, eh?" said Steerforth. "I say, young Copperfield, you're going it!"

I smiled because he smiled, but I was a little troubled in my mind, too.

"Well!" said Steerforth, "I'll do the best in my power for you. I can go out when I like, and I'll smuggle thc prog in." With these words he put the money in his pocket, and kindly told me he would take care it would be all right.

He was as good as his word, if that were all right which I had a secret misgiving was nearly all wrong—for when we went up-stairs to bed, he produced the whole seven shillings' worth, and laid it out on my bed in the moonlight, saying:

"There you are, young Copperfield, and a royal spread you've got."

How well I recollect our sitting there, talking in whispers: or their talking, and my respectfully listening, I ought rather to say; the moonlight falling a little way into the room and the greater part of us in shadow. A certain mysterious feeling steals over me again, and I listen to all they tell me with a vague feeling of solemnity and awe, which makes me glad that they are all so near, and frightens me (though I feign to laugh) when Traddles pretends to see a ghost in the corner.

I heard all kinds of things about the school and all belonging to it. I heard that Mr. Creakle was the sternest and most severe of masters; that he knew nothing himself, but the art of slashing, being more ignorant (J. Steerforth said) than the lowest boy in the school.

I heard that the man with the wooden leg, Tungay, had come into the scholastic line with Mr. Creakle, in consequence of his having done a deal of dishonest work for him, and knowing his secrets.

But the greatest wonder that I heard of Mr. Creakle was, there being one boy in the school on whom he never ventured to lay a hand, and that boy being J. Steerforth.

I heard that Mr. Sharp and Mr. Mell were both supposed to be wretchedly paid; and that when there was hot and cold meat for dinner at Mr. Creakle's table, Mr. Sharp was always expected to say he preferred cold; which was corroborated by J. Steerforth, the only parlour-boarder.

The hearing of all this, and a good deal more, outlasted the banquet some time. The greater part of the guests had gone to bed and we, who had remained whispering and listening half undressed, at last betook ourselves to bed too.

"Good night, young Copperfield," said Steerforth. "I'll take care of you."

"You're very kind," I gratefully returned.

"You haven't got a sister, have you?" said Steerforth, yawning.

"No," I answered.

"That's a pity," said Steerforth. "If you had one, I should think she would have been a pretty, timid, little, bright-eyed sort of girl. I should have liked to know her. Good-night, young Copperfield."

"Good-night, Sir," I replied.

I thought of him very much after I went to bed, and raised myself to look at him where he lay in the moonlight, with his handsome face turned up, and his head reclining easily on his arm.

CHAPTER VII

MY "FIRST HALF" AT SALEM HOUSE

SCHOOL began in earnest next day. A profound impression was made upon me, I remember, by the roar of voices in the schoolroom suddenly becoming hushed as death when Mr. Creakle entered after breakfast, and stood in the doorway looking round upon us like a giant in a story-book surveying his captives.

Tungay stood at Mr. Creakle's elbow.

Mr. Creakle was seen to speak, and Tungay was heard, to this effect:

"Now, boys, this is a new half. Take care what you're about, in this new half. Come fresh up to the lessons, I advise you, for I come fresh up to the punishment. I won't flinch. It will be of no use your rubbing yourselves; you won't rub the marks out that I shall give you. Now get to work, every boy!"

When this dreadful exordium was over, and Tungay had stumped out again, Mr. Creakle came to where I sat, and told me that if I were famous for biting, he was famous for biting, too. He then showed me the cane, and asked me what I thought of *that,* for a tooth? Was it a sharp tooth, hey? Was it a double tooth, hey? Had it a deep prong, hey? Did it bite, hey? Did it bite? At every question he gave me a fleshy cut with it that made me writhe, and I was very soon in tears also.

Not that I mean to say these were special marks of distinction. On the contrary half of the establishment was writhing and crying, before the day's work began; and how much of it had writhed and cried before the day's work was over, I am really afraid to recollect, lest I should seem to exaggerate.

I should think there never can have been a man who enjoyed his profession more than Mr. Creakle did.

Here I sit at the desk watching his eye—humbly watching his eye. I have plenty to do. I don't watch his eye in idleness, but because I am morbidly attracted to it, a dread desire to know what he will do next, and whether it will be my turn to suffer, or somebody else's. A lane of small boys beyond me, with the same interest in his eye, watch it too. A moment afterwards an unhappy culprit, found guilty of imperfect exercise, approaches at his command. The culprit falters excuses, and professes a determination to do better to-morrow. Mr. Creakle cuts a joke before he beats him, and we laugh at it—miserable little dogs, we laugh, with our visages as white as ashes, and our hearts sinking into our boots.

Here I am in the playground, with my eye still fascinated by him, though I can't see him. If he looks out through the glass, the boldest boy (Steerforth excepted) stops in the middle of a shout or yell, and becomes contemplative. One day, Traddles (the most unfortunate boy in the world) breaks that window accidentally with a ball. I shudder at this moment with the tremendous sensation of seeing it done.

Poor Traddles! In a tight sky-blue suit that made his arms and legs like German sausages, or roly-poly puddings, he was the merriest and most miserable of all the boys. He was always being caned—I think he was caned every day that half-year, excepting one holiday Monday when he was only ruler'd on both hands—and was always going to write to his uncle about it, and never did. After laying his head on the desk for a little while, he would cheer up somehow, begin to laugh again, and draw skeletons all over his slate, before his eyes were dry. I used at first to wonder what comfort Traddles found in drawing skeletons, but I believe he only did it because they were easy, and didn't want any features.

He was very honourable, Traddles was, and held it as a solemn duty in the boys to stand by one another. He suffered for this on several occasions; and particularly once, when Steerforth laughed in church, and the Beadle thought it was Traddles, and took him out. He never said who was the real offender, though he smarted for it next day, and was imprisoned so many hours that he came forth with a whole churchyardful of skeletons swarming all over his Latin Dictionary. But he had his reward. Steerforth said there was nothing of the sneak in Traddles, and we all felt that to be the highest praise. For my part, I could have gone through a good deal (though I was much less brave than Traddles, and nothing like so old) to have won such a recompense.

Steerforth continued his protection of me, and proved a very useful friend, since nobody dared to annoy one whom he honoured with his countenance. He couldn't—or at all events he didn't—defend me from Mr. Creakle, but whenever I had been treated worse than usual, he always told me that I wanted a little of his pluck, and that he wouldn't have stood it himself; which I felt he intended for encouragement, and considered to be very kind of him. There was one advantage, and only one that I know of, in Mr. Creakle's severity. He found my placard in his way when he came up or down behind the form on which I sat, and wanted to make a cut at me in passing; for this reason it was soon taken off, and I saw it no more.

An accidental circumstance cemented the intimacy between Steerforth and me, in a manner that inspired me with great pride and satisfaction, though it sometimes led to inconvenience. It happened on one occasion that I hazarded the observation that something or somebody—I forget what now—was like something or somebody in *Peregrine Pickle*. He said nothing at the time; but when I was going to bed at night, asked me if I had got that book?

I told him no, and explained how it was that I had read it, and all those other books of which I have made mention.

"And do you recollect them?" Steerforth said.

"Oh, yes," I replied.

"Then I tell you what, young Copperfield," said Steerforth. "You shall tell 'em to me. I can't get to sleep very early at night, and I generally wake rather early in the morning. We'll go over 'em one after another. We'll make some regular *Arabian Nights* of it."

I felt extremely flattered by this arrangement, and we commenced that very evening.

The drawback was, that I was often sleepy at night, or out of spirits, and then it was rather hard work, and it must be done; for to disappoint or to displease Steerforth was of course out of the question. In the morning, too, it was tiresome to be roused and forced into a long story before the getting-up bell rang; but Steerforth was resolute; and as he explained to me, in return, anything in my tasks that was too hard for me, I was no loser by the transaction. Let me do myself justice, however. I was moved by no selfish motive. I admired and loved him, and his approval was return enough. It was so precious to me, that I look back on these trifles, now, with an aching heart.

Whatever I had within me that was romantic and dreamy, was encouraged by so much story-telling in the dark; and in that respect the pursuit may not have been very profitable to me. But the consciousness that this accomplishment of mine was bruited about among the boys, and attracted a good deal of notice to me stimulated me to exertion. In a school carried on by sheer cruelty there is not likely to be much learnt. I believe our boys were, generally, as ignorant a set as any schoolboys in existence; they were too much troubled and knocked about to learn. But my little vanity, and Steerforth's help, urged me on somehow; and without saving me from much, if anything, in the way of punishment, made me, for the time I was there, an exception to the general body, insomuch that I did steadily pick up some crumbs of knowledge.

In this I was much assisted by Mr. Mell, who had a liking for me that I am grateful to remember.

One afternoon, when we were all harassed into a state of dire confusion, and Mr. Creakle was laying about him dreadfully, Tungay came in, and called out in his usual strong way: "Visitors for Copperfield!"

A few words were interchanged between him and Mr. Creakle, as, who the visiters were, and what room they were to be shown into; and then I, who had, according to custom, stood up on the announcement being made, and felt quite faint with astonishment, was told to go by the back stairs and get a clean frill on, before I repaired to the dining-room. These orders I obeyed, and when I got to the parlour-door, and thought that it might be my mother—I had only thought of Mr. or Miss Murdstone until then—I drew back my hand from the lock, and stopped to have a sob before I went in.

At first I saw nobody; but feeling a pressure against the door I looked round it, and there, to my amazement, were Mr. Peggotty and Ham. I could not help laughing; but we shook hands in a very cordial way; and I laughed and laughed, until I pulled out my pocket-handkerchief and wiped my eyes.

Mr. Peggotty showed a great concern when he saw me do this, and nudged Ham to say something.

"Cheer up, Mas'r Davy bor'!" said Ham, in his simpering way. "Why, how you have growed!"

"Am I grown?" I said.

"Growed, Mas'r Davy bor'? Ain't he growed!" said Ham.

"Ain't he growed!" said Mr. Peggotty.

They made me laugh again by laughing at each other, and then we all three laughed until I was in danger of crying again.

"Do you know how mama is, Mr. Peggotty?" I said. "And how my dear, dear, old Peggotty is?"

"Oncommon," said Mr. Peggotty.

"And little Em'ly, and Mrs. Gummidge?"

"On—common," said Mr. Peggotty.

There was a silence. Mr. Peggotty, to relieve it, took

A long story before the gettin-up bell rang.

two prodigious lobsters, and an enomous crab, and a large canvas bag of shrimps, out of his pockets, and piled them up in Ham's arms.

"You see," said Mr. Peggotty, "knowing as you was partial to a little relish with your wittles when you was along with us, we took the liberty. Mrs. Gummidge biled 'em. Yes," said Mr. Peggotty, slowly, "Mrs. Gummidge, I do assure you, she biled 'em."

I expressed my thanks. Mr. Peggotty, after looking at Ham, who stood smiling sheepishly over the shell-fish, without making any attempt to help him, said:

"We come, you see, in one of our Yarmouth lugs to Gravesen'. My sister she wrote to me if ever I chanced to come to Gravesen', I was to come over and inquire for Mas'r Davy, and give her dooty, humbly wishing him well, and reporting of the fam'ly. Little Em'ly, you see, she'll write to my sister when I go back."

I thanked Mr. Peggotty heartily; and said, with a consciousness of reddening, that I supposed little Em'ly was altered too.

"She's getting to be a woman, that's wot she's getting to be," said Mr. Peggotty. "Ask *him*."

He meant Ham, who beamed with delight and assent over the bag of shrimps.

"Her pretty face!" said Mr. Peggotty, with his own shining like a light.

"Her learning!" said Ham.

"Her writing!" said Mr. Peggotty. "Why it's as black as jet! And so large it is, you might see it anywheres."

It was perfectly delightful to behold Mr. Peggotty when he thought of his little favourite.

Ham was quite as earnest as he. I dare say they would have said much more about her, if they had not been abashed by the unexpected coming in of Steerforth, who, seeing me in a corner speaking with two strangers, stopped and said: "I didn't know you were here, young Copperfield!" and crossed by us on his way out. I called to him as he was going, "Don't go, Steerforth, if you please. These are two Yarmouth boatmen—very kind, good people—who are relations of my nurse, and have come from Gravesend to see me."

"Aye, aye?" said Steerforth, returning. "I am glad to see them. How are you both?"

There was an ease in his manner—a gay and light manner it was, but not swaggering—which I still believe to have borne a kind of enchantment with it. I could not but see how pleased they were with him, and how they seemed to open their hearts to him in a moment.

"You must let them know at home, if you please, Mr. Peggotty," I said, "when that letter is sent, that Mr. Steerforth is very kind to me, and that I don't know what I should ever do here without him."

"Nonsense!" said Steerforth, laughing. "You mustn't tell them anything of the kind."

"And if Mr. Steerforth ever comes into Norfolk or Suffolk, Mr. Peggotty," I said, "while I am there, you may depend upon it I shall bring him to Yarmouth, if he will let me, to see your house. You never saw such a good house, Steerforth. It's made out of a boat!"

"Made out of a boat, is it?" said Steerforth. "It's the right sort of house for such a thorough-built boatman."

"So 'tis, Sir, so 'tis, Sir," said Ham, grinning. "You're right, young gen'lm'n. Mas'r Davy, bor', gen'lm'n's right. A thorough-built boatman! Hor, hor! That's what he is, too!"

Mr. Peggotty was no less pleased than his nephew.

"Well, sir," he said, bowing and chuckling, and tucking in the ends of his neckerchief at his breast: "I thankee, Sir, I thankee!

"I'm obleeged to you, Sir, for your welcoming manner of me. I'm rough, Sir, but I'm ready—least ways, I *hope* I'm ready, you understand. My house ain't much for to see, Sir, but it's hearty at your service if ever you should come along with Mas'r Davy to see it."

Ham echoed this sentiment, and we parted with them in the heartiest manner.

We transported the shell-fish up into our room unobserved, and made a great supper that evening. But Traddles couldn't get happily out of it. He was too unfortunate even to come through a supper like anybody else. He was taken ill in the night, and after being drugged with black draughts and blue pills, to an extent which Demple (whose father was a doctor) said was enough to undermine a horse's constitution, received a caning and six chapters of Greek Testament for refusing to confess.

The rest of the half-year is a jumble in my recollection of the daily strife and struggle of our lives. I well remember though, how the distant idea of the holidays began to come towards us, and to grow and grow. How from counting months, we came to weeks, and then to days; and how I then began to be afraid that I should not be sent for, and learnt from Steerforth that I *had* been sent for. How the breaking-up day changed its place fast, at last, from the week after next to next week, this week, the day after to-morrow, to-morrow, to-day, to-night—when I was inside the Yarmouth mail, and going home.

CHAPTER VIII

MY HOLIDAYS. ESPECIALLY ONE HAPPY AFTERNOON

When we arrived before day at the inn where the mail stopped, which was not the inn where my friend the waiter lived, I was shown up to a nice little bedroom, with DOLPHIN painted on the door.

Mr. Barkis, the carrier, was to call for me in the morning at nine o'clock. He received me exactly as if not five minutes had elapsed since we were last together.

As soon as I and my box were in the cart, and the carrier was seated, the lazy horse walked away with us all at his accustomed pace.

"You look very well, Mr. Barkis," I said.

Mr. Barkis rubbed his cheek with his cuff, and then looked at his cuff, but made no other acknowledgment of the compliment.

"I gave your message, Mr. Barkis," I said. "I wrote to Peggotty.

"Ah!" said Mr. Barkis.

"Wasn't it right, Mr. Barkis?" I asked, after a little hesitation.

"Why, no," said Mr. Barkis.

"Not the message?"

"The message was right enough, perhaps," said Mr. Barkis, "but it come to an end there."

Not understanding what he meant, I repeated inquisitively: "Came to an end, Mr. Barkis?"

"Nothing come of it," he explained. "No answer. When a man says he's willin', it's as much as to say, that man's a waitin' for a answer."

"Well, Mr. Barkis?"

"Well," said Mr. Barkis, "that man's been a waitin' for a answer ever since."

"Have you told her so, Mr. Barkis?"

"N—no," growled Mr. Barkis. "I ain't got no call to go and tell her so. I never said six words to her myself. *I* ain't a goin' to tell her so."

"Would you like me to do it, Mr. Barkis?" said I, doubtfully.

"You might tell her, if you would," said Mr. Barkis, "that Barkis was a waitin' for a answer. Says you—what name is it?"

"Her name?"

"Ah!" said Mr. Barkis, with a nod of his head.

"Peggotty."

"Chrisen name? Or nat'ral name?" said Mr. Barkis.

"Oh, it's not her Christian name. Her Christian name is Clara."

"Is it though?" said Mr. Barkis.

"Well!" he resumed at length. "Says you, 'Peggotty! Barkis is a waitin' for a answer.' Says she, perhaps, 'Answer to what?' Says you, 'To what I told you.' 'What is that?' says she. 'Barkis is willin', says you."

This extremely artful suggestion, Mr. Barkis accompanied with a nudge of his elbow that gave me quite a stitch in my side. After that he slouched over his horse in his usual manner; and made no other reference to the subject except, half an hour afterwards, taking a piece of chalk from his pocket, and writing up, inside the tilt of the cart, "Clara Peggotty"—apparently as a private memorandum.

Ah, what a strange feeling it was to be going home when it was not home, and to find that every object I looked at, reminded me of the happy old home, which was like a dream I could never dream again! But there I was; and soon I was at our house, and the carrier put my box down at the garden-gate, and left me.

I walked along the path towards the house, glancing at the windows, and fearing at every step to see Mr. Murdstone or Miss Murdstone lowering out of one of them. No face appeared, however; and I went in with a quiet, timid step.

When I set foot in the hall my mother was singing in a low tone. I think I must have lain in her arms, and heard her singing so to me when I was but a baby.

I went softly into the room. She was sitting by the fire, suckling an infant, whose tiny hand she held against her neck.

I spoke to her, and she started, and cried out. But seeing me, she called me her dear Davy, her own boy! and coming half across the room to meet me, kneeled down upon the ground and kissed me, and laid my head down on her bosom near the little creature that was nestling there, and put its hand up to my lips.

I wish I had died. I wish I had died then, with that feeling in my heart! I should have been more fit for Heaven than I ever have been since.

"He is your brother," said my mother, fondling me. "Davy, my pretty boy! My poor child!" Then she kissed me more and more, and clasped me round the neck. This she was doing when Peggotty came running in, and bounced down on the ground beside us, and went mad about us both for a quarter of an hour.

It seemed that I had not been expected so soon, the carrier being much before his usual time. It seemed, too, that Mr. Murdstone and Miss Murdstone had gone out upon a visit and would not return before night. I had never hoped for this, and I felt, for the time, as if the old days were come back.

We dined together by the fireside. Peggotty was in attendance to wait upon us, but my mother wouldn't let her do it, and made her dine with us. I had my own old plate, with a brown view of a man-of-war in full sail upon it, which Peggotty would not have had broken, she said, for a hundred pounds. I had my own old mug with David on it, and my own old little knife and fork that wouldn't cut.

While we were at table, I thought it a favourable occasion to tell Peggotty about Mr. Barkis, who, before I had finished what I had to tell her, began to laugh, and throw her apron over her face.

"Peggotty," said my mother. "What's the matter?"

"Oh, drat the man!" cried Peggotty. "He wants to marry me."

"It would be a very good match for you; wouldn't it?" said my mother.

"Oh! I don't know," said Peggotty. "Don't ask me. I wouldn't have him if he was made of gold. Nor I wouldn't have anybody."

"Then, why don't you tell him so, you ridiculous thing?" said my mother.

"Tell him so," retorted Peggotty, looking out of her apron. "He has never said a word to me about it. He knows better. If he was to make so bold as say a word to me, I should slap his face."

Her own was as red as ever I saw it, or any other face, I think; but she only covered it again, for a few moments at a time, when she was taken with a violent fit of laughter; and after two or three of those attacks, went on with her dinner.

I remarked that my mother, though she smiled when Peggotty looked at her, became more serious and thoughtful. I had seen at first that she was changed. Her face was very pretty still, but it looked careworn, and too delicate; and her hand was so thin and white that it seemed to me to be almost transparent. But the change to which I now refer was in her manner, which became anxious and fluttered. At last she said, putting out her hand, and laying it affectionately on the hand of her old servant:

"Peggotty dear, you are not going to be married?"

"Me, ma'am?" returned Peggotty, staring. "Lord bless you, no!"

"Not just yet?" said my mother, tenderly.

"Never!" cried Peggotty.

My mother took her hand and said:

"Don't leave me, Peggotty. Stay with me. It will not be for long, perhaps. What should I ever do without you!"

"Me leave you, my precious!" cried Peggotty. "Not for all the world and his wife. Why, what's put that in your silly little head?" For Peggotty had been used of old to talk to my mother sometimes, like a child.

But my mother made no answer, except to thank her, and Peggotty went running on in her own fashion.

"Me leave you? Peggotty go away from you? No, no, no," said Peggotty, shaking her head, and folding her arms; "not she, my dear. It isn't that there ain't some Cats that would be well enough pleased if she did, but they sha'n't be pleased. They shall be aggravated. I'll stay with you till I am a cross cranky old woman. And when I'm too deaf, and too lame, and too blind, and too mumbly for want of teeth, to be of any use at all, then I shall go to my Davy, and ask him to take me in."

"And Peggotty," says I, "I shall be glad to see you, and I'll make you as welcome as a queen."

"Bless your dear heart!" cried Peggotty. "I know you will!" And she kissed me beforehand, in grateful acknowledgement of my hospitality.

We sat round the fire, and talked delightfully. I told them what a hard master Mr. Creakle was, and they pitied me very much. I told them what a fine fellow Steerforth was, and what a patron of mine, and Peggotty said she would walk a score of miles to see him. I took the little baby in my arms when it was awake, and nursed it lovingly. When it was asleep again, I crept close to my mother's side, according to my old custom, and sat with my arms embracing her waist, and my little red cheek on her shoulder, and once more felt her beautiful hair drooping over me—like an angel's wing as I used to think, and was very happy indeed.

It was almost ten o'clock before we heard the sound of wheels. We all got up then; and my mother said hurriedly that, as it was so late, and Mr. and Miss Murdstone approved of early hours for young people, perhaps I had better go to bed. I kissed her, and went up-stairs with my candle directly, before they came in.

I felt uncomfortable about going down to breakfast in the morning, as I had never set eyes on Mr. Murdstone since the day when I committed my memorable offence. However, as it must be done, I went down, after two or three false starts half-way, and as many runs back on tiptoe to my own room, and presented myself in the parlour.

He was standing before the fire with his back to it, while Miss Murdstone made the tea. He looked at me steadily as I entered, but made no sign of recognition whatever.

I went up to him, after a moment of confusion, and said: "I beg your pardon, sir. I am very sorry for what I did, and I hope you will forgive me."

"I am glad to hear you are sorry, David," he replied.

The hand he gave me was the hand I had bitten. I could not restrain my eye from resting for an instant on a red spot upon it; but it was not so red as I turned, when I met that sinister expression in his face.

"How do you do, ma'am?" I said to Miss Murdstone.

"Ah, dear me!" sighed Miss Murdstone, giving me the tea-caddy scoop instead of her fingers. "How long are the holidays?"

"A month, ma'am."

"Counting from when?"

"From to-day, ma'am."

"Oh!" said Miss Murdstone. "Then here's *one* day off."

She kept a calendar of the holidays in this way, and every morning checked a day off in exactly the same manner. She did it gloomily until she came to ten, but when she got into two figures she became more hopeful, and, as the time advanced, even jocular.

On one occasion my mother, who had been looking at the baby's eyes as it lay upon her lap, said:

"Davy! come here!" and looked at mine.

I saw Miss Murdstone lay her beads down.

"I declare," said my mother, gently, "they are exactly

alike. I suppose they are mine. But they are wonderfully alike."

"What are you talking about, Clara?" said Miss Murdstone.

"My dear Jane," faltered my mother, a little abashed by the harsh tone of this inquiry, "I find that the baby's eyes and Davy's are exactly alike."

"Clara!" said Miss Murdstone, rising angrily, "you are a positive fool sometimes."

"My dear Jane," remonstrated my mother.

"A positive fool," said Miss Murdstone. "Who else could compare my brother's baby with your boy? They are not at all alike. They are exactly unlike. I hope they will ever remain so." With that she stalked out, and made the door bang after her.

In short, I was not a favourite with Miss Murdstone. In short, I was not a favourite there with anybody, not even with myself; for those who did like me could not show it, and those who did not showed it so plainly that I had a sensitive consciousness of always appearing constrained, boorish, and dull.

I had perception enough to know that my mother was not only ceaselessly afraid of her own offending, but of my offending, and uneasily watched their looks if I only moved. Therefore I resolved to keep myself as much out of their way as I could; and many a wintry hour did I hear the church-clock strike, when I was sitting in my cheerless bedroom, wrapped in my little great-coat, poring over a book.

In the evening, sometimes, I went and sat with Peggotty in the kitchen. There I was comfortable, and not afraid of being myself. But neither of these resources was approved of in the parlour.

"David," said Mr. Murdstone, one day after dinner when I was going to leave the room as usual, "I am sorry to observe that you are of a sullen disposition."

"As sulky as a bear!" said Miss Murdstone.

I stood still, and hung my head.

"Now, David," said Mr. Murdstone, "a sullen obdurate disposition is, of all tempers, the worst."

"And the boy's is, of all such dispositions that ever I have seen," remarked his sister, "the most confirmed and stubborn. I think, my dear Clara, even you must observe it?"

"I beg your pardon, my dear Jane," said my mother, "but are you quite sure—I am certain you'll excuse me, my dear Jane—that you understand Davy?"

"I should be somewhat ashamed of myself, Clara," returned Miss Murdstone, "if I could not understand the boy, or any boy. I do lay claim to common sense."

"No doubt, my dear Jane," returned my mother, "your understanding is very vigorous."

"We'll say I don't understand the boy, Clara," returned Miss Murdstone. "He is much too deep for me. But perhaps my brother's penetration may enable him to have some insight into his character. And I believe my brother was speaking on the subject when we—not very decently—interrupted him."

"I think, Clara," said Mr. Murdstone, in a low grave voice, "that there may be better and more dispassionate judges of such a question than you."

"Edward," replied my mother, timidly, "you are a far better judge of all questions than I pretend to be. Both you and Jane are. I only said——"

"You only said something weak and inconsiderate," he replied. "Try not do it again, my dear Clara."

My mother's lips moved, as if she answered "Yes, my dear Edward," but she said nothing aloud.

"I was sorry, David, I remarked," said Mr. Murdstone, "to observe that you are of a sullen disposition. You must endeavour, Sir, to change it. We must endeavour to change it for you."

"I beg your pardon, Sir," I faltered. "I have never meant to be sullen since I came back."

"Don't take refuge in a lie, Sir!" he returned so fiercely that I saw my mother involuntarily put out her trembling hand as if to interpose between us. "You have withdrawn yourself in your sullenness to your own room. You know, now, once for all, that I require you to be here, and not there. You know me, David. I will have it done."

Miss Murdstone gave a hoarse chuckle.

"I will not have this room shunned as if it were infected, at the pleasure of a child," he continued. "Sit down."

He ordered me like a dog, and I obeyed like a dog.

"One thing more," he said. "You are not to associate with servants. I disapprove of such company as Mistress Peggotty. Now, David, you understand me, and you know what will be the consequence if you fail to obey me to the letter."

I knew well—better perhaps than he thought, as far as my poor mother was concerned—and I obeyed him to the letter. I retreated to my own room no more; I took refuge with Peggotty no more; but sat wearily in the parlour day after day looking forward to night, and bedtime.

What irksome constraint I underwent, sitting in the same attitude hours upon hours, afraid to move an arm or a leg lest Miss Murdstone should complain of my restlessness.

What meals I had in silence and embarrassment, always feeling that there were a knife and fork too many, and those mine; an appetite too many, and that mine; a plate and chair too many, and those mine; a somebody too many, and that I!

What evenings, when the candles came, and I was expected to employ myself, but not daring to read an entertaining book, pored over some hard-headed harder-hearted treatise on arithmetic; what a heavy relief it was to hear Miss Murdstone hail the first stroke of nine at night, and order me to bed!

Thus the holidays lagged away, until the morning came when Miss Murdstone said: "Here's the last day off!" and gave me the closing cup of tea of the vacation.

I was not sorry to go. I had lapsed into a stupid state; but I was recovering a little and looking forward to Steerforth, albeit Mr. Creakle loomed behind him. Again Mr. Barkis appeared at the gate, and again Miss Murdstone in her warning voice, said: "Clara!" when my mother bent over me, to bid me farewell.

I kissed her, and my baby brother, and was very sorry then; but not sorry to go away, for the gulf between us was there, and the parting was there, every day.

I was in the carrier's cart when I heard her calling to me. I looked out, and she stood at the garden-gate alone, holding her baby up in her arms for me to see.

So I lost her. So I saw her afterwards, in my sleep at school—a silent presence near my bed—looking at me with the same intent face—holding up her baby in her arms.

CHAPTER IX

I HAVE A MEMORABLE BIRTHDAY

I PASS over all that happened at school, until the anniversary of my birthday came round in March. Except that Steerforth was more to be admired than ever, I remember nothing.

It is even difficult for me to believe that there was a gap of full two months between my return to Salem House and the arrival of that birthday.

It was after breakfast, and we had been summoned in from the playground, when Mr. Sharp entered and said:

"David Copperfield is to go into the parlour."

I expected a hamper from Peggotty, and brightened at the order.

"Don't hurry, David," said Mr. Sharp. "There's time enough, my boy, don't hurry."

I might have been surprised by the feeling tone in which he spoke, if I had given it a thought; but I gave it none. I hurried away to the parlour and there I found Mrs. Creakle with an opened letter.

"David Copperfield," said Mrs. Creakle, leading me to a sofa, and sitting down beside me. "I have something to tell you, my child."

I looked at her earnestly.

"When you came away from home at the end of the vacation," said Mrs. Creakle, after a pause, "were they all well?" After another pause, "Was your mama well?"

I trembled and still looked at her earnestly, making no attempt to answer.

"Because," said she, "I grieve to tell you that your mama is very ill."

A mist rose between Mrs. Creakle and me. Then I felt the burning tears run down my face.

"She is very dangerously ill," she added.

I knew all now.

"She is dead."

There was no need to tell me so. I had already broken out into a desolate cry.

She was very kind to me. She kept me there all day, and left me alone sometimes; and I cried, and wore myself to sleep, and awoke and cried again. When I could cry no more, I began to think.

I thought of our house shut up and hushed. I thought of the little baby who, they believed, would die too. I thought of my father's grave and of my mother lying there beneath the tree.

I was to go home next night. We had no story-telling that evening, and Traddles insisted on lending me his pillow. I don't know what good he thought it would do me, for I had one of my own; but it was all he had to lend, poor fellow, except a sheet of letter-paper full of skeletons; and that he gave me at parting.

I left Salem House upon the morrow afternoon. I little thought then that I left it, never to return. We did not get into Yarmouth before nine or ten o'clock in the morning. I looked out for Mr. Barkis, but he was not there; and instead of him a fat little old man with rusty little bunches of ribbons at the knees of his breeches came puffing up to the coach-window, and said:

"Master Copperfield?"

"Yes, Sir."

"Will you come with me, young Sir, if you please," he said.

I put my hand in his and we walked to a shop on which was written, OMER, DRAPER, TAILOR, HABERDASHER, FUNERAL FURNISHER, &c. It was a close and stifling little shop; full of all sorts of clothing, made and unmade. We went into a little back-parlour behind the shop, where we found three young women at work on a quantity of black materials.

"Well," said Mr. Omer, "I think I'll measure this young scholar. Would you walk into the shop, Master Copperfield?"

I preceded Mr. Omer, and after showing me a roll of cloth which he said was too good mourning for anything short of parents, he took my various dimensions, and put them down in a book.

He then called down a little break-neck range of steps behind a door: "Bring up that tea and bread-and-butter!" which, after some time, appeared on a tray, and turned out to be for me.

"Do you know how my little brother is, Sir?" I inquired. Mr. Omer shook his head.

"He is in his mother's arms," said he.

"Oh, poor little fellow! Is he dead?"

"Don't mind it more than you can help," said Mr. Omer. "Yes, the baby's dead."

My wounds broke out afresh at this intelligence. I left the scarcely tasted breakfast, and went and rested my head on another table hastily cleared lest I should spot the mourning, lying there, with my tears.

The chaise soon came round to the front of the shop, and the old man sat in front to drive. When we reached home, I dropped out behind, as quickly as possible. I was in Peggotty's arms before I got to the door, and she took me into the house. Her grief burst out when she first saw me; but she controlled it soon, and spoke in whispers, and walked softly as if the dead could be disturbed.

Mr. Murdstone took no heed of me when I went into the parlour, where he was, but sat by the fireside, weeping silently, and pondering in his elbow-chair. Miss Murdstone, who was busy at her writing-desk, gave me her cold finger-nails, and asked me, in an iron whisper, if I had been measured for my mourning.

I said: "Yes."

"And your shirts," said Miss Murdstone; "have you brought 'em home?"

"Yes, ma'am, I have brought home all my clothes."

Her brother took a book sometimes, but never read it that I saw. He would open it and look at it but would remain for a whole hour without turning the leaf and then put it down and walk to and fro in the room. He very seldom spoke to her, and never to me.

In these days before the funeral, I saw but little of Peggotty, except that, in passing up or down stairs, I always found her close to the room where my mother and her baby lay, and except that she came to me every night, and sat by my bed's head while I went to sleep.

If the funeral had been yesterday, I could not recollect it better. The very air of the best parlour, the faint sweet smell of cake, the odour of our black clothes. Mr. Chillip is in the room, and comes to speak to me.

"And how is Master David?" he says, kindly.

I cannot tell him very well. I give him my hand, which he holds in his.

"Dear me!" says Mr. Chillip, meekly smiling. "Our little friends grow out of our knowledge, ma'am?"

This is to Miss Murdstone, who makes no reply.

And now the bell begins to sound, and Mr. Omer and another come to make us ready. . . . We stand around the grave. Now there is a solemn hush; and while we stand bare-headed, I hear the voice of the clergyman, saying: "I am the Resurrection and the Life, saith the Lord!" Then I hear sobs; and, standing apart among the lookers-on, I see that good and faithful servant, whom of all the people upon earth I love the best, and unto whom my childish heart is certain that the Lord will one day say: "Well done."

I knew that Peggotty would come to me in my room. The stillness of the time was suited to us both. She sat down by my side upon my little bed; and holding my hand, told me all that she had to tell.

"She was never well," said Peggotty, "and not happy.

When her baby was born, I thought at first she would get better, but she was more delicate every day.

"The last time that I saw her like her own old self was the night when you came home, my dear. The day you went away, she said to me, 'I never shall see my pretty darling again.'

"She never told her husband what she told me till one night, a little more than a week before it happened, when she said to him: 'My dear, I think I am dying.'

" 'It's off my mind now, Peggotty,' she told me, when I laid her in her bed that night. 'He will believe it more and more, poor fellow, every day for a few days, and then it will be past.'

"On the last night she said, 'Tell my dearest boy that his mother blessed him not once, but a thousand times.' "

Thus ended Peggotty's narration. From the moment of my knowing of the death of my mother I remembered her only as the young mother of my earliest impressions, who had been used to wind her bright curls round and round her finger, and to dance with me at twilight in the parlour. In her death she winged her way back to her calm untroubled youth, and cancelled all the rest.

CHAPTER X

I BECOME NEGLECTED, AND AM PROVIDED FOR

THE first act of business Miss Murdstone performed when the day of the solemnity was over, and light was freely admitted into the house, was to give Peggotty a month's warning. Much as Peggotty would have disliked such a service, I believe she would have retained it, for my sake, in preference to the best upon earth. She told me we must part, and told me why; and we condoled with one another, in all sincerity.

As to me or my future, not a word was said. I mustered courage once, to ask Miss Murdstone when I was going back to school; and she answered drily, she believed I was not going back at all. I was told nothing more. I was very anxious to know what was going to be done with me, and so was Peggotty; but neither she nor I could pick up any information on the subject.

There was one change in my condition, which, while it relieved me a great deal, might have made me yet more uncomfortable about the future. It was this. The constraint that had been put upon me was quite abandoned. I was so far from being required to keep my dull post in the parlour, that on several occasions, when I took my seat there, Miss Murdstone frowned to me to go away. I was so far from being warned off from Peggotty's society, that, provided I was not in Mr. Murdstone's, I was never sought out or inquired for. At first I was in daily dread of his taking my education in hand again, or of Miss Murdstone's devoting herself to it; but I soon began to think that all I had to anticipate was neglect.

One evening when I was warming my hands at the

kitchen fire, Peggotty said, "I have tried, my dear, to get a suitable service here, in Blunderstone; but there's no such a thing, my love."

"And what do you mean to do, Peggotty?" says I, wistfully.

"I expect I shall be forced to go to Yarmouth," replied Peggotty, "and live there."

I said, brightening a little, "I shall see you sometimes, my dear old Peggotty, there. You won't be quite at the other end of the world, will you?"

"Contrary ways, please God!" cried Peggotty, with great animation. "As long as you are here, my pet, I shall come over every week of my life to see you. One day every week of my life!"

I felt a great weight taken off my mind by this promise; but even this was not all, for Peggotty went on to say: "I'm a going, Davy, you see, to my brother's first, for another fortnight's visit. Now, I have been thinking, that perhaps you might be let to go along with me."

If anything could have given me pleasure it would have been this project.

Miss Murdstone soon came out to take an evening grope in the store-closet and Peggotty broached the topic.

"The boy will be idle there," said Miss Murdstone, looking into a pickle-jar, "but he would be anywhere, in my opinion. It is of paramount importance that my brother should not be disturbed or made uncomfortable. I suppose I had better say yes."

The permission was never retracted; for when the month was out, Peggotty and I were ready to depart.

Mr. Barkis came into the house for Peggotty's boxes. I had never known him to pass the garden-gate before, but on this occasion he came to the house. Peggotty was naturally in low spirits at leaving what had been her home so many years, and she got into the cart, and sat in it with her handkerchief at her eyes. So long as she remained in this condition, Mr. Barkis gave no sign of life whatever. But when she began to look about her, and to speak to me, he nodded his head and grinned several times.

"It's a beautiful day, Mr. Barkis!" I said, as an act of politeness.

"It ain't bad," said Mr. Barkis.

"Peggotty is quite comfortable now, Mr. Barkis," I remarked, for his satisfaction.

"Is she, though?" said Mr. Barkis.

After reflecting about it, with a sagacious air, Mr. Barkis eyed her, and said:

"*Are* you pretty comfortable?"

Peggotty laughed, and answered in the affirmative.

"But really and truly, you know. Are you?" growled Mr. Barkis, sliding nearer to her on the seat, and nudging her with his elbow. "Are you? Really and truly, pretty comfortable? Are you? Eh?" At each of these inquiries Mr. Barkis shuffled nearer to her, and gave her another nudge; so that at last we were all crowded together in the left-hand corner of the cart, and I was so squeezed that I could hardly bear it.

Peggotty calling his attention to my sufferings, Mr. Barkis gave me a little more room at once, but he seemed to think he had hit upon a wonderful expedient for expressing himself in a neat, agreeable, and pointed manner, without inventing conversation. He manifestly chuckled over it for some time. By-and-by he turned to Peggotty again, and repeating, "Are you pretty comfortable, though?" bore down upon us as before, until the breath was nearly wedged out of my body. By-and-by he made another descent upon us with the same inquiry, and the same result. At length, I got up whenever I saw him coming, and standing on the foot-board, pretended to look at the prospect; after which I did very well.

But as we drew nearer to the end of our journey, he had more to do and less time for gallantry; and when we got on Yarmouth pavement, we were all too much shaken and jolted to have any leisure for anything else.

Mr. Peggotty and Ham waited for us at the old place.

They received me and Peggotty in an affectionate manner, and shook hands with Mr. Barkis. They each took one of Peggotty's trunks, and we were going away, when Mr. Barkis solemnly made a sign to me with his forefinger to come under an archway.

"I say," growled Mr. Barkis, "it was all right."

I looked up into his face, and answered, with an attempt to be very profound: "Oh!"

"It didn't come to a end there," said Mr. Barkis, nodding confidentially. "It was all right."

Again I answered, "Oh!"

"You know who was willin'," said my friend. "It was Barkis, and Barkis only."

I nodded assent.

"It's all right," said Mr. Barkis, shaking hands; "I'm a friend of yourn. You made it all right, first. It's all right."

In his attempts to be particularly lucid, Mr. Barkis was so extremely mysterious that I might have stood looking in his face for an hour but for Peggotty's calling me away. As we were going along, she asked me what he had said; and I told her he had said it was all right.

"Like his impudence," said Peggotty, "but I don't mind that! Davy dear, what should you think if I was to think of being married?"

"Why—I suppose you would like me as much then, Peggotty, as you do now?" I returned, after a little consideration.

Greatly to the astonishment of the passengers in the street, the good soul was obliged to stop and embrace me on the spot, with many protestations of her unalterable love.

"Tell me what should you say, darling?" she asked again, when this was over, and we were walking on.

"If you were thinking of being married—to Mr. Barkis, Peggotty?"

"Yes," said Peggotty.

"I should think it would be a very good thing. For then you know, Peggotty, you would always have the horse and cart to bring you over to see me, and could come for nothing, and be sure of coming."

"The sense of the dear!" cried Peggotty. "What I have been thinking of, this month back! Yes, my precious; and I think I should be more independent altogether, you see. Barkis is a good plain creatur'," said Peggotty, "and if I tried to do my duty by him, I think it would be my fault if I wasn't—if I wasn't pretty comfortable," said Peggotty, laughing heartily.

This quotation from Mr. Barkis was so appropriate, and tickled us both so much, that we laughed again and again, and were quite in a pleasant humour when we came within view of Mr. Peggotty's cottage.

It looked just the same, except that it may, perhaps, have shrunk a little in my eyes; and Mrs. Gummidge was waiting at the door as if she had stood there ever since. All within was the same, down to the seaweed in the blue mug in my bedroom. I went into the outhouse to look about me; and the very same lobsters, crabs, and crawfish possessed by the same desire to pinch the world in general, appeared to be in the same state of conglomeration in the same old corner.

But there was no little Em'ly to be seen, so I asked Mr. Peggotty where she was.

"She's at school, Sir," said Mr. Peggotty. "She'll be home," looking at the Dutch clock, "in from twenty minutes to half-an-hour's time."

Mrs. Gummidge moaned.

"Cheer up, Mawther!" cried Mr. Peggotty.

"I feel it more than anybody else," said Mrs. Gummidge; "I'm a lone lorn creetur', and she used to be a'most the only think that didn't go contrairy with me."

Mrs. Gummidge, whimpering and shaking her head, applied herself to blowing the fire. Mr. Peggotty, looking round upon us, said in a low voice: "The old 'un!" From this I rightly conjectured that no improvement had taken place since my last visit in the state of Mrs. Gummidge's spirits.

Now, the whole place was, or it should have been, quite as delightful a place as ever; and yet it did not impress me in the same way. I felt rather disappointed with it. Perhaps it was because little Em'ly was not at home. I knew the way by which she would come, and presently found myself strolling along the path to meet her.

A figure appeared in the distance before long, and I soon knew it to be Em'ly. But when she drew nearer, and I saw her blue eyes looking bluer, and her dimpled face looking brighter, and her whole self prettier and gayer, a curious feeling came over me that made me pretend not to know her, and pass by as if I were looking at something a long way off.

Little Em'ly didn't care a bit. She saw me well enough; but instead of turning round and calling after me, ran away laughing. This obliged me to run after her and we were very near the cottage before I caught her.

"Oh, it's you, is it?" said little Em'ly.

"Why, you knew who it was, Em'ly," said I.

"And didn't *you* know who it was?" said Em'ly. I was going to kiss her, but she covered her cherry lips with her hands, and said she wasn't a baby now, and ran away, laughing more than ever, into the house.

She seemed to delight in teasing me, which was a change in her I wondered at very much. The tea-table was ready, and our little locker was put out in its old place, but instead of coming to sit by me, she went and bestowed her company upon that grumbling Mrs. Gummidge: and on Mr. Peggotty's inquiring why, rumpled her hair all over her face to hide it, and would do nothing but laugh.

Little Em'ly was spoiled by them all; and by no one more than Mr. Peggotty himself. But she was so affectionate and sweet-natured, and had such a pleasant manner of being both sly and shy at once, that she captivated me more than ever.

She was tender-hearted, too; for when an allusion was made by Mr. Peggotty to the loss I had sustained, the tears stood in her eyes, and she looked at me so kindly that I felt quite thankful to her.

"And how's your friend, Sir?" said Mr. Peggotty to me.

"Steerforth?" said I.

"That's the name!" cried Mr. Peggotty, turning to Ham. "I knowed it was something in our way."

"You said it was Rudderford," observed Ham, laughing.

"Well!" retorted Mr. Peggotty. "And ye steer with a rudder, don't ye? It ain't fur off. How is he, Sir?"

"He was very well indeed when I came away, Mr. Peggotty."

"There's a friend!" said Mr. Peggotty, stretching out his pipe. "There's a friend, if you talk of friends! Why, Lord love my heart alive, if it ain't a treat to look at him!"

"Then, he's such a generous, fine, noble fellow," said I, quite carried away by my favourite theme, "I am sure I can never feel thankful enough for the generosity with which he has protected me, so much younger and lower in the school than himself."

The days passed pretty much as they had passed before, except that little Em'ly and I seldom wandered on the beach now. She had tasks to learn, and needlework to do; and was absent during a great part of each day. But I felt that we should not have had these old wanderings, even if it had been otherwise. She liked me, but she laughed at me, and tormented me; and when I went to meet her, stole home another way, and was laughing at the door when I came back, disappointed.

On the very first evening after our arrival, Mr. Barkis appeared with a bundle of oranges tied up in a handkerchief. As he made no allusion of any kind to this, he was supposed to have left it behind him by accident when he went away; until Ham, running after him to restore it, came back with the information that it was intended for Peggotty. After that occasion he appeared every evening at exactly the same hour, and always with a little bundle, to which he never alluded, and which he regularly put behind the door, and left there. These offerings were most various and eccentric. Among them I remember a huge pin-cushion, half a bushel or so of apples, a pair of jet earrings, some Spanish onions, a box of dominoes, a canary bird and cage, and a leg of pickled pork.

At length, when the term of my visit was nearly expired, it was given out that Peggotty and Mr. Barkis were going to make a day's holiday together, and that little Em'ly and I were to accompany them. We were all astir betimes in the morning; and while we were yet at breakfast Mr. Barkis appeared in the distance, driving a chaise-cart.

Peggotty was dressed as usual, in her neat and quiet mourning; but Mr. Barkis bloomed in a new blue coat, of which the tailor had given him such a good measure that the collar was so high that it pushed his hair up on end on the top of his head. His bright buttons, too, were of the largest size. Rendered complete by drab pantaloons and a buff waistcoat, I thought Mr. Barkis a phenomenon of respectability.

Away we went on our holiday excursion; and the first thing we did was to stop at a church, where Mr. Barkis tied the horse to some rails, and went in with Peggotty, leaving little Em'ly and me alone in the chaise.

Mr. Barkis and Peggotty were a good while in the church, but came out at last, and then we drove away into the country. As we were going along, Mr. Barkis turned to me, and said, with a wink:

"What name was it as I wrote up in the cart?"

"Clara Peggotty," I answered.

"What name would it be as I should write up now, if there was a tilt here?"

"Clara Peggotty, again?" I suggested.

"Clara Peggotty BARKIS!" he returned, and burst into a roar of laughter that shook the chaise.

In a word, they were married, and had gone into the church for no other purpose. Peggotty was a little confused when Mr. Barkis made this abrupt announcement and could not hug me enough in token of her unimpaired

Barkis appeared every evening at exactly the same hour.

affection; but she soon became herself again, and said she was very glad it was over.

We drove to a little inn where we were expected, and where we had a very comfortable dinner, and passed the day with great satisfaction. If Peggotty had been married every day for the last ten years, she could hardly have been more at her ease about it; it made no sort of difference in her; she was just the same as ever, and went out for a stroll with little Em'ly and me before tea, while Mr. Barkis philosophically smoked his pipe.

Well, we came to the old boat again in good time at night; and there Mr. and Mrs. Barkis bade us good-bye, and drove away snugly to their own home. I felt then, for the first time, that I had lost Peggotty.

Mr. Peggotty and Ham knew what was in my thoughts as well as I did, and were ready with some supper and their hospitable faces to drive it away. Little Em'ly came and sat beside me on the locker for the only time in all that visit; and it was altogether a wonderful close to a wonderful day.

With morning came Peggotty, who after breakfast, took me to her own home, and a beautiful little home it was. I must have been most impressed by a certain old bureau of some dark wood with a retreating top which opened, let down, and became a desk, within which was a large quarto edition of Foxe's *Book of Martyrs*. I was chiefly edified by the pictures, which were numerous, and represented all kinds of dismal horrors; but the Martyrs and Peggotty's house have been inseparable in my mind ever since, and are now.

I took leave of Mr. Peggotty, and Ham, and Mrs. Gummidge, and little Em'ly, that day; and passed the night at Peggotty's in a little room in the roof (with the crocodile-book on a shelf by the bed's head), which was to be always mine, Peggotty said, and should always be kept for me in exactly the same state.

I felt the truth and constancy of my dear old nurse, with all my heart, and thanked her as well as I could.

I went home in the morning with herself and Mr. Barkis in the cart. They left me at the gate, not easily or lightly; and it was a strange sight to me to see the cart go on, taking Peggotty away, and leaving me at the house in which there was no face to look on mine with love or liking any more.

And now I fell into a state of neglect, which I cannot look back upon without compassion. I fell at once into a solitary condition,—apart from all friendly notice, apart from the society of all other boys of my own age, apart from all companionship but my own spiritless thoughts.

What would I have given, to have been sent to the hardest school that ever was kept!—to have been taught something, anyhow, anywhere!

I was not actively ill-used. I was not beaten, or starved; but day after day, week after week, month after month, I was coldly neglected. I was seldom allowed to visit Peggotty. Faithful to her promise, she either came to see me, or met me somewhere near, once every week, and never empty-handed; but many and bitter were the disappointments I had, in being refused permission to pay a visit to her at her house. Some few times I was allowed to go there; and then I found out that Mr. Barkis was something of a miser, or, as Peggotty dutifully expressed it, was "a little near," and kept a heap of money in a box under his bed, which he pretended was only full of coats and trousers; so that Peggotty had to prepare a long and elaborate scheme, a very Gunpowder Plot, for every Saturday's expenses.

I had been out, one day, loitering somewhere, when, turning the corner of a lane near our house, I came upon Mr. Murdstone walking with a gentleman I knew to be Mr. Quinion.

Looking back as I turned into the front garden, I saw Mr. Murdstone leaning against the wicket of the churchyard, and Mr. Quinion talking to him. They were both looking after me, and I felt that they were speaking of me.

Mr. Quinion lay at our house that night. After breakfast, the next morning, I had put my chair away, and was going out of the room, when Mr. Murdstone called me back.

"David," said Mr. Murdstone, "to the young this is a world for action; not for moping and droning in."

"—As you do," added his sister.

"Jane Murdstone, leave it to me, if you please. I say, David, to the young this is a world for action, and not for moping and droning in. It is especially so for a young boy of your disposition, which requires a great deal of correcting——"

"For stubbornness won't do here," said his sister. "What it wants is, to be crushed. And crushed it must be. Shall be, too!"

He gave her a look, half in remonstrance, half in approval, and went on:

"I suppose you know, David, that I am not rich. At any rate, you know it now. You have received some considerable education already. Education is costly; and even if it were not, and I could afford it, I am of opinion that it would not be at all advantageous to you to be kept at a school. What is before you, is a fight with the world; and the sooner you begin it, the better."

I think it occurred to me that I had already begun it.

"You have heard the 'counting-house' mentioned sometimes," said Mr. Murdstone.

"The counting-house, Sir?" I repeated.

"Of Murdstone and Grinby, in the wine trade," he replied. I suppose I looked uncertain, for he went on hastily, "Mr. Quinion manages that business."

I glanced at the latter deferentially.

"Mr. Quinion suggests that it gives employment to some other boys, and that he sees no reason why it shouldn't, on the same terms, give employment to you. Those terms are, that you will earn enough to provide for your eating and drinking, and pocket-money. Your lodging (which I have arranged for) will be paid by me. So will your washing."

"Which will be kept down to my estimate," said his sister.

"Your clothes will be looked after for you, too," said Mr. Murdstone; "as you will not be able, yet awhile, to get them for yourself. So you are now going to London, David, with Mr. Quinion to begin the world on your own account."

"In short, you are provided for," observed his sister; "and will please to do your duty."

Behold me, on the morrow, in a much-worn little white hat, with a black crape round it, a black jacket, and a pair of hard stiff corduroy trousers—behold me so attired, and with my little worldly all before me in a small trunk, sitting in the post-chaise that was carrying Mr. Quinion to the London coach at Yarmouth.

CHAPTER XI

I BEGIN LIFE ON MY OWN ACCOUNT, AND DON'T LIKE IT

Murdstone and Grinby's warehouse was at the waterside. It was a crazy old house with a wharf of its own, abutting on the water when the tide was in, and on the mud when the tide was out, and literally overrun with rats. Its panelled rooms, discoloured with the dirt and smoke of a hundred years; its decaying floors and staircase; the squeaking and scuffling of the old grey rats down in the cellars; and the dirt and rottenness of the place are all before me, just as they were in the evil hour when I went among them for the first time, with my trembling hand in Mr. Quinion's.

Murdstone and Grinby's trade was among a good many kinds of people, but an important branch of it was the supply of wines and spirits to certain packet ships. A great many empty bottles were one of the consequences, and certain men and boys were employed to examine them against the light, and reject those that were flawed, and to rinse and wash them. When the empty bottles ran short, there were labels to be pasted on full ones, or corks to be fitted to them, or seals to be put upon the corks, or finished bottles to be packed in casks. All this work was my work, and of the boys employed upon it I was one.

There were three or four of us, counting me. On the first morning the oldest of the regular boys was summoned to show me my business. His name was Mick Walker, and he wore a ragged apron and a paper cap. He informed me that our principal associate would be another boy whom he introduced by the—to me—extraordinary name of Mealy Potatoes. I discovered, however, that this youth had not been christened by that name, but that it had been bestowed upon him in the warehouse, on account of his complexion, which was pale or mealy. Mealy's father was a waterman, who had the additional distinction of being a fireman at one of the large theatres; where some young relation of Mealy's—I think his little sister—did Imps in the Pantomimes.

No words can express the secret agony of my soul as I sank into this companionship and felt my hopes of growing up to be a learned and distinguished man crushed in my bosom. The deep sense I had of being utterly without hope cannot be written. As often as Mick Walker went away in the course of that forenoon, I mingled my tears with the water in which I was washing the bottles; and sobbed as if there were a flaw in my own breast, and it were in danger of bursting.

The counting-house clock was at half-past twelve when Mr. Quinion tapped at the counting-house window, and beckoned to me to go in. I went in, and found there a stoutish, middle-aged person, with no more hair upon his head (which was a large one, and very shining) than there is upon an egg. His clothes were shabby, but he had an imposing shirt-collar on. He carried a jaunty sort of a stick, with a large pair of rusty tassels to it.

"This," said Mr. Quinion, in allusion to myself, "is he."

"This," said the stranger with a certain indescribable air of doing something genteel, "is Master Copperfield. I hope I see you well, Sir?"

I said I was very well, and hoped he was.

"I am," said the stranger, "thank Heaven, quite well. I have received a letter from Mr. Murdstone, in which he mentions that he would desire me to receive into an apartment of my house, which is to be let as a—in short," said the stranger, with a smile and in a burst of confidence, "as a bedroom—the young beginner whom I have now the pleasure to——" and the stranger waved his hand.

"This is Mr. Micawber," said Mr. Quinion to me. "Mr.

Micawber is known to Mr. Murdstone. He takes orders for us on commission, when he can get any, and he will receive you as a lodger."

"My address," said Mr. Micawber, "is Windsor Terrace, City Road. I—in short," said Mr. Micawber, with the same genteel air, and in another burst of confidence—"I live there."

I made him a bow.

"Under the impression," said Mr. Micawber, "that you might have some difficulty in penetrating the arcana of the Modern Babylon—in short," said Mr. Micawber, in another burst of confidence, "that you might lose yourself—I shall be happy to call this evening, and instal you in the knowledge of the nearest way."

I thanked him with all my heart.

"At what hour," said Mr. Micawber, "shall I——"

"At about eight," said Mr. Quinion.

"At about eight," said Mr. Micawber. "I beg to wish you good day, Mr. Quinion. I will intrude no longer."

So he put on his hat, and went out with his cane under his arm: very upright, and humming a tune.

At the appointed time in the evening, Mr. Micawber reappeared, and we walked to our house, as I suppose I must now call it, together; Mr. Micawber impressing the names of streets, and the shapes of corner houses upon me, as we went along, that I might find my way back, easily, in the morning.

Arrived at his house in Windsor Terrace (which I noticed was shabby like himself, but also, like himself, made all the show it could), he presented me to Mrs. Micawber, a thin and faded lady, not at all young, who was sitting in the parlour with a baby at her breast. This baby was one of twins; and I may remark here that one of them was always taking refreshment.

There were two other children; Master Micawber, aged about four, and Miss Micawber, aged about three. These, and a dark-complexioned young woman, who was servant to the family, and informed me, that she was "a Orfling," completed the establishment. My room was at the top of the house, at the back, and very scantily furnished.

"I never thought," said Mrs. Micawber, when she came up, twin and all, to show me the apartment, and sat down to take breath, "before I was married, when I lived with papa and mama, that I should ever find it necessary to take a lodger. But Mr. Micawber being in difficulties, all considerations of private feeling must give way."

I said: "Yes, ma'am."

"Mr. Micawber's difficulties are almost overwhelming just at present," said Mrs. Micawber; "and whether it is possible to bring him through them, I don't know. When I lived at home with papa and mama I really should have hardly understood what the word meant, in the sense in which I now employ it, but experimentia does it—as papa used to say."

Poor Mrs. Micawber! She said she had tried to exert herself; and so, I have no doubt, she had. The centre of the street-door was perfectly covered with a great brass-plate, on which was engraved "Mrs. Micawber's Boarding Establishment for Young Ladies"; but I never found that any young lady had ever been to school there; or that any young lady ever came, or proposed to come; or that the least preparation was ever made to receive any young lady. The only visitors I ever saw or heard of, were creditors. *They* used to come at all hours, and some of them were quite ferocious. One dirty-faced man, I think he was a boot-maker, used to edge himself into the passage as early as seven o'clock in the morning, and call up the stairs to Mr. Micawber—"Come! You ain't out yet, you know. You just pay us, d'ye hear? Come!" At these times, Mr. Micawber would be transported with grief and mortification, even to the length (as I was once made aware by a scream from his wife) of making motions at himself with a razor; but within half-an-hour afterwards, he would polish up his shoes and go out, humming a tune. Mrs. Micawber was quite as elastic. On one occasion I saw her lying (of course with a twin) under the grate in a swoon, with her hair all torn about her face; but I never knew her more cheerful than she was, that very same night, over a veal-cutlet, telling me stories about her papa and mama, and the company they used to keep.

In this house, and with this family, I passed my leisure time. My breakfast of a penny loaf and a pennyworth of milk, I provided. I kept another small loaf, and a modicum of cheese, on a particular shelf of a particular cupboard, to make my supper on when I came back at night.

I was so young and childish that often, in going to Murdstone and Grinby's, of a morning, I could not resist the stale pastry put out for sale at half-price at the pastry-cooks' doors, and spent in that, the money I should have kept for my dinner. Then, I went without my dinner, or bought a roll or a slice of pudding.

I know I do not exaggerate the scantiness of my resources or the difficulties of my life. I know that if a shilling were given me by Mr. Quinion at any time, I spent it in a dinner or a tea. I know that I worked from morning until night and I know that I lounged about the streets, insufficiently fed. I know that, but for the mercy of God, I might easily have been a little robber or a little vagabond.

How much I suffered, it is, as I have said already, utterly beyond my power to tell. But I kept my own counsel, and I did my work. I knew from the first, that, if I could not do my work as well as any of the rest, I could not hold myself above contempt.

Mr. Micawber's difficulties were an addition to the distressed state of my mind. In my forlorn state I became quite attached to the family, and used to walk about, busy with Mrs. Micawber's calculations of ways and means, and heavy with the weight of Mr. Micawber's debts.

A curious equality of friendship sprang up between me and these people, notwithstanding the ludicrous disparity in our years. But I never allowed myself to accept any invitation to eat and drink with them until Mrs. Micawber took me into her entire confidence. This she did one evening as follows:

"Master Copperfield," said Mrs. Micawber, "I make no stranger of you, and therefore do not hesitate to say that Mr. Micawber's difficulties are coming to a crisis."

It made me very miserable to hear it, and I looked at Mrs. Micawber's red eyes with the utmost sympathy.

"With the exception of the heel of a Dutch cheese—which is not adapted to the wants of a young family"—said Mrs. Micawber, "there is really not a scrap of anything in the larder. What I mean to express is, that there is nothing to eat in the house."

"Dear me!" I said, in great concern.

I had two or three shillings of my week's money in my pocket—and I hastily produced them, and begged Mrs. Micawber to accept of them as a loan. But that lady, kissing me, replied that she couldn't think of it.

"No, my dear Master Copperfield," said she, "far be it from my thoughts! But you can render me another kind of service, if you will; and a service I will thankfully accept of."

I begged Mrs. Micawber to name it.

"I have parted with the plate myself," said Mrs. Micawber. "Six tea, two salt, and a pair of sugars, I have at different times borrowed money on, in secret, with my own hands. There are still a few trifles that we could part with. Mr. Micawber's feelings would never allow *him* to dispose of them. Master Copperfield, if I might ask you——"

I understood Mrs. Micawber now, and begged her to make use of me to any extent. I began to dispose of the more portable articles of property that very evening; and went out on a similar expedition almost every morning, before I went to Murdstone and Grinby's.

Mr. Micawber had a few books on a little chiffonier, which he called the library; and those went first. I carried them, one after another, to a bookstall in the City Road and sold them for whatever they would bring.

At the pawnbroker's shop, too, I began to be very well known. The principal gentleman who officiated behind the counter, took a good deal of notice of me; and often got me, I recollect, to decline a Latin noun or adjective, or to conjugate a Latin verb, in his ear, while he transacted my business. After all these occasions Mrs. Micawber made a little treat, which was generally a supper; and there was a peculiar relish in these meals which I well remember.

At last Mr. Micawber's difficulties came to a crisis, and he was arrested early one morning, and carried over to the King's Bench Prison. He told me, as he went out of the house, that the God of day had now gone down upon him—and I really thought his heart was broken and mine too. But I heard, afterwards, that he was seen to play a lively game at skittles, before noon.

On the first Sunday after he was taken there, I was to go and see him, and have dinner with him. I was to ask my way to such a place, and just short of that place I should see such another place, and just short of that I should see a yard, which I was to cross, and keep straight on until I saw a turnkey. All this I did.

Mr. Micawber was waiting for me within the gate, and we went up to his room (top story but one), and cried very much. He solemnly conjured me, I remember, to take warning by his fate; and to observe that if a man had twenty pounds a year for his income, and spent nineteen pounds nineteen shillings and sixpence, he would be happy, but that if he spent twenty pounds one he would be miserable. After which he borrowed a shilling of me, gave me a written order on Mrs. Micawber for the amount, and put away his pocket-handkerchief, and cheered up.

We sat before a little fire, with two bricks put within the rusted grate, one on each side, to prevent its burning too many coals; until another debtor, who shared the room with Mr. Micawber, came in from the bakehouse with the loin of mutton which was our joint-stock repast.

There was something gipsy-like and agreeable in the dinner, and early in the afternoon I went home to comfort

Mrs. Micawber with an account of my visit. She fainted when she saw me return, and made a little jug of egg-hot afterwards to console us while we talked it over.

I don't know how the household furniture came to be sold or who sold it, except that *I* did not. Sold it was, however, and carried away in a van; except the beds, a few chairs, and the kitchen-table. With these possessions we encamped, as it were, in the two parlours of the emptied house; Mrs. Micawber, the children, the Orfling, and myself. At last Mrs. Micawber resolved to move into the prison, where Mr. Micawber had now secured a room to himself. So I took the key of the house to the landlord, who was very glad to get it; and the beds were sent over to the King's Bench, except mine, for which a little room was hired outside. Mine was a quiet back-garret with a sloping roof, commanding a pleasant prospect of a timber-yard, and when I took possession of it, with the reflection that Mr. Micawber's troubles had come to a crisis at last, I thought it quite a paradise.

All this time I was working at Murdstone and Grinby's in the same common way, and with the same common companions, and with the same sense of unmerited degradation. I led the same secretly unhappy life in the same lonely, self-reliant manner. The only changes I am conscious of are, firstly, that I had grown more shabby, and secondly, that I was now relieved of the weight of Mr. and Mrs. Micawber's cares; for some relatives or friends had engaged to help them and they lived more comfortably in the prison than they had lived for a long while out of it.

At last Mrs. Micawber informed me that "her family" had decided that Mr. Micawber should apply for his release under the Insolvent Debtors' Act, which would set him free, she expected, in about six weeks.

"And then," said Mr. Micawber, who was present, "I have no doubt I shall, please Heaven, begin to live in a perfectly new manner, if—in short, if anything turns up."

CHAPTER XII

LIKING LIFE ON MY OWN ACCOUNT NO BETTER, I FORM A GREAT RESOLUTION

In due time, Mr. Micawber's petition was ripe for hearing, and that gentleman was ordered to be discharged. His creditors were not implacable; and Mrs. Micawber informed me that even the revengeful bootmaker had declared in open court that he bore him no malice, but that when money was owing to him he liked to be paid. He said he thought it was human nature.

Mr. Micawber returned to the King's Bench when his case was over, as some fees were to be settled, while Mrs. Micawber and I had a lamb's fry.

As I could hardly hope for a more favourable opportunity I said to Mrs. Micawber:

"May I ask, ma'am, what you and Mr. Micawber intend to do, now that Mr. Micawber is out of his difficulties, and at liberty? Have you settled yet?"

"My family," said Mrs. Micawber, "are of the opinion that Mr. Micawber should quit London, and exert his talents in the country. Mr. Micawber is a man of great talent, Master Copperfield."

I said I was sure of that.

"Of great talent," repeated Mrs. Micawber. "My family are of opinion, that, something might be done in the Custom House. The influence of my family being local, it is their wish that Mr. Micawber should go down to Plymouth.

"That he may be ready?" I suggested.

"Exactly," returned Mrs. Micawber. "That he may be ready, in case of anything turning up."

"And do you go too, ma'am?"

The events of the day had made Mrs. Micawber hysterical, and she shed tears as she replied:

"I never will desert Mr. Micawber. Mr. Micawber may have concealed his difficulties from me. The pearl necklace and bracelets which I inherited from mama, have been disposed of for less than half their value. But I never will desert Mr. Micawber. No!" cried Mrs. Micawber, "I never will do it!"

I felt quite uncomfortable—as if Mrs. Micawber supposed I had asked her to do anything of the sort!—and sat looking at her in alarm.

"Mr. Micawber has his faults. I do not deny that he is improvident," she went on, "but I never will desert Mr. Micawber!"

Mrs. Micawber having now raised her voice into a perfect scream, I was so frightened that I ran off to Mr. Micawber with the tidings that Mrs. Micawber was in an alarming state, upon which he immediately burst into tears, and came away with me.

"Emma, my angel!" cried Mr. Micawber, running into the room; "what is the matter?"

"I never will desert you, Micawber!" she exclaimed.

"My life!" said Mr. Micawber, taking her in his arms. "I am perfectly aware of it."

Mr. Micawber was soon so overcome, that he mingled his tears with hers and mine; until he begged me to do him the favour of taking a chair on the staircase, while he got her into bed. So I sat at the staircase window, until he came out and joined me.

"How is Mrs. Micawber now, Sir?" I said.

"Very low," said Mr. Micawber; "reaction. We stand alone now."

Mr. Micawber pressed my hand, and groaned, and afterwards shed tears. I was greatly touched, but Mr. and Mrs. Micawber were so used to their old difficulties, I think, that they felt quite shipwrecked when they were released from them, and I never saw them half so wretched as on this night.

But through all the lowness of spirits I plainly discerned that Mr. and Mrs. Micawber were going away from London. It was in my walk home that night, and in the sleepless hours which followed, that the thought first occurred to me which afterwards shaped itself into a settled resolution.

The very next day showed me that Mrs. Micawber had not spoken of their going away without warrant. They took a lodging for a week; at the expiration of which time they were to start for Plymouth. Mr. Micawber himself came down to the counting-house, in the afternoon, to tell Mr. Quinion. And Mr. Quinion, calling in Tipp the carman quartered me prospectively on him—by our mutual consent, as he had every reason to think; for I said nothing, though my resolution was now taken.

I passed my evenings with Mr. and Mrs. Micawber and I think we became fonder of one another as the time went on. On the last Sunday, they invited me to dinner; and we had a loin of pork and apple sauce, and a pudding.

Next morning I met the whole family at the coach-office, and saw them, with a desolate heart, take their places outside, at the back.

"Master Copperfield," said Mrs. Micawber, "God bless you! I never can forget all that, you know, and I never would if I could."

"Copperfield," said Mr. Micawber, "farewell! Every happiness and prosperity! In case of anything turning up (of which I am rather confident), I shall be extremely happy if it should be in my power to improve your prospects."

I think, as Mrs. Micawber sat at the back of the coach, with the children, and I stood in the road looking wistfully at them, a mist cleared from her eyes, and she saw what a little creature I really was. She beckoned to me to climb up, with quite a new and motherly expression in her face, and gave me just such a kiss as she might have given to her own boy. I had barely time to get down again before the coach started, and I could hardly see the family for the handkerchiefs they waved. It was gone in a minute, and I went to begin my weary day at Murdstone and Grinby's.

But with no intention of passing many more weary days there. No. I had resolved to run away.—To go, by some means or other, down into the country, to the only relation I had in the world, Miss Betsey.

As I did not even know where Miss Betsey lived, I wrote to Peggotty, and asked her, incidentally, if she remembered. In the course of that letter, I told Peggotty that I had a particular occasion for half a guinea; and that if she could lend me that sum I should be very much obliged to her, and would tell her afterwards what I had wanted it for.

Peggotty's answer soon arrived, and was, as usual, full of affectionate devotion. She enclosed the half-guinea (I was afraid she must have had a world of trouble to get it out of Mr. Barkis's box), and told me that Miss Betsey lived near Dover, and I resolved to set out at the end of that week.

Being a very honest little creature, I considered myself bound to remain until Saturday night; and, as I had been paid a week's wages in advance when I first came there, not to receive my stipend. For this express reason, I had borrowed the half-guinea for my travelling expenses. Accordingly, when the Saturday night came I shook Mick Walker by the hand; asked him to say to Mr. Quinion that I had gone to move my box to Tipp's; and, bidding a last good night to Mealy Potatoes, ran away.

My box was at my old lodging and as I went I looked about me for some one who would help me to carry it to the booking-office.

There was a long-legged young man, with a very little empty donkey-cart, standing near, whose eye I caught and who hoped "I should know him agin"—in allusion no doubt, to my staring at him. I stopped to assure him that I had not done so in bad manners, but uncertain whether he might like a job.

The young man sat upon my box and rattled away.

"Wot job?" said the long-legged young man.

"To move a box," I answered.

"Wot box?" said the long-legged young man.

I told him mine, which I wanted him to take to the Dover coach-office.

"Done!" said the long-legged young man.

There was a defiant manner about this young man that I did not much like; as the bargain was made, however, I took him up-stairs to the room I was leaving, and we brought the box down, and put it in his cart. Now, I was unwilling to put the direction-card on there, lest any of my landlord's family should detain me; so I said to the young man that I would be glad if he would stop for a minute, when he came to the dead-wall of the King's Bench prison. The words were no sooner out of my mouth, than he rattled away, and I was quite out of breath with running and calling after him, when I caught him at the place appointed.

Being much flushed and excited, I tumbled my half-guinea out of my pocket in pulling the card out. I put it in my mouth for safety and had just tied the card on when I felt myself violently chucked under the chin by the long-legged young man, and saw my half-guinea fly out of my mouth into his hand.

"Wot!" said the young man, seizing me by my jacket collar, with a frightful grin. "This is a pollis case, is it? You're a going to bolt, are you? Come to the pollis!"

"You give me my money back, if you please," said I, very much frightened; "and leave me alone."

"Come to the pollis!" said the young man.

"Give me my box and money, will you?" I cried, bursting into tears.

The young man still replied: "Come to the pollis!" and was dragging me against the donkey in a violent manner, when he jumped into the cart, sat upon my box, and, exclaiming that he would drive to the pollis straight, rattled away harder than ever.

I ran after him as fast as I could, but I had no breath

to call out with, and should not have dared to call out, now, if I had. I narrowly escaped being run over, twenty times at least, in half a mile. Now I lost him, now I saw him, now I lost him, now I was cut at with a whip, now shouted at, now down in the mud, now up again, now running into somebody's arms, now running headlong at a post. At length, confused by fright and heat, I left the young man to go where he would with my box and money; and, panting and crying, but never stopping, faced about for Greenwich, which I had understood was on the Dover Road: taking very little more out of the world, towards the retreat of my aunt, Miss Betsey, than I had brought into it, on the night when my arrival gave her so much umbrage.

CHAPTER XIII

THE SEQUEL OF MY RESOLUTION

For anything I know, I may have had some wild idea of running all the way to Dover! My scattered senses were soon collected as to that point for I came to a stop in the Kent Road and here sat down on a door-step, quite exhausted and with hardly breath enough to cry for the loss of my box and half-guinea.

It was by this time dark; I heard the clocks strike ten, as I sat resting. But it was a summer night, fortunately, and fine weather. When I had recovered my breath, and had got rid of a stifling sensation in my throat, I rose up and went on. I had no notion of going back.

But my standing possessed of only three-halfpence in the world troubled me none the less, and I trudged on miserably until I happened to pass a little shop, where it was written up that ladies' and gentlemen's wardrobes were bought. The master of this shop was sitting at the door in his shirt-sleeves, smoking.

My late experiences with Mr. and Mrs. Micawber suggested to me that here might be a means of keeping off the wolf for a little while. I went up the next bye-street, took off my waistcoat, rolled it neatly under my arm, and came back to the shop-door. If you please, Sir," I said, "I am to sell this for a fair price."

Mr. Dolloby—Dolloby was the name over the shop-door, at least—took the waistcoat, went into the shop, followed by me, spread the waistcoat on the counter and ultimately said:

"What do you call a price, now, for this here little weskit?"

"Would eighteenpence be?"—I hinted, after some hesitation.

Mr. Dolloby rolled it up again, and gave it me back. "I should rob my family," he said, "if I was to offer ninepence for it."

My circumstances being so very pressing, however, I said I would take ninepence for it, if he pleased. Mr. Dolloby, not without some grumbling, gave ninepence. I walked out of the shop, the richer by that sum, and the poorer by a waistcoat. But when I buttoned my jacket, that was not much. Indeed, I foresaw pretty clearly that my jacket would go next, and that I should have to make the best of my way to Dover in a shirt and a pair of trousers.

A plan had occurred to me for passing the night, which was, to lie behind the wall at the back of my old school, in a corner where there used to be a haystack. I imagined it would be a kind of company to have the boys, and the bedroom where I used to tell the stories, so near me: although the boys would know nothing of my being there, and the bedroom would yield me no shelter.

It cost me some trouble to find out Salem House; but I found it, and I found a haystack in the corner, and I lay down by it. Never shall I forget the lonely sensation of first lying down, without a roof above my head!

The warm beams of the sun, and the ringing of the getting-up bell at Salem House, awoke me. If I could have hoped that Steerforth was there, I would have lurked about until he came out alone; but I knew he must have left long since. Traddles still remained, perhaps, but it was very doubtful, so I crept away from the wall as Mr. Creakle's boys were getting up, and struck into the Dover Road.

I got, that Sunday, through three-and-twenty miles on the straight road, though not very easily, for I was new to that kind of toil. I see myself, as evening closes in, coming over the bridge at Rochester, footsore and tired, and eating bread that I bought for supper.

I sought no shelter but the sky; and toiling into Chatham, crept upon a sort of grass-grown battery where a sentry was walking to and fro. Here I lay down, near a cannon; and, happy in the society of the sentry's footsteps, slept soundly until morning.

Very stiff and sore of foot I was in the morning; but under this difficulty, as under all the other difficulties of my journey, I seemed to be led on by my fanciful picture of my mother in her youth, before I came into the world. It always kept me company. It was there when I lay down to sleep; it was with me on my waking in the morning; it went before me all day. When I came, at last, upon the bare, wide downs near Dover, it relieved the solitary aspect of the scene with hope; and not until I actually set foot in the town itself, on the sixth day of my flight, did it desert me. But then when I stood in the place so long desired, it seemed to vanish like a dream, and to leave me helpless and dispirited.

I inquired about my aunt among the boatmen first, and received various answers. One said that she was seen to mount a broom, in the last high wind, and make direct for Calais. The fly-drivers, among whom I inquired next, were equally jocose and equally disrespectful; and the shopkeepers generally replied, without hearing what I had to say, that they had got nothing for me. My money was all gone, I had nothing left to dispose of; I was hungry, thirsty, and worn out; and seemed as distant from my end as if I had remained in London.

The morning had worn away in these inquiries, and I was sitting on the step of an empty shop when a fly-driver, coming by with his carriage, dropped a horsecloth. Something good-natured in the man's face, as I handed it up, encouraged me to ask him if he could tell me where Miss Trotwood lived;

"Trotwood," said he. "Let me see. I know the name, too. Old lady?"

"Yes," I said, "rather."

"Pretty stiff in the back?" said he.

"Yes," I said. "I should think it very likely."

"Carries a bag?" said he—"bag with a good deal of room in it—is gruffish, and comes down upon you, sharp?"

My heart sank within me as I acknowledged the undoubted accuracy of this description.

"Why then, I tell you what," said he. "If you go up there," pointing with his whip towards the heights, "and keep right on till you come to some houses facing the sea, I think you'll hear of her. My opinion is, she won't stand anything, so here's a penny for you."

I accepted the gift thankfully, and bought a loaf with it. Dispatching this refreshment by the way, I walked on a good distance. At length I went into a little shop and inquired if they could have the goodness to tell me where Miss Trotwood lived. I addressed myself to a man behind the counter who was weighing some rice for a young woman; but the latter turned round quickly.

"My mistress?" she said. "What do you want with her, boy?"

"I want," I replied, "to speak to her, if you please."

"To beg of her, you mean," retorted the damsel.

"No," I said, "indeed." But suddenly remembering that in truth I came for no other purpose, I felt my face burn.

My aunt's handmaiden put her rice in a little basket and walked out of the shop; telling me that I could follow her. I followed and we soon came to a very neat little cottage with cheerful bow-windows: in front of it, a small square gravelled court or garden full of flowers, carefully tended, and smelling deliciously.

"This is Miss Trotwood's," said the young woman. "Now you know; and that's all I have got to say." With which words she hurried into the house and left me standing at the garden-gate, looking disconsolately towards the parlour-window, where a muslin curtain partly undrawn, a large round green screen or fan fastened on the window-sill, a small table, and a great chair, suggested to me that my aunt might be at that moment seated in awful state.

My shoes were by this time in a woeful condition. My hat (which had served me for a night-cap, too) was crushed and bent. My shirt and trousers, stained and torn besides, might have frightened the birds from my aunt's garden. My hair had known no comb or brush since I left London. In this plight I waited to introduce myself to my formidable aunt.

The unbroken stillness of the parlour-window leading me to infer that she was not there, I lifted up my eyes to the window above it, where I saw a florid, pleasant looking gentleman, with a grey head, who shut up one eye in a grotesque manner, nodded his head at me several times, shook it at me as often, laughed, and went away.

I was so much discomposed by this unexpected behaviour, that I was on the point of slinking off when there came out of the house a lady with her handkerchief tied over her cap, and a pair of gardening gloves on her hands, and carrying a great knife. I knew her immediately to be Miss Betsey, for she came stalking out of the house exactly as my poor mother had so often described her stalking up our garden at Blunderstone Rookery.

"Go away!" said Miss Betsey, shaking her head, and making a distant chop in the air with her knife. "Go along! No boys here!"

I watched her, with my heart at my lips, as she marched to a corner of her garden, and stooped to dig up some little root there. Then, without a scrap of courage, but with a great deal of desperation, I went softly in and stood beside her, touching her with my finger.

"If you please, ma'am," I began.

She started and looked up.

"If you please, aunt."

"Eh?" exclaimed Miss Betsey, in a tone of amazement I have never heard approached.

"If you please, aunt, I am your nephew."

"Oh, Lord!" said my aunt. And sat flat down in the garden path.

"I am David Copperfield, of Blunderstone, in Suffolk—

where you came, on the night when I was born, and saw my dear mama. Since she died I have been slighted, and taught nothing, and thrown upon myself, and put to work not fit for me. It made me run away to you. I was robbed and have walked all the way." Here my self-support gave way all at once, and I broke into a passion of crying.

My aunt sat on the gravel, staring at me, until I began to cry; when she got up in a great hurry, collared me, and took me into the parlour. Her first proceeding there was to bring out several bottles, and pour some of the contents of each into my mouth. (I am sure I tasted aniseed, water, anchovy sauce, and salad dressing.) When she had administered these, as I was still unable to control my sobs, she put me on the sofa; and then sitting herself down behind, ejaculated at intervals, "Mercy on us!"

After a time she rang the bell. "Janet," said my aunt, when her servant came in. "Go up-stairs, give my compliments to Mr. Dick, and say I wish to speak to him."

Janet looked a little surprised to see me lying on the sofa, but went on her errand. My aunt, with her hands behind her, walked up and down the room, until the gentleman who had squinted at me from the upper window came in laughing.

"Mr. Dick," said my aunt, "don't be a fool, because nobody can be more discreet than you can, when you choose."

The gentleman was serious immediately.

"Mr. Dick," said my aunt, "you have heard me mention David Copperfield?"

"David Copperfield?" said Mr. Dick, "*David* Copperfield? Oh yes, to be sure. David, certainly."

"Well," said my aunt, "this is his boy, his son."

"His son?" said Mr. Dick. "David's son? Indeed!"

"Yes," pursued my aunt, "and he has run away. Ah! His sister, Betsey Trotwood, never would have run away." My aunt shook her head, confident in the character of the girl who never was born.

"Oh! you think she wouldn't have run away?" said Mr. Dick.

"Bless and save the man," exclaimed my aunt, sharply, "how he talks! Don't I know she wouldn't? She would have lived with her godmother, and we should have been devoted to one another. Where should his sister, Betsey Trotwood, have run from, or to?"

"Nowhere," said Mr. Dick.

"Well then," returned my aunt, "here you see young David Copperfield, and the question I put to you is, what shall I do with him?"

"What shall you do with him?" said Mr. Dick, feebly, scratching his head. "Oh! do with him?"

"Yes," said my aunt, with a grave look, and her forefinger held up. "Come! I want some very sound advice."

"Why, if I was you," said Mr. Dick, looking vacantly at me, "I should——" The contemplation of me seemed to inspire him with a sudden idea, and he added, briskly, "I should wash him!"

"Janet," said my aunt, turning round with a quiet triumph, which I did not then understand, "Mr. Dick sets us all right. Heat the bath!"

Although I was deeply interested in this dialogue, I could not help observing my aunt, Mr. Dick, and Janet, while it was in progress.

My aunt was a tall, hard-featured lady, but by no means ill-looking. There was an inflexibility in her face, in her voice, and carriage, but her features were handsome. I particularly noticed that she had a very quick, bright eye. Her hair, which was grey, was arranged in two plain divisions, under a mob-cap. She wore at her side a gentleman's gold watch; she had some linen at her throat not unlike a shirt-collar, and things at her wrists like little shirt-wristbands.

Mr. Dick, as I have already said, was grey-headed and florid: I should have said all about him, in saying so, had not his head been curiously bowed—not by age; it reminded me of one of Mr. Creakle's boys' heads after a beating—and his grey eyes prominent and large, with a strange kind of watery brightness in them.

Janet was a pretty blooming girl, of about nineteen or twenty, and a perfect picture of neatness. She was one of a series of protégées whom my aunt had taken into her service expressly to educate in a renouncement of mankind, and who had generally completed their abjuration by marrying the baker.

Janet had gone away to get the bath ready, when my aunt, to my great alarm, became in one moment rigid with indignation, and had hardly voice to cry out, "Janet! Donkeys!"

Upon which, Janet came running up the stairs, darted out on a little piece of green in front, and warned off two saddle-donkeys, lady-ridden, while my aunt, rushing out of the house, seized the bridle of a third animal laden with a bestriding child, turned him, led him forth, and boxed the ears of the unlucky urchin.

To this hour I don't know whether my aunt had any lawful right of way over that patch of green; but she had settled it in her own mind that she had. The one great outrage of her life was the passage of a donkey over that immaculate spot. Jugs of water were kept ready to be discharged on the offending boys; sticks were behind the door; and incessant war prevailed. There were three alarms before the bath was ready. These interruptions were the more ridiculous to me, because she was giving me broth out of a table-spoon at the time, and while my mouth was yet open to receive the spoon, she would put it back into the basin, cry "Janet! Donkeys!" and go out to the assault.

The bath was a great comfort. When I had bathed, they enrobed me in a shirt and a pair of trousers belonging to Mr. Dick, and tied me up in two or three great shawls. Feeling very faint and drowsy, I soon lay down on the sofa again and fell asleep.

We dined soon after I awoke, I sitting at table and moving my arms with considerable difficulty. All this time, I was deeply anxious to know what my aunt was going to do with me; but she took her dinner in profound silence, except when she occasionally said, "Mercy upon us!"

The cloth being drawn, and some sherry put upon the table, my aunt sent up for Mr. Dick again, who looked as wise as he could when she requested him to attend to my story, which she elicited from me, gradually, by a course of questions.

"Whatever possessed that poor unfortunate Baby, that she must go and be married again," said my aunt, when I had finished, "*I* can't conceive."

"Perhaps she fell in love with her second husband," Mr. Dick suggested.

"Fell in love!" repeated my aunt. "What do you mean? What business had she to do it?"

"Perhaps," Mr. Dick simpered, after thinking a little, "she did it for pleasure."

"Pleasure, indeed!" replied my aunt. "A mighty pleasure for the poor Baby to fix her simple faith upon any dog of a fellow, certain to ill-use her in some way or other.

"And then there's that woman with the Pagan name," said my aunt, "that Peggotty, *she* goes and gets married next. I only hope," said my aunt, shaking her head, "that her husband will beat her well."

I could not bear to hear my old nurse so decried. I told my aunt that indeed she was mistaken. That Peggotty was the best, the truest, the most faithful, most devoted, and most self-denying friend and servant in the world; who had ever loved me dearly, who had ever loved my mother dearly. I broke down as I was trying to say that I would have gone to her for shelter, but for her humble station, which made me fear that I might bring some trouble on her—I broke down, I say, as I was trying to say so, and laid my face in my hands upon the table.

"Well, well!" said my aunt, "the child is right to stand by those who have stood by him.—Janet! Donkeys!"

I thoroughly believed that but for those unfortunate donkeys, we should have come to a good understanding;

for my aunt had laid her hand on my shoulder, and the impulse was upon me to embrace her and beseech her protection. But the interruption put an end to all softer ideas.

After tea, we sat at the window until dusk, when Janet set candles, and a backgammon-board, on the table, and pulled down the blinds.

"Now, Mr. Dick," said my aunt, with her grave look, and her forefinger up as before, "I am going to ask you another question. Look at this child."

"David's son?" said Mr. Dick, with an attentive, puzzled face.

"Exactly so," returned my aunt. "What would you do with him, now?"

"Do with David's son?" said Mr. Dick.

"Ay," replied my aunt, "with David's son."

"Oh!" said Mr. Dick. "Yes. Do with—I should put him to bed."

"Janet!" cried my aunt, with the same complacent triumph that I had remarked before. "Mr. Dick sets us all right. If the bed is ready, we'll take him up to it."

Janet reporting it to be quite ready, I was taken up to it; kindly, but in some sort like a prisoner; my aunt going in front, and Janet bringing up the rear.

The room was a pleasant one, at the top of the house, overlooking the sea, on which the moon was shining brilliantly. After I had said my prayers I remember the sensation of gratitude and rest which the sight of the white-curtained bed—and how much more the lying softly down upon it, nestling in the snow-white sheets!—inspired. I remember how I thought of all the solitary places under the night sky where I had slept, and how I prayed that I never might be houseless any more, and never might forget the houseless. I remember how I seemed to float, then, away into the world of dreams.

CHAPTER XIV

MY AUNT MAKES UP HER MIND ABOUT ME

On going down in the morning, I found my aunt musing so profoundly over the breakfast-table, with her elbow on the tray, that the contents of the urn had overflowed the teapot. I felt sure that I had been the subject of her reflections, and was more than ever anxious to know her intentions towards me.

When she had finished her breakfast, my aunt leaned back in her chair, folded her arms, and contemplated me with such attention that I was overpowered by embarrassment. Not having finished my own breakfast, I attempted to hide my confusion by proceeding with it; but my knife tumbled over my fork, my fork tripped up my knife, and I choked myself with my tea.

"Hallo!" said my aunt, after a long time.

I looked up, and met her sharp bright glance respectfully.

"I have written to him," said my aunt.

"To——?"

"To your father-in-law," said my aunt.

"Does he know where I am, aunt?" I inquired, alarmed.

"I have told him," said my aunt, with a nod.

"Shall I—be—given up to him?" I faltered.

"I don't know," said my aunt. "We shall see."

"Oh! I can't think what I shall do," I exclaimed, "if I have to go back to Mr. Murdstone!"

"I don't know anything about it," said my aunt, shaking her head. "I can't say, I am sure. We shall see."

My spirits sank under these words, and I became very heavy of heart. My aunt put on a coarse apron, washed up the teacups; next she swept up the crumbs; next dusted and arranged the room. When all these tasks were performed she took off the apron, brought out her work-box and sat down to work.

"I wish you'd go up-stairs," said my aunt, as she threaded her needle, "and give my compliments to Mr. Dick, and I'll be glad to know how he gets on with his Memorial."

I rose with all alacrity.

"I suppose," said my aunt, "you think Mr. Dick a short name, eh?"

"I thought it was rather a short name, yesterday," I confessed.

"You are not to suppose that he hasn't got a longer name," said my aunt, with a loftier air. "Babley—Mr. Richard Babley. But don't you call him by it, whatever you do. He can't bear his name. That's a peculiarity of his. Mr. Dick is his name here, and everywhere else, now—if he ever went anywhere else, which he don't. So take care, child, you don't call him anything but Mr. Dick."

I promised to obey, and went up-stairs with my message. I found him with a long pen, and his head almost laid upon the paper. He was so intent that I had leisure to observe the large paper kite in a corner, the bundles of manuscript, the number of pens, and, above all, the ink (which he seemed to have in, in half-gallon jars by the dozen), before he observed my being present.

"Ha!" said Mr. Dick, laying down his pen. "How does the world go? I'll tell you what," he added, in a lower tone, "It's a mad world. Mad as Bedlam, boy!"

I delivered my message.

"Well," said Mr. Dick, in answer, "my compliments to her, and I—I believe I have made a start. You have been to school?"

"Yes, Sir," I answered; "for a short time."

"Do you recollect the date," said Mr. Dick, looking earnestly at me, and taking up his pen to note it down, "when King Charles the First had his head cut off?"

My aunt folded her arms and contemplated me.

I said I believed it happened in the year sixteen hundred and forty-nine.

"Well," returned Mr. Dick, scratching his ear with his pen. "So the books say; but I don't see how that can be. Because, if it were so long ago, how could the people about him have made that mistake of putting some of the trouble out of *his* head, after it was taken off, into *mine?*"

I was very much surprised but could give no information.

"It's very strange," said Mr. Dick, "that I never can get that quite right. But no matter! There's time enough! My compliments to Miss Trotwood, I am getting on very well indeed."

I was going away, when he directed my attention to the kite.

"What do you think of that for a kite?" he said.

I answered that it was a beautiful one. It must have been as much as seven feet high.

"I made it. We'll go and fly it, you and I," said Mr. Dick. "Do you see this?"

He showed me that it was covered with manuscript, very closely written.

"There's plenty of string," said Mr. Dick, "and when it flies high, it takes the facts a long way. That's my manner of diffusing 'em."

"Well, child," said my aunt, when I went down-stairs. "And what of Mr. Dick, this morning?"

I informed her that he sent his compliments, and was getting on very well indeed.

"What do you think of him?" said my aunt.

"Is he—is Mr. Dick—I ask because I don't know, aunt—is he at all out of his mind, then?" I stammered.

"Not a morsel," said my aunt.

"Oh, indeed!" I observed faintly.

"He has been *called* mad," said my aunt, "and nice people they were, who had the audacity to call him mad. Mr. Dick is a sort of distant connexion of mine. If it hadn't been for me, his own brother would have shut him up for life."

My aunt smoothed her dress and shook her head.

"He had a favourite sister," said my aunt. "But she did what they all do—took a husband. And *he* did what they all do—made her wretched. It had such an effect upon Mr. Dick that it threw him into a fever. Did he say anything to you about King Charles the First, child?"

"Yes, aunt."

"Ah!" said my aunt, "That's his allegorical way of expressing it. He connects his illness with great disturbance, and that's the figure which he chooses to use. And why shouldn't he?"

I said: "Certainly, aunt."

"It's not a business-like way of speaking," said my aunt, "and that's why I insist that there shan't be a word about it in his Memorial."

"Is it a Memorial about his own history that he is writing, aunt?"

"Yes, child," said my aunt. "He is memorialising the Lord Chancellor, or the Lord Somebody or other—about his affairs. He hasn't been able to draw it up yet, but it don't signify; it keeps him employed."

In fact, I found out afterwards that Mr. Dick had been for upwards of ten years endeavouring to keep King Charles the First out of the Memorial; but he had been constantly getting into it, and was there now.

"I say again," said my aunt, "nobody knows what that man's mind is except myself. If he likes to fly a kite sometimes, what of that! Franklin used to fly a kite."

I must say that her championship of poor harmless Mr. Dick not only inspired my young breast with some selfish hope for myself, but warmed it unselfishly towards her.

The anxiety I underwent before a reply could be received to my aunt's letter to Mr. Murdstone, was extreme. At length my aunt informed me, to my infinite terror, that he was coming the next day.

On the next day my aunt sat at work in the window,

and I sat by until pretty late in the afternoon, when to my consternation I beheld Miss Murdstone, on a side-saddle, ride deliberately over the sacred piece of green, and stop in front of the house.

"Go along with you!" cried my aunt, shaking her head and her fist at the window. "How dare you trespass? Go along! Oh! you bold-faced thing!"

My aunt was so exasperated that I really believe she was unable to dart out. I seized the opportunity to inform her who it was; and that the gentleman now coming was Mr. Murdstone himself.

"I don't care who it is!" cried my aunt. "I won't be trespassed upon. Go away! Janet, turn him round. Lead him off!" and I saw a hurried battle, in which the donkey stood resisting everybody, with all his four legs planted different ways, while Janet tried to pull him round by the bridle, Mr. Murdstone tried to lead him on, Miss Murdstone struck at Janet with a parasol, and several boys shouted vigorously. But my aunt, suddenly descrying among them, the young malefactor who was the donkey's guardian, rushed out, pounced upon him, captured him, dragged him, with his jacket over his head and his heels grinding the ground, into the garden, and, calling upon Janet to fetch the constables, held him there. This, however, did not last long; for the young rascal, being expert at dodges, soon went whooping away, taking his donkey with him.

Miss Murdstone had dismounted, and was now waiting with her brother at the bottom of the steps. My aunt marched past them into the house, with great dignity, and took no notice of their presence, until they were announced by Janet.

"Shall I go away, aunt?" I asked, trembling.

"No, Sir," said my aunt. "Certainly not!" With which she pushed me into a corner near her, and fenced me in with a chair. This position I continued to occupy, and from it I now saw Mr. and Miss Murdstone enter the room.

"Oh!" said my aunt, "I was not aware at first to whom I had the pleasure of objecting. But I don't allow anybody to ride over that turf."

"Your regulation is rather awkward to strangers," said Miss Murdstone.

"Is it!" said my aunt.

Mr. Murdstone began: "Miss Trotwood!"

"I beg your pardon," observed my aunt with a keen look. "You are *the* Mr. Murdstone?"

"I am," said Mr. Murdstone.

"Janet," said my aunt, ringing the bell, "my compliments to Mr. Dick, and beg him to come down."

Until he came, my aunt sat perfectly upright. When he came, my aunt performed the ceremony of introduction.

"Mr. Dick. An old and intimate friend. On whose judgment," said my aunt, with emphasis, as an admonition to Mr. Dick, who was biting his forefinger and looking rather foolish, "I rely."

Mr. Dick took his finger out of his mouth, on this hint, and stood among the group, with a grave and attentive expression of face. My aunt inclined her head to Mr. Murdstone, who went on:

"Miss Trotwood. On the receipt of your letter, I considered it an act of greater justice to myself to answer it in person. This unhappy boy who has run away from his friends and his occupation, has been the occasion of much domestic trouble. He has a sullen, rebellious spirit; a violent temper; and an intractable disposition."

"It can hardly be necessary for me to confirm anything stated by my brother," said Miss Murdstone; "but of all the boys in the world, I believe this is the worst boy."

"Strong!" said my aunt, shortly.

"But not at all too strong for the facts," returned Miss Murdstone.

"Ha!" said my aunt. "Well, Sir? What have you got to say next?"

"Merely this, Miss Trotwood," he returned. "I am here to take David back, to dispose of him as I think proper, and to deal with him as I think right. Now I must caution you that if you step in between him and me, now, you must step in, Miss Trotwood, for ever. I am here, for the first and last time, to take him away. Is he ready to go?"

To this address, my aunt had listened with the closest attention. When he had finished, she said:

"Are you ready to go, David?"

I answered no, and entreated her not to let me go, but to befriend and protect me.

"Mr. Dick," said my aunt, "what shall I do with this child?"

Mr. Dick considered, hestitated, brightened, and rejoined, "Have him measured for a suit of clothes directly."

"Mr. Dick," said my aunt triumphantly, "give me your hand, for your common sense is invaluable." Having shaken it with great cordiality, she pulled me towards her and said to Mr. Murdstone:

"You can go when you like; I'll take my chance with the boy. If he's all you say he is, at least I can do as much for him then, as you have done. But I don't believe a word of it."

"Miss Trotwood," rejoined Mr. Murdstone, shrugging his shoulders, as he rose, "if you were a gentleman——"

"Bah! Stuff and nonsense!" said my aunt. "Don't talk to me!"

"How exquisitely polite!" exclaimed Miss Murdstone, rising. "Overpowering, really!"

"Do you think I don't know," said my aunt, "what kind of life you must have led that poor, unhappy, misdirected baby? Mr. Murdstone, you were a tyrant, and you broke her heart. She was a loving baby, and you gave her the wounds she died of. That is the truth for your comfort, and you and your instruments may make the most of it."

"Good day, Sir," said my aunt, "and good-bye! Good day to you, too, ma'am," said my aunt, turning suddenly upon his sister. "Let me see you ride a donkey over *my* green again, and as sure as you have a head upon your shoulders, I'll knock your bonnet off, and tread upon it!"

It would require a painter to depict my aunt's face as she delivered herself of this very unexpected sentiment, and Miss Murdstone's face as she heard it. But the manner was so fiery, that Miss Murdstone, without a word in answer, discreetly put her arm through her brother's, and walked haughtily out of the cottage; my aunt remaining in the window looking after them, prepared, I have no doubt, to carry her threat into instant execution.

No attempt at defiance being made, however, my aunt's face gradually relaxed, and became so pleasant, that I was emboldened to kiss and thank her; which I did with both my arms clasped round her neck.

"You'll consider yourself guardian, jointly with me, of this child, Mr. Dick," said my aunt.

"I shall be delighted," said Mr. Dick, "to be the guardian of David's son."

"Very good," returned my aunt, "*That's* settled. I have been thinking, do you know, Mr. Dick, that I might call him Trotwood?"

"Certainly, certainly. Call him Trotwood, certainly," said Mr. Dick. "David's son's Trotwood."

"Trotwood Copperfield, you mean," returned my aunt.

"Yes, to be sure. Yes. Trotwood Copperfield," said Mr. Dick a little abashed.

Thus I began my new life, in a new name, and with everything new about me.

CHAPTER XV

I MAKE ANOTHER BEGINNING

Mr. Dick and I soon became the best of friends, and very often, when his day's work was done, we went out together to fly the great kite.

It was quite an affecting sight, I used to think, to see him with the kite when it was up a great height in the air. He never looked so serene as he did then. I used to fancy, as I sat by him of an evening, on a green slope, that it lifted his mind out of its confusion, and bore it into the skies. As he wound the string in, he seemed to wake gradually out of a dream; and I remember to have seen him take the kite up, and look about him in a lost way, as if they had both come down together.

While I advanced in friendship and intimacy with Mr. Dick, I did not go backward in the favour of his staunch friend.

"Trot," said my aunt one evening, when the backgammon-board was placed as usual for herself and Mr. Dick, "we must not forget your education."

This was my only subject of anxiety, and I felt quite delighted by her referring to it.

"Should you like to go to school at Canterbury?" said my aunt.

I replied that I should like it very much, as it was so near her.

"Good," said my aunt. "Should you like to go to-morrow?"

I was not surprised by the suddenness of the proposal, and said: "Yes."

"Good," said my aunt again. "Janet, hire the grey pony and chaise to-morrow morning at ten o'clock, and pack up Master Trotwood's clothes to-night."

I was greatly elated by these orders; but my heart smote me when I witnessed their effect on Mr. Dick, who was so low-spirited and played so ill that my aunt, after giving him several raps on the knuckles with her dice-box, shut up the backgammon-board, and declined to play with him any more. But, on hearing that I should sometimes come over on a Saturday, and that he could sometimes come and see me on a Wednesday, he revived; and vowed to make another kite for those occasions, of proportions greatly surpassing the present one. In the morning we parted in a most affectionate manner, and Mr. Dick did not go into the house until my aunt had driven me out of sight.

My aunt drove the grey pony through Dover in a masterly manner, making a point of not letting him have his own way in any respect. When we came into the country road, she permitted him to relax a little, however; and looking at me asked me whether I was happy?

"Very happy indeed, thank you, aunt," I said.

She was much gratified; and both her hands being occupied, patted me on the head with her whip.

"Is it a large school, aunt?" I asked.

"Why, I don't know," said my aunt. "We are going to Mr. Wickfield's first."

"Does *he* keep a school?" I asked.

"No, Trot," said my aunt. "He keeps an office."

I asked for no more information, and we conversed on other subjects until we came to Canterbury, where we stopped before a very old house bulging out over the road.

When the pony-chaise stopped at the door I saw a cadaverous face appear at a small window on the ground floor, and quickly disappear. The low arched door then opened, and the face came out. It belonged to a red-haired person—a youth of fifteen, but looking much older—whose hair was cropped close; who had hardly any eyebrows, and no eyelashes, and eyes of a red-brown. He was high-shouldered and bony, and had a long, lank, skeleton hand.

"Is Mr. Wickfield at home, Uriah Heep?" said my aunt.

"Mr. Wickfield's at home, ma'am," said Uriah Heep, "if you'll please to walk in there"; and we got out and went into a long low parlour. Opposite to the tall old chimney-piece, were two portraits: one of a gentleman with grey hair and black eyebrows; the other, of a lady, with a very placid and sweet expression.

A door at the farther end of the room opening, a gentleman entered, at sight of whom I turned to the first-mentioned portrait again, to make quite sure that it had not come out of its frame.

"Miss Betsey Trotwood," said the gentleman, "pray walk in. I was engaged for a moment, but you'll excuse my being busy. You know my motive. I have but one in life."

Miss Betsey thanked him, and we went into his office.

"This is my nephew," said my aunt.

"Wasn't aware you had one, Miss Trotwood," said Mr. Wickfield.

"I have adopted him," said my aunt, with a wave of her hand, "and I have brought him here, to put him to a school where he may be thoroughly well taught, and well treated. Now tell me where that school is, and what it is, and all about it."

"Before I can advise you properly," said Mr. Wickfield, "what's your motive in this?"

"Deuce take the man!" exclaimed my aunt. "Always fishing for motives! Why, to make the child happy and useful. You don't suppose, I hope, that you are the only plain dealer in the world?"

"Ay, but I have only one motive in life, Miss Trotwood," he rejoined, smiling. "Other people have dozens. The best school? Whatever the motive, you want the best?"

My aunt nodded assent.

"At the best we have," said Mr. Wakefield, considering, "your nephew couldn't board just now."

"But he could board somewhere else, I suppose?" suggested my aunt.

Mr. Wickfield thought I could. After a little discussion, he proposed to take my aunt to the school; also, to take her to two or three houses where he thought I could be boarded. We were all three going out together, when he stopped and said:

"Our little friend here might have some motive for objecting. I think we had better leave him behind."

I said I would gladly remain behind, if they pleased; and returned into Mr. Wickfield's office.

My aunt and Mr. Wickfield came back, after a pretty long absence. They were not so successful as I could have wished; for though the advantages of the school were undeniable, my aunt had not approved of any of the boarding-houses.

"It's very unfortunate," said my aunt. "I don't know what to do, Trot."

"I'll tell you what you can do, Miss Trotwood," said Mr. Wickfield.

"What's that?" inquired my aunt.

"Leave your nephew here, for the present. He won't disturb me at all. It's a capital house for study."

My aunt evidently liked the offer, though she was delicate of accepting it. So did I.

"Come, Miss Trotwood," said Mr. Wickfield. "This is the way out of the difficulty. You may pay for him, if you like. We won't be hard about terms, but you shall pay if you will."

"On that understanding," said my aunt, "though it doesn't lessen the real obligation, I shall be very glad to leave him."

"Then come and see my little housekeeper," said Mr. Wickfield.

We accordingly went up a wonderful old staircase, and into a shady old drawing-room that seemed to be all nooks and corners.

Mr. Wickfield tapped at a door, and a girl of about my

own age came quickly out and kissed him. On her face, I saw immediately the placid and sweet expression of the lady whose picture had looked at me down-stairs. Although her face was quite bright and happy, there was a tranquillity about it, and about her—a quiet, good, calm spirit—that I never have forgotten; that I never shall forget.

This was his little housekeeper, his daughter Agnes, Mr. Wickfield said. When I heard how he said it, and saw how he held her hand, I guessed what the one motive of his life was. She listened to her father as he told her about me, and proposed that we should go upstairs and see my room. We all went together, she before us. A glorious old room it was, with oak beams, and diamond panes; and the broad balustrade going all the way up to it.

My aunt was as happy as I, and we went down to the drawing-room again, well pleased. As she would not hear of staying to dinner, some lunch was provided for her, and Agnes went back to her governess, and Mr. Wickfield to his office. So we were left to take leave of one another without any restraint.

"Trot," said my aunt in conclusion, "be a credit to yourself, to me, and Mr. Dick, and Heaven be with you!"

I could only thank her, again and again, and send my love to Mr. Dick.

"Never," said my aunt, "be mean; never be false; never be cruel. Avoid those three vices, Trot, and I can always be hopeful of you."

I promised, as well as I could, that I would not abuse her kindness or forget her admonition.

"The pony's at the door," said my aunt, "and I am off! Stay here."

With these words she embraced me hastily, and went out, shutting the door. At first I almost feared I had displeased her; but when I saw how dejectedly she got into the chaise, and drove away, I understood her better.

By five o'clock, which was Mr. Wickfield's dinner-hour,

I had mustered up my spirits again, and was ready for my knife and fork. The cloth was only laid for us two; but Agnes went down with her father, and sat opposite to him at table. I doubted whether he could have dined without her.

In the course of the evening I rambled a little way along the street, that I might have another peep at the old houses, and the grey Cathedral. As I came back, I saw Uriah Heep, and, feeling friendly towards everybody, spoke to him, and at parting, gave him my hand. But oh, what a clammy hand his was! I rubbed mine afterwards, to warm it, *and to rub his off*.

CHAPTER XVI

I AM A NEW BOY IN MORE SENSES THAN ONE

NEXT morning, after breakfast, I entered on school life again. I went, accompanied by Mr. Wickfield, to the scene of my future studies—a grave building in a courtyard—and was introduced to my new master, Doctor Strong.

Doctor Strong looked almost as rusty as the tall iron rails and gates outside the house. He was in his library with his clothes not particularly well brushed, and his hair not particularly well combed, sitting at work. Not far off was a very pretty young lady—whom he called Annie, and who was his daughter, I supposed. We were going out to the school-room when Doctor Strong himself enlightened me.

"By the bye, Wickfield," he said, "you have not found any suitable provision for my wife's cousin yet?"

"No," said Mr. Wickfield. "No. Not yet."

"I could wish it done as soon as it *can* be done, Wickfield," said Doctor Strong, "for Jack Maldon is needy, and idle, and of those two bad things, worse things sometimes come."

"I believe," said Mr. Wickfield with some hesitation, "I penetrate your motive, and it makes the thing more difficult."

"My motive," returned Doctor Strong, "is to make some suitable provision for a cousin, and an old playfellow, of Annie's."

"Yes, I know," said Mr. Wickfield, "at home or abroad."

"Ah!" replied the Doctor, apparently wondering why he emphasized those words so much. "At home or abroad."

"Have you no choice?" asked Mr. Wickfield.

"No," returned the Doctor.

"No?" with astonishment.

"Not the least."

"No motive," said Mr. Wickfield, "for meaning abroad, and not at home?"

"No," returned the Doctor.

"I am bound to believe you, and of course I do believe you," said Mr. Wickfield. "But I confess I entertained another impression."

Doctor Strong regarded him with a puzzled and doubting look, which almost immediately subsided into a smile that gave me great encouragement; for it was full of amiability and sweetness, and there was a simplicity in it, and indeed in his whole manner, very attractive and hopeful to a young scholar like me.

The schoolroom was a pretty large hall, on the quietest side of the house. About five-and-twenty boys were studiously engaged at their books when we went in, but they rose to give the Doctor good morning, and remained standing when they saw Mr. Wickfield and me.

"A new boy, young gentlemen," said the Doctor; "Trotwood Copperfield."

Adams, who was the head-boy, then stepped out of his place and welcomed me. He was very affable and good-humoured; and he showed me my place, and presented me to the masters, in a gentlemanly way that would have put me at my ease, if anything could.

It seemed to me so long, however, since I had been among such boys, or among any companions of my own age, except Mick Walker and Mealy Potatoes, that I felt as strange as ever I have done in all my life. I felt distrustful of my slightest look and gesture; shrunk within myself whensoever I was approached by one of my new school-fellows; and hurried off, the minute school was over.

But there was such an influence in Mr. Wickfield's old house, that when I knocked at it, with my new school-books under my arm, I began to feel my uneasiness softening away. As I went up to my airy old room, the grave shadow of the staircase seemed to fall upon my doubts and fears. I sat there, sturdily conning my books, until dinner-time (we were out of school for good at three); and went down, hopeful of becoming a passable sort of boy yet.

Agnes was in the dining-room, waiting for her father. She met me with her pleasant smile, and asked me how I liked the school. I told her I should like it very much, I hoped; but I was a little strange to it at first.

When we had dined, we went up-stairs again, where everything went on exactly as on the previous day. Agnes set the glasses and decanters in the same corner, and Mr. Wickfield drank a good deal. Agnes played the piano to him, sat by him, and worked and talked, and played dominoes with me. In good time she made tea; and afterwards, when I brought down my books, looked into them, and showed me what was the best way to understand them.

She having left us for the night, I gave Mr. Wickfield my hand, preparatory to going away myself. But he checked me and said: "Should you like to stay with us, Trotwood, or to go elsewhere?"

"To stay," I answered, quickly.

"You are sure?"

"If you please. If I may!"

"Stay with us, Trotwood, eh?" he said. "I am glad of it. It is wholesome to have you here, wholesome perhaps for all of us."

"I am sure it is for me, Sir," I said. "I am so glad to be here."

"That's a fine fellow!" said Mr. Wickfield. "As long as you are glad to be here, you shall stay here." He shook hands with me upon it, and told me that when I had anything to do at night after Agnes had left us, or when I wished to read, I was free to come down to his room and to sit with him. I thanked him and, as he went down soon afterwards, I went down too.

But, seeing a light in the little round office, and immediately feeling myself attracted towards Uriah Heep, who had a sort of fascination for me, I went in there instead. I found Uriah reading a great fat book, with such attention, that his lank forefinger followed up every line as he read.

"You are working late to-night, Uriah," says I.

"Yes, Master Copperfield. No, I am not doing office-work, Master Copperfield," said Uriah.

"What work, then?" I asked.

"I am improving my legal knowledge, Master Copperfield," said Uriah. "I am going through Tidd's *Practice*. Oh, what a writer Mr. Tidd is, Master Copperfield!"

"I suppose you are quite a great lawyer?" I said, after looking at him for some time.

"Me, Master Copperfield?" said Uriah. "Oh, no! I am the umblest person going. My mother is likewise a very umble person. We live in a numble abode, Master Copperfield, but have much to be thankful for. How much have I to be thankful for in living with Mr. Wickfield!"

I asked Uriah if he had been with Mr. Wickfield long?

"I have been with him going on four years, Master Copperfield," said Uriah. "How much have I to be thankful for, in Mr. Wickfield's kind intention to give me my articles.

"Then, when your articled time is over, you'll be a regular lawyer, I suppose?" said I.

"With the blessing of Providence, Master Copperfield," returned Uriah.

"Perhaps you'll be a partner in Mr. Wickfield's business, one of these days," I said, to make myself agreeable; "and it will be Wickfield and Heep, or Heep late Wickfield."

"Oh no, Master Copperfield," returned Uriah, shaking his head, "I am much too umble for that!"

Being, at last, ready to leave the office for the night, he asked me if it would suit my convenience to have the light put out; and on my answering "Yes," instantly extinguished it. After shaking hands with me—his hand felt

In the evening Agnes played the piano to him.

like a fish, in the dark—he opened the door into the street a very little, and crept out, and shut it, leaving me to grope my way back into the house: which cost me some trouble and a fall over his stool.

I got a little the better of my uneasiness when I went to school next day, and so shook it off by degrees, that in less than a fortnight I was quite at home, and happy, among my new companions. I was awkward enough in their games, and backward enough in their studies; but I went to work very hard, both in play and in earnest, and gained great commendation.

Doctor Strong's was an excellent school; as different from Mr. Creakle's as good is from evil. It was ordered with an appeal, in everything, to the honour and good faith of the boys. We all felt that we had a part in the management of the place. Hence, we soon became warmly attached to it and learnt with a good will, desiring to do it credit. We had noble games out of hours, and plenty of liberty; but we were well spoken of in the town, and rarely did any disgrace to the reputation of Doctor Strong and Doctor Strong's boys.

Some of the higher scholars boarded in the Doctor's house, and through them I learned some particulars of the Doctor's history—as, how he had not yet been married twelve months to the beautiful young lady whom he had married for love; for she had not a sixpence, and had a world of poor relations (so our fellows said) ready to swarm the Doctor out of house and home. Also, how the Doctor's cogitating manner was attributed to his being always engaged in looking out for Greek roots; which, I supposed to be botanical until I understood that they were roots of words, with a view to a new Dictionary. Adams, our head-boy had made a calculation of the time this Dictionary would take in completing at the Doctor's rate of going. He considered that it might be done in one thousand six hundred and forty-nine years, counting from the Doctor's last, or sixty-second, birthday.

But the Doctor himself was the idol of the whole school.

He was the kindest of men. He would have taken his gaiters off his legs, to give away. In fact, there was a story current among us that on a frosty day, one winter-time, he actually did bestow his gaiters on a beggar-woman, who occasioned some scandal in the neighbourhood by exhibiting a fine infant from door to door, wrapped in those garments.

It was very pleasant to see the Doctor with his pretty young wife. He had a fatherly, benignant way of showing his fondness for her, which seemed in itself to express a good man. She appeared to me to take great care of the Doctor, and to like him very much, though I never thought her vitally interested in the Dictionary: some cumbrous fragments of which the Doctor always carried in his pockets, and in the lining of his hat.

I saw a good deal of Mrs. Strong, both because she had taken a liking for me and because she was very fond of Agnes, and was often backwards and forwards at our house.

Mrs. Strong's mama was a lady I took great delight in. Her name was Mrs. Markleham; but our boys used to call her the Old Soldier, on account of her generalship, and the skill with which she marshalled great forces of relations against the Doctor. She was a little, sharp-eyed woman, who used to wear, when she was dressed, one unchangeable cap, ornamented with some artificial flowers, and two artificial butterflies supposed to be hovering above the flowers.

I observed the Old Soldier to pretty good advantage, on a night which is made memorable to me by something else I shall relate. It was the night of a little party at the Doctor's, which was given on the occasion of Mr. Jack Maldon's departure for India; Mr. Wickfield having at length arranged the business. It happened to be the Doctor's birthday, too. We had had a holiday, had made presents to him in the morning, had made a speech to him through the head-boy, and had cheered him until we were hoarse, and until he had shed tears. And now, in the evening, Mr. Wickfield, Agnes, and I, went to have tea with him.

Mr. Jack Maldon was there, before us. Mrs. Strong, dressed in white, with cherry-coloured ribbons, was playing the piano, when we went in; and he was leaning over her to turn the leaves.

"I have forgotten, Doctor," said Mrs. Strong's mama, when we were seated, "to pay you the compliments of the day. Allow me to wish you many happy returns."

"I thank you, ma'am," replied the Doctor.

"Many, many, many, happy returns," said the Old Soldier. "Not only for your own sake, but for Annie's and John Maldon's and many other people's. It seems but yesterday to me, John, when you were a little creature, making baby love to Annie."

"My dear mama," said Mrs. Strong, "never mind that now."

"Annie, don't be absurd," returned her mother. "It is well for you, John, that your cousin *is* the wife of the Doctor. You have found in him an influential and kind friend."

The Doctor, in the goodness of his heart, waved his hand as if to make light of it. But Mrs. Markleham changed her chair for one next the Doctor's, and putting her fan on his coat-sleeve, said:

"No, really, my dear Doctor, you must excuse me if I appear to dwell on this rather, because I feel so very strongly. You are a blessing to us. You really are a boon, you know."

"Nonsense, nonsense," said the Doctor.

"No, no, I beg your pardon," retorted the Old Soldier. "With nobody present, but Mr. Wickfield, I cannot consent to be put down. What I am saying, is what I said when you first overpowered me with surprise by proposing for Annie."

"Aye, aye," returned the Doctor, good-humouredly. "Never mind."

"But I *do* mind," said the Old Soldier, laying her fan

upon his lips. "I mind very much. Well! I spoke to Annie, and I said, 'My dear, here's Doctor Strong has positively been and made you an offer.' I said, 'Now, Annie, is your heart free?' 'Mama,' she said crying, 'I hardly know if I have a heart at all.' 'Then, my dear,' I said, 'it's free.' 'Mama,' said Annie, still crying, 'I honour and respect him so much, that I think I will have him.' So it was settled. And then, and not till then, I said to Annie, 'Annie, Doctor Strong will represent the head of our family and will be, in short, a boon to it.' "

The daughter had sat quite silent during this speech, with her eyes fixed on the ground. She now said very softly, in a trembling voice:

"Mama, I hope you have finished?"

"No, my dear Annie," returned the Soldier, "I have not quite finished. I complain that you are a little unnatural towards your own family. Now, my dear Doctor, do look at that silly wife of yours."

As the Doctor turned his kind face towards her, she drooped her head more. I noticed that Mr. Wickfield looked at her steadily.

"When I happened to say to that naughty thing, the other day," pursued her mother, shaking her head and her fan at her, playfully, "that there was a family circumstance she might mention to you, she said, that to mention it was to ask a favour; and that, as you were too generous, she wouldn't."

"Annie, my dear," said the Doctor. "That was wrong. It robbed me of a pleasure."

"Almost the very words I said to her!" exclaimed her mother. "Now really, another time, when she won't, I have a great mind, my dear Doctor, to tell you myself."

"I shall be glad if you will," returned the Doctor.

"Shall I?"

"Certainly."

"Well, then, I will!" said the Old Soldier. "That's a bargain." And having carried her point, she tapped the Doctor's hand several times with her fan (which she kissed first), and returned triumphantly to her former station.

Mrs. Strong was a very pretty singer: as I knew, who often heard her singing by herself. But, whether she was afraid to sing before people, or was out of voice that evening, it was certain that she couldn't sing at all. The good Doctor said she was nervous, and to relieve her, proposed a round game at cards; of which he knew as much as of the art of playing the trombone. We had a merry game, not made the less merry by the Doctor's mistakes, of which he committed an innumerable quantity.

At supper, we were hardly so gay. The Doctor, however, was well pleased, and had no suspicion but that we were all at the utmost height of enjoyment.

"Annie, my dear," said he, looking at his watch, and filling his glass, "it is past your cousin Jack's time, and we must not detain him, since time and tide—both concerned in this case—wait for no man. Mr. Jack Maldon, you have a long voyage, and a strange country, before you. I shall not weary you with good advice. You have long had a good model before you, in your cousin Annie. Imitate her virtues."

Mrs. Markleham fanned herself, and shook her head.

"Farewell, Mr. Jack," said the Doctor, standing up; on which we all stood up. "A prosperous voyage out, a thriving career abroad, and a happy return home!"

We all drank the toast, and all shook hands with Mr. Jack Maldon; after which he hastily took leave of the ladies who were there, and hurried to the door. I was very near the chaise when it rolled away; and I had a lively impression made upon me, in the midst of the noise and dust, of having seen Mr. Jack Maldon rattle past with an agitated face, and something cherry-coloured in his hand.

I went back into the house, where I found the guests in a group discussing how Mr. Jack Maldon had gone away, and how he had borne it. In the midst of these remarks, Mrs. Markleham cried: "Where's Annie?"

No Annie was there; and when they called to her, no Annie replied. But all pressing out of the room to see what was the matter, we found her lying on the hall floor. There was a great alarm, until it was found that she was in a swoon, and that the swoon was yielding; when the Doctor, who had lifted her head upon his knee, put her curls aside with his hand, and said, looking around:

"Poor Annie! She's so faithful and tender-hearted! It's the parting from her favourite cousin. Ah! It's a pity! I am very sorry!"

When she opened her eyes, she arose with assistance: turning her head to lay it on the Doctor's shoulder—or to hide it, I don't know which. She said she would rather be among us; so they brought her in, looking very white and weak, and sat her on a sofa.

"Annie, my dear," said her mother. "You have lost a bow. Will anybody be so good as to find a ribbon; a cherry-coloured ribbon?"

It was the one she had worn at her bosom. We all looked for it; I myself looked everywhere, I am certain; but nobody could find it.

"Do you recollect where you had it last, Annie?" said her mother.

She answered that she had had it safe, a little while ago, she thought, but it was not worth looking for.

Nevertheless, it was looked for in a desultory way, until she was quite well, and the company took their departure.

We walked very slowly home, Mr. Wickfield scarcely raising his eyes from the ground. When we reached our own door, Agnes discovered that she had left her little reticule behind. Delighted to be of any service to her, I ran back to fetch it.

I went into the supper-room where it had been left, which was dark. But a door between that and the Doctor's study being open, I passed on there, to say what I wanted, and to get a candle.

The Doctor was sitting in his easy-chair by the fireside, and his young wife was on a stool at his feet. The Doctor was reading aloud out of that interminable Dictionary, and she was looking up at him. But, with such a face as I never saw. It was so beautiful in its form, so ashy pale, so full of a horror of I don't know what. Penitence, humiliation, love, I see them all; and in them all, I see that horror of I don't know what.

My entrance roused her. It disturbed the Doctor too, for when I went back to replace the candle he was patting her head, in his fatherly way, and saying he was a merciless drone and he would have her go to bed.

But she asked him, in a rapid, urgent manner, to let her stay. To let her feel assured that she was in his confidence that night. And, as she turned again towards him, I saw her cross her hands upon his knee, and look up at him something quieted, as he resumed his reading.

It made a great impression on me, and I remembered it a long time afterwards, as I shall have occasion to narrate when the time comes.

CHAPTER XVII

SOMEBODY TURNS UP

It had not occurred to me to mention Peggotty since I ran away; but of course I wrote her a letter almost as soon as I was housed at Dover, and another when my aunt took me under her protection. On my being settled at Doctor Strong's I wrote to her again. I could never have derived anything like the pleasure from spending a half-guinea that Mr. Dick had given me, that I felt in sending a gold half-guinea to Peggotty!

To these communications Peggotty replied promptly. I made out without much difficulty, that she could not take quite kindly to my aunt yet. We never knew a person, she wrote; but to think that Miss Betsey would seem to be so different from what she had been thought to be, was a Moral!—That was her word.

She gave me one piece of intelligence that affected me very much, namely, that there had been a sale of the furniture at our old house, and that Mr. and Miss Murdstone were gone away, and the house was shut up, to be let or sold.

While I was yet new at Doctor Strong's, my aunt made several excursions to see me, and always at unseasonable hours, but finding me well employed, and hearing that I rose fast in the school, she soon discontinued these visits. I saw her on a Saturday, every third or fourth week, when I went over to Dover for a treat; and I saw Mr. Dick every alternate Wednesday, when he arrived by stage-coach at noon, to stay until next morning.

"Trotwood," said Mr. Dick with an air of mystery, one Wednesday; "who's the man that hides near our house and frightens her?"

"Frightens my aunt, Sir?"

Mr. Dick nodded. "I thought nothing would have frightened her," he said, "for she's——" here he whispered softly, "don't mention it—the wisest and most wonderful of women. The first time he came was—let me see—sixteen hundred and forty-nine was the date of King Charles's execution, I think you said, sixteen hundred and forty-nine?"

"Yes, sir."

"I can't make it out," said Mr. Dick, shaking his head. "There's something wrong, somewhere. However, it was very soon after the mistake was made of putting some of the trouble out of King Charles's head into my head, that the man first came. I was walking out with Miss Trotwood after tea, just at dark, and there he was, close to our house."

I asked what he was doing.

"Well, he wasn't there at all," said Mr. Dick, "until he came up behind her, and whispered. Then she turned round and fainted, and I stood still and looked at him, and he walked away; but that he should have been hiding ever since (in the ground or somewhere), is the most extraordinary thing!"

"*Has* he been hiding ever since?" I asked.

"To be sure he has," retorted Mr. Dick, nodding his head gravely. "Never came out, till last night! He came up behind her again."

"And did he frighten my aunt again?"

"All of a shiver," said Mr. Dick. "Held by the palings. Cried. But, Trotwood, why did she give him money?"

"He was a beggar, perhaps."

Mr. Dick shook his head, and having replied a great many times "No beggar, no beggar, no beggar, Sir!" went on to say, that from his window he had afterwards seen my aunt give this person money, who then slunk away—into the ground again, as he thought probable—and was seen no more.

These Wednesdays were the happiest days of Mr. Dick's

life; and he never had anything more to tell of the man who could frighten my aunt.

Mr. Dick soon became known to every boy in the school; and though he never took an active part in any game but kite-flying, was deeply interested in all our sports. How often have I seen him, intent upon a match at marbles or pegtop, hardly breathing at the critical times.

He was a universal favourite! He could make a boat out of anything, from a skewer upwards. He could fashion Roman chariots from old court cards; make spoked wheels out of cotton reels, and birdcages of old wire.

Mr. Dick's renown was not long confined to us. After a few Wednesdays, Doctor Strong himself made some inquiries of me about him, and I told him all my aunt had told me; which interested the Doctor so much that he requested to be presented to him. This ceremony I performed; and the Doctor begging Mr. Dick, whensoever he should not find me at the coach-office, to come on there, and rest himself until our morning's work was over, it soon passed into a custom. He became more and more familiar until, at last, he would come into the school and wait. He always sat in a particular corner, on a particular stool, which was called "Dick," after him. Mr. Dick thought the Doctor the most subtle and accomplished philosopher of any age, and even when he and the Doctor had struck up quite a friendship, and would walk together by the hour, Mr. Dick would pull off his hat at intervals to show his respect. How it ever came about, that the Doctor began to read out scraps of the famous Dictionary, in these walks, I never knew. However, it passed into a custom too; and Mr. Dick, listening with a face shining with pride and pleasure, believed the Dictionary to be the most delightful book in the world.

One Thursday morning, when I was about to walk with Mr. Dick from the hotel to the coach-office before going back to school (for we had an hour's school before breakfast), I met Uriah in the street, who reminded me of the promise I had made to take tea with himself and his mother; adding, with a writhe, "But I didn't expect you to keep it, Master Copperfield, we're so very umble."

I really had not yet been able to make up my mind whether I liked Uriah or detested him, but I felt it quite an affront to be supposed proud, and said I only wanted to be asked.

"Oh, if that's all, Master Copperfield," said Uriah, "and it really isn't our umbleness that prevents you, will you come this evening?"

I said I would come with pleasure. So, at six o'clock that evening I announced myself as ready.

"Mother will be proud, indeed," he said, as we walked away together. "Or she would be proud, if it wasn't sinful, Master Copperfield."

"Yet you didn't mind supposing *I* was proud this morning," I returned.

"Oh dear, no, Master Copperfield!" returned Uriah. "Oh, believe me, no! Such a thought never came into my head! I shouldn't have deemed it at all proud if you had thought *us* too umble for you. Because we are so very umble."

"Have you been studying much law lately?" I asked, to change the subject.

"Oh, Master Copperfield," he said, with an air of self-denial, "my reading is hardly to be called study. I have passed an hour or two in the evening, sometimes, with Mr. Tidd.

"Rather hard, I suppose?" said I.

"He is hard to *me* sometimes," returned Uriah. "But I don't know what he might be to a gifted person."

We entered a low, old-fashioned room and found there Mrs. Heep, who was the dead image of Uriah, only short. She received me with the utmost humility, and apologised to me for giving her son a kiss, observing that, lowly as they were, they had their natural affections, which they hoped would give no offence to any one.

"This is a day to be remembered, my Uriah, I am sure," said Mrs. Heep, making the tea, "when Master Copperfield pays us a visit."

I felt embarrassed; but I was sensible, too, of being entertained as an honoured guest, and I thought Mrs. Heep an agreeable woman.

"My Uriah," said Mrs. Heep, "has looked forward to this, Sir, a long while. He had his fears that our umbleness stood in the way, and I joined in them myself. Umble we are, umble we have been, umble we shall ever be," said Mrs. Heep.

"I am sure you have no occasion to be so, ma'am," I said, "unless you like."

"Thank you, Sir," retorted Mrs. Heep. "We know our station and are thankful in it."

I found that Mrs. Heep gradually got nearer to me, and that Uriah gradually got opposite to me, and that they respectfully plied me with the choicest of the eatables on the table. Presently they began to talk about aunts, and then I told them about mine; and about fathers and mothers, and then I told them about mine; and then Mrs. Heep began to talk about fathers-in-law, and then I began to tell her about mine; but stopped, because my aunt had advised me to observe a silence on that subject. A tender young cork, however, would have had no more chance against a pair of corkscrews, or a tender young tooth against a pair of dentists, than I had against Uriah and Mrs. Heep. They wormed things out of me that I had no desire to tell, with a certainty I blush to think of: the more especially as I took some credit to myself for being so confidential, and felt that I was quite the patron of my two respectful entertainers.

They were very fond of one another: that was certain. But the skill with which the one followed up whatever the other said, was a touch of art. When there was nothing more to be got out of me about myself (for on the Murdstone and Grinby life, and on my journey, I was dumb), they began about Mr. Wickfield and Agnes. Now it was the excellence of Mr. Wickfield, now my admiration of Agnes; now the extent of Mr. Wickfield's business and resources, now our domestic life after dinner; now, the wine that Mr. Wickfield took, the reason why he took it, and the pity that it was he took so much; now one thing, now another; and all the time I found myself letting out something or other that I had no business to let out.

I had begun to be a little uncomfortable when a figure coming down the street passed the door—came back again, looked in, and walked in, exclaiming loudly, "Copperfield! Is it possible?"

It was Mr. Micawber! It was Mr. Micawber, with his eye-glass, and his walking-stick, and his genteel air, and the condescending roll in his voice, all complete!

"My dear Copperfield," said Mr. Micawber, putting out his hand, "this is indeed a meeting which is calculated to impress—in short, it is a most extraordinary meeting. Walking along the street, reflecting upon the probability of something turning up, I find a young but valued friend turn up. Copperfield, my dear fellow, how do you do?"

I cannot say—I really can*not* say—that I was glad to see Mr. Micawber *there;* but I was glad to see him too, and shook hands with him heartily, inquiring how Mrs. Micawber was.

"Thank you," said Mr. Micawber, waving his hand as of old, and settling his chin in his shirt-collar. "She is tolerably convalescent. The twins no longer derive their sustenance from Nature's founts—in short," said Mr. Micawber, in one of his bursts of confidence, "they are weaned—and Mrs. Micawber is, at present, my travelling companion. She will be rejoiced, Copperfield, to renew her acquaintance."

I said I should be delighted to see her.

"You are very good," said Mr. Micawber.

Mr. Micawber then smiled, settled his chin again, and looked about him.

"I have discovered my friend Copperfield," said Mr. Micawber genteelly, "not in solitude, but partaking of a social meal in company with a widow lady, and one who is—in short, her son. I shall esteem it an honour to be presented."

I could do no less than make Mr. Micawber known to Uriah Heep and his mother; which I accordingly did. As they abased themselves before him, Mr. Micawber took a seat, and waved his hand in his most courtly manner.

"Any friend of my friend Copperfield's," said Mr. Micawber, "has a personal claim upon myself."

"We are too umble, Sir," said Mrs. Heep, "to be the friends of Master Copperfield. We are thankful to him for his company; also to you, Sir, for your notice."

"Ma'am," returned Mr. Micawber, with a bow, "you are very obliging; and what are you doing, Copperfield? Still in the wine trade?"

I was excessively anxious to get Mr. Micawber away; and replied, with my hat in my hand, and a very red face, I have no doubt, that I was a pupil at Doctor Strong's.

"A pupil?" said Mr. Micawber, raising his eyebrows. "I am extremely happy to hear it. A mind like my friend Copperfield's"—to Uriah and Mrs. Heep—"is a rich soil—in short," said Mr. Micawber, smiling, in another burst of confidence, "it is an intellect capable of getting up the classics to any extent."

"Shall we go and see Mrs. Micawber, Sir?" I said, to get Mr. Micawber away.

"If you will do her that favour, Copperfield," replied Mr. Micawber. "I have no scruple in saying in the presence of our friends here, that I am a man who has contended against pecuniary difficulties." I knew he was certain to say something of this kind. "Sometimes I have risen superior to my difficulties. Sometimes my difficulties have—in short, have floored me. But at no time," said Mr. Micawber, "have I enjoyed a higher satisfaction than in pouring my griefs (if I may describe difficulties by that word) into the bosom of my friend Copperfield."

Mr. Micawber closed this handsome tribute by saying, "Mr. Heep! Good evening. Mrs. Heep! Your servant,"

Mr. Micawber, with his eye-glass and his walking-stick and his genteel air.

and then walking out with me in his most fashionable manner, and humming a tune as we went.

It was a little inn where Mr. Micawber put up, and he occupied a little room in it strongly flavoured with tobacco-smoke. Here, recumbent on a small sofa was Mrs. Micawber, to whom Mr. Micawber entered first, saying, "My dear, allow me to introduce to you a pupil of Dr. Strong's."

Mrs. Micawber was amazed, but very glad to see me. I was very glad to see her too, and, after an affectionate greeting on both sides, sat down on the small sofa near her.

"My dear," said Mr. Micawber, "if you will mention to Copperfield what our present position is, I will go and look at the paper the while, and see whether anything turns up among the advertisements."

"I thought you were at Plymouth, ma'am," I said to Mrs. Micawber, as he went out.

"My dear Master Copperfield," she replied, "we went to Plymouth. But, talent is not wanted in the Custom House. Apart from which," said Mrs. Micawber, "I will not disguise from you, my dear Master Copperfield, that when that branch of my family became aware that Mr. Micawber was accompanied by myself, and by little Wilkins and his sister, and by the twins, our reception was cool."

"Dear me!" I said.

"Yes," said Mrs. Micawber, "our reception was, decidedly, cool. There is no doubt about it."

I said, and thought, that they ought to be ashamed of themselves.

"Still, so it was," continued Mrs. Micawber. "But one obvious course was left. To borrow of that branch of my family the money to return to London, and to return."

"Then you all came back again, ma'am?" I said.

"We all came back again," replied Mrs. Micawber. "Since then, I have consulted other branches of my family on the course which is the most expedient for Mr. Micawber to take—for," said Mrs. Micawber, argumentatively, "it is clear that a family of six cannot live upon air."

"Certainly, ma'am," said I.

"The opinion of those other branches of my family," pursued Mrs. Micawber, "is, that Mr. Micawber should turn his attention to coals."

"To what, ma'am?"

"To coals," said Mrs. Micawber. "To the coal trade. Mr. Micawber was induced to think, that there might be an opening for a man of his talent in the Medway Coal Trade. Then, the first step was, to come and *see* the Medway. Which we came and saw. I say 'we' Master Copperfield; for," said Mrs. Micawber with emotion, "I never will desert Mr. Micawber."

I murmured my admiration and approbation.

"We came," repeated Mrs. Micawber, "and saw the Medway. My opinion of the coal trade on that river is, that it may require talent, but that it certainly requires capital. Talent, Mr. Micawber has; capital, Mr. Micawber has not. Being so near here, Mr. Micawber was of opinion that it would be rash not to come on, and see the Cathedral. Firstly, on account of its being so well worth seeing; and secondly, on account of the great probability of something turning up in a cathedral town. We have been here," said Mrs. Micawber, "three days. Nothing has, as yet, turned up, and it may not surprise you, my dear Master Copperfield, to know that we are at present waiting for a remittance from London, to discharge our pecuniary obligation at this hotel. Until the arrival of that remittance," said Mrs. Micawber with much feeling, "I am cut off from my home (I allude to lodgings in Pentonville), from my boy and girl, and from my twins."

I felt the utmost sympathy for Mr. and Mrs. Micawber and said as much to Mr. Micawber who now returned; adding that I only wished I had money enough, to lend them the amount they needed. When I took my leave of them, they both pressed me so much to come and dine before they went away, that I could not refuse.

As I was looking out of the window that same evening, it surprised me, and made me rather uneasy, to see Mr.

Micawber and Uriah Heep walk past, arm in arm. But I was still more surprised, when I went to the little hotel next day to find, from what Mr. Micawber said, that he had gone home with Uriah.

"And I'll tell you what, my dear Copperfield," said Mr. Micawber, "if I had known that young man when my difficulties came to a crisis, I believe my creditors would have been a great deal better managed than they were."

I hardly understood how this could have been, seeing that Mr. Micawber had paid them nothing at all. Neither did I like to inquire if they had talked much about me; but I was uncomfortable about it and often thought about it afterwards.

We had a beautiful little dinner and I never saw anybody so thoroughly jovial as Mr. Micawber. Consequently, I was not prepared, at seven o'clock next morning, to receive the following communication, dated a quarter of an hour after I had left him:—

"My dear Young Friend:

"The die is cast—all is over. Hiding the ravages of care with a sickly mask of mirth, I have not informed you, this evening, that there is no hope of the remittance! I have discharged the pecuniary liability contracted at this establishment, by giving a note of hand. When it becomes due, it will not be taken up. The result is destruction.

"This is the last communication, my dear Copperfield, you will ever receive.

"From
"The
"Beggared Outcast,
"Wilkins Micawber."

I was so shocked that I ran off directly towards the little hotel with the intention of trying to soothe Mr. Micawber with a word of comfort. But half-way there, I met the London Coach with Mr. and Mrs. Micawber up behind; Mr. Micawber, the very picture of tranquil enjoyment, eating walnuts out of a paper bag. As they did not see me, I thought it best, all things considered, not to see them. So, with a great weight off my mind, I turned into a by-street, and felt, upon the whole, relieved that they were gone: though I still liked them very much, nevertheless.

CHAPTER XVIII

A RETROSPECT

My school-days! The unseen, unfelt progress of my life—from childhood up to youth! Let me think, as I look back, whether there are any marks along its course, by which I can remember how it ran.

I am not the last boy in the school. I have risen, in a few months, over several heads. But the first boy seems to me a mighty creature, afar off. He is not my private friend and public patron, as Steerforth was; but I hold him in a reverential respect. I chiefly wonder what he'll be, when he leaves Dr. Strong's, and what mankind will do to maintain any place against him.

But who is this that breaks upon me? This is Miss Shepherd, whom I love.

Miss Shepherd is a boarder at the Misses Nettingalls' establishment. I adore Miss Shepherd. She is a little girl with a round face and curly flaxen hair.

For some time, I am doubtful of Miss Shepherd's feelings, but at length we meet at the dancing-school. I have Miss Shepherd for my partner. I touch Miss Shepherd's glove, and feel a thrill go up the right arm of my jacket, and come out at my hair. I say nothing tender to Miss Shepherd, but we understand each other.

Why do I secretly give Miss Shepherd twelve Brazil nuts for a present, I wonder? Soft, seedy biscuits, also; and oranges innumerable. Once, I kiss Miss Shepherd in the cloak room. Ecstasy! What are my agony and indignation next day, when I hear that the Misses Nettingall have stood Miss Shepherd in the stocks for turning in her toes!

How do I ever come to break with her? I can't conceive. And yet, a coolness grows between Miss Shepherd and myself. Whispers reach me of Miss Shepherd having said she wished I wouldn't stare so, and having avowed a preference for Master Jones—for Jones! a boy of no merit whatever! At last, one day, I meet the Misses Nettingalls' establishment out walking. Miss Shepherd makes a face as she goes by, and laughs to her companion. All is over. The devotion of a life—it seems a life—is at an end.

I am higher in the school and Doctor Strong refers to me in public as a promising young scholar. Mr. Dick is wild with joy, and my aunt remits me a guinea by the next post.

The shade of a young butcher rises, the terror of the youth of Canterbury. He is a broad-faced, bull-necked young butcher, with an injurious tongue. His main use of this tongue is, to disparage Doctor Strong's young gentlemen. He waylays the smaller boys to punch their unprotected heads, and calls challenges after me in the open streets. For these sufficient reasons I resolve to fight the butcher.

It is a summer evening, down in a green hollow. I meet the butcher by appointment. I am attended by a select body of our boys; the butcher, by two other butchers, a young publican, and a sweep. The butcher and myself stand face to face. In a moment the butcher lights ten thousand candles out of my left eyebrow. In another moment, I don't know where the wall is, or where I am, or where anybody is. Sometimes I see the butcher, bloody, but confident; sometimes I see nothing, and sit gasping on my second's knee; sometimes I go in at the butcher madly, and cut my knuckles open against his face, without appearing to discompose him at all. At last I awake, very queer about the head, and see the butcher walking off, congratulated by the two other butchers and the sweep and publican, and putting on his coat as he goes; from which I augur, justly, that the victory is his.

I am taken home in a sad plight, and I have beef-steaks

put to my eyes, and am rubbed with vinegar and brandy, and find a great white puffy place bursting out on my upper lip, which swells immoderately. For three or four days I remain at home, a very ill-looking subject, with a green shade over my eyes; and I should be very dull, but that Agnes condoles with me, and reads to me, and makes the time light and happy. Agnes thinks I couldn't have done otherwise than fight the butcher, while she shrinks and trembles at my having fought him.

Time has stolen on unobserved and *I* am the head-boy, now! I look down on the line of boys below me, with a condescending interest in such of them as bring to my mind the boy I was myself, when I first came there.

I wear a gold watch and chain, a ring upon my little finger, and a long-tailed coat. Am I in love again? I am. I worship the eldest Miss Larkins.

The eldest Miss Larkins is not a little girl. She is a tall, fine figure of a woman. Perhaps the eldest Miss Larkins may be about thirty. My passion for her is beyond all bounds.

The eldest Miss Larkins knows officers. I see them speaking to her in the street. She laughs and talks, and seems to like it. I spend a good deal of my spare time in walking up and down to meet her.

I think continually about my age. Say I am seventeen, and say that seventeen is young for the eldest Miss Larkins, what of that! Besides, I shall be one-and twenty in no time almost. I regularly take walks outside Mr. Larkins's house in the evening. I even walk, on two or three occasions, in a sickly, spoony manner, round and round the house after the family are gone to bed, wishing that a fire would burst out; that the assembled crowd would stand appalled; that I, dashing through them with a ladder, might save the eldest Miss Larkins in my arms, go back for something she had left behind, and perish in the flames.

Sometimes brighter visions rise before me. I picture myself taking courage to make a declaration to Miss Larkins. I picture Miss Larkins sinking her head upon my shoulder, and saying, "Oh, Mr. Copperfield, can I believe my ears!" I picture Mr. Larkins saying, "My dear Copperfield, my daughter has told me all. Here are twenty thousand pounds. Be happy!"

"Trotwood," says Agnes, one day after dinner. "Who do you think is going to be married to-morrow? Some one you admire."

"Not you, I suppose, Agnes?"

"Not me!" raising her cheerful face from the music she is copying. "The eldest Miss Larkins."

I am terribly dejected for about a week or two. I take off my ring, I wear my worst clothes, and I frequently lament. Being, by that time, rather tired of this kind of life, and having received new provocation from the butcher, I go out with the butcher, and gloriously defeat him.

This, and the resumption of my ring, are the last marks I can discern, now, in my progress to seventeen.

CHAPTER XIX

I LOOK ABOUT ME, AND MAKE A DISCOVERY

MY school-days drew to an end, and the time came for my leaving Doctor Strong's. I had been very happy there, I had a great attachment for the Doctor, and I was eminent in that little world. For these reasons I was sorry to go; but for others reasons I was glad. Misty ideas of being a young man, of the wonderful things to be seen and done lured me away, and life was more like a great fairy story, which I was just about to begin to read, than anything else.

My aunt and I had held many grave deliberations on the calling to which I should be devoted. For a year or more I had endeavoured to find a satisfactory answer to her often repeated question, "What I would like to be?" But I had no particular liking, that I could discover, for anything.

"Trot, I tell you what, my dear," said my aunt, one morning, "as we must not make a mistake, I think we had better take a little breathing time. In the meanwhile, you must try to look at it from a new point of view, and not as a schoolboy."

"I will, aunt."

"It has occurred to me," pursued my aunt, "that a little change may be useful in helping you to know your own mind. Suppose you were to take a little journey now. Suppose you were to go down into the old part of the country again, for instance, and see that—that out-of-the-way woman with the savagest of names," said my aunt, rubbing her nose, for she could never thoroughly forgive Peggotty for being so called.

"Of all things in the world, aunt, I should like it best!"

"Well," said my aunt, "that's lucky, for I should like it too. But it's rational that you should like it. And I am persuaded that whatever you do, Trot, will always be rational."

"I hope so, aunt."

"But what I want you to be, Trot," resumed my aunt, "—I don't mean physically, but morally—is, a firm fellow. A fine firm fellow, with a will of your own. With resolution," said my aunt, shaking her cap at me, and clenching her hand. "With determination. With character, Trot."

I intimated that I hoped I should be what she described.

"That you may begin to have a reliance upon yourself," said my aunt, "I shall send you upon your trip alone. I did think, once, of Mr. Dick's going with you; but, on second thought, I shall keep him to take care of me."

Mr. Dick, for a moment, looked a little disappointed; until the honour and dignity of having to take care of the most wonderful woman in the world restored the sunshine to his face.

"Besides," said my aunt, "there's the Memorial."

"Oh, certainly," said Mr. Dick, in a hurry, "I intend, Trotwood, to get that done immediately. And then it will go in, you know—and then——," said Mr. Dick, after pausing a long time, "there'll be a pretty kettle of fish!"

In pursuance of my aunt's kind scheme, I was fitted out and tenderly dismissed upon my expedition. At parting, my aunt gave me some good advice, and a good many kisses; and said that I was at liberty to do what I would, for three weeks or a month.

I went to Canterbury first, that I might take leave of Agnes and Mr. Wickfield, and also of the good Doctor. Agnes was very glad to see me, and told me that the house had not been like itself since I had left it.

"I am sure I am not like myself when I am away," said I. "Though that's not saying much. Every one who knows you, consults with you, and is guided by you, Agnes."

"Every one who knows me spoils me, I believe," she answered smiling.

"No. It's because you are like no one else."

"You talk," said Agnes, breaking into a pleasant laugh, as she sat at work, "as if I were the late Miss Larkins."

We had gone on, so far, in a mixture of jest and earnest, but Agnes, now suddenly lifting up her eyes to mine, and speaking in a different manner, said:

"Trotwood, there is something that I want to ask you. Something I would ask, I think, of no one else. Have you observed any gradual alteration in Papa?"

I had observed it, and had often wondered whether she had too.

"Tell me what it is," she said, in a low voice.

"I think—shall I be quite plain, Agnes, liking him so much?"

"Yes," she said.

"I think he does himself no good by the habit that has increased upon him. He is often very nervous, or I fancy so."

"It is not fancy," said Agnes, shaking her head.

"I have remarked that when he is least like himself, he is most certain to be wanted on some business."

"By Uriah," said Agnes.

"Yes; and the sense of being unfit for it seems to make him so uneasy, that next day he is worse."

Her hand passed softly before my lips while I was yet speaking, and in a moment she had met her father at the door of the room. The expression of her face, as they both looked towards me, I felt to be very touching. She was, at once, so proud of him and devoted to him, yet so compassionate and sorry, and so reliant upon me to be so, too; that nothing she could have said would have expressed more to me, or moved me more.

We were to drink tea at the Doctor's. We went there at the usual hour; and round the study fireside found the Doctor, and his young wife, and her mother. The Doctor, who made as much of my going away as if I were going to China, received me as an honoured guest.

"I shall not see many more new faces in Trotwood's stead, Wickfield," said the Doctor, warming his hands; "I am getting lazy, and want ease. I shall relinquish all my young people in another six months, and lead a quieter life."

"You have said so, any time these ten years, Doctor," Mr. Wickfield answered.

"But now I mean to do it," returned the Doctor, "so you'll soon have to arrange contracts."

"And to take care," said Mr. Wickfield, "that you're not imposed on, eh? Well! I am ready."

"I shall have nothing to think of, then," said the Doctor, with a smile, "but my Dictionary; and Annie."

As Mr. Wickfield glanced towards her she seemed to me to avoid his look with such unwonted timidity, that his attention became fixed upon her.

"There is a post come in from India, I observe," he said, after a short silence.

"By-the-by! and letters from Mr. Jack Maldon!" said the Doctor.

"Indeed!"

"Poor dear Jack!" said Mrs. Markleham, shaking her head. "That trying climate! Like living, they tell me, on a sand-heap, underneath a burning-glass! He looked strong, but he wasn't."

"Do I gather from what you say, ma'am, that Mr. Maldon is ill?" asked Mr. Wickfield.

"I'll!" replied the Old Soldier. "My dear Sir, he's all sorts of things."

"Except well?" said Mr. Wickfield.

"Except well, indeed!" said the Old Soldier. "He has had dreadful strokes of the sun, no doubt, and jungle fevers and agues, and every kind of thing you can mention."

Mr. Wickfield now asked what Mr. Jack Maldon had actually written and to whom he had written it?

"Why, here," said Mrs. Markleham, taking a letter from

the chimney-piece above the Doctor's head, "the dear fellow says to the Doctor himself—where is it? Oh!—'I am sorry to inform you that my health is suffering severely, and that I fear I may be reduced to the necessity of returning home for a time, as the only hope of restoration.' That's pretty plain, poor fellow! But Annie's letter is plainer still. Annie, show me that letter again."

The letter was reluctantly produced.

"Now let us see," said Mrs. Markleham, putting her glass to her eye, 'The remembrance of old times, my dearest Annie'—and so forth—it's not there. Now I have found it. '*You* may not be surprised to hear, Annie,—that I have undergone so much in this distant place, as to have decided to leave it at all hazards. What I have endured, and do endure here, is insupportable.' And but for the promptitude of that best of creatures," said Mrs. Markleham, telegraphing the Doctor as before, and refolding the letter, "it would be insupportable to me to think of."

Mr. Wickfield said not one word but sat severely silent. Long after other topics occupied us, he remained so; seldom raising his eyes, unless to rest them for a moment, with a thoughtful frown, upon the Doctor, or his wife, or both.

The Doctor was very fond of music. Agnes sang with great sweetness and expression, and so did Mrs. Strong. They sang together, and played duets together, and we had quite a little concert. But I remarked that Mr. Wickfield seemed to dislike the intimacy between her and Agnes, and to watch it with uneasiness.

Morning brought with it my parting from the old house. I should be there again soon, no doubt; I might sleep again —perhaps often—in my old room; but the old time was past. I was heavier at heart than I cared to show to Uriah Heep; who was so officious to help me, that I uncharitably thought him mighty glad that I was going.

I got away from Agnes and her father, somehow with a show of being very manly, and took my seat upon the box of the London coach. It was curious and interesting, to be sitting up there, behind four horses: well educated, well dressed, and with plenty of money in my pocket; and to look out for the places where I had slept on my weary journey. I had abundant occupation for my thoughts, in every landmark on the road. When we came, at last, within a stage of London, and passed Salem House where Mr. Creakle had laid about him with a heavy hand, I would have given all I had, for lawful permission to get down and thrash him, and let all the boys out like so many caged sparrows.

We went to the Golden Cross, at Charing Cross. A waiter showed me into the coffee-room; and a chambermaid introduced me to my small bedchamber, which smelt like a hackney-coach, and was shut up like a family vault. I was painfully conscious of my youth, for nobody stood in any awe of me at all: the chambermaid being utterly indifferent to my opinions and the waiter being familiar with me, and offering advice!

Being in a pleasant frame of mind, I resolved to go to the play. It was Covent Garden Theatre that I chose; and there I saw *Julius Cæsar* and the new *Pantomime*. To have all those noble Romans alive before me, and walking in and out for my entertainment, instead of being the stern taskmasters they had been at school, was a most novel and delightful effect. But the mingled reality and mystery of the whole show, the poetry, the lights, the music and brilliant scenery, were so dazzling that when I came out into the rainy street, at twelve o'clock, I felt as if I had come from the clouds to a bawling, splashing, umbrella-struggling, muddy, miserable world.

I stood in the street for a little while, as if I really were a stranger upon earth; but the unceremonious pushing and hustling that I received soon recalled me to myself, and put me in the road back to the hotel, where, after some porter and oysters, I still sat at past one o'clock, with my eyes on the coffee-room fire.

I was so filled with the play, and with the past that I don't know when the figure of a handsome well-formed young man, dressed with a tasteful easy negligence which

I stood as if I were really a stranger upon earth.

I have reason to remember very well, became a real presence to me.

At last I rose to go to bed and in going towards the door, I passed the person who had come in, and saw him plainly. I turned directly, came back, and looked again. He did not know me, but I knew him in a moment.

At another time I might have wanted the confidence to speak to him, and might have put it off until next day, and might have lost him. But, in the then condition of my mind my old love for him overflowed my breast so freshly and spontaneously, that I went up to him at once, with a fast-beating heart, and said:

"Steerforth! won't you speak to me?"

He looked at me—just as he used to look, sometimes—but I saw no recognition in his face.

"You don't remember me, I am afraid," said I.

"My God!" he suddenly exclaimed. "It's little Copperfield!"

I grasped him by both hands, and could not let them go.

"I never, never, never was so glad! My dear Steerforth, I am so overjoyed to see you!"

"And I am rejoiced to see you, too!" he said, shaking my hands heartily. "Why, Copperfield, old boy, how do you come to be here?"

"I came here by the Canterbury coach, to-day. I have been adopted by an aunt down in that part of the country and have just finished my education there. How do *you* come to be here, Steerforth?"

"Well, I am what they call an Oxford man," he returned,—"and I am on my way now to my mother's. You're a devilish amiable-looking fellow, Copperfield. Not altered in the least!"

"I knew *you* immediately," I said; "but you are more easily remembered."

He laughed as he ran his hand through the clustering curls of his hair, and said gaily:

"Yes, I am on an expedition of duty. My mother lives a little way out of town: and the roads being in a beastly condition, and our house tedious enough, I remained here to-night instead of going on.—Holloa, you Sir!"

This was addressed to the waiter, who now came forward deferentially.

"Where have you put my friend, Mr. Copperfield?" said Steerforth.

"Beg your pardon, Sir?"

"Where does he sleep? What's his number? You know what I mean," said Steerforth.

"Well, Sir," said the waiter, with an apologetic air, "Mr. Copperfiield is at present in forty-four, Sir."

"And what the devil do you mean," retorted Steerforth, "by putting Mr. Copperfield into a little loft over a stable?"

"Why, you see we wasn't aware, Sir," returned the waiter, still apologetically, "as Mr. Copperfield was anyways particular. We can give Mr. Copperfield seventy-two, Sir, if it would be preferred. Next to you, Sir."

"Of course it would be preferred," said Steerforth. "And do it at once."

The waiter immediately withdrew to make the exchange. Steerforth, very much amused at my having been put into forty-four, laughed again, and invited me to breakfast with him next morning at ten o'clock—an invitation I was only too proud and happy to accept.

I found my new room a great improvement on my old one, it not being at all musty, and having an immense four-post bedstead in it. Here, among pillows enough for six, I soon fell asleep in a blissful condition, and dreamed of ancient Rome, Steerforth, and friendship, until the early morning coaches, rumbling out of the archway underneath, made me dream of thunder and the gods.

CHAPTER XX

STEERFORTH'S HOME

It was not in the coffee-room that I found Steerforth expecting me, but in a snug, red-curtained apartment, where the fire burnt bright, and a fine hot breakfast was set forth.

"Now, Copperfield," said Steerforth, when we were alone, "I should like to hear what you are doing, and where you are going, and all about you."

Glowing with pleasure to find that he had still this interest in me, I told him how my aunt had proposed the little expedition that I had before me, and whither it tended.

"As you are in no hurry, then," said Steerforth, "come home with me to Highgate, and stay a day or two. You will be pleased with my mother—she is a little vain and prosy about me, but that you can forgive her—and she will be pleased with you."

"I should like to be as sure of that, as you are kind enough to say you are," I answered, smiling.

"Oh!" said Steerforth, "every one who likes me, has a claim on her that is sure to be acknowledged."

"Then I think I shall be a favourite," said I.

"Good!" said Steerforth. "Come and prove it. We will go and see the lions for an hour or two—it's something to have a fresh fellow like you to show them to, Copperfield—and then we'll journey out to Highgate by the coach."

Lunch succeeded to our sight-seeing, and the short winter day wore away so fast, that it was dusk when the stage-coach stopped with us at an old brick house at Highgate. An elderly lady with a handsome face was in the doorway as we alighted; and greeting Steerforth as "My dearest James," folded him in her arms. To this lady he presented me as his mother, and she gave me a stately welcome.

It was a genteel old-fashioned house, very quiet and orderly. From the windows of my room I saw all London lying in the distance like a great vapour, with here and there some lights twinkling through it. I had only time, in dressing, to glance at the solid furniture, and some pictures of ladies with powdered hair, when I was called to dinner.

There was a second lady in the dining-room, of a slight short figure, dark, and not agreeable to look at, but with some appearance of good looks too. She had black hair and eager black eyes, and was thin, and had a scar upon her lip. It was an old scar which had once cut through her mouth but was now barely visible except above and on her upper lip.

She was introduced as Miss Dartle, and both Steerforth and his mother called her Rosa. I found that she lived there, and had been for a long time Mrs. Steerforth's companion. Before dinner was done, Mrs. Steerforth speaking to me about my intention of going down into Suffolk, I said how glad I should be, if Steerforth would only go there with me; and explaining to him that I was going to see my old nurse, and Mr. Peggotty's family, I reminded him of the boatman whom he had seen at school.

"Oh! That bluff fellow!" said Steerforth. "He had a son with him, hadn't he?"

"No. That was his nephew," I replied; "whom he adopted, though, as a son. He has a very pretty little niece too, whom he adopted as a daughter. In short, his house (or rather his boat, for he lives in one, on dry land) is full of people who are objects of his generosity and kindness. You would be delighted to see that household."

"Should I?" said Steerforth. "Well, I think I should. It would be worth a journey (not to mention the pleasure of a journey with you, Daisy), to see that sort of people together, and to make one of 'em."

David Copperfield at eighteen years of age.

My heart leaped with a new hope of pleasure. But Miss Dartle now broke in:

"Oh, but, really? Do tell me. Are they, though?" she said.

"Are they what? And are who what?" said Steerforth.

"That sort of people. Are they really animals and clods, and beings of another order? I want to know *so* much."

"Why, there's a pretty wide separation between them and us," said Steerforth, with indifference. "They are not to be expected to be as sensitive as we are. They are wonderfully virtuous, I dare say. But they have not very fine natures, and they are not easily wounded."

"Really!" said Miss Dartle. "Well, I don't know, now, when I have been better pleased than to hear that. It's such a delight to know that, when they suffer, they don't feel!"

I believed that Steerforth had said what he had in jest, or to draw Miss Dartle out; and I expected him to say as much when she was gone, and we two were sitting before the fire. But he merely asked me what I thought of her.

"She is very clever, is she not?" I asked.

"Clever! She brings everything to a grindstone," said Steerforth, "and sharpens it. She has worn herself away by constant sharpening. She is all edge."

"What a remarkable scar that is upon her lip!" I said.

Steerforth's face fell, and he paused a moment.

"Why, the fact is," he returned, "*I* did that."

"By an unfortunate accident!"

"No. I was a young boy, and she exasperated me, and I threw a hammer at her. A promising young angel I must have been!"

I was deeply sorry to have touched on such a painful theme, but that was useless now.

"She has borne the mark ever since, as you see," said Steerforth, "and she'll bear it to her grave."

I could not help glancing at the scar with a painful interest when we went in to tea. It was not long before I observed that it was the most susceptible part of her face, and that, when she turned pale, that mark altered first. There was a little altercation between her and Steerforth about a cast of the dice at backgammon, when I thought her, for one moment, in a storm of rage; and then I saw it start forth like the old writing on the wall.

When the evening was pretty far spent, Steerforth promised that he would seriously think of going down into the country with me. There was no hurry, he said; a week hence would do; and his mother hospitably said the same. While we were talking, he more than once called me Daisy; which brought Miss Dartle out again.

"But really, Mr. Copperfield," she asked, "is it a nickname? And why does he give it you? Is it—eh?—because he thinks you young and innocent? I am so stupid in these things."

I coloured in reply that I believed it was.

"Oh!" said Miss Dartle. "Now I am glad to know that! He thinks you young and innocent; and so you are his friend? Well, that's quite delightful!"

She went to bed soon after this, and Mrs. Steerforth retired too. Steerforth and I, after lingering for half an hour over the fire, talking about Traddles and all the rest of them at old Salem House, went upstairs together.

I found the fire burning clear in my room, and the curtains drawn close. I sat down to meditate on my happiness, when I found a likeness of Miss Dartle looking eagerly at me from above the chimney-piece.

I undressed quickly and went to bed. But as I fell asleep, I could not forget that she was still there, looking.

CHAPTER XXI

LITTLE EM'LY

THERE was a servant named Littimer in that house, a man who, I understood, was usually with Steerforth, and had come into his service at the University. I believe there never existed a more respectable-looking man. He was soft-footed, deferential, always at hand when wanted, and never near when not wanted; but his great claim to consideration was his respectability. He had rather a stiff neck, and rather a tight smooth head, but every peculiarity that he had he made respectable. If his nose had been upside-down, he would have made that respectable.

Littimer was in my room in the morning before I was up. When I undrew the curtains and looked out of bed, I saw him, standing my boots right and left in the first dancing position, and blowing specks of dust off my coat as he laid it down like a baby.

I gave him good morning, and asked him what o'clock it was. He took out of his pocket the most respectable hunting-watch I ever saw, and said, if I pleased, it was half-past eight.

"Mr. Steerforth will be glad to hear how you have rested, Sir."

"Thank you," said I, "very well indeed. Is Mr. Steerforth quite well?"

"Thank you, Sir, Mr. Steerforth is tolerably well. Is there anything more I can have the honour of doing for you, Sir?"

"Nothing, I thank you."

"I thank *you,* Sir, if you please;" and with that he went out.

Every morning we held exactly this conversation: never

any more, never any less; and yet, invariably whenever he was by, I felt myself the greenest and most inexperienced of mortals.

I am particular about this man, because he made a particular effect on me at that time, and because of what took place thereafter.

The week passed away in a most delightful manner. Steerforth made up his mind to go with me into the country, and the day arrived for our departure. He had been doubtful at first whether to take Littimer or not, but decided to leave him at home.

I was so concerned for the honour of Yarmouth, that when Steerforth said, as we drove through its dark streets to the inn, that it was a good, queer, out-of-the-way kind of hole, I was highly pleased. We went to bed on our arrival, and breakfasted late in the morning. Steerforth, who was in great spirits, had been strolling about the beach before I was up, and had made acquaintance, he said, with half the boatmen in the place. Moreover, he had seen, in the distance, what he was sure must be the identical house of Mr. Peggotty.

"When do you propose to introduce me there, Daisy?" he said. "I am at your disposal."

"Why, I was thinking that this evening would be a good time, Steerforth, when they are all sitting round the fire."

"So be it!" returned Steerforth. "This evening. Now what are you going to do? You are going to see your nurse, I suppose?"

"Why, yes," I said, "I must see Peggotty first of all."

"Well," replied Steerforth, looking at his watch. "Suppose I deliver you up to be cried over for a couple of hours. Is that long enough?"

I answered, laughing, that I thought we might get through it in that time, but that he must come also.

"I'll come anywhere you like," said Steerforth, "or do anything you like. Tell me where to come to, and in two hours I'll produce myself."

I gave him minute directions for finding the residence of Mr. Barkis, and went out alone.

The streets looked small, of course. But I found nothing changed, until I came to Mr. Omer's shop. OMER AND JORAM was now written up, where OMER used to be; but the inscription, DRAPER, TAILOR, HABERDASHER, FUNERAL FURNISHER, &c., remained as it was.

"Is Mr. Omer at home?" said I, entering. "I should like to see him, for a moment, if he is."

Soon Mr. Omer, shorter-winded, but not much older-looking, stood before me.

"Servant, Sir," said Mr. Omer. "What can I do for you, Sir?"

"You can shake hands with me, Mr. Omer, if you please," said I, putting out my own. "You were very good-natured to me once."

"Was I though?" returned the old man. "I'm glad to hear it, but I think my memory has got as short as my breath, for I don't remember you."

"Don't you remember your coming to the coach to meet me, and my having breakfast here, and our riding out to Blunderstone together?"

"Why, Lord bless my soul!" exclaimed Mr. Omer, "you don't say so! Dear me, yes; the party was a lady, I think?"

"My mother," I rejoined.

"To—be—sure," said Mr. Omer, touching my waistcoat with his forefinger, "and there was a little child too! Over at Blunderstone it was, of course. Dear me! Dear me! Yes, to be sure. Let me see," said Mr. Omer. "Barkis's the carrier's wife—Peggotty's the boatman's sister—she was in service there, sure?"

My answering in the affirmative gave him great satisfaction.

"Well, Sir, " said Mr. Omer, "we've got a young relation of hers here that has as elegant a taste in the dressmaking business, I don't believe there's a Duchess in England can touch her."

"Not little Em'ly?" said I, involuntarily.

"Em'ly's her name," said Mr. Omer, "and she's little, too. But if you'll believe me, she has such a face of her own that half the women in this town are mad against her."

"You see," he said, breathing with difficulty, "an ill-natured story got about, that Em'ly wanted to be a lady. Now, my opinion is, that it came on account of her sometimes saying that if she was a lady, she would like to do so-and-so for her uncle—don't you see?—and buy him such-and-such fine things."

"I assure you, Mr. Omer, she has said so to me," I returned eagerly, "when we were both children."

Mr. Omer nodded his head and rubbed his chin. "Just so. Moreover, she was rather what might be called wayward—a little spoiled. So when she got a situation," said Mr. Omer, "to keep a fractious old lady company, they didn't very well agree. At last she came here, apprenticed for three years. Nearly two of 'em are over, and she has been as good a girl as ever was. Worth any six!"

As he had spoken in a subdued tone I had no doubt that Em'ly was near. On my asking, Mr. Omer nodded towards the door of the parlour, and, looking through the glass, I saw her sitting at her work. I saw her, a most beautiful little creature, with enough of wilfulness in her bright face to justify what I had heard, but with nothing in her pretty looks, I am sure, but what was meant for goodness and for happiness.

"Wouldn't you like to step in," said Mr. Omer, "and speak to her?"

I was too bashful to do so then, and taking leave of Mr. Omer, went away to my dear old Peggotty's.

Here she was, in the tiled kitchen, cooking dinner! The moment I knocked at the door she opened it, and asked me what I pleased to want. I looked at her with a smile, but she gave me no smile in return. I had never ceased to write to her, but it must have been seven years since we had met.

"Is Mr. Barkis at home, ma'am?" I said.

"He's at home, Sir," returned Peggotty, "but he's bad abed with the rheumatics."

"Don't he go over to Blunderstone now?" I asked.

"When he's well he do," she answered.

"Do *you* ever go there, Mrs. Barkis?"

She looked at me more attentively.

"Because I want to ask a question about a house there, that they call the—what is it?—the Rookery," said I.

She took a step backward, and put out her hands in an undecided frightened way.

"Peggotty!" I cried to her.

She cried, "My darling boy!" and we both burst into tears, and were locked in one another's arms. What extravagances she committed; what laughing and crying over me; what pride she showed, I have not the heart to tell.

"Barkis will be so glad," said Peggotty, wiping her eyes with her apron, "that it'll do him more good than pints of liniment. May I go and tell him you are here? Will you come up and see him, my dear?"

Of course I would. He received me with absolute enthusiasm. He was too rheumatic to be shaken hands with, but he begged me to shake the tassel on the top of his nightcap, which I did most cordially.

"What name was it as I wrote up in the cart, Sir?" said Mr. Barkis, with a slow rheumatic smile.

"Ah! Mr. Barkis, we had some grave talks about that matter, hadn't we?"

"I was willin' a long time, Sir?" said Mr. Barkis.

"A long time," said I.

"And I don't regret it," said Mr. Barkis. "Do you remember what you told me once, about her making all the apple parsties and doing all the cooking?"

"Yes, very well," I returned.

"It was as true," said Mr. Barkis, "as turnips is. It was as true," said Mr. Barkis, nodding his nightcap, which was his only means of emphasis, "as taxes is. And nothing's truer than them. Nothing's truer than them," repeated

Mr. Barkis, "a man as poor as I am, finds that out. I'm a very poor man, Sir."

"I am sorry to hear it, Mr. Barkis."

"A very poor man, indeed I am," said Mr. Barkis.

Here his right hand came slowly and feebly from under the bedclothes and took hold of a stick which was loosely tied to the side of the bed. After some poking about Mr. Barkis poked it against a box.

"Old clothes," said Mr. Barkis.

"Oh!" said I.

"I wish it was Money, Sir," said Mr. Barkis.

"I wish it was, indeed," said I.

"But it AIN'T," said Mr. Barkis, opening both his eyes as wide as possible.

I expressed myself quite sure of that, and Mr. Barkis, turning his eyes more gently to his wife, said:

"She's the usefullest and best of women, C. P. Barkis. My dear, you'll get a dinner to-day, for company; something good to eat and drink, will you?"

I should have protested but that I saw Peggotty extremely anxious I should not.

"I have got a trifle of money somewhere about me, my dear," said Mr. Barkis, "but I'm a little tired. If you and Mr. David will leave me for a short nap, I'll try and find it when I wake."

When we got outside the door, Peggotty informed me that Mr. Barkis always resorted to this same device before producing a single coin, and that he endured unheard-of agonies in crawling out of bed alone, and taking it from that unlucky box.

I prepared Peggotty for Steerforth's arrival, and it was not long before he came. His genial manner, his handsome looks, his natural gift of adapting himself to whomsoever he pleased bound her to him wholly in five minutes.

He stayed there with me to dinner. He went into Mr. Barkis's room like light and air, brightening and refreshing it as if he were healthy weather. When Peggotty spoke of what she called my room, and of its being ready for me at night, and of her hoping I would occupy it, before I could so much as look at him, Steerforth said: "Of course, you'll sleep here, and I shall sleep at the hotel."

It was settled at once.

He maintained all his delightful qualities to the last, until we started forth, at eight o'clock, for Mr. Peggotty's boat. I walked beside him, over the dark wintry sands; the wind sighing around us mournfully.

"This is a wild kind of place, Steerforth, is it not?"

"Dismal enough in the dark," he said; "and the sea roars as if it were hungry for us. Is that the boat, where I see a light yonder?"

"That's the boat," said I.

"And it's the same I saw this morning," he returned. "I came straight to it, by instinct, I suppose."

We said no more but made softly for the door and went in.

A murmur of voices had been audible at the moment of our entrance, a clapping of hands: which I was surprised to see, proceeded from the generally disconsolate Mrs. Gummidge. But Mrs. Gummidge was not the only person there who was unusually excited. Mr. Peggotty, his face lighted up, held his rough arms wide open, as if for little Em'ly to run into them; Ham held little Em'ly by the hand; little Em'ly herself blushing and shy, but delighted with Mr. Peggotty's delight, as her joyous eyes expressed, was stopped by our entrance (for she saw us first) in the very act of springing from Ham to nestle in Mr. Peggotty's embrace.

The little picture was so instantaneously dissolved by our going in, that one might have doubted whether it had ever been. I was in the midst of the astonished family, face to face with Mr. Peggotty, and holding out my hand to him, when Ham shouted:

"Mas'r Davy! It's Mas'r Davy!"

In a moment we were all shaking hands with one another, and asking one another how we did, and telling one another how glad we were to meet, and all talking at once.

"Why, that you two gent'lman—gent'lmen growed—should come to this here roof to-night," said Mr. Peggotty, "is such a thing as never happened afore, I do rightly believe!"

After delivering this speech all in a breath, Mr. Peggotty put one of his large hands rapturously on each side of his niece's face, and kissing it a dozen times, laid it with a gentle pride and love upon his broad chest. Then he let her go; and as she ran into the little chamber, he looked round upon us, quite out of breath.

"If you two gent'lmen, gent'lmen growed," said Mr. Peggotty, "don't excuse me for being in a state of mind, when you understand matters, I'll arks your pardon. Em'ly knows I'm a going to tell and has made off. Would you be so good as look arter her, Mawther, for a minute?"

Mrs. Gummidge nodded and disappeared.

"This here little Em'ly of ours," said Mr. Peggotty, "ain't my child; I never had one; but I couldn't love her more. You understand! I couldn't do it!"

"I quite understand," said Steerforth.

"I know you do, Sir," returned Mr. Peggotty, "and thankee again. But neither of you can't fully know what she has been, is, and will be, to my loving 'art.

Mr. Peggotty ruffled his hair with both hands and went on.

"There was a certain person as had know'd our Em'ly, from the time when her father was drownded," said Mr. Peggotty, "something o' my own build—rough—a good deal o' the sou'-wester in him—but, a honest sort of a chap, with his 'art in the right place."

I thought I had never seen Ham grin to anything like the extent to which he sat grinning at us now.

"What does this here blessed tarpaulin go and do," said Mr. Peggotty, "but he loses that there 'art of his to our little Em'ly. Well! I counsels him to speak to Em'ly. He's big enough, but he's bashfuller than a little un, and he don't like. So *I* speak. 'What! *Him!'* says Em'ly. *Him* that I've know'd so many years, and like so much. Oh,

Mr. Peggotty put one of his large hands rapturously on each side of his niece's face.

Uncle! I never can have *him!*' Then I aways to him, and I says, 'I wish it could have been so, but it can't, and wot I say to you is, Be as you was with her, like a man.' And he was—honourable and manful—for two year going on, and we was just the same at home here as afore."

"All of a sudden—as it might be to-night—comes little Em'ly from her work, and him with her! There ain't so much in *that,* because he takes care on her, like a brother, arter dark, and afore dark, and at all times. But this tarpaulin chap, he takes hold of her hand, and he cries out to me, joyful, 'Look here! This is to be my little wife!' And she says, half bold and half shy, and half a laughing and half a crying, 'Yes, Uncle! If you please. I'll be as good a little wife as I can to him, for he's a dear, good fellow!' Then Missis Gummidge, she claps her hands like a play, and you come in."

I thought it affecting to see such a sturdy fellow as Ham was now, trembling in the strength of what he felt. I thought the simple confidence reposed in us by Mr. Peggotty affecting. How far my emotions were influenced by the recollections of my childhood, I don't know. I know that I was filled with pleasure by all this; but, that a very little would have changed it to pain.

Therefore, if it had depended upon me, to touch the prevailing chord among them I should have made a poor hand of it. But it depended upon Steerforth; and he did it with such address, that in a few minutes we were all as easy and as happy as it was possible to be.

"Mr. Peggotty," he said, "you are a thoroughly good fellow, and deserve to be as happy as you are to-night. My hand upon it! Ham, I give you joy, my boy. My hand upon that, too! Daisy, stir the fire, and Mr. Peggotty, unless you can induce your gentle niece to come back, I shall go."

So Mr. Peggotty went to fetch little Em'ly and then Ham went. Presently they brought her to the fireside, very shy,—but she soon became more assured when she found how gently and respectfully Steerforth spoke to her; how he talked to Mr. Peggotty of boats, and ships, and tides, and fish; how delighted he was with the boat and all belonging to it, until we were all talking away without any reserve.

Em'ly, indeed, said little all the evening; but she looked, and listened, and she was charming. As to Mrs. Gummidge, he roused that victim of despondency with a success never attained by any one else (so Mr. Peggotty informed me), since the decease of the old one.

It was almost midnight when we tock our leave. We parted merrily; and as they all stood crowded round the door, I saw the sweet blue eyes of little Em'ly peeping after us, from behind Ham, and heard her soft voice calling to us to be careful how we went.

"A most engaging little beauty!" said Steerforth, taking my arm. "Well! It's a quaint place, and they are quaint company."

"How fortunate we are, too," I returned, "to witness their happiness in that intended marriage!"

"That's rather a chuckle-headed fellow for the girl; isn't he?" said Steerforth.

He had been so hearty with him, and with them all, that I felt a shock in this unexpected and cold reply. But turning quickly upon him, and seeing a laugh in his eyes, I answered, much relieved:

"Ah, Steerforth! It's well for you to joke about the poor! But I know better. I know that there is not a joy or sorrow of such people, that can be indifferent to you. And I admire and love you for it, Steerforth, twenty times the more!"

He stopped, and looking in my face, said: "Daisy, I believe you are in earnest, and are good. I wish we all were!" Next moment he was gaily singing as we walked back to Yarmouth.

CHAPTER XXII

SOME OLD SCENES, AND SOME NEW PEOPLE

Steerforth and I stayed for more than a fortnight in that part of the country. We were very much together, I need not say; but occasionally we were asunder for some hours at a time. My occupation of Peggotty's spare-room put a constraint upon me, from which he was free, and thus it came about, that I heard of his making little treats for the fishermen at Mr. Peggotty's house of call, "The Willing Mind," after I was in bed, and of his being afloat wrapped in fisherman's clothes, whole moonlight nights, and coming back when the morning tide was at flood.

Another cause of our being sometimes apart was that I had naturally an interest in revisiting the old familiar scenes of my childhood. It was with a singular jumble of sadness and pleasure that I used to linger about my native place, but when Steerforth and I were happily seated over our dinner by a blazing fire, it was delicious to think of having been there.

In coming back from these long walks, Mr. Peggotty's house being not a hundred yards out of my tracks, I always looked in as I went by. Steerforth was pretty sure to be there expecting me, and we went on together through the frosty air and gathering fog towards the twinkling lights of the town.

One dark evening, when I was later than usual—for I had that day been making my parting visit to Blunderstone, as we were now about to return home—I found him alone in Mr. Peggotty's house, sitting thoughtfully before the fire.

He gave such a start when I put my hand upon his shoulder, that he made me start too.

"You come upon me," he said, almost angrily, "like a reproachful ghost."

"I was obliged to announce myself somehow," I replied. "How late you are! Where have you been?"

"I have been taking leave of my usual walk," said I.

"And I have been sitting here," said Steerforth, glancing round the room, "thinking. David, I wish to God I had had a judicious father these last twenty years!"

There was a passionate dejection in his manner that quite amazed me.

"It would be better to be this poor Peggotty, or his lout of a nephew," he said, getting up, "than to be myself, myself that I have been, within the last half hour!"

I was so confounded by the alteration in him, that I could only observe him in silence. At length he began to laugh—fretfully at first, but soon with returning gaiety.

"Tut, it's nothing, Daisy! nothing! What old women call the horrors, have been creeping over me from head to foot. I have been afraid of myself."

"You are afraid of nothing else, I think," said I.

"Perhaps not, and yet may have enough to be afraid of too," he answered. "Well! So it goes by! But I tell you, my good fellow, once more, that it would have been well for me (and for more than me) if I had had a steadfast and judicious father!"

His face was always full of expression, but I never saw it express such a dark kind of earnestness as when he said these words.

"So much for that!" he said, making as if he tossed something light into the air with his hand, "And now for dinner."

His spirits were again at their usual flow, and he was full of vivacious conversation as we went along.

"And so," he said, gaily, "we abandon this buccaneer life to-morrow, do we?"

"So we agreed," I returned.

"Ay! there's no help for it, I suppose," said Steerforth. "I have almost forgotten that there is anything to do in the world but to go out tossing on the sea here. I could pass a reasonably good examination already, as a pilot in these waters, I think. You know I have bought a boat down here?"

"What an extraordinary fellow you are, Steerforth!" I exclaimed, stopping—for this was the first I had heard of it. "When you may never care to come near the place again!"

"I don't know that," he returned. "I have taken a fancy to the place. At all events," walking me briskly on, "I have bought a boat—and Mr. Peggotty will be master of her in my absence."

"Now I understand you, Steerforth!" said I, exultingly. "You pretend to have bought it for yourself, but you have really done so to confer a benefit on him. My dear kind Steerforth, how can I tell you what I think of your generosity?"

"Tush!" he answered, turning red. "The less said the better. She must be newly rigged and I shall leave Littimer behind to see it done. Did I tell you Littimer had come down?"

"No."

"Oh, yes!" This morning. I'll have the boat christened again."

"By what name?" I asked.

"The Little Em'ly."

I could not help showing in my face how much it pleased me.

"But see here," he said, looking before us, "where the original little Em'ly comes! And that fellow with her, eh? Upon my soul, he's a true knight. He never leaves her!"

Ham was a boat-builder in these days, having improved a natural ingenuity in that handicraft, until he had become a skilled workman. We stopped to speak to them, and when they passed on we looked after them fading away in the light of a young moon.

Suddenly there passed us—evidently following them, a young woman whose approach we had not observed. She was lightly dressed; looked haggard, and flaunting, and poor; but seemed, for the time, to have nothing in her mind but going after them.

"That is a black shadow to be following the girl," said Steerforth, standing still; "what does it mean?"

He spoke in a low voice that sounded almost strange to me, and he wondered about it, in some broken expressions, several times, in the short remainder of our walk; and only seemed to forget it when the light of fire and candle shone upon us, seated warm and merry, at table.

Littimer was there, and had his usual effect upon me. We had almost finished dinner, when taking a step or two towards the table, from the corner where he kept his watch upon us, or rather upon me, as I felt, he said to his master:

"I beg your pardon, Sir. Miss Mowcher is down here."

"Why, what on earth does *she* do here?" said Steerforth.

"She informs me that she makes one of her professional visits here, every year, Sir. I met her in the street this afternoon, and she wished to know if she might have the honor of waiting on you after dinner, Sir."

"Do you know the giantess in question, Daisy?" inquired Steerforth.

I was obliged to confess that Miss Mowcher and I were wholly unacquainted.

"Then you shall know her," said Steerforth. "When Miss Mowcher comes, show her in."

The cloth had been removed some half an hour, and we were sitting over our decanter of wine before the fire, when the door opened, and Littimer announced:

"Miss Mowcher!"

I looked at the doorway and saw nothing. I was still looking at the doorway when, to my infinite astonishment, there came waddling round a sofa which stood between me and it, a pursy dwarf, of about forty, or forty-five, with a very large head, a pair of roguish grey eyes, and extremely little arms. She was so short that she stood at a common-sized chair as at a table, resting a bag she carried on the seat. This lady—dressed in an off-hand easy style—broke into a torrent of words.

"What! My flower!" she pleasantly began, shaking her large head at him. "You're there, are you! Oh, you naughty boy, fie for shame, what do you do so far from home? Up to mischief, I'll be bound.

"Oh my stars and what's-their-names!" she went on. "After a flight of stairs, it gives me as much trouble to draw every breath I want, as if it was a bucket of water."

She had by this time drawn the chair to her side, and was busily engaged in producing from the bag (plunging in her short arm to the shoulder at every dive) a number of small bottles, combs, bits of flannel, little pairs of curling irons, and other instruments, which she tumbled in a heap upon the chair. From this employment she suddenly desisted, and said to Steerforth, much to my confusion:

"Who's your friend?"

"Mr. Copperfield," said Steerforth; "he wants to know you."

"Well, then, he shall! I thought he looked as if he did!" returned Miss Mowcher, waddling up to me, bag in hand, and laughing on me as she came. "Face like a peach!" standing on tiptoe to pinch my cheek as I sat. "Quite tempting! I'm very fond of peaches. Happy to make your acquaintance, Mr. Copperfield, I'm sure."

I said that the happiness was mutual.

"Well, well!" she said, "this is not business. Come, Steerforth, let's explore the polar regions, and have it over."

She then selected two or three of the little instruments, and a little bottle, and asked (to my surprise) if the table would bear. On Steerforth's replying in the affirmative, she pushed a chair against it, and begging the assistance of my hand, mounted up, pretty nimbly, to the top, as if it were a stage.

Steerforth sat himself down and submitted his head to her inspection. To see Miss Mowcher standing over him, looking at his rich profusion of brown hair through a large round magnifying glass, which she took out of her pocket, was a most amazing spectacle.

"*You're* a pretty fellow!" said Miss Mowcher, after a brief inspection. "You'd be as bald as a friar in twelve months, but for me. Just half-a-minute, my young friend, and we'll give you a polishing that shall keep your curls on for the next ten years!"

With this, she began rubbing and scraping on the crown of Steerforth's head in the busiest manner I ever witnessed, talking all the time.

"Ah!" she said. "I haven't seen a pretty woman since I've been here, Jemmy."

"We could show her one, I think?" said Steerforth, addressing his eyes to mine. "Eh, Daisy?"

"Yes, indeed," said I.

"Aha?" cried the little creature, glancing sharply at my face and then peeping round at Steerforth's. "A sister of yours, Mr. Copperfield?"

"No," said Steerforth, before I could reply. "Nothing of the sort."

"Is her name Polly?"

The elfin suddenness with which she pounced upon me with this question, and a searching look, quite disconcerted me for a moment.

"No, Miss Mowcher," I replied. Her name is Emily."

"Aha?" she cried exactly as before. "Umph? What a rattle I am! Mr. Copperfield, ain't I volatile?"

I said, in a graver manner: "She is as virtuous as she is pretty. She is engaged to be married to a most worthy and deserving man in her own station of life. I esteem her for her good sense, as much as I admire her for her good looks."

"Well said!" cried Steerforth. "Hear! I admire her—as my friend does—exceedingly. If it were not that I might appear to disparage her intended, I would add, that to *me* she seems to be throwing herself away."

Miss Mowcher listened to these words with her head on one side, and her eye in the air. When he ceased, she became brisk again in an instant, and rattled away with surprising volubility.

"Oh! And that's all about it, is it?" she exclaimed. "Very well; *very* well! Ah! What's that game at forfeits? I love my love with an E, because she's enticing; I hate her with an E, because she's engaged. Her name's Emily, and she lives in the east? Ha! Ha! Ha! Mr. Copperfield, ain't I volatile?"

Not waiting for any reply, she continued:

"There! If ever any scapegrace was trimmed and touched up to perfection, you are, Steerforth. If Mr. Copperfield will take the chair, I'll operate on him."

But finding that I was proof against the blandishments of the small bottle which she held up before one eye, Miss Mowcher requested the aid of my hand to descend from her elevated station. Thus assisted, she skipped down with much agility.

"The fee," said Steerforth, "is——"

"Five bob," replied Miss Mowcher, "and dirt cheap, my chicken. Ain't I volatile, Mr. Copperfield?"

I replied politely: "Not at all." But I thought she was rather so, when she tossed up his two half-crowns like a goblin pieman, caught them, dropped them in her pocket, and gave it a loud slap.

With the bag slung over her arm, she waddled to the door; where she stopped to inquire if she should leave us a lock of her hair. "Ain't I volatile?" she added, as a commentary on this offer, and departed.

That evening, when I came to Mr. Barkis's house, I was surprised to find Ham walking up and down in front of it, and still more surprised to learn from him that little

Em'ly was inside. I naturally inquired why he was not there too.

"Why, you see, Mas'r Davy," he rejoined, in a hesitating manner, "Em'ly, she's talking to some'un in here. It's a young woman, Sir—a young woman that Em'ly knowed once, and doen't ought to know no more."

"Did I see her to-night, Ham, on the sands, after we met you?"

"It's like you did, Mas'r Davy. Not that I know'd then, she was theer, Sir, but along of her creeping soon arterwards under Em'ly's little winder, and whisp'ring 'Em'ly, Em'ly, for Christ's sake have a woman's heart towards me. I was once like you!'"

"What did Em'ly do?"

"Says Em'ly, 'Martha, is it you? Oh, Martha, can it be you!'—for they had sat at work together many a day, at Mr. Omer's."

"I recollect her now!" cried I. "I recollect her quite well!"

"Martha Endell," said Ham. "She wanted to speak to Em'ly. Em'ly couldn't speak to her theer, for her loving uncle was come home, and he wouldn't—no, Mas'r Davy," said Ham, with great earnestness, "he couldn't, tender-hearted as he is, see them two together, for all the treasures in the sea."

I felt how true this was.

"So Em'ly writes in pencil on a bit of paper," he pursued, "and gives it to her out o' winder to bring here. 'Show that,' she says, 'to my aunt, Mrs. Barkis, and she'll set you down by her fire, till uncle is gone out, and I can come.' By-and-by she tells me what I tells you, Mas'r Davy, and asks me to bring her. I can't deny her, when the tears is on her face."

He put his hand into the breast of his shaggy jacket, and took out with great care a pretty little purse.

"And if I could deny her when the tears was on her face, Mas'r Davy," said Ham, tenderly adjusting it on the rough palm of his hand, "How could I deny her when she give me this to carry for her—knowing what she brought it for?"

I shook him warmly by the hand when he had put it away again, and we walked up and down for a minute or two, in silence. The door opened then, and Peggotty appeared, beckoning to Ham to come in. I would have kept away, but she came after me, entreating me to come in too.

The girl was near the fire, with her head and one arm lying on a chair. Not a word was spoken when we first went in; and the Dutch clock on the dresser seemed, in the silence, to tick twice as loud as usual.

Em'ly spoke first.

"Martha wants," she said to Ham, "to go to London."

"What will she do there?" inquired Ham.

"She will try to do well," said little Em'ly.

"I'll try," said Martha, "if you'll help me away. Oh!" with a dreadful shiver, "take me out of these streets, where the whole town knows me from a child!"

As Em'ly held out her hand to Ham, I saw him put in it a little canvas bag. She took it, as if she thought it were her purse, but finding her mistake turned and showed it to him.

"It's all yourn, Em'ly," I could hear him say. "I haven't nowt in all the wureld that ain't yourn, my dear."

The tears rose freshly in her eyes, but she turned away, and went to Martha. I saw her stooping over her, and putting money in her bosom. She whispered something, and asked was that enough? "More than enough," the other said, and took her hand and kissed it.

Then Martha arose, and gathering her shawl about her, covering her face with it, and weeping aloud, went slowly to the door.

As the door closed, little Em'ly looked at us three in a hurried manner, and then hid her face in her hands, and fell to sobbing.

"Doen't, Em'ly!" said Ham, tapping her gently on the shoulder. "Doen't, my dear! You doen't ought to cry so, pretty!"

"Oh, Ham!" she exclaimed, still weeping pitifully, "I am not as good a girl as I ought to be!"

"Yes, yes, I'm sure. Poor little tender heart," said Ham.

"No! no! no!" cried little Em'ly, sobbing, and shaking her head. "I am not as good a girl as I ought to be. Not near! not near!" and still she cried, as if her heart would break.

She got calmer by degrees, while Peggotty recalled her stray ringlets, dried her eyes, and made her neat again.

I saw her do, that night, what I had never seen her do before. I saw her innocently kiss her chosen husband on the cheek, and creep close to his bluff form as if it were her best support.

CHAPTER XXIII

I CHOOSE A PROFESSION

In the morning, while we were at breakfast, a letter was delivered to me from my aunt. As it contained matter on which I thought Steerforth could advise me, I resolved to make it a subject of discussion on our journey home. For the present we had enough to do, in taking leave of all our friends. Mr. Barkis was far from being the last among them, in his regret at our departure; and Peggotty and all her family were full of grief. The whole house of Omer and Joram turned out to bid us good-bye; and there were so many seafaring volunteers in attendance on Steerforth that if we had had the baggage of a regiment we should hardly have wanted porters to carry it.

"Do you stay long here, Littimer?" said I, as he stood waiting to see the coach start.

"No, Sir," he replied; "probably not very long, Sir."

"He can hardly say, just now," observed Steerforth, carelessly. "He knows what he has to do, and he'll do it."

"That I am sure he will," said I.

Littimer touched his hat and I felt about eight years old. He touched it once more, wishing us a good journey; and we left him standing on the pavement, as respectable a mystery as any pyramid in Egypt.

For some little time we held no conversation, Steerforth being unusually silent. At length becoming gay and talkative in a moment, he pulled me by the arm:

"Find a voice, David. What about the letter?"

"Oh!" said I. "It's from my aunt."

"And what does she say?"

"Why, she reminds me, Steerforth," said I, "that I came out on this expedition to look about me, and to think a little."

"Which, of course, you have done?"

"Indeed I can't say I have. To tell you the truth I had forgotten it."

"What says our aunt?" inquired Steerforth. "Does she suggest anything?"

"Why, yes," said I. "She asks me, here, if I think I should like to be a proctor? What do you think of it?"

"Well, I don't know," replied Steerforth, coolly. "You may as well do that as anything else, I suppose."

"What *is* a proctor, Steerforth?" said I.

"'Why, he is a sort of monkish attorney," replied Steerforth. "He is, to courts held in Doctors' Commons—a lazy old nook near St. Paul's Churchyard—what solicitors are to the courts of law. I can tell you best what he is, by telling you what Doctors' Commons is. It's a little out-of-the-way place that has an ancient monopoly in suits about people's wills and people's marriages, and disputes among ships and boats. On the whole, I would recommend you to take to Doctors' Commons kindly, David."

I quite made up my mind to do so. I then told Steerforth that my aunt was in town awaiting me (as I found from her letter). When we came to our journey's end, he went home, engaging to call upon me next day but one; and I found my aunt. If I had been round the world since we parted, we could hardly have been better pleased to meet again.

Supper was comfortably served, and when the table was cleared Janet assisted her to arrange her hair, to put on her nightcap, which was of a smarter construction than usual ("in case of fire," my aunt said), and to fold her gown back over her knees, these being her usual preparations for warming herself before going to bed. I then made her, according to certain established regulations, a glass of hot white wine and water, and a slice of toast cut into long thin strips. With these accompaniments we were left alone to finish the evening, my aunt looking benignantly on me, from among the borders of her nightcap.

"Well, Trot," she began, "what do you think of the proctor plan?"

"I have thought about it, my dear aunt, and I have talked about it with Steerforth. I like it very much indeed."

"Come," said my aunt. "That's cheering."

"I have only one difficulty, aunt."

"Say what it is, Trot," she returned.

"Why, I want to ask, aunt, whether it would not be very expensive?"

"It will cost," returned my aunt, "to article you, just a thousand pounds."

"Now, my dear aunt," said I, drawing my chair nearer, "I am uneasy in my mind about that. You have expended a great deal on my education, and have been the soul of generosity. Surely there are some ways in which I might begin life with hardly any outlay, and yet begin with a good hope of getting on by resolution and exertion. Are you sure that it would not be better to try that course?"

My aunt finished eating the piece of toast on which she was engaged, and then replied:

"Trot, my child, if I have any object in life, it is to provide for your being a good, a sensible, and a happy man. I am bent upon it—so is Dick."

She stopped for a moment to take my hand between hers, and went on.

"It's in vain, Trot, to recall the past, unless it works some influence upon the present. Perhaps I might have been better friends with your poor father. Perhaps I might have been better friends with your mother, even after your sister Betsey Trotwood disappointed me. When you came to me, a little runaway boy, perhaps I thought so. From that time until now, Trot, you have ever been a credit to me. I have no other claim upon my means; at least"—here to my surprise she hesitated, and was confused—"no,

I have *no* other claim upon my means—and you are my adopted child. Only be a loving child to me in my age, and bear with my whims; and you will do more for an old woman whose prime of life was not so happy as it might have been, than ever that old woman did for you. All is understood between us now, Trot," said my aunt. "Give me a kiss, and we'll go to the Commons after breakfast to-morrow."

At about midday, we set out for the office of Messrs. Spenlow and Jorkins, in Doctors' Commons. My aunt gave me her purse to carry for her, which had ten guineas in it and some silver.

We made a pause at the toy-shop in Fleet Street, to see the giants of Saint Dunstan's strike upon the bells—and then went on towards St. Paul's Churchyard, when I found that my aunt greatly accelerated her speed. I observed, at the same time, that a lowering ill-dressed man who had stopped and stared at us in passing, was coming so close after us, as to brush against her.

"Trot!" cried my aunt, in a terrified whisper, and pressing my arm. "I don't know what I am to do."

"Don't be alarmed," said I. "Step into a shop, and I'll soon get rid of this fellow."

"No, no, child!" she returned. "Don't speak to him for the world. I entreat, I order you!"

"Good Heaven, aunt!" said I. "He is nothing but a sturdy beggar."

"You don't know what he is!" replied my aunt. "Don't look at him but get me a coach, my dear, and wait for me in St. Paul's Churchyard."

"Wait for you?" I repeated.

"Yes," rejoined my aunt. "I must go alone. I must go with him."

"With him, aunt? This man?"

"I am in my senses," she replied, "and I tell you I *must*. Get me a coach!"

I was sensible that I had no right to refuse compliance, and called a hackney chariot. My aunt sprang in and the man followed. She waved her hand to me to go away, so earnestly that I turned from them at once.

What Mr. Dick had told me now came into my mind. I could not doubt that this was the person of whom he had made such mysterious mention. After half an hour I saw the chariot coming back. The driver stopped beside me, and my aunt was sitting in it alone.

She desired me to get into the chariot, and to tell the coachman to drive slowly up and down a little while. She said no more, except, "My dear child, never ask me what it was, and don't refer to it," until she had perfectly regained her composure. On her giving me her purse to pay the driver, I found that all the guineas were gone, and only the loose silver remained.

Doctors' Commons was approached by a little low archway. Before we had taken many paces down the street beyond it, the noise of the city seemed to melt, as if by magic, into a softened distance. A few dull courts and narrow ways brought us to the offices of Spenlow and Jorkins; in the vestibule of which three or four clerks were at work.

As we were left to look about us while Mr. Spenlow was fetched, I availed myself of the opportunity. The furniture of the room was old-fashioned and dusty; and on the top of the writing-table were a great many bundles of papers and immense manuscript Books of Evidence, strongly bound, and tied together in massive sets. All this looked tolerably expensive, I thought, and gave me an agreeable notion of a proctor's business. I was casting my eyes over these and many similar objects, when Mr. Spenlow, in a black gown trimmed with white fur, came hurrying in.

He was a little light-haired gentleman, with the stiffest of white cravats and shirt-collars. He must have taken a great deal of pains with his whiskers, which were accurately curled.

"And so, Mr. Copperfield, you think of entering into our profession," he said.

I bowed my acknowledgments, and said that I presumed I should have an opportunity of trying how I liked it, before I bound myself to it irrevocably.

"Oh surely! surely!" said Mr. Spenlow. "We always, in this house, propose a month. I should be happy, myself, to propose two months—three—but I have a partner. Mr. Jorkins."

"And the premium, Sir," I returned, "is a thousand pounds."

"And the premium, stamp included, is a thousand pounds," said Mr. Spenlow. "As I have mentioned to Miss Trotwood, I am bound to respect Mr. Jorkins's opinions. Mr. Jorkins thinks a thousand pounds too little, in short."

"I suppose, Sir," said I, "that if an articled clerk were particularly useful, it is not the custom, in the later years of his time, to allow him any——"

"No. Mr. Jorkins is immovable," Mr. Spenlow answered, anticipating the word "salary."

I was quite dismayed by the idea of this terrible Jorkins. But I found out afterwards that he was a mild man whose place in the business was to keep himself in the background, and be constantly exhibited by name as the most obdurate and ruthless of men.

My aunt and I had another long talk about my plans, when we were safely housed; and as I knew she was anxious to get home, I urged her not to be uncomfortable on my account, but to leave me to take care of myself.

"I have not been here a week to-morrow, without considering that too, my dear," she returned. "There is a set of chambers in the Adelphi, Trot, which ought to suit you."

With this brief introduction, she produced from her pocket an advertisement, setting forth that in Buckingham Street in the Adelphi there was to be let furnished, with a view of the river, a singularly desirable and compact set of chambers. Terms moderate, and could be taken for a month only, if required.

"Why, this is the very thing, aunt!" said I.

"Then come," replied my aunt, immediately resuming the bonnet she had a minute before laid aside. "We'll go and look at 'em."

Away we went. The advertisement directed us to apply to Mrs. Crupp on the premises, and we rung the area bell. It was not until we had rung three or four times that Mrs. Crupp appeared, being a stout lady with a flounce of flannel petticoat below a nankeen gown.

"Let us see these chambers of yours, if you please, ma'am," said my aunt.

"For this gentleman?" said Mrs. Crupp, feeling in her pocket for her keys.

"Yes, for my nephew," said my aunt.

"And a sweet set they is for sich!" said Mrs. Crupp.

So we went up-stairs.

They were on the top of the house and consisted of a little half-blind entry, a little stone-blind pantry, a sitting room, and a bedroom. The furniture was rather faded, but quite good enough for me; and, sure enough, the river was outside the windows.

My aunt, seeing how enraptured I was with the premises, took them for a month, with leave to remain for twelve months when that time was out. I need only add, that she made a handsome provision for all my possible wants during my month of trial; that Steerforth, to my great disappointment and hers too, did not make his appearance before she went away; and that I saw her safely seated in the Dover coach, exulting in the coming discomfiture of the vagrant donkeys.

CHAPTER XXIV

MY FIRST DISSIPATION

It was a wonderfully fine thing to have that lofty castle to myself, and to walk about town with the key of my house in my pocket! I must say, too, that there were times when it was very dreary.

After two days and nights, I felt as if I had lived there for a year, and yet I was not an hour older, but was quite as much tormented by my own youthfulness as ever.

Steerforth not yet appearing, I left the Commons early on the third day, and walked out to Highgate. Mrs. Steerforth was very glad to see me, and said that he had gone away with one of his Oxford friends to see another who lived near St. Albans, but that she expected him to return to-morrow.

I was taking my coffee and roll in the morning, when Steerforth himself walked in.

"My dear Steerforth," cried I, "I began to think I should never see you again!"

"I was carried off, by force of arms," said Steerforth, "the very next morning after I got home. Why, Daisy, what a rare old bachelor you are here!"

I showed him over the establishment, with no little pride, and he commended it highly.

"But you shall have some breakfast!" said I, with my hand on the bell-rope.

"No, no!" said Steerforth. "Don't ring! I can't!"

"But you'll come back to dinner?" said I.

"I can't, upon my life. I *must* remain with these two fellows. We are all three off together to-morrow morning."

"Then bring them here to dinner," I returned, for it occurred to me that I really ought to have a little house-warming. I therefore made him promise positively in the names of his two friends, and we appointed six o'clock as the dinner-hour.

When he was gone, I rang for Mrs. Crupp, and acquainted her with my desperate design. Mrs. Crupp said what she would recommend would be this. A pair of hot roast fowls—from the pastry-cook's; a dish of stewed beef, with vegetables—from the pastry-cook's; two little corner things, as a raised pie and dish of kidneys—from the pastry-cook's; a tart, and (if I liked) a shape of jelly—from the pastry-cook's. This, Mrs. Crupp said, would leave her at full liberty to concentrate her mind on the potatoes, and to serve up the cheese and celery as she could wish to see it done.

These preparations happily completed, I bought a little dessert in Covent Garden Market, and gave a rather extensive order at a retail wine-merchant's.

One of Steerforth's friends was named Grainger, and the other Markham. They were both very gay and lively fellows.

"I hope you have both brought appetites with you?" said Steerforth.

"Upon my honour," returned Markham, "town seems to sharpen a man's appetite. A man is hungry all day long."

Being a little embarrassed at first, and feeling much too young to preside, I made Steerforth take the head of the table and seated myself opposite to him. Everything was very good; we did not spare the wine; and he exerted himself so brilliantly to make the thing pass off well, that there was no pause in our festivity.

I began, by being singularly cheerful and light-hearted. I went on, by passing the wine faster and faster yet, and continually starting up with a corkscrew to open more wine, long before any was needed. I proposed Steerforth's health. I said he was my dearest friend, the protector of my boyhood and the companion of my prime. I finished by saying, "I'll give you Steerforth! God bless him! Hurrah!" I broke my glass in going round the table to shake hands with him, and I said (in two words) "Steerforth, you'retheguidingstarofmyexistence."

Somebody was leaning out of my bedroom window and feeling the air upon his face. Now, somebody was unsteadily contemplating his features in the looking-glass. I was very pale; my eyes had a vacant appearance; and my hair looked drunk.

Somebody said to me, "Let us go to the theatre, Copperfield!" To be sure. The very thing. Come along! But they must excuse me if I saw everybody out first, and turned the lamp off—in case of fire.

Owing to some confusion in the dark, the door was gone. I was feeling for it in the window-curtains, when Steerforth, laughing, took me by the arm and led me out.

A very foggy night, with great rings round the lamps in the streets! Steerforth said, "You are all right, Copperfield, are you not?" and I told him, "Neverberrer."

Shortly afterwards, we were in a very hot theatre. There was a great stage and there were people upon it, talking about something or other, but not at all intelligibly. There was an abundance of bright lights, and there was music. The whole building looked to me, as if it were learning to swim.

We resolved to go to the dress-boxes, where the ladies were. Then I was being ushered into one of these boxes, and found myself saying something as I sat down, and the people about me crying "Silence!" and—what! yes!—Agnes in the same box, with a lady and gentleman whom I didn't know. I see her face now, with its indelible look of regret and wonder.

"Agnes!" I said, thickly.

"Hush!" she answered. "You disturb the company."

I looked at her again by-and-by, and saw her shrink into her corner, and put her gloved hand to her forehead.

"Agnes!" I said. "I'mafraidyou'renorwell."

"Yes, yes. Do not mind me, Trotwood," she returned. "Listen! For my sake. ask your friends to take you home."

She had so far improved me that I felt ashamed, and with a short "Goori!" (which I intended for "Good-night!") got up and went away. They followed, and I stepped at once out of the box-door into my bedroom, where only Steerforth was with me, helping me to undress.

How somebody, lying in my bed, lay saying and doing all this over again, at cross purpose, in a feverish dream all night—the bed a rocking sea that was never still!

But the agony of mind, the remorse, and shame I felt, when I became conscious next day! My horror of having committed a thousand offences I had forgotten, and which nothing could ever expiate—my recollection of that indelible look which Agnes had given me—the torturing impossibility of communicating with her—my racking head—the smell of smoke, the sight of glasses, the impossibility of going out, or even getting up! Oh, what a day it was!

CHAPTER XXV

GOOD AND BAD ANGELS

I WAS going out at my door on the morning after that deplorable day of headache, sickness, and repentance, when I saw a ticket-porter coming up-stairs, with a letter.

"T. Copperfield, Esquire," said the ticket-porter, touching his hat with his little cane.

I told him I was T. Copperfield, Esquire, and he gave me the letter, which he said required an answer. It was a very kind note. All it said was, "My dear Trotwood. I am staying at the house of papa's agent, Mr. Waterbrook in Ely Place, Holborn. Will you come and see me to-day, at any time you like to appoint? Ever yours affectionately, AGNES."

It took me such a long time to write an answer at all to my satisfaction, that I don't know what the ticket-porter can have thought, unless he thought I was learning to write. After many attempts, I wrote, "My dear Agnes. Your letter is like you, and what could I say of it that would be higher praise than that? I will come at four o'clock. Affectionately and sorrowfully, T. C."

Although I left the office at half-past three, and was prowling about the place of appointment within a few minutes afterward, the appointed time was exceeded by a full quarter of an hour, before I could muster up sufficient desperation to pull the bell-handle of Mr. Waterbrook's house.

I was shown into a pretty but rather close drawing-room, and there sat Agnes, netting a purse.

She looked so quiet and good that I yielded to my self-reproach and shame, and—in short, made a fool of myself. I cannot deny that I shed tears.

"If it had been any one but you, Agnes," said I, "I should not have minded it half so much. But that it should have been *you* who saw me!"

She put her hand upon my arm for a moment; and I felt so befriended and comforted, that I could not help moving it to my lips, and gratefully kissing it.

"Sit down," said Agnes, cheerfully. "Don't be unhappy, Trotwood. If you cannot confidently trust me, whom will you trust?"

"Ah, Agnes!" I returned. "You are my good Angel!"

She smiled rather sadly, I thought, and shook her head.

"Yes, Agnes, my good Angel! Always!"

"If I were, indeed, Trotwood," she returned, "there is one thing that I should set my heart on very much."

I looked at her inquiringly.

"On warning you," said Agnes, with a steady glance, "against your bad Angel."

"My dear Agnes," I began, "if you mean Steerforth——"

"I do, Trotwood," she returned.

"Then, Agnes, you wrong him very much. My dear Agnes! Now, is it not unjust, and unlike you, to judge him from what you saw of me the other night?"

"I do not," she quietly replied.

"From what, then?"

"From many things—trifles in themselves, but they do not seem to me to be so, when they are put together. I judge him, partly from your account of him, Trotwood, and your character, and the influence he has over you."

I sat looking at her as she cast her eyes down on her work, and Steerforth, in spite of all my attachment to him, darkened in that tone.

"It is very bold in me," said Agnes, looking up again, "who can know so little of the world, to give you my advice so confidently. But I am certain that what I say is right. I am quite sure that you have made a dangerous friend."

Again I looked at her and again his image, though it was still fixed in my heart, darkened.

"I am not so unreasonable as to expect," said Agnes, after a little while, "that you will, or that you can, change a sentiment that is rooted in your trusting disposition. You ought not hastily to do that. I only ask you, Trotwood, as often as you think of me—to think of what I have said."

"And when, Agnes," said I, "will you forgive me the other night?"

"When I recall it," said Agnes.

She would have dismissed the subject so, but I insisted on telling her how it happened. It was a great relief to me to do this, and to enlarge on the obligation that I owed to Steerforth for his care of me when I was unable to take care of myself.

"You must not forget," said Agnes, calmly changing the conversation, "that you are always to tell me when you fall into trouble."

Then she asked me if I had seen Uriah.

"Uriah Heep?" said I. "No. Is he in London?"

"He was in London a week before me. I am afraid on disagreeable business, Trotwood."

"On some business that makes you uneasy, Agnes, I see," said I. "What can that be?"

Agnes laid aside her work, and replied, looking pensively at me:

"I believe he is going to enter into partnership with papa."

"What? Uriah? That mean, fawning fellow!" I cried, indignantly. "Have you made no remonstrance? You must not allow your father to take such a mad step. You must prevent it."

Agnes shook her head with a faint smile at my warmth; and then replied:

"You remember our last conversation about papa? It was not long after that when he gave me the first intimation of what I tell you. It was sad to see his inability to conceal that it was forced upon him."

"Forced upon him, Agnes! Who forces it upon him?"

"Uriah," she replied, after a moment's hesitation. "He has mastered papa's weaknesses, fostered them, and taken advantage of them, until—Trotwood—until papa is afraid of him."

There was more that she might have said; more that she knew, or that she suspected; I clearly saw.

"His ascendancy over papa," said Agnes, "is very great. He professes humility and gratitude, but his position is really one of power, and I fear he makes a hard use of his power."

I said he was a hound, which, at the moment, was a great satisfaction to me.

"At the time I speak of," pursued Agnes, "papa was bowed down by care; but he seemed relieved by this expedient, though hurt and ashamed."

"And how did you receive it, Agnes?"

"I did, Trotwood," she replied, "what I hope was right. Feeling sure that it was necessary for papa's peace that the sacrifice be made, I entreated him to make it. Oh, Trotwood!" cried Agnes, putting her hands before her face, as her tears started, "I almost feel as if I had been papa's enemy, instead of his loving child. I know how his anxious thoughts of me have shadowed his life, and weakened his strength and energy, by turning them always upon one idea. If I could ever set this right!"

I had never before seen Agnes cry. It made me so sorry that I could only say, "Pray, Agnes, don't! Don't, my dear sister!"

But Agnes was too superior to me in character and purpose to be long in need of my entreaties. The beautiful, calm manner came back again, as if a cloud had passed from a serene sky.

"We are not likely to remain alone much longer," said Agnes; "and while I have an opportunity, let me earnestly entreat you, Trotwood, to be friendly to Uriah. Don't repel him. Think first of papa and me!"

Agnes had no time to say more, for the room-door opened,

and Mrs. Waterbrook, who was a large lady—or who wore a large dress: I don't exactly know which—came sailing in. I had a dim recollection of having seen her at the theatre, but she appeared to remember me perfectly, and still to suspect me of being in a state of intoxication.

Finding by degrees, however, that I was sober, Mrs. Waterbrook softened towards me, and invited me to dinner next day. I accepted the invitation, and took my leave.

When I went, next day, I found Uriah Heep among the company, in a suit of black, and in deep humility. He told me, when I shook hands with him, that he was proud to be noticed by me, and he hovered about me in his gratitude all the rest of the evening.

There were other guests, but there was one who attracted my attention before he came in, on account of my hearing him announced as Mr. Traddles! My mind flew back to Salem House; and could it be Tommy, I thought, who used to draw the skeletons!

I looked for Mr. Traddles with unusual interest. He was a sober, steady-looking young man of retiring manners, with a comic head of hair; and either my vision deceived me, or it was the old unfortunate Tommy.

When dinner was announced, Uriah, Traddles, and I went down last and it gave me an opportunity of making myself known to Traddles who greeted me with great fervour.

Traddles and I were separated at table, and the dinner was long. I was glad indeed to get up-stairs to Agnes and to introduce Traddles to her. As he was obliged to leave early, on account of going away next morning for a month, I had not nearly so much conversation with him as I could have wished; but we exchanged addresses, and promised ourselves the pleasure of another meeting when he should come back to town.

Agnes was going away within a few days. This caused me to remain until all the company were gone. I have said that the company were all gone; but I ought to have excepted Uriah who had never ceased to hover near us.

He was close beside me, when I walked away from the house, and in remembrance of the entreaty Agnes had made, I asked him if he would come home to my rooms, and have some coffee.

"Oh, really, Master Copperfield," he rejoined,—"I beg your pardon, Mister Copperfield—I don't like that you should put a constraint upon yourself to ask a numble person like me."

"There is no constraint in the case," said I. "Will you come?"

"I should like to, very much," replied Uriah, with a writhe.

"Well, then, come along!" said I.

As he sat on my sofa, with his long knees drawn up under his coffee-cup, and a snaky undulation pervading his frame, I decided that I disliked him intensely.

"You have heard something, I des-say, of a change in my expectations, Master Copperfield—I should say, Mister Copperfield?" observed Uriah.

"Yes," said I, "something."

"Ah! I thought Miss Agnes would know of it!" he quietly returned. "Oh, thank you, Master—Mister Copperfield!"

I could have thrown my bootjack at him for having entrapped me into the disclosure of anything concerning Agnes.

"What a prophet you have shown yourself, Mister Copperfield!" pursued Uriah. "Don't you remember saying to me once, that perhaps I should be a partner in Mr. Wickfield's business?"

"I recollect talking about it," said I, "though I certainly did not think it very likely then."

"Oh! who *would* have thought it likely, Mister Copperfield!" returned Uriah, enthusiastically. "I am sure I didn't myself."

"But the umblest persons, Master Copperfield," he presently resumed, "may be the instruments of good. I am glad to think I have been the instrument of good to Mr.

Wickfield, and that I may be more so. Oh, what a worthy man he is, Mister Copperfield, but how imprudent he has been!"

"I am sorry to hear it," said I, "on all accounts."

"Decidedly so, Mister Copperfield," replied Uriah. "On all accounts. Miss Agnes's above all!"

"So, Mr. Wickfield," said I, "has been imprudent, has he, Mr. Heep?"

"Oh, very imprudent indeed, Master Copperfield," returned Uriah. "But I wish you'd call me Uriah, if you please. It's like old times."

"Well! Uriah," said I, bolting it out with some difficulty.

"Thank you," he returned, with fervour. "Thank you, Master Copperfield! It's like the blowing of old breezes or the ringing of old bellses to hear *you* say Uriah. Was I making any observation?"

"About Mr. Wickfield," I suggested.

"Oh! Yes, truly," said Uriah. "Ah! Great imprudence, Master Copperfield. If any one else had been in my place during the last few years, by this time he would have had Mr. Wickfield (oh, what a worthy man he is, Master Copperfield, too!) under his thumb. Un-der-his thumb," said Uriah, very slowly.

"Master Copperfield," he began again, "you will not think the worse of my umbleness, if I make a little confidence to you, Master Copperfield? Will you?"

"Oh no," said I, with an effort.

"Thank you! Miss Agnes, Master Copperfield——"

"Well, Uriah?"

"You thought her looking very beautiful to-night, Master Copperfield?"

"I thought her looking as she always does: superior, in all respects, to every one around her," I returned.

"Oh, thank you!" he cried.

"Not at all," I said, loftily. "There is no reason why you should thank me."

"Why that, Master Copperfield," said Uriah, "is, in fact, the confidence that I am going to take the liberty

He sat on my sofa with his long knees drawn up under his coffee cup.

of reposing. Umble as I am, the image of Miss Agnes has been in my breast for years. Oh, Master Copperfield, with what a pure affection do I love the ground my Agnes walks on!"

I believe I had a delirious idea of seizing the red-hot poker out of the fire, and running him through with it.

A timely observation of the sense of power that there was in his face, did more to bring back to my remembrance the entreaty of Agnes, in its full force, than any effort I could have made. I asked him, whether he had made his feelings known to Agnes.

"Oh, no, Master Copperfield!" he returned; "oh dear, no! Not to any one but you. I rest a good deal of hope on her observing how useful I am to her father. I think she may come, on his account, to be kind to me."

I fathomed the depth of the rascal's whole scheme, and understood why he laid it bare.

"If you'll have the goodness to keep my secret, Master Copperfield, and not, in general, to go against me, I shall take it as a particular favour. There's no hurry at present, you know," Uriah proceeded, in his slimy way. "My Agnes is very young still; and Mother and me will have to work our way upwards, and make a good many arrangements, before it would be quite convenient. Oh, it's such a relief, you can't think, to know that you are certain (as you wouldn't wish to make unpleasantness in the family) not to go against me!"

He took the hand which I dared not withhold, and having given it a damp squeeze, referred to his pale-faced watch.

"Dear me!" he said, "it's past one. The 'ouse that I am stopping at will have gone to bed these two hours."

"I am sorry," I returned, "that there is only one bed here."

"Oh, don't think of mentioning beds, Master Copperfield! But *would* you have any objections to my laying down before the fire?"

"If it comes to that," I said, "pray take my bed, and I'll lie down before the fire."

His repudiation of this offer was shrill! As no arguments had the least effect, I was obliged to make the best arrangements I could, for his repose before the fire. The mattress of the sofa (which was a great deal too short for his lank figure), the sofa pillows, a blanket, the table-cover, a clean breakfast cloth, and a great-coat, made him a bed and covering, for which he was more than thankful. Having lent him a night-cap in which he made such an awful figure, that I have never worn one since, I left him to his rest.

I never shall forget that night! I never shall forget how I turned and tumbled; how I wearied myself with thinking about Agnes and this creature; how I considered what could I do, and what ought I to do; how I could come to no other conclusion than that the best course for her peace, was to do nothing, and to keep to myself what I had heard.

CHAPTER XXVI

I FALL INTO CAPTIVITY

I SAW no more of Uriah Heep until the day when Agnes left town. I was at the coach-office to take leave of her and see her go; and there was he, returning to Canterbury by the same conveyance. At the coach-window, as at the dinner-party, he hovered about us like a great vulture; gorging himself on every syllable that I said to Agnes, or Agnes said to me.

I could not get over this farewell glimpse of them for a long time. Whenever I fell into a thoughtful state, this subject was sure to present itself, and all my uneasiness was sure to be redoubled.

I had ample leisure to refine upon my uneasiness: for Steerforth was at Oxford and I was very much alone. I believe I had at this time some lurking distrust of Steerforth. I wrote to him most affectionately, but I think I was glad, upon the whole, that he could not come to London just then.

In the meantime, days and weeks slipped away. On the day when I was articled, no festivity took place, beyond my having sandwiches and sherry into the office for the clerks, and going alone to the theatre at night. Mr. Spenlow remarked on this occasion that he should have been happy to have seen me at his house at Norwood, but for his domestic arrangements being in some disorder, on account of the expected return of his daughter from finishing her education at Paris. But, he intimated that when she came home he should hope to have the pleasure of entertaining me. I knew that he was a widower with one daughter, and expressed my acknowledgments.

Mr. Spenlow was as good as his word. In a week or

two, he said, that if I would do him the favour to come down next Saturday, and stay till Monday, he would be extremely happy. Of course I said I *would* do him the favour; and he was to drive me down in his phaeton, and to bring me back.

We had an adjourned cause that day—and as the evidence was just twice the length of Robinson Crusoe, it was rather late in the day before Mr. Spenlow and I drove away in the phaeton.

There was a lovely garden to Mr. Spenlow's house; and it was so beautifully kept, that I was quite enchanted.

We went into the house, which was cheerfully lighted up. "Where is Miss Dora?" said Mr. Spenlow to the servant. "Dora!" I thought. "What a beautiful name!"

We turned into a room near at hand and I heard a voice say, "Mr. Copperfield, my daughter Dora, and my daughter Dora's confidential friend!" All was over in a moment. I was a captive and a slave. I loved Dora Spenlow to distraction!

"I," observed a well-remembered voice, "have seen Mr. Copperfield before."

The speaker was not Dora. No; the confidential friend, Miss Murdstone!

I don't think I was much astonished. To the best of my judgment, no capacity of astonishment was left in me. I said, "How do you do, Miss Murdstone? I hope you are well." She answered, "Very well." I said, "How is Mr. Murdstone?" She replied, "My brother is robust, I am obliged to you."

Mr. Spenlow then put in his word: "I am glad to find," he said, "Copperfield, that you and Miss Murdstone are already acquainted."

"Mr. Copperfield and myself," said Miss Murdstone, with severe composure, "are connexions. We were once slightly acquainted. It was in his childish days. I should not have known him."

I replied that I should have known her, anywhere. Which was true enough.

"Miss Murdstone has had the goodness," said Mr. Spenlow to me, "to accept the office—if I may so describe it—of my daughter Dora's confidential friend."

What a state of mind I was in at dinner. I don't remember who was there, except Dora. I have not the least idea what we had for dinner, besides Dora. I sat next to her. I talked to her. She had the most delightful little voice, the gayest little laugh, the pleasantest and most fascinating little ways, that ever led a lost youth into hopeless slavery. She was rather diminutive altogether. So much the more precious, I thought.

When she went out of the room with Miss Murdstone I fell into a reverie, only disturbed by the cruel apprehension that Miss Murdstone would disparage me to her.

My apprehensions were revived when we went into the drawing-room, but I was relieved of them in an unexpected manner.

"David Copperfield," said Miss Murdstone, beckoning me aside into a window. "A word."

I confronted Miss Murdstone alone.

"David Copperfield," said Miss Murdstone, "I need not enlarge upon family circumstances. They are not a tempting subject."

"Far from it, ma'am," I returned.

"David Copperfield, I shall not attempt to disguise the fact that I formed an unfavourable opinion of you in your childhood. I am not the creature of circumstance or change. I may have my opinion of you. You may have your opinion of me."

I inclined my head, in my turn.

"But it is not necessary," said Miss Murdstone, "that these opinions should come into collision here. Let us meet here as distant acquaintances. It is quite unnecessary that either of us should make the other the subject of remark. Do you approve of this?"

"Miss Murdstone," I returned, "I think you and Mr. Murdstone used me very cruelly, and treated my mother with great unkindness. But I quite agree in what you propose."

Miss Murdstone bent her head. Then, just touching the back of my hand with the tips of her cold, stiff fingers, she walked away.

All I know of the rest of the evening is, that I heard the empress of my heart sing enchanted ballads in the French language, generally to the effect that, whatever was the matter, we ought always to dance, Ta ra la, Ta ra la! accompanying herself on a glorified instrument, resembling a guitar. That when Miss Murdstone took her into custody and led her away, she smiled and gave me her delicious hand. That I retired to bed in a most maudlin state of mind, and got up in a crisis of feeble infatuation.

It was a fine morning, and early, and I thought I would go and take a stroll. On my way through the hall, I encountered her little dog, who was called Jip—short for Gipsy. I approached him tenderly, for I loved even him; but he showed his whole set of teeth and wouldn't hear of the least familiarity.

I had not been walking long, when I turned a corner, and met her. I tingle again from head to foot as my recollection turns that corner.

"You—are—out early, Miss Spenlow," said I.

"It's so stupid at home," she replied. "Besides, it's the brightest time of the whole day. Don't you think so?"

I said (not without stammering) that it was very bright to me then, though it had been very dark to me a minute before.

"Do you mean a compliment?" said Dora, "or that the weather has really changed?"

I stammered worse than before, in replying that I meant no compliment, but the plain truth; though I was not aware of any change having taken place in the weather. It was in the state of my own feelings, I added bashfully.

I never saw such curls—how could I, for there never were such curls!—as those she shook out to hide her blushes.

The little dog came running along the walk. She took him up in her arms—oh, my goodness!—and caressed him.

"You are not very intimate with Miss Murdstone, are you?" said Dora.

"No," I replied. "Not at all so."

"She is a tiresome creature," said Dora, pouting. "I am sure *I* don't want a protector. Jip can protect me a great deal better than Miss Murdstone,—can't you, Jip, dear?"

He only winked lazily, when she kissed his ball of a head.

"It is very hard, because we have not a kind Mama, that we are to have, instead, a sulky, gloomy old thing like Miss Murdstone, always following us about—isn't it, Jip? Never mind, Jip. We won't be confidential, and we'll tease her, and not please her,—won't we, Jip?"

Miss Murdstone had been looking for us. She found us here, and took Dora's arm in hers, and marched us in to breakfast.

We had a quiet day. No company, a walk, a family dinner of four, and an evening of looking over books and pictures; Miss Murdstone with a homily before her, and her eye upon us, keeping guard vigilantly. Ah! Little did Mr. Spenlow imagine, when he sat opposite to me after dinner that day, with his pocket-handkerchief over his head, how fervently I was embracing him, in my fancy, as his son-in-law!

We departed early in the morning, for we had a Salvage case coming on in the Admiralty Court. Dora was at the breakfast-table to make the tea again, however; and I had the melancholy pleasure of taking off my hat to her in the phaeton, as she stood on the doorstep with Jip in her arms.

Within the first week of my passion, I bought four sumptuous waistcoats and took to wearing straw-coloured kid gloves. I walked miles upon miles daily in the hope of seeing her. I walked about the streets where the best shops for ladies were, I haunted the Bazaar, I fagged through the Park. On rare occasions, I saw her. Perhaps I saw her glove waved in a carriage window; perhaps I met her, walked with her and Miss Murdstone a little way, and spoke to her.

Mrs. Crupp must have been a woman of penetration; for when this attachment was but a few weeks old she found it out!

"Cheer up, Sir," said Mrs. Crupp. "I can't abear to see you so, Sir. I know what it is, Sir. There's a lady in the case."

"Mrs. Crupp?" I returned, reddening.

"Oh, bless you!" said Mrs. Crupp, nodding encouragement. "Never say die, Sir! Keep a good heart, and know your own value. If you was to take to something, Sir," said Mrs. Crupp, "if you was to take to skittles, now, which is 'ealthy, you might find it divert your mind, and do you good."

With these words, Mrs. Crupp, with a majestic curtsey, retired.

CHAPTER XXVII

TOMMY TRADDLES

It may have been in consequence of Mrs. Crupp's advice that it came into my head, next day, to go and look after Traddles. An indescribable character of faded gentility that attached to the house I sought reminded me of Mr. and Mrs. Micawber.

"Does Mr. Traddles live here?" I inquired.

A mysterious voice from the end of the passage replied "Yes."

"Is he at home?" said I.

Again the mysterious voice replied in the affirmative, and I walked in and up-stairs.

Traddles was on the landing to meet me. He was delighted to see me, and gave me welcome, with great heartiness, to his little room. It was extremely neat, though sparely furnished. His table was covered with papers, and he was hard at work. In a corner of the room was something neatly covered up with a large white cloth. I could not make out what that was.

"Traddles," said I, shaking hands with him again, after I had sat down, "I am delighted to see you."

"I am delighted to see *you,* Copperfield," he returned. "It was because I was thoroughly glad to see you when we met in Ely Place that I gave you this address instead of my address at chambers."

"Oh! You have chambers?" said I.

"Why, I have the fourth of a room and a passage, and the fourth of a clerk," returned Traddles.

His old good temper and something of his old unlucky fortune also, I thought, smiled at me in the smile with which he made this explanation.

"You are reading for the bar, Mr. Waterbrook informed me?" said I.

"Why, yes," said Traddles, "I am reading for the bar. It's some time since I was articled, but the payment of that hundred pounds was a great pull. A great pull!" said Traddles, with a wince, as if he had had a tooth out.

"Do you know what I can't help thinking of, Traddles, as I sit here looking at you?" I asked him.

"No," said he.

"That sky-blue suit you used to wear."

"Lord, to be sure!" cried Traddles, laughing, "Dear me! Well! Those were happy times, weren't they?"

"I think our schoolmaster might have made them happier," I returned.

"Perhaps he might," said Traddles. "But dear me, there was a good deal of fun going on. Ha, ha, ha! Old Creakle! I should like to see him again, too!"

"He was a brute to you, Traddles," said I, indignantly.

"Do you think so?" returned Traddles. "Really? Perhaps he was, rather. But it's all over, a long while."

"You were brought up by an uncle, then?" said I.

"Of course I was!" said Traddles. "The one I was always going to write to. And always didn't, eh! Ha, ha, ha! He died soon after I left school."

"Indeed!"

"Yes. He had made me his heir. But he didn't like me when I grew up, and so he married his housekeeper."

"Did you get nothing, Traddles?"

"Oh dear yes!" said Traddles. "I got fifty pounds. I had never been brought up to any profession, and at first I was at a loss. However, I began to make abstracts, and do that sort of work. So, by little and little I managed to scrape up the hundred pounds," said Traddles. "Now, Copperfield, it's so pleasant to see you, that I sha'n't conceal anything. Therefore you must know that I am engaged."

Engaged! Oh Dora!

This flower-pot and stand she bought herself. This little round table I bought!

"She is a curate's daughter," said Traddles; "one of ten, down in Devonshire, a little older than me, but the dearest girl! I dare say ours is likely to be a rather long engagement, but our motto is 'Wait and hope!'"

Traddles rose from his chair, and, with a triumphant smile, put his hand upon the white cloth I had observed.

"However," he said, "it's not that we haven't made a beginning towards housekeeping. "Here," drawing the cloth off, "are two pieces of furniture to commence with. This flower-pot and stand, she bought herself. You put that in a parlour-window with a plant in it, and—and there you are! This little round table with the marble top *I* bought. You want to lay a book down, you know—and there you are again!" said Traddles. "It's an admirable piece of workmanship—firm as a rock! It's not a great deal towards the furnishing, but it's something, and I assure you she's the dearest girl!"

"I am quite certain of it," said I.

"In the meantime," said Traddles, coming back to his chair; "I get on as well as I can. I don't make much, but I don't spend much. In general, I board with the people down-stairs, who are very agreeable. Both Mr. and Mrs. Micawber are excellent company."

"Mr. and Mrs. Micawber!" I repeated. "Why, I am intimately acquainted with them!"

I begged Traddles to ask his landlord to walk up; and Mr. Micawber, not a bit changed—his tights, his stick, his shirt-collar, and his eye-glass, all the same as ever—came into the room with a genteel and youthful air.

"I beg your pardon, Mr. Traddles," said Mr. Micawber, "I was not aware that there was any individual, alien to this tenement, in your sanctum." And he slightly bowed to me, and pulled up his shirt-collar.

"How do you do, Mr. Micawber?" said I.

"Sir," said Mr. Micawber, "you are exceedingly obliging. I am *in statu quo*."

"And Mrs. Micawber?" I pursued.

"Sir," said Mr. Micawber, "she is also, thank God, *in statu quo*."

Mr. Micawber had not known me, though he had stood face to face with me. But now, seeing me smile, he cried, "Is it possible! Have I the pleasure of again beholding Copperfield!" and shook me by both hands with the utmost fervour.

"Good Heaven, Mr. Traddles!" said Mr. Micawber, "to think that I should find you acquainted with the friend of my youth! My dear!" calling over the banisters to Mrs. Micawber, while Traddles looked not a little amazed at this description of me. "Here is a gentleman in Mr. Traddles's apartment, whom he wishes to have the pleasure of presenting to you, my love!"

"You find us, Copperfield," said Mr. Micawber, with one eye on Traddles, "at present established, on what may be designated as a small and unassuming scale. You find me, fallen back, *for* a spring; and I have every reason to believe that a vigorous leap will shortly be the result."

I was expressing my satisfaction, when Mrs. Micawber came in; a little more slatternly than she used to be but still with some preparation of herself for company, and with a pair of brown gloves on.

We had half-an-hour's talk, all together, and Mr. Micawber was very anxious that I should stay to dinner. But I imagined that I detected calculation relative to the extent of the cold meat, in Mrs. Micawber's eye, and resisted all persuasion.

But I told Traddles, and Mr. and Mrs. Micawber, that they must appoint a day when they would come and dine with me. An appointment was made that suited all, and then I took my leave.

Mr. Micawber accompanied me to the corner of the street.

"My dear Copperfield," said Mr. Micawber, "I am at present engaged in the sale of corn upon commission. It is not an avocation of a remunerative description—in other words, it does *not* pay—and some temporary embarrassments of a pecuniary nature have been the consequence. I am, however, delighted to add that I have now an immediate prospect of something turning up (I am not at liberty to say in what direction), which I trust will enable me to provide, permanently, both for myself and for your friend Traddles, in whom I have an unaffected interest."

Mr. Micawber then shook hands with me again, and left me.

CHAPTER XXVIII

MR. MICAWBER'S GAUNTLET

THE day arrived on which I was to entertain my newly-found old friends. I did not repeat my former extensive preparations. I merely provided a pair of soles, a small leg of mutton, and a pigeon-pie.

Having laid in the materials for a bowl of punch, to be compounded by Mr. Micawber; having provided a bottle of lavender-water, a paper of mixed pins, and a pincushion, to assist Mrs. Micawber in her toilette at my dressing-table, and having laid the cloth with my own hands, I awaited the result with composure.

At the appointed time, my three visitors arrived together. Mr. Micawber with a new ribbon to his eye-glass: Mrs. Micawber with her cap in a whity-brown paper parcel; Traddles carrying the parcel and supporting Mrs. Micawber on his arm. They were all delighted with my residence.

"My dear Copperfield," said Mr. Micawber, "this is luxurious. This is a way of life which reminds me of the period when I was myself in a state of celibacy."

I informed Mr. Micawber that I relied upon him for a bowl of punch, and led him to the lemons. It was wonderful to see his face shining at us out of a thin cloud of delicate fumes, as he stirred, and mixed, and tasted. As to Mrs. Micawber, I don't know whether it was the effect of the cap, or the lavender-water, or the pins, but she came out of my room, comparatively speaking, lovely. And the lark was never gayer than that excellent woman.

I suppose that Mrs. Crupp, after frying the soles, was taken ill, because we broke down at that point. The leg of mutton came up very red within, and very pale without. The pigeon-pie was delusive, the crust being full of lumps and bumps, with nothing particular underneath. In short, the banquet was such a failure that I should have been quite unhappy if I had not been relieved by a bright suggestion from Mr. Micawber.

"My dear friend Copperfield," said Mr. Micawber, "if you will allow me to take the liberty of remarking that there are few comestibles better, in their way, than a Devil, and that I believe, with a little division of labour, we could accomplish a good one, I would put it to you, that this little misfortune may be easily repaired."

There was a gridiron in the pantry. We had it in, in a twinkling, and immediately applied ourselves to carrying Mr. Micawber's idea into effect. Traddles cut the mutton into slices; Mr. Micawber covered them with pepper, mustard, salt, and cayenne; I put them on the gridiron, turned them with a fork, and took them off, under Mr. Micawber's direction; and Mrs. Micawber heated, and continually stirred, some mushroom ketchup in a little saucepan. When we had slices enough done to begin upon, we fell to, with our sleeves still tucked up at the wrist, more slices sputtering and blazing on the fire, and our attention divided between the mutton on our plates, and the mutton then preparing.

What with the novelty of this cookery, the excellence of it, the being so amused, and in the midst of such a tempting noise and savour, we reduced the leg of mutton to the bone.

We were at the height of our enjoyment, and were all busily engaged endeavouring to bring the last batch of slices to a state of perfection when I was aware of a strange presence in the room, and my eyes encountered those of the staid Littimer, standing hat in hand before me.

"What's the matter?" I involuntarily asked.

"I beg your pardon, Sir, I was directed to come in. Is my master not here, Sir?"

"No."

"Have you not seen him, Sir?"

"No. Did he tell you you would find him here?"

"Not exactly so, Sir. I beg, Sir, that you will be seated, and allow me to do this." With which he took the fork and bent over the gridiron.

We became in a moment the meekest of the meek. Mr. Micawber, humming a tune, to show that he was quite at ease, subsided into his chair, with the handle of a hastily concealed fork sticking out of the bosom of his coat. Mrs. Micawber put on her brown gloves, and assumed a genteel languor. Traddles ran his greasy hands through his hair and stared in confusion on the table-cloth. As for me, I was a mere infant at the head of my own table.

Meanwhile Littimer took the mutton off the gridiron, and gravely handed it round. We all took some but we merely made a show of eating it. As we severally pushed away our plates, he noiselessly removed them, and set on the cheese. He took that off, too, when it was done with; cleared the table; gave us our wine-glasses.

"Can I do anything more, Sir?"

I thanked him and said, No; but would he take no dinner himself?

"None, I am obliged to you, Sir."

He was moving softly to the door, when I said:

"Oh! Littimer!"

"Sir!"

"Did you remain long at Yarmouth, that time?"

"Not particularly so, Sir."

"You saw the boat completed?"

"Yes, Sir. I remained behind on purpose to see the boat completed."

"I know! Mr. Steerforth has not seen it yet, I suppose?"

"I really can't say, Sir. I think—but I really can't say Sir. I wish you good night, Sir."

He comprehended everybody present, in a respectful bow with which he followed these words, and disappeared. My visitors seemed to breathe more freely when he was gone, and my own relief was very great.

Mr. Micawber roused me by bestowing many encomiums on the absent Littimer as a thoroughly admirable servant. "But punch, my dear Copperfield," said Mr. Micawber, tasting it, "like time and tide, waits for no man. My love, will you give me your opinion?"

Mrs. Micawber pronounced it excellent.

"Then I will drink," said Mr. Micawber, "to the days when my friend Copperfield and myself were younger, and fought our way in the world side by side."

Mr. Micawber took a pull at his punch. So we all did: Traddles evidently lost in wondering at what distant time Mr. Micawber and I could have been comrades in the battle of the world.

"As we are quite confidential here, Mr. Copperfield," said Mrs. Micawber, "I should much like to have your opinion on Mr. Micawber's prospects. For corn," said Mrs. Micawber argumentatively, "may be gentlemanly, but it is not remunerative."

We were all agreed upon that.

"Then," said Mrs. Micawber, who prided herself on taking a clear view of things, "then I ask myself this question: If corn is not to be relied upon, what is? Are coals to be relied upon? Not at all."

Mr. Micawber, leaning back in his chair with his hands in his pockets, nodded his head.

"The articles of corn and coals," said Mrs. Micawber, "being equally out of the question, I naturally look round the world, and say, 'What is there in which a person of Mr. Micawber's talent is likely to succeed?' And I exclude commission, because commission is not a certainty. What is best suited to a person of Mr. Micawber's peculiar temperament is, I am convinced, a certainty."

Traddles and I both expressed, by a feeling murmur, that this was no doubt true.

"What do I deduce from this?" Mrs. Micawber went on

to say. "Am I wrong in saying, it is clear that we must live?"

I answered "Not at all!" and Traddles answered "Not at all!"

"Just so," returned Mrs. Micawber. "Now I am convinced that things cannot be expected to turn up of themselves. We must, in a measure, assist to turn them up."

Both Traddles and I applauded it highly.

"Very well," said Mrs. Micawber. "Then what do I recommend? Here is Mr. Micawber with a variety of qualifications—with great talent——"

"Really, my love," said Mr. Micawber.

"And here is Mr. Micawber without any suitable position or employment. Where does that responsibility rest? Clearly on society. It appears to me, my dear Mr. Copperfield," said Mrs. Micawber, forcibly, "that what Mr. Micawber has to do, is to throw down the gauntlet to society, and say, in effect, 'Show me who will take that up.' "

I ventured to ask Mrs. Micawber how this was to be done.

"By advertising," said Mrs. Micawber—"in all the papers. It appears to me, that what Mr. Micawber has to do is to describe himself plainly and to put it thus: '*Now* employ me, on remunerative terms, and address, post-paid, to W. M., Post Office, Camden Town.' "

"This idea of Mrs. Micawber's, my dear Copperfield," said Mr. Micawber, "is, in fact, the Leap to which I alluded, when I last had the pleasure of seeing you."

"Advertising is rather expensive," I remarked, dubiously.

"Exactly so!" said Mrs. Micawber. "It is for that reason especially, that I think Mr. Micawber ought to raise a certain sum of money on a bill, take that bill into the Money Market and dispose of it for what he can get. I recommend Mr. Micawber, my dear Mr. Copperfield, to regard it as an investment and to make up his mind to *any* sacrifice."

I felt, but I am sure I don't know why, that this was self-denying and devoted in Mrs. Micawber, and I uttered a murmur to that effect. Traddles, who took his tone from me, did likewise.

Later in the evening, Mrs. Micawber made tea for us in a most agreeable manner, and it was between ten and eleven o'clock when Mrs. Micawber rose to replace her cap in the whity-brown paper parcel, and to put on her bonnet. Mr. Micawber took the opportunity to slip a letter into my hand. I also took the opportunity to detain Traddles for a moment on the top of the stairs.

"Traddles," said I, "Mr. Micawber don't mean any harm, poor fellow; but, if I were you, I wouldn't lend him anything."

"My dear Copperfield," returned Traddles, smiling, "I haven't got anything to lend."

"You have got a name, you know," said I.

"Oh! You call *that* something to lend?" returned Traddles, with a thoughtful look.

"Certainly."

"Oh!" said Traddles. "Yes, to be sure! but—I am afraid I have lent him that already."

"I hope there will be nothing wrong about it," said I.

"I hope not," said Traddles. "He told me, only the other day, that it was provided for. That was Mr. Micawber's expression. 'Provided for.' "

I returned to my fireside, and was musing, half gravely and half laughing, on the character of Mr. Micawber and the old relations between us, when I heard a quick step ascending the stairs. At first I thought it was Traddles; but as the step approached, I knew it, and felt my heart beat high, and the blood rush to my face, for it was Steerforth's.

I was never unmindful of Agnes. But when he entered, and stood before me with his hand out I felt ashamed of having doubted one I loved so heartily.

"Why, Daisy, old boy, dumb-foundered!" laughed Steerforth. His bright glance went merrily round the room, as he took the seat on the sofa opposite to me, and stirred the fire into a blaze.

"I was so surprised at first," said I, "that I had hardly breath to greet you with, Steerforth."

"Well, the sight of me *is* good for sore eyes, as the Scotch say," replied Steerforth, "and so is the sight of you, Daisy. How are you, my Bacchanal?"

"I am very well," said I; "and not at all Bacchanalian to-night, though I confess to another party of three."

"All of whom I met in the street, talking loud in your praise," returned Steerforth.

During most of this short dialogue, when he had not been speaking in a wild vivacious manner, he had sat idly beating on the lump of coal with the poker. I observed that he did the same thing while I was getting out the remains of the pigeon-pie and so forth.

"Why, Daisy, here's a supper for a king!" he exclaimed. "I shall do it justice, for I have come from Yarmouth."

"I thought you came from Oxford?"

"Not I," said Steerforth. "I have been seafaring."

"Littimer was here to-day, to inquire for you," I remarked.

"Littimer is a greater fool than I thought him, to have been inquiring for me at all," said Steerforth, jovially pouring out a glass of wine, and drinking to me.

"So you have been at Yarmouth, Steerforth! Have you been there long?"

"No," he returned. "An escapade of a week or so."

"And how are they all? Of course, little Emily is not married yet?"

"Not yet. Going to be, I believe—in so many weeks, or months, or something or other. I have not seen much of 'em. By-the-by, I have a letter for you."

"From whom?"

"Why, from your old nurse," he returned. "It's all over with poor Barkis, I am afraid. I saw a little apothecary there—surgeon, or whatever he is—who brought your worship into the world. His opinion was, that the carrier was making his last journey rather fast."

The letter was from Peggotty; something less legible than usual, and brief. While I deciphered it, Steerforth continued to eat and drink.

"It's a bad job," he said, when I had done; "but people die every minute, and we mustn't be scared by the common lot. No! Ride on! Rough-shod if need be, smooth-shod if that will do, but ride on! Ride on over all obstacles, and win the race!"

"And win what race?" said I.

"The race that one has started in," said he.

"I tell you what, Steerforth," said I, "if your high spirits will listen to me. I think I will go down and see my old nurse. It is not that I can do her any good, but she is so attached to me that it will be a comfort to her."

His face was thoughtful, and he sat considering a little before he answered, in a low voice, "Well! Go. You can do no harm."

"You have just come back," said I, "and it would be in vain to ask you to go with me?"

"Quite," he returned. "I am for Highgate to-night. I have not seen my mother this long time, and it lies upon my conscience. You mean to go to-morrow, I suppose?" he said, holding me out at arm's length, with a hand on each of my shoulders.

"Yes, I think so."

"Well, then, don't go till next day and pass as much of to-morrow as you can with us! Come! Say the next day! I want you to stand between Rosa Dartle and me, and keep us asunder."

"Would you love each other too much, without me?"

"Yes; or hate," laughed Steerforth; "Come! Say the next day!"

I said the next day; and he put on his great-coat and lighted his cigar, and set off to walk home.

I was undressing in my own room, when Mr. Micawber's

letter tumbled on the floor. It was dated an hour and a half before dinner.

"Sir—for I dare not say, my dear Copperfield:

"The undersigned is Crushed.

"The present communication is penned within the personal range of an individual in legal possession of the premises, under a distress for rent. His inventory includes, not only the chattels and effects belonging to the undersigned, but also those appertaining to Mr. Thomas Traddles, lodger.

"If any drop of gloom were wanted in the overflowing cup, it would be found in the fact, that a friendly acceptance granted to the undersigned, by the before-mentioned Mr. Thomas Traddles, for the sum of £23 4*s.* 9½*d.* is overdue, and is *not* provided for.

"It would be a work of supererogation to add, that dust and ashes are for ever scattered

"On
"The
"Head
"Of

"Wilkins Micawber."

CHAPTER XXIX

I VISIT STEERFORTH AT HIS HOME, AGAIN

I MENTIONED to Mr. Spenlow in the morning, that I wanted leave of absence for a short time; and as I was not in the receipt of any salary, and consequently was not obnoxious to the implacable Jorkins, there was no difficulty about it.

Mrs. Steerforth was pleased to see me, and so was Rosa Dartle. I was agreeably surprised to find that Littimer was not there, and that we were attended by a modest little parlour-maid, with blue ribbons in her cap. But what I particularly observed was the close and attentive watch Miss Dartle kept upon me; and the lurking manner in which she seemed to compare my face with Steerforth's, and Steerforth's with mine.

"You have been a long time," she said, "without coming here. Is your profession really so engaging and interesting as to absorb your whole attention?"

I replied that I liked it well enough, but that I certainly could not claim so much for it.

"Oh! You mean it is a little dry, perhaps?"

Well, I replied; perhaps it *was* a little dry.

"Oh! and that's the reason why you want excitement, and all that?" said she. "Ah! very true! But isn't it a little—Eh?—for him; I don't mean you?"

A quick glance of her eye towards the spot where Steerforth was walking, with his mother, showed me whom she meant; but beyond that, I was quite lost.

"Don't it make him, perhaps, a little more remiss than usual in his visits to his blindly-doting—eh?"

"It certainly is not the fact," said I, perplexed, "that I am accountable for Steerforth's having been away from home longer than usual—if he has been. I have not seen him this long while, until last night."

"No?"

"Indeed, Miss Dartle, no!"

As she looked full at me, I saw the marks of the old wound lengthen out until it cut through the disfigured lip, and down the face. There was something positively awful to me in this, and in the brightness of her eyes, as she said, looking fixedly at me:

"What is he doing?"

I repeated the words more to myself than her, being so amazed.

"What is he doing?" she said, with an eagerness that seemed enough to consume her like a fire.

"Miss Dartle," I returned, "I know of nothing in Steerforth different from what there was when I first came here. I firmly believe there is nothing."

As she still stood looking fixedly at me, a twitching or throbbing came into that cruel mark. She put her hand upon it hurriedly and saying, in a quick, fierce, passionate way, "I swear you to secrecy about this!" said not a word more.

One other little circumstance connected with Miss Dartle I must not omit. During the whole of this day, but especially at dinner, Steerforth exerted himself with his utmost skill to charm this singular creature into a pleasant and pleased companion. I saw her try, more and more faintly, but always angrily, to resist the captivating power that he possessed; and finally, I saw her smile become quite gentle and we all sat about the fire, talking and laughing together.

We did not remain in the dining-room more than five minutes after her departure. "She is playing her harp," said Steerforth, softly, at the drawing-room door, "and nobody but my mother has heard her do that, I believe, these three years." He said it with a curious smile, which

She drew it to her and played and sang.

was gone directly; and we went into the room and found her alone.

"Don't get up," said Steerforth (which she had already done); "be kind for once, and sing us an Irish song."

"What do you care for an Irish song?" she returned.

"Much!" said Steerforth. "Much more than for any other. Sing us an Irish song, Rosa! and let me sit and listen as I used to do."

He sat himself near the harp. She stood beside it for some little while. At length she sat down, and drew it to her with one sudden action, and played and sang.

I don't know what it was that made that song the most unearthly I have ever heard in my life. I was dumb when she leaned beside the harp again, playing it, but not sounding it, with her right hand.

A minute more, and Steerforth had put his arm laughingly about her, and had said, "Come, Rosa, for the future we will love each other very much!" And she had struck him, and had thrown him off with the fury of a wild cat, and had burst out of the room.

Rosa did not come back; and no mention was made of her, until I went with Steerforth into his room to say Good-night. Then I expressed my astonishment and asked if he could guess what it was that she had taken so much amiss, so suddenly.

"Oh, Heaven knows," said Steerforth. "I told you she took everything, herself included, to a grindstone, and sharpened it. She is always dangerous. Good-night!"

"Good-night!" said I, "my dear Steerforth! I shall be gone before you wake in the morning. Good-night!"

He was unwilling to let me go; and stood, holding me, with a hand on each of my shoulders.

"Daisy, if anything should ever separate us, you must think of me at my best, old boy. Come! Let us make that bargain. Think of me at my best."

I was up with the dull dawn, and having dressed as quietly as I could, looked into his room. He was fast asleep; lying, easily, with his head upon his arm, as I had often seen him asleep at school, and thus, in this silent hour, I left him.

——Never more, oh God forgive you, Steerforth! to touch that passive hand in love and friendship. Never. never, more!

CHAPTER XXX

A LOSS

I GOT down to Yarmouth in the evening, went to the inn, dined, and engaged my bed.

It was ten o'clock when I went out. Many of the shops were shut, and the town was dull. When I came to Omer and Joram's I found the shutters up, but the shop door standing open. As I could obtain a view of Mr. Omer inside, I entered, and asked him how he was.

"Why, bless my life and soul!" said Mr. Omer. "How do you find yourself? Take a seat."

Mr. Omer had placed a chair. He now sat down again, very much out of breath.

"I am sorry to have heard bad news of Mr. Barkis," said I. "Do you know how he is to-night?"

"The very question I should have put to you, Sir," returned Mr. Omer, "but on account of delicacy. It's one of the drawbacks of our line of business. When a party's ill, we *can't* ask how the party is."

The difficulty had not occurred to me. On its being mentioned I recognised it, however, and said as much. Mr. Omer, with a very complacent and amiable face then said, resuming his first point:

"Accordingly we're obleeged, in ascertaining how Barkis goes on, to limit ourselves to Em'ly. Minnie and Joram have just stepped down to the houses, in fact, (she's there, after hours, helping her aunt a bit), to ask her how he is to-night; and if you was to please to wait till they come back, they'd give you full partic'lers."

I thanked him, observing that I would wait, and inquired how little Emily was?

"Well, Sir," said Mr. Omer, "I tell you truly, I shall be glad when her marriage has taken place."

"Why so?" I inquired.

"Well, she's unsettled at present," said Mr. Omer. "It ain't that she's not as pretty as ever, for she's prettier. It ain't that she don't work as well as ever, for she does. But somehow she wants heart."

Mr. Omer's face and manner went for so much, that I could conscientiously nod my head, as divining his meaning, and he went on:

"We have talked it over a good deal, her uncle and myself, and her sweetheart and myself, and I consider it is principally on account of her being unsettled. You must always recollect of Em'ly," said Mr. Omer, shaking his head gently, "that she's a most extraordinary affectionate little thing. Well, Sir, her cousin—you know it's a cousin she's going to be married to?"

"Oh yes," I replied. "I know him well."

"Of course you do," said Mr. Omer. "Well, Sir! Her cousin being, as it appears, in good work, and well to do, went and took as comfortable a little house as you or I could wish to clap eyes on. That little house is now furnished, right through, as neat and complete as a doll's parlour; and but for Barkis's illness having taken this bad turn, poor fellow, they would have been man and wife —I dare say, by this time. As it is, there's a postponement."

"And Emily, Mr. Omer?" I inquired. "Has she become more settled?"

"Why that, you know," he returned, rubbing his double chin again, "can't naturally be expected. It's an uncertain state of matters, you see."

"I see," said I.

Mr. Omer, hearing his daughter's footstep, touched me with his pipe. She and her husband came in immediately afterwards.

Their report was, that Mr. Barkis was "as bad as bad could be!" and that Mr. Chillip had mournfully said that the College of Physicians, the College of Surgeons, and Apothecaries' Hall couldn't help him.

Hearing this, I determined to go to the house at once. My low tap at the door was answered by Mr. Peggotty. He was not so much surprised to see me as I had expected. I remarked this in Peggotty, too, when she came down, and I think, in the expectation of that dread surprise, all other changes and surprises dwindled into nothing.

I shook hands with Mr. Peggotty, and passed into the kitchen. Little Emily was sitting by the fire, with her hands before her face. Ham was standing near her.

"Em'ly, my dear," cried Mr. Peggotty. "See here! Here's Mas'r Davy come! What, cheer up, pretty! Not a wured to Mas'r Davy?"

There was a trembling upon her, that I can see now. The coldness of her hand when I touched it, I can feel yet. Then she glided from the chair, and, creeping to the other side of her uncle, bowed herself upon his breast.

"It's such a loving 'art," said Mr. Peggotty, smoothing her rich hair with his great hard hand. "It's getting late, my dear and here's Ham come fur to take you home. What, Em'ly? Eh, my pretty?"

The sound of her voice had not reached me, but he bent his head as if he listened to her, and then said:

"Let you stay with your uncle, Moppet? When your husband that'll be so soon is here fur to take you home? Now a person wouldn't think it," said Mr. Peggotty, looking round at both of us, with infinite pride; "but the sea ain't more salt in it than she has fondness in her for her uncle!"

"Em'ly's in the right in that, Mas'r Davy!" said Ham. "Lookee here! As Em'ly wishes of it, and as she's hurried and frightened, like, besides, I'll leave her till morning. Let me stay too!"

"No, no," said Mr. Peggotty. "You doen't ought to watch and work both. That won't do. You go home and turn in."

Ham yielded to this persuasion, and took his hat to go.

Even when he kissed her,—and I never saw him approach her, but I felt that nature had given him the soul of a gentleman,—she seemed to cling closer to her uncle.

"Now, I'm a going up-stairs to tell your aunt as Mas'r Davy's here, and that'll cheer her up a bit," he said. "What? You'll go along with me?—Well! come along with me—come!"

I had leisure to think, before the kitchen-fire, of pretty little Em'ly's dread of death—which, added to what Mr. Omer had told me, I took to be the cause of her being so unlike herself—before Peggotty came down.

Peggotty took me in her arms, and blessed and thanked me over and over again for being such a comfort to her. She then entreated me to come up-stairs, sobbing that Mr. Barkis had always liked me, and that she believed, in case of his coming to himself again, he would brighten up at sight of me.

The probability of his ever doing so appeared to be very small. He was lying with his head and shoulders out of bed, half resting on the box which had cost him so much pain and trouble. Time and the world were slipping from beneath him, but the box was there; and the last words he had uttered were (in an explanatory tone) "Old clothes!"

"Barkis, my dear!" said Peggotty, almost cheerfully: bending over him. "Here's my dear boy, Master Davy, that you sent messages by, you know! Won't you speak to Master Davy?"

He was as mute and senseless as the box.

"He's going out with the tide," said Mr. Peggotty to me.

I repeated in a whisper, "With the tide?"

"People can't die, along the coast," said Mr. Peggotty, "except when the tide's pretty nigh out. They can't be born, unless it's pretty nigh in. He's a going out with the tide."

We remained there, watching him, a long time. When he at last began to wander he was muttering about driving me to school.

"He's coming to himself," said Peggotty. "Barkis, my dear!"

"C. P. Barkis," he cried faintly. "No better woman anywhere!"

"Look! Here's Master Davy!" said Peggotty. For he now opened his eyes.

I was on the point of asking him if he knew me, when he tried to stretch out his arm, and said to me, distinctly, with a pleasant smile:

"Barkis is willin'!"

And, it being low water, he went out with the tide.

CHAPTER XXXI

A GREATER LOSS

It was not difficult for me, on Peggotty's solicitation, to resolve to stay where I was, until after the remains of the poor carrier should have made their last journey to Blunderstone.

I may claim the merit of having originated the suggestion that Mr. Barkis' will should be looked for in the box. After some search, it was found in there, at the bottom of a horse's nose-bag; wherein (besides hay) there was discovered an old gold watch, eighty-seven guineas and a half, two hundred and ten pounds, in perfectly clean banknotes; an old horse-shoe, a bad shilling, a piece of camphor, and an oyster-shell.

For years and years, Mr. Barkis had carried this box, on all his journeys, every day.

He had hoarded, I found, to good purpose. His property in money amounted to nearly three thousand pounds. Of this he bequeathed the interest of one thousand to Mr. Peggotty for his life; on his decease, the principal to be equally divided between Peggotty, little Emily, and me. All the rest he bequeathed to Peggotty.

I felt myself quite a proctor when I read this document aloud. I examined the will, pronounced it perfectly formal in all respects, made a pencil-mark or so in the margin, and thought it rather extraordinary that I knew so much.

In this abstruse pursuit; in making an account for Peggotty; in arranging all the affairs; and in being her adviser on every point; I passed the week before the funeral. I did not see little Emily in that interval, but they told me she was to be quietly married in a fortnight.

On the day of the funeral I walked over to Blunderstone early in the morning, and was in the churchyard when it came, attended only by Peggotty and her brother. It was very quiet. We walked about the churchyard for an hour, after all was over; and pulled some young leaves from the tree above my mother's grave.

A dread falls on me here. I cannot bear to think of what did come, upon that memorable night; of what must come again, if I go on.

We were all to meet in the old boathouse. Ham would bring Emily at the usual hour. The brother and sister would be expecting us, when the day closed in, at the fireside.

I parted from them at the wicket-gate of the churchyard and walked back towards Yarmouth. I stayed to dine at a decent alehouse, some mile or two from the Ferry, and thus the day wore away, and it was evening. Rain was falling heavily and it was a wild night; but there was a moon behind the clouds, and it was not dark.

Mr. Peggotty's house looked very comfortable indeed. Mr. Peggotty had smoked his evening pipe, and there were preparations for some supper by-and-by. In her own old place sat Peggotty, once more, looking (but for her dress) as if she had never left it. Mrs. Gummidge appeared to be fretting a little, in her old corner; and consequently looked quite natural, too.

"You're first of the lot, Mas'r Davy!" said Mr. Peggotty, with a happy face. "Sit ye down, Sir. It ain't o' no use saying welcome to you, but you're welcome, kind and hearty."

"Thank you, Mr. Peggotty, I am sure of that. Well, Peggotty!" said I, giving her a kiss. "And how are you, old woman?"

"Ha, ha!" laughed Mr. Peggotty, sitting down beside us. "There's not a woman in the wureld, Sir—as I tell her—that need to feel more easy in her mind than her! She done her dooty by the departed, and the departed know'd it; and the departed done what was right by her—and—and—and it's *all* right!"

Mrs. Gummidge groaned.

"Cheer up, my pretty mawther!" said Mr. Peggotty. Then he glanced at the Dutch clock, rose, snuffed the candle, and put it in the window.

"Theer!" said Mr. Peggotty, cheerily. "Theer we are, Missis Gummidge! Lighted up, accordin' to custom! That candle, you see," said Mr. Peggotty, "meets two objects. She says, says Em'ly, 'Theer's home!' And likewise, says Em'ly, 'My uncle's theer!' Fur if I ain't theer, I never have no light showed. At the present minute, when I see the candle sparkle up, I says to myself, 'She's a looking at it! Em'ly's a coming!'" said Mr. Peggotty, "fur here she is!"

It was only Ham.

"Wheer's Em'ly?" said Mr. Peggotty.

Ham made a motion with his head, as if she were outside. Mr. Peggotty took the light from the window and was busily stirring the fire, when Ham, who had not moved, said:

"Mas'r Davy, will you come out a minute, and see what Em'ly and me has got to show you?"

We went out. As I passed him at the door, I saw, to my astonishment and fright, that he was deadly pale. He pushed me hastily into the open air, and closed the door upon us.

"Ham! what's the matter?"

"Mas'r Davy!——" Oh, for his broken heart, how dreadfully he wept!

I was paralyzed by the sight of such grief. I could only look at him.

"Em'ly's run away! Oh, Mas'r Davy, think *how* she's run away, when I pray my good and gracious God to kill her (her that is so dear above all things) sooner than let her come to ruin and disgrace."

I saw the door move. Mr. Peggotty thrust forth his

face; and never could I forget the change that came upon it when he saw us, if I were to live five hundred years.

I remember a great wail and cry, and the women hanging about him, and we all standing in the room; I with a paper in my hand, which Ham had given me; Mr. Peggotty, with his vest torn open, his hair wild, his face and lips quite white, looking fixedly at me.

"Read it, Sir," he said, in a low shivering voice. "Slow, please."

In the midst of the silence of death, I read:

"'When you, who love me so much better than I ever have deserved, even when my mind was innocent, see this, I shall be far away.'"

"I shall be fur away," he repeated slowly. "Stop! Em'ly fur away. Well!"

"'When I leave my dear home—oh, my dear home!—it will be never to come back, unless he brings me back a lady. Oh, if you knew how my heart is torn. If even you, that I have wronged so much, could only know what I suffer! Oh, don't remember we were ever to be married—but try to think as if I died when I was little. Pray Heaven have compassion on my uncle! Tell him that I never loved him half so dear. Love some good girl, that will be true to you, and worthy of you. God bless all! My parting love to uncle. My last tears, and my last thanks, for uncle!'"

That was all.

He stood, long after I had ceased to read, still looking at me. Ham spoke to him. Mr. Peggotty was so far sensible of *his* affliction, that he wrung his hand; but, otherwise, he remained in the same state.

Slowly, at last, he moved his eyes from my face. Then he said, in a low voice:

"Who's the man?"

"Mas'r Davy!" implored Ham. "Go out a bit. You doen't ought to hear it, Sir."

I sank down in a chair, and tried to utter some reply; but my tongue was fettered.

"For some time past," Ham faltered, "there's been a

servant about here, at odd times. There's been a gen'lm'n too."

Mr. Peggotty stood fixed as before, but now looking at him.

"The servant," pursued Ham, "was seen along with—our poor girl—last night. Doen't stay, Mas'r Davy, doen't!"

I felt Peggotty's arm round my neck, but I could not have moved if the house had been about to fall upon me.

"A strange chay and hosses was outside town, this morning," Ham went on. "The servant went to it, and come from it. When he went to it again, Em'ly was nigh him. The t'other was inside."

"For the Lord's love," said Mr. Peggotty, falling back, "doen't tell me his name's Steerforth!"

"Mas'r Davy," exclaimed Ham, in a broken voice, "it ain't no fault of yourn—but his name is Steerforth, and he's a damned villain!"

Mr. Peggotty moved no more, until he seemed to wake again, all at once, and pulled down his rough coat from its peg in a corner.

"Bear a hand with this!" he said, impatiently. "Bear a hand and help me. Now give me that theer hat!"

Ham asked him whither he was going.

"I'm a going to seek my Em'ly. I'm a going, first, to stave in that theer boat, and sink it where I would have drownded *him*, if I had had one thought of what was in him! I'm a going to seek my niece."

"Where?" cried Ham.

"Anywhere! I'm a going to find my poor niece in her shame, and bring her back."

"No, no!" cried Mrs. Gummidge. "No, no, Dan'l. Seek her in a little while, but not as you are now. Sit ye down, and let us speak a word about them times when she was first an orphan, and when Ham was too, and when I was a poor widder woman, and you took me in. It'll soften your poor heart, Dan'l, for you know the promise, 'As you have done it unto one of the least of these, you have done it unto me'; and that can never fail under this roof!"

He was quite passive now; and when I heard him crying, the impulse to go down upon my knees, and ask their pardon, and curse Steerforth, yielded to a better feeling, and I cried too.

CHAPTER XXXII

THE BEGINNING OF A LONG JOURNEY

THE news of what had happened soon spread through the town. Many were hard upon her, some few were hard upon him, but towards her second father and her lover there was but one sentiment: a respect for them in their distress, which was full of gentleness and delicacy.

It was on the beach, close down by the sea, that I found those two. They looked worn; and I thought Mr. Peggotty's head was bowed in one night more than in all the years I had known him. But they were as grave and steady as the sea itself.

"We have had a mort of talk, Sir," said Mr. Peggotty to me, when we had all three walked a little while in silence, "of what we ought and doen't ought to do. But we see our course now."

"My dooty here, Sir," said Mr. Peggotty, "is done. I'm a going to seek my——" he stopped, and went on in a firmer voice: "I'm a going to seek her. That's my dooty evermore."

He shook his head when I asked him where he would seek her, and inquired if I were going to London to-morrow? I told him that I was ready.

"I'll go along with you, Sir," he rejoined, 'if you're agreeable, to-morrow."

We walked again, for a while, in silence.

"Ham," he presently resumed, "he'll hold to his present work, and go and live along with my sister. The old boat yonder——"

"Will you desert the old boat, Mr. Peggotty?"

"No, Sir, no; I doen't mean as it should be deserted. Fur from that."

We walked again for a while, as before, until he explained:

"My wishes is, Sir, as it shall look, day and night, winter and summer, as it has always looked, since she fust know'd it. If ever she should come a wandering back, and peep in, then, maybe, Mas'r Davy, seein' none but Missis Gummidge there, she might take heart to creep in, trembling, and rest her weary head where it was once so gay."

I could not speak to him in reply, though I tried.

"Every night," said Mr. Peggotty, "the candle must be stood in its old pane of glass, that if ever she should see it, it may seem to say 'Come back, my child, come back!' If ever there's a knock, Ham (partic'ler a soft knock), arter dark, at your aunt's door, doen't you go nigh it. Let it be her—not you—that sees my fallen child!"

We approached the old boat, and entered. Mrs. Gummidge was busy preparing breakfast. She took Mr. Peggotty's hat, and placed his seat for him, and spoke so comfortably and softly, that I hardly knew her.

"Dan'l, my good man," said she, "you must eat and drink, and keep up your strength. Try, that's a dear soul!"

When she had served us all she employed herself in repairing some clothes belonging to Mr. Peggotty, and neatly folding and packing them in an old oilskin bag, such as sailors carry. Meanwhile, she continued talking, in the same quiet manner:

"All times and seasons, you know, Dan'l," said Mrs. Gummidge, "I shall be allus here, and everythink will look accordin' to your wishes."

"You'll be a solitary woman I'm afeerd!" said Mr. Peggotty.

"No, no, Dan'l," she returned, "I shan't be that. Doen't you mind me. I shall have enough to do to keep a Beein' for you" (Mrs. Gummidge meant a home)—"to keep a Beein' here for any that may hap to come back, Dan'l."

What a change in Mrs. Gummidge! She was another

woman. She was so devoted, so forgetful of herself, and so regardful of the sorrow about her, that I held her in a sort of veneration. The work she did that day! toiling under weights she was quite unequal to and fagging to and fro on all sorts of unnecessary errands. In short, I left her, when I went home to Peggotty's at night, the prop and staff of Mr. Peggotty's affliction.

Peggotty—all untired by her late anxieties and sleepless nights, was at her brother's, where she meant to stay till morning. An old woman, who had been employed about the house for some weeks past, was the house's only occupant besides myself. I sent her to bed; and sat down before the kitchen fire a little while, to think about all this.

I was recalled by a knock at the door. There was a knocker upon the door, but it was not that which had made the sound. The tap was from a hand, and low down, as if it were given by a child. I opened the door; and at first looked down, to my amazement, on nothing but a great umbrella. But presently I discovered underneath it, Miss Mowcher.

"Miss Mowcher!" said I. "What is the matter?"

She motioned to me to shut the umbrella for her; and passing me hurriedly, went into the kitchen. When I had closed the door, and followed, with the umbrella in my hand, I found her sitting on the corner of the fender, swaying herself backwards and forwards, and chafing her hands upon her knees like a person in pain.

Quite alarmed, I exclaimed again, "Pray tell me, Miss Mowcher, what is the matter! are you ill?"

"My dear young soul," returned Miss Mowcher, squeezing her hands upon her heart one over the other. "I am ill here. To think that I might have known it and perhaps prevented it, if I hadn't been a thoughtless fool!"

"I am surprised," I began, "to see you so distressed and serious——" when she interrupted me.

"Yes, it's always so!" she said. "They are all surprised, these inconsiderate young people, to see any natural feeling in a little thing like me. Yes, yes, that's the way."

"It may be, with others," I returned, "but I do assure you it is not with me. I said, without consideration, what I thought."

"What can I do?" returned the little woman, standing up, and holding out her arms to show herself. "See! I must live. I do no harm. If there are people so unreflecting or so cruel, as to make a jest of me, what is left for me to do but to make a jest of myself, them, and everything? If I do so, whose fault is that? Mine?"

No. Not Miss Mowcher's, I perceived.

"I saw you in the street just now," Miss Moucher pursued, "and came after you. Do you remember what Steerforth said to me about this unfortunate girl, that time when I saw you both at the inn?"

I remembered very well, having had it in my thoughts many times that day. I told her so.

"May the Father of all Evil confound him," said the little woman, "and ten times more confound that wicked servant; but I believed it was *you* who had a boyish passion for her!"

"I?" I repeated.

"Child, child!" cried Miss Mowcher, wringing her hands impatiently, "why did you praise her so, and blush, and look disturbed?"

I could not conceal from myself that I had done this, though for a reason very different from her supposition.

"What did I know?" said Miss Mowcher. "When his man told me that 'Young Innocence' (so he called you) had set his heart upon her, and she was giddy and liked him, but his master was resolved that no harm should come of it—more for your sake than for hers—how could I *but* believe him? Oh! Oh! Oh! They were afraid of my finding out the truth," exclaimed Miss Mowcher, trotting up and down the kitchen, "because I am a sharp little thing—and they deceived me altogether, and I gave the poor unfortunate girl a letter, which I fully believed was the beginning of her ever speaking to Littimer, who was left behind on purpose!"

I stood amazed at the revelation of all this perfidy, looking at Miss Mowcher as she walked up and down the kitchen until she was out of breath.

"My country rounds," she added at length, "brought me to Norwich, Mr. Copperfield, the night before last. What I happened to find out there, about their secret way of coming and going, without you—led to my suspecting something wrong. I was here this morning. Oh, oh, oh! too late!"

"I must go," she said at last. "It's late. Now, mind!" turning back on her way to the door, and looking shrewdly at me, "I have some reason to suspect that they are gone abroad. But if ever they return, if ever any one of them returns, while I am alive, I am likely to find it out soon. Whatever I know, you shall know. If ever I can do anything to serve the poor betrayed girl, I will do it faithfully, please Heaven! And Littimer had better have a bloodhound at his back, than little Mowcher!"

I gave Miss Mowcher my hand, with a very different opinion of her from that which I had hitherto entertained, and opened the door to let her out. It was not a trifling business to get the great umbrella up, and properly balanced in her grasp; but at last I successfully accomplished this, and saw it go bobbing down the street through the rain.

In the morning I was joined by Mr. Peggotty and by my old nurse, and we went at an early hour to the coach-office, where Mrs. Gummidge and Ham were waiting to take leave of us.

"Mas'r Davy," Ham whispered, drawing me aside, while Mr. Peggotty was stowing his bag among the luggage, "his life is quite broke up. He's bound upon a voyage that'll last, on and off, all the rest of his days unless he finds what he's a seeking of. I am sure you'll be a friend to him, Mas'r Davy?"

"I will indeed," said I, shaking hands with Ham earnestly.

"Thankee. One thing furder. I'm in good employ, you know, Mas'r Davy, and money's of no use to me no more, except to live. If you can lay it out for him, I shall do my work with a better 'art. Though as to that, Sir," and he spoke very steadily, "I shall work at all times, like a man, and act the best that lays in my power."

When we got to our journey's end, our first pursuit was to look about for a little lodging for Peggotty, where her brother could have a bed. We were so fortunate as to find one, very clean and cheap, only two streets removed from me.

Mr. Peggotty had made a communication to me on the way to London for which I was not unprepared. It was, that he purposed first seeing Mrs. Steerforth. As I felt bound to assist him in this, I wrote to her that night, and I ventured to express a hope that she would not refuse to see him in his heavy trouble.

At the appointed time, we stood at the door. No Littimer appeared. The pleasanter face which had replaced his answered to our summons, and went before us to the drawing-room. Mrs. Steerforth was sitting there. Rosa Dartle glided, as we went in, from another part of the room, and stood behind her chair.

I saw, directly, in his mother's face, that she knew from himself what he had done. She sat upright in her arm-chair, with a stately, immovable, passionless air. She looked very steadfastly at Mr. Peggotty and he looked quite as steadfastly at her. Rosa Dartle's keen glance comprehended all of us. For some moments not a word was spoken. She motioned to Mr. Peggotty to be seated. He said, in a low voice, "I'd sooner stand." And this was succeeded by another silence, which she broke thus:

"I know, with deep regret, what has brought you here. What do you want of me? What do you ask me to do?"

He put his hat under his arm, and feeling in his breast for Emily's letter, took it out, unfolded it, and gave it to her.

"Please to read that, ma'am."

She read it, and returned it to him.

"'Unless he brings me back a lady,'" said Mr. Peggotty,

tracing out that part with his finger. "I come to know, ma'am, whether he will keep his wured?"

"No," she returned.

"Why not?" said Mr. Peggotty.

"It is impossible. He would disgrace himself. She is far below him."

"Raise her up!" said Mr. Peggotty.

"Since you oblige me to speak more plainly, her humble connexions would render such a thing impossible."

"Hark to this, ma'am," he returned, slowly and quietly. "You know what it is to love your child. So do I. You doen't know what it is to lose your child. I do. Save her from this disgrace, and not one of us that she's growed up among will ever look upon her pritty face again. We'll be content to let her be, to trust her to her husband,—to her little children, p'raps,—and bide the time when all of us shall be alike in quality afore our God!"

The rugged eloquence with which he spoke, was not devoid of all effect. She still preserved her proud manner, but there was a touch of softness in her voice, as she answered:

"I justify nothing. But I am sorry to repeat, it is impossible. Nothing is more certain than that it never can take place, and never will. If there is any other compensation——"

"I am looking at the likeness of the face," interrupted Mr. Peggotty, with a steady but a kindling eye, "so treacherous, that I go half wild when I think of it. If the likeness of that face don't turn to burning fire, at the thought of offering money to me for my child's blight and ruin, it's as bad."

She changed now, in a moment. An angry flush overspread her features; and she said:

"What compensation can you make to *me* for opening such a pit between me and my son?"

Miss Dartle softly touched her, and bent down her head to whisper, but she would not hear a word.

"No, Rosa, not a word! Let the man listen to what

I say! My son, who has been the object of my life—to take up in a moment with a miserable girl, and avoid me! To repay my confidence with systematic deception, for her sake, and quit me for her!"

Again Rosa Dartle tried to soothe her; again ineffectually.

"I say, Rosa, not a word! Let him put away his whim now, and he is welcome back. Let him not put her away now, and he never shall come near me, living or dying, unless, being rid of her for ever, he comes humbly to me and begs for my forgiveness."

While I heard and saw the mother as she said these words, I seemed to hear and see the son, defying them.

She now observed to me, aloud, that it was useless to hear more, or to say more. She rose to leave the room, when Mr. Peggotty signified that it was needless.

"I have no more to say, ma'am," he remarked, as he moved towards the door. "I come here with no hope, and I take away no hope. This has been too evil a house fur me and mine, fur me to be in my right senses and expect it."

We had, on our way out, to cross a paved hall, and the day being sunny, a pair of glass doors leading to the garden were thrown open. Rosa Dartle, entering this way with a noiseless step, addressed herself to me:

"You do well," she said, "indeed, to bring this fellow here!"

Such a concentration of rage and scorn as darkened her face and flashed in her jet-black eyes, I could not have thought compressible even into that face.

"This is a fellow," she said, "to champion and bring here, is he not? Why do you bring this man here?"

"He is a deeply injured man, Miss Dartle," I replied. "You may not know it."

"I know that James Steerforth has a false, corrupt heart, and is a traitor. But what need I know or care about this fellow, and his common niece?"

"Miss Dartle," I returned, "you deepen the injury. You do him a great wrong."

"I do him no wrong," she returned. "They are a depraved, worthless set. I would have her whipped!"

Mr. Peggotty passed on, without a word, and went out at the door.

"Oh, shame, Miss Dartle! shame!" I said indignantly.

"I would have his house pulled down. I would have her branded on the face, drest in rags, and cast out in the streets to starve. I detest her. If I could hunt her to her grave, I would."

The mere vehemence of her words can convey but a weak impression of the passion by which she was possessed, though her voice, instead of being raised, was lower than usual. I have seen passion in many forms, but never in such a form as that.

When I joined Mr. Peggotty, he was walking slowly and thoughtfully down the hill. He told me, as soon as I came up with him, that he meant "to set out on his travels," that night.

We went back to the little lodging and there I found an opportunity of repeating to Peggotty what he had said to me. We all three dined together off a beefsteak pie, and after dinner we sat for an hour or so without talking much. Then Mr. Peggotty got up, slung his bag about him, took his hat and stick, and bade us both "Good-bye!"

"All good attend you, dear old woman," he said, embracing Peggotty, "and you too, Mas'r Davy!" shaking hands with me. "I'm a going to seek her, fur and wide. If she should come home while I'm away, or if I should bring her back, my meaning is, that she and me shall live and die where no one can't reproach her. If any hurt should come to me, remember that the last words I left for her was, 'My unchanged love is with my darling child, and I forgive her!'"

He said this solemnly, bare-headed; then, putting on his hat, he went down the stairs, and away.

CHAPTER XXXIII

BLISSFUL

All this time I had gone on loving Dora harder than ever. My love was so much on my mind, and it was so natural to me to confide in Peggotty, that I imparted to her my great secret. Peggotty was strongly interested, but audaciously prejudiced in my favour, and quite unable to understand why I should have any misgivings. "The young lady might think herself well off," she observed, "to have such a beau. And as to her Pa," she said, "what *did* the gentleman expect, for gracious sake!"

Taking the management of Peggotty's affairs into my own hands, with no little pride, I proved Mr. Barkis's will, and soon got everything into an orderly train. Her business being settled, I took her down to the office one morning to pay her bill. Mr. Spenlow had stepped out to get a gentleman sworn for a marriage license, but I knew he would be back directly.

We were a little like undertakers, as regarded Probate transactions; generally making it a rule to look more or less cut up, when we had to deal with clients in mourning. In a similar feeling of delicacy, we were always blithe and light-hearted with the license clients. Therefore I hinted to Peggotty that she would find Mr. Spenlow much recovered from the shock of Mr. Barkis's decease; and indeed he came in like a bridegroom.

But neither Peggotty nor I had eyes for him, when we saw, in company with him, Mr. Murdstone.

"Ah, Copperfield?" said Mr. Spenlow. "You know this gentleman, I believe?"

I made my gentleman a distant bow, and Peggotty barely

recognized him. He was, at first, somewhat disconcerted to meet us two together; but quickly decided what to do, and came up to me.

"I hope," he said, "that you are doing well?"

"It can hardly be interesting to you," said I. "Yes, if you wish to know."

He addressed himself to Peggotty.

"And you," said he. "I am sorry to observe that you have lost your husband."

"It's not the first loss I have had in my life, Mr. Murdstone," replied Peggotty, trembling from head to foot. "I am glad to hope that there is nobody to blame for this one."

"Ha!" said he. "You have done your duty?"

"I have not worn anybody's life away," said Peggotty. "No, Mr. Murdstone, I have not worrited and frightened any sweet creetur to an early grave!"

He eyed her gloomily—remorsefully I thought—for an instant; and said, turning his head towards me, but looking at my feet instead of my face:

"I do not expect that you, who always rebelled against my just authority should owe me any good-will now. There is an antipathy between us——"

"An old one, I believe?" said I, interrupting him.

He smiled and shot as evil a glance at me as could come from his dark eyes.

"It rankled in your baby breast," he said. "It embittered the life of your mother. You are right. I hope you may correct yourself."

Here he ended the dialogue, which had been carried on in a low voice, paid the money for his license; and, went out of the office.

Mr. Spenlow did not appear to know what the connexion between Mr. Murdstone and myself was, which I was glad of, remembering what I did of the history of my poor mother.

"Rather a good marriage this, I believe?" said Mr. Spenlow.

I explained that I knew nothing about it.

"Indeed!" he said. "Speaking from the few words Mr. Murdstone dropped, I should say it was rather a good marriage."

"Do you mean that there is money, Sir?" I asked.

"Yes," said Mr. Spenlow, "I understand there's money. Beauty too, I am told."

"Indeed! Is his new wife young?"

"Just of age," said Mr. Spenlow. "So lately, that I should think they had been waiting for that."

"Lord deliver her!" said Peggotty. So very emphatically and unexpectedly, that we were all three discomposed. Peggotty then returned to her lodging, and Mr. Spenlow and I went into Court.

It came about that Mr. Spenlow told me this day week was Dora's birthday, and he would be glad if I would come down and join a little picnic on the occasion. I went out of my senses immediately, and passed the intervening period in a state of dotage.

I committed every possible absurdity in the way of preparation for this blessed event. I turn hot when I remember the cravat I bought. I sent down by the Norwood Coach the night before, a delicate little hamper, amounting in itself almost to a declaration. There were crackers in it with the tenderest mottoes that could be got for money. At six in the morning, I was in Covent Garden Market, buying a bouquet for Dora. At ten I was on horseback (I hired a gallant grey, for the occasion), with the bouquet in my hat, to keep it fresh, trotting down to Norwood.

I suppose that when I saw Dora in the garden and pretended not to see her, and rode past the house pretending to be anxiously looking for it, I committed two small fooleries which other young gentlemen in my circumstances might have committed. But oh! when I *did* find the house, and *did* dismount at the garden gate, what a spectacle she was, among the butterflies, in a white chip bonnet and a dress of celestial blue!

There was a young lady with her. Her name was Miss Mills, and Dora called her Julia. She was the bosom friend of Dora. Happy Miss Mills!

Jip was there, and Jip *would* bark at me again. When I presented my bouquet, he gnashed his teeth with jealousy.

"Oh, thank you, Mr. Copperfield! What dear flowers!" said Dora.

I had had an intention of saying that I thought them beautiful before I saw them so near *her*. But I couldn't manage it. She was too bewildering.

Then Dora held my flowers to Jip to smell. Then Jip growled, and wouldn't smell them. Then Dora laughed, and held them a little closer to Jip, to make him. Then Jip laid hold of a bit of geranium with his teeth, and worried imaginary cats in it. Then Dora beat him, and pouted, and said, "My poor beautiful flowers!" as compassionately, I thought, as if Jip had laid hold of me. I wished he had!

"You'll be so glad to hear, Mr. Copperfield," said Dora, "that that cross Miss Murdstone is not here. She has gone to her brother's marriage, and will be away at least three weeks. Isn't that delightful?"

I said I was sure it must be delightful to her, and all that was delightful to her was delightful to me.

"She is the most disagreeable thing I ever saw," said Dora.

But now Mr. Spenlow came out of the house and we all walked from the lawn towards the carriage.

I shall never have such a ride again. I have never had such another. There were only those three, their hamper, my hamper, and the guitar-case, in the phaeton; and, of course, the phaeton was open; and I rode behind it, and Dora sat with her back to the horses, looking towards me. The sun shone Dora, and the birds sang Dora. The south wind blew Dora, and the wild flowers in the hedges were all Doras, to a bud.

I don't know how long we were going, and to this hour

I know as little where we went. It was a green spot, on a hill, carpeted with soft turf. There were shady trees, and heather, and, as far as the eye could see, a rich landscape.

It was a trying thing to find people here, waiting for us; and my jealousy, even of the ladies, knew no bounds. But all those of my own sex—especially one impostor, three or four years my elder, with a red whisker, were my mortal foes.

We all unpacked our baskets, and employed ourselves in getting dinner ready. Red Whisker pretended he could make a salad (which I don't believe), and obtruded himself on public notice.

Red Whisker made his salad (I wondered how they could eat it. Nothing should have induced *me* to touch it!) and by-and-bye, I saw him eating his dinner at the feet of Dora!

I have but an indistinct idea of what happened for some time after this. I attached myself to a young creature in pink and flirted with her desperately.

There was a general breaking up of the party, while the remnants of the dinner were being put away; and I strolled off by myself among the trees, in a raging and remorseful state. I was debating whether I should pretend that I was not well, and fly, when Dora and Miss Mills met me.

"Mr. Copperfield," said Miss Mills, "you are dull."

"And Dora," said Miss Mills, "*you* are dull."

Oh dear no! Not in the least.

"Mr. Copperfield and Dora," said Miss Mills, "enough of this. Do not allow a trivial misunderstanding to wither the blossoms of spring."

I hardly knew what I did, but I took Dora's little hand and kissed it—and she let me! I kissed Miss Mills's hand; and we all seemed to go straight up to the seventh heaven.

We did not come down again. We stayed up there all the evening. I was happier than ever when the party broke up, and the other people went their several ways, and we went ours through the still evening and the dying light, with sweet scents rising up around us. Mr. Spenlow being fast asleep in a corner of the carriage, I rode by the side and talked to Dora.

That sagacious Miss Mills, too, what a kind thing *she* did!

"Mr. Copperfield," said Miss Mills, "come to this side of the carriage a moment,—if you can spare a moment."

Behold me, on my gallant grey, bending at the side of Miss Mills, with my hand upon the carriage door!

"Dora is coming to stay with me the day after to-morrow. If you would like to call, I am sure papa would be happy to see you."

Norwood was many miles too near, and we reached it many hours too soon; but Mr. Spenlow came to himself and said, "You must come in, Copperfield, and rest!" In the light room, Dora blushing looked so lovely, that I could not tear myself away, but sat there staring, in a dream, until the snoring of Mr. Spenlow inspired me with sufficient consciousness to take my leave. So we parted; I riding all the way to London with the farewell touch of Dora's hand still light on my own.

When I awoke next morning, I was resolute to declare my passion to Dora, and know my fate. I passed three days in a luxury of wretchedness.

At last, arrayed for the purpose at a vast expense, I went to Miss Mills's. Mr. Mills was not at home. Miss Mills was at home. Miss Mills would do.

I was shown into a room up-stairs. Jip was there. Miss Mills was copying music and Dora was painting flowers. Miss Mills was conversational for a few minutes, and then got up, and left the room.

I began to think I would put it off till to-morrow.

"I hope your poor horse was not tired," said Dora. "It was a long way for him."

I began to think I would do it to-day.

"It was a long way for *him,*" said I, "for *he* had nothing to uphold him on the journey."

I had Dora in my arms.

"Wasn't he fed, poor thing?" asked Dora.

I began to think I would put it off till to-morrow.

"Ye—yes," I said, "I mean he had not the unutterable happiness that I had in being so near you."

Dora bent her head over her drawing, and said, after a little while—I had sat, in the interval, in a burning fever—

"You didn't seem to be sensible of that happiness yourself, at one time of the day."

I saw now that it must be done on the spot.

I don't know how I did it. I had Dora in my arms. I told her how I loved her. I told her I should die without her. Jip barked madly all the time.

Well, well! Dora and I were sitting on the sofa by-and-by, quiet enough, and Jip was lying in her lap, winking peacefully at me. It was off my mind. I was in a state of perfect rapture. Dora and I were engaged.

CHAPTER XXXIV

MY AUNT ASTONISHES ME

While I had been away from home lately, Traddles had called twice or thrice. Finding Peggotty within, he had established a good-humoured acquaintance with her, and had stayed to have a little chat with her about me. So Peggotty said; but I am afraid that chat was all on her own side, and of immoderate length!

On a certain afternoon of his own appointing he punctually appeared at my door.

"My dear Traddles," said I, "I am delighted to see you at last, and very sorry I have not been at home before. But I have been so much engaged——"

"Yes, yes, I know," said Traddles, "of course. Yours lives in London, I think."

"What did you say?"

"She—excuse me—Miss D., you know," said Traddles, colouring in his great delicacy, "lives in London, I believe?"

"Oh yes. Near London."

"Mine, perhaps you recollect, lives down in Devonshire—one of ten."

"Is she the eldest?" I inquired.

"Oh dear, no," said Traddles. "The eldest is a Beauty. Not, of course, but that Sophy is beautiful too in my eyes. But when I say the eldest is a Beauty, I mean she really is a——splendid, you know," said Traddles.

"Is Sophy the youngest?" I hazarded.

"Oh dear, no!" said Traddles. "The two youngest are only nine and ten. Sophy educates 'em."

"The second daughter, perhaps?" I hazarded.

"No," said Traddles. "Sarah's the second. Sarah has

something the matter with her spine, poor girl. Sophy nurses her. Sophy's the fourth."

"Is the mother living?"

"Oh yes. But she has lost the use of her limbs. Sophy takes her place. She is quite as much a mother to her as to the other nine."

I felt the greatest admiration for the virtues of this young lady; and to prevent the good-nature of Traddles from being imposed upon, to the detriment of their joint prospects, inquired how Mr. Micawber was?

"He is quite well, Copperfield, thank you," said Traddles. "I am not living with him at present."

"No?"

"No. You see the truth is," said Traddles, in a whisper, "he has changed his name to Mortimer and he don't come out till after dark—and then in spectacles. There was an execution put into our house, for rent. I have been living in a furnished apartment since then, and the Mortimers have been very private indeed. I hope you won't think it selfish, Copperfield, if I mention that the broker carried off my little round table with the marble top, and Sophy's flower-pot and stand?"

"What a hard thing!" I exclaimed indignantly.

"It was a—it was a pull," said Traddles, with his usual wince at that expression. "Now, I have kept my eye since, upon the broker's shop," said Traddles, "and at last to-day I find them put out for sale. If the broker saw *me*, bless you, he'd ask any price for them! What has occurred to me, is, that perhaps you wouldn't object to ask that good nurse of yours to come with me to the shop—I can show it her from round the corner—and make the best bargain for them that she can!"

I told him that my old nurse would be delighted, but on one condition, that he should grant no more loans to Mr. Micawber.

"My dear Copperfield," said Traddles, "I have already done so, because I begin to feel that I have been positively unjust to Sophy. My word being passed to myself, there is no longer any apprehension; but I pledge it to you, too. That first unlucky obligation, I have paid. The second obligation is not yet due. Mr. Micawber don't tell me that it *is* provided for, but he says it *will be*."

I never shall forget Traddles peeping round the corner of the street while Peggotty was bargaining for the precious articles! The end of the negotiation was, that she bought the property on tolerably easy terms, and Traddles was transported with pleasure.

"I am very much obliged to you, indeed," said Traddles, on hearing it was to be sent that night. "If I might ask one other favour, I hope you would not think it absurd, Copperfield?"

I said beforehand, certainly not.

"Then if you *would* be good enough," said Traddles to Peggotty, "to get the flower-pot now, I think I should like (it being Sophy's, Copperfield) to carry it home myself!"

Peggotty was glad to get it for him, and he went his way carrying the flower-pot affectionately in his arms.

We then turned back towards my chambers. On our way up-stairs, we were both very much surprised to find my outer door standing open and to hear voices inside. We went into the sitting-room. What was my amazement to find my aunt and Mr. Dick! My aunt sitting on a quantity of luggage, with her two birds before her, and her cat on her knee, like a female Robinson Crusoe, drinking tea. Mr. Dick leaning thoughtfully on a great kite with more luggage piled about him!

"My dear aunt!" I cried. "Why, what an unexpected pleasure!"

We cordially embraced; and Mr. Dick and I cordially shook hands; and Mrs. Crupp, who was busy making tea cordially said she had knowed well as Mr. Copperfull would have his heart in his mouth, when he see his dear relations.

"Holloa!" said my aunt to Peggotty, who quailed before her awful presence. "How are *you?*"

"You remember my aunt, Peggotty?" said I.

"For the love of goodness, child," exclaimed my aunt, "don't call the woman by that South Sea Island name. What's your name now,—P.?"

"Barkis, ma'am," said Peggotty, with a curtsey.

"Well! That's human," said my aunt. "How d'ye do, Barkis? I hope you're well?"

"Let me draw the sofa here, or the easy chair, aunt," said I. "Why should you be so uncomfortable?"

"Thank you, Trot," replied my aunt, "I prefer to sit upon my property." Here my aunt looked hard at Mrs. Crupp, and observed, "We needn't trouble you to wait, ma'am."

"Shall I put a little more tea in the pot afore I go, ma'am?" said Mrs. Crupp.

"No, thank you, ma'am," replied my aunt.

"Would you let me fetch another pat of butter, ma'am?" said Mrs. Crupp.

"Nothing, ma'am," returned my aunt.

Mrs. Crupp, who had been incessantly smiling to express sweet temper, gradually smiled herself, one-sided herself, and rubbed herself, out of the room.

I knew my aunt sufficiently well to know that she had something of importance on her mind. As I knew she would only speak in her own good time, I sat down near her, and spoke to the birds, and played with the cat, and was as easy as I could be.

"Trot," said my aunt at last, "you needn't go, Barkis!—Trot, have you got to be firm, and self-reliant?"

"I hope so, aunt."

"What do you think?" inquired Miss Betsey.

"I think so, aunt."

"Then why, my love," said my aunt, looking earnestly at me, "why do you think I prefer to sit upon this property of mine to-night?"

I shook my head, unable to guess.

"Because," said my aunt, "it's all I have. Because I'm ruined, my dear!"

If the house, and every one of us, had tumbled out into

the river together, I could hardly have received a greater shock. I was roused from my amazement by her falling on my neck and crying that she only grieved for me. In another moment she suppressed this emotion; and said with an aspect more triumphant than dejected:

"We must meet reverses boldly. We must learn to act the play out. We must live misfortune down, Trot!"

CHAPTER XXXV

DEPRESSION

As soon as I could recover my presence of mind, I proposed to Mr. Dick to take possession of the bed which Mr. Peggotty had lately vacated. I tried to ascertain whether Mr. Dick had any understanding of the causes of this sudden and great change in my aunt's affairs. As I might have expected, he had none at all. The only account he could give of it, was, that my aunt had said to him, "Now, Dick, are you really and truly the philosopher I take you for?" That then he had said, Yes, he hoped so. That then my aunt had said, "Dick, I am ruined." That then he had said, "Oh, indeed!" That then my aunt had praised him highly. And that then they had come to me, and had had bottled porter and sandwiches on the road.

Mr. Dick was so very complacent that I am sorry to say I was provoked into explaining to him that ruin meant distress, want, and starvation; but, I was soon bitterly reproved by seeing his face turn pale while he fixed upon me a look of such unutterable woe, that it might have softened a far harder heart than mine. I took infinitely greater pains to cheer him up again than I had taken to depress him, but the fright I had given him proved too much for his best attempt at concealment. All the evening his eyes wandered to my aunt's face, with an expression of the most dismal apprehension, as if he saw her growing thin on the spot. I detected him in the act of pocketing fragments of his bread and cheese; I have no doubt for the purpose of reviving us with those savings, when we should have reached an advanced stage of attenuation.

My aunt, on the other hand, was in a composed frame of mind. She was to have my bed, and I was to lie in the sitting-room, to keep guard over her.

"Trot, my dear," said my aunt, when she saw me making preparations for compounding her usual night-draught, "not wine, my dear. Ale."

"But there is wine here, aunt."

"Keep that, in case of sickness," said my aunt. "Ale for me."

My aunt being resolute, I went out and got the ale myself. I parted from Mr. Dick at the corner of the street, with his kite at his back, a monument of misery.

My aunt was walking up and down the room when I returned. I warmed the ale and made the toast. When it was ready for her, she was ready for it, with her night-cap on, and the skirt of her gown turned back on her knees.

"Trot," said she, "I don't care for strange faces in general, but I rather like that Barkis of yours, do you know!"

"It's better than a hundred pounds to hear you say so!" said I.

"Barkis is uncommonly fond of you, Trot. The poor fool has been begging and praying about handing over some of her money—because she has got too much of it. A simpleton!" she put her tumbler on my knee and said: "Oh, Trot, Trot! And so you fancy yourself in love! Do you?"

"Fancy, aunt!" I exclaimed, as red as I could be. "I adore her!"

"Dora, indeed!" returned my aunt. "And you mean to say the little thing is very fascinating, I suppose?"

"My dear aunt," I replied, "no one can form the least idea what she is!"

"Ah! And not silly?" said my aunt.

"Silly, aunt!"

I made her toast.

It had never once entered my head for a moment, to consider whether she was or not.

"Well, well!" said my aunt. "I only ask. And so you think you are to go through a party-supper-table kind of life, like two pretty pieces of confectionery, do you, Trot?"

She asked me this so kindly, and with such a gentle air, half playful and half sorrowful, that I was quite touched.

"We are young and inexperienced, aunt, I know," I replied. "But we love one another truly. If I thought Dora could ever love anybody else, or cease to love me; or that I could ever love anybody else, or cease to love her; I don't know what I should do—go out of my mind, I think!"

"Ah, Trot!" said my aunt, shaking her head, and smiling gravely, "Blind, blind, blind!"

"However," she continued, "though it is a girl and boy attachment, we'll be serious about it. There's time enough for it to come to anything!"

This was not very comforting to a rapturous lover; but I was glad to have my aunt in my confidence, and after a tender good-night she took her nightcap into my bedroom.

How miserable I was, when I lay down! How I thought and thought about being poor; about the chivalrous necessity of telling Dora and releasing her from her engagement; about how I should contrive to live during the long term of my articles; about doing something to assist my aunt, and seeing no way of doing anything; about coming down to wear a shabby coat, and to be able to carry Dora no little presents, and to ride no gallant greys! How exceedingly miserable I was, that night!

There was an old Roman bath in those days at the bottom of one of the streets out of the Strand—in which I have had many a cold plunge. Dressing myself as quietly as I could, and leaving Peggotty to look after my aunt, I tumbled head foremost into it, and then went for a walk to Hampstead. I had a hope that this brisk treatment might freshen my wits a little; and I think it did them good, for I soon came to the conclusion that the first step I ought to take was to try if my articles could be cancelled and the premium recovered.

I arrived at the office so soon that I had half an hour's loitering about the Commons, before Mr. Spenlow came in, crisp and curly.

"How are you, Copperfield?" said he. "Fine morning!"

"Beautiful morning, Sir," said I. "Could I say a word to you before you go into Court?"

"By all means," said he. "Come into my room."

"I am sorry to say," said I, "that I have some rather disheartening intelligence from my aunt. She has met with some large losses. In fact, she has very little left, indeed."

"You as-tound me, Copperfield!" cried Mr. Spenlow.

I shook my head. "Indeed, Sir," said I, "her affairs are so changed, that I wished to ask you whether it would be possible—at a sacrifice on our part of some portion of the premium, of course," I put in this, on the spur of the moment—"to cancel my articles?"

"I am extremely sorry to hear this, Copperfield," said Mr. Spenlow. "Extremely sorry. It is not usual to cancel articles for any such reason. It is not a convenient precedent at all. At the same time——"

"You are very good, Sir," I murmured, anticipating a concession.

"Not at all," said Mr. Spenlow. "At the same time, I was going to say, if I had not a partner—Mr. Jorkins——"

My hopes were dashed in a moment, but I made another effort.

"Do you think Sir," said I, "if I were to mention it to Mr. Jorkins——"

Mr. Spenlow shook his head discouragingly. "Mr. Jorkins is *not* a man to respond to a proposition of this peculiar nature. You know what he is!"

I am sure I knew nothing about him, except that he came very late of a day, and went away very early; that he never appeared to be consulted about anything; and that he had a dingy little black-hole of his own up-stairs, where no business was ever done.

"Would you object to my mentioning it to him, Sir?" I asked.

"By no means," said Mr. Spenlow. "I cannot have the least objection to your mentioning it to Mr. Jorkins, Copperfield, if you think it worth while."

Availing myself of this permission, I went up to Mr. Jorkins's room, and evidently astonished Mr. Jorkins very much.

"Come in, Mr. Copperfield," said Mr. Jorkins. "Come in!"

I went in, and sat down; and stated my case. Mr. Jorkins was not by any means the awful creature one might have expected, but a large, mild, smooth-faced man of sixty.

"You have mentioned this to Mr. Spenlow, I suppose?" said Mr. Jorkins.

I answered Yes.

"He said I should object?" asked Mr. Jorkins.

I was obliged to admit that Mr. Spenlow had considered it probable.

"I am sorry to say, Mr. Copperfield, I can't advance your object," said Mr. Jorkins, nervously. "The fact is—but I have an appointment at the Bank."

With that he rose in a great hurry, when I made bold to say that I feared, then, there was no way of arranging the matter?"

"No!" said Mr. Jorkins. "Oh, no! I object, you know. If Mr. Spenlow objects——"

"Personally, he does not object, Sir," said I.

"Oh! Personally!" repeated Mr. Jorkins, in an impatient manner. "I assure you there's an objection, Mr. Copperfield. I—I really have got an appointment at the Bank." With that he fairly ran away; and it was three days before he showed himself in the Commons again.

I waited until Mr. Spenlow came in, and then described what had passed; giving him to understand that I was not hopeless of his being able to soften the adamantine Jorkins.

"Copperfield," returned Mr. Spenlow, with a gracious smile, "Mr. Jorkins has a way of stating his objections which often deceives people. No, Copperfield!" shaking his head. "Mr. Jorkins is not to be moved, believe me!"

I was completely bewildered between Mr. Spenlow and Mr. Jorkins, but I saw with sufficient clearness that there was obduracy somewhere in the firm, and that the recovery of my aunt's thousand pounds was out of the question. In a state of despondency I left the office, and went homeward.

I was trying to familiarise my mind with the worst, when a hackney chariot stopping at my very feet, occasioned me to look up. The face I had never seen without a feeling of serenity and happiness was smiling on me.

"Agnes!" I joyfully exclaimed. "Oh, my dear Agnes, of all people in the world, what a pleasure to see you!"

"Is it, indeed?" she said, in her cordial voice.

"Where are you going?"

She was going to my rooms to see my aunt. The day being very fine, I dismissed the coachman, and we walked on together. She was like Hope embodied, to me. She was not alone, she said. Her papa was with her—and Uriah Heep.

"Does he exercise the same influence over Mr. Wickfield still, Agnes?"

Agnes shook her head. "There is such a change at home," said she. "They live with us now."

"They?" said I.

"Mr. Heep and his mother. The chief evil of their presence in the house," said Agnes, "is that I cannot be as near papa as I could wish, and cannot watch over him, if that is not too bold a thing to say, as closely as I would."

We found my aunt alone and she received us with unimpaired good humour. We began to talk about her losses, and I told them what I had tried to do that morning.

"Which was injudicious, Trot," said my aunt, "but well meant. You are a generous boy and I am proud of you, my dear. So far so good. Now, Trot and Agnes, let us look the case of Betsey Trotwood in the face, and see how it stands."

"Betsey Trotwood," said my aunt, "had a certain property. She thought she was wiser, now, than her man of business, who was not such a good man of business by this time, as he used to be—I am alluding to your father, Agnes—and she took it into her head to lay it out for herself. So she took her pigs," said my aunt, "to a foreign market; and a very bad market it turned out to be. First, she lost in the mining way, and then she lost in the diving way, and then she lost in the mining way again, and, last of all, to set the thing entirely to rights, she lost in the banking way. Least said, soonest mended."

"Dear Miss Trotwood, is that all the history?" said Agnes.

"I hope it's enough, child," said my aunt. "If there had been more money to lose I dare say Betsey would have contrived to throw that after the rest. But, there was no more money, and there's no more story."

"Is that all?" repeated my aunt. "Why, yes, that's all, except 'And she lived happy ever afterwards.' Perhaps I may add that of Betsey yet, one of these days. Now, Agnes, you have a wise head. So have you, Trot, in some things. What's to be done? Here's the cottage, will produce, say seventy pounds a-year. Well!—That's all we've got."

"Then," said my aunt, after a rest, "there's Dick. He's good for a hundred a year, but of course that must be expended on himself. How can Trot and I do best, upon our means? What do you say, Agnes?"

Agnes inquired if my rooms were held for any long term?

"They are not to be got rid of, for six months at least," said my aunt. "I have a little ready money; and I agree with you, the best thing we can do, is to live the term out here, and get Dick a bedroom hard by."

"I have been thinking, Trotwood," said Agnes, diffidently, "that if you had time——"

"I have a good deal of time, Agnes. I have abundance of time."

"I know you would not mind," said Agnes, "the duties of a secretary. Dr. Strong has come to live in London;

and he asked papa, I know, if he could recommend him one."

I was scarcely more delighted with the prospect of earning my own bread, than with the hope of earning it under my old master; in short, acting on the advice of Agnes, I sat down and wrote a letter to the Doctor, stating my object, and appointing to call on him next day at ten in the forenoon. This I went and posted, myself, without losing a minute.

When I came back, I found my aunt's birds hanging, just as they had hung so long in the parlour window of the cottage, and even the round green fan screwed on to the window-sill. I knew who had done all this, by its seeming to have quietly done itself, and I was thinking how little even Peggotty seemed to do with a good deal of bustle, and how much Agnes did without any bustle at all, when a knock came at the door.

"I think," said Agnes, turning pale, "it's papa."

I opened the door, and admitted, not only Mr. Wickfield, but Uriah Heep. I had not seen Mr. Wickfield for some time. I was prepared for a great change in him, but his appearance shocked me.

It was not that he had lost his good looks, or his old bearing of a gentleman—for that he had not—but the thing that struck me most was, that with the evidences of his native superiority still upon him, he should submit himself to that crawling impersonation of meanness, Uriah Heep.

He appeared to be only too conscious of it himself. When he came in, he stood still; and with his head bowed.

"Well, Wickfield!" said my aunt; and he looked up at her. "I have been telling your daughter how well I have been disposing of my money for myself, because I couldn't trust it to you. Agnes is worth the whole firm, in my opinion."

"If I may umbly make the remark," said Uriah Heep, with a writhe, "I fully agree with Miss Betsey Trotwood, and should be only too appy if Miss Agnes was a partner."

"You're a partner yourself, you know," returned my aunt, "and that's about enough for you, I expect. How do you find yourself, Sir?"

Mr. Heep, uncomfortably clutching the blue bag he carried, replied that he was pretty well, he thanked my aunt, and hoped she was the same.

"And you, Master—I should say, Mister Copperfield," pursued Uriah, "I hope I see you well!"

Here he shook hands with me: standing at a good distance, and lifting my hand up and down like a pump-handle.

"And how do you think we are looking, Master Copperfield,—I should say, Mister?" fawned Uriah. "Years don't tell much in our firm, Master Copperfield, except in raising up the umble, and in developing," he added, as an afterthought, "the beautiful, namely, Miss Agnes."

"Uriah Heep," said Mr. Wickfield, in a monotonous forced way, "is active in the business, Trotwood."

"Oh, what a reward it is," said Uriah, drawing up one leg, "to be so trusted in!"

"Uriah Heep is a great relief to me," said Mr. Wickfield, in the same dull voice. "It's a load off my mind, Trotwood, to have such a partner."

"You are not going, papa?" said Agnes anxiously. "Will you not walk back with Trotwood and me?"

"I am bespoke myself," said Uriah, "on business. But I leave my partner to represent the firm. Miss Agnes, ever yours! I wish you good-day, Master Copperfield, and leave my umble respects to Miss Betsey Trotwood."

With these words he retired, kissing his great hand, and leering at us like a mask.

CHAPTER XXVI

ENTHUSIASM

I BEGAN the next day with another dive into the Roman bath, and then started for Highgate. I was not dispirited now. My whole manner of thinking of our late misfortune was changed. What I had to do, was, to show my aunt that her past goodness to me had not been thrown away; by going to work with a resolute and steady heart.

When I approached the Doctor's cottage, I saw him walking in the garden at the side, gaiters and all, as if he had never left off walking since the days of my pupilage. I made bold to open the gate and walk after him, so as to meet him when he should turn round. When he did, and came towards me, he looked at me thoughtfully for a few moments, evidently without thinking about me at all; and then his benevolent face expressed extraordinary pleasure, and he took me by both hands.

"Why, my dear Copperfield," said the Doctor; "you are a man! How do you do? I am delighted to see you!"

I hoped he was well, and Mrs. Strong too.

"Oh dear, yes!" said the Doctor; "Annie's quite well, and she'll be delighted to see you. You were always her favourite. And—yes, to be sure—you recollect Mr. Jack Maldon, Copperfield?"

"Perfectly, Sir."

"Of course," said the Doctor. "To be sure. *He's* pretty well, too."

"Has he come home, Sir?" I inquired.

"From India?" said the Doctor. "Yes. Mr. Jack Maldon couldn't bear the climate, my dear. Mrs. Markleham—you have not forgotten Mrs. Markleham?"

Forgotten the Old Soldier! And in that short time!

"Mrs. Markleham," said the Doctor, "was quite vexed about him, poor thing; so we have got him at home again; and we have bought him a little Patent place, which agrees with him much better."

I knew enough of Mr. Jack Maldon to suspect from this account that it was a place where there was not much to do, and which was pretty well paid. The Doctor, walking up and down with his hand on my shoulder, and his kind face turned encouragingly to mine, went on:

"Now, my dear Copperfield, in reference to this proposal of yours, don't you think you could do better? You achieved distinction, you know, when you were with us. You are qualified for many good things."

I became very glowing and urged my request strongly:

"Well, well," said the Doctor. "But, my good young friend, what's seventy pounds a year?"

"It doubles our income, Doctor Strong," said I.

"Dear me!" replied the Doctor. "To think of that!"

"My dear tutor, if you will take my mornings and evenings, and can think it worth seventy pounds a year, you will do me such a service as I cannot express."

"Dear me!" said the Doctor, innocently. "Dear, dear! And when you can do better, you will? On your word, now?"

"On my word, Sir!" I returned, answering in our old school manner.

"Then be it so," said the Doctor.

"And I shall be twenty times happier, Sir," said I, with —I hope innocent—flattery, "if my employment is to be on the Dictionary."

The Doctor stopped, smilingly clapped me on the shoulder again, and exclaimed, "My dear young friend, you have hit it. It *is* the Dictionary!"

How could it be anything else! His pockets were as full of it as his head. It was sticking out of him in all directions.

Our plans being thus arranged to our mutual satisfaction,

the Doctor took me into the house to present me to Mrs. Strong. They had postponed their breakfast on my account, and we sat down together. We had not been seated long, before a gentleman on horseback came to the gate, and came into the breakfast parlour, whip in hand. It was Mr. Jack Maldon; and he was not at all improved by India, I thought.

"Mr. Jack!" said the Doctor. "Copperfield!"

Mr. Jack Maldon shook hands with me with an air of languid patronage.

"Have you breakfasted, Mr. Jack?" said the Doctor.

"I hardly ever take breakfast, Sir," he replied, with his head thrown back in an easy chair. "I find it bores me."

"Is there any news to-day?" inquired the Doctor.

"Nothing at all, Sir," replied Mr. Maldon. "There's a long statement, Sir, about a murder, but somebody is always being murdered and I didn't read it."

"I came out to inquire whether Annie would like to go to the opera to-night," said Mr. Maldon, turning to her.

The Doctor, ever pleased with what was likely to please his young wife, turned to her and said:

"You must go, Annie. You must go."

"I would rather not," she said to the Doctor. "I would much rather remain at home."

Without looking at her cousin, she then addressed me, and asked me about Agnes, and whether she should see her, and was so much disturbed, that I wondered how even the Doctor, buttering his toast, could be blind to what was so obvious.

But he saw nothing. He told her, good-naturedly, that she was young and ought to be amused. Moreover, he said, he wanted to hear her sing all the new songs to him; and how could she do that well, unless she went? So the Doctor persisted in making the engagement for her, and Mr. Jack Maldon was to come back to dinner.

I was curious to find out next morning, whether she had been. She had not, but had gone out in the afternoon to see Agnes, and had prevailed upon the Doctor to go with her; and they had walked home by the fields, the Doctor told me, the evening being delightful.

I was pretty busy now; up at five in the morning, and home at nine or ten at night. But I had infinite satisfaction in being so closely engaged, and felt enthusiastically that the more I tired myself, the more I was doing to deserve Dora. She was coming to see Miss Mills in a few days, and I deferred all I had to tell her until then; merely informing her in my letters (all our communications were secretly forwarded through Miss Mills), that I had much to tell her.

Burning with impatience to do something more, I went to see Traddles. I took Mr. Dick with me, because he had begun to fret and worry himself out of spirits and appetite, as having nothing useful to do. In this condition, he felt more incapable of finishing the Memorial than ever; and the harder he worked at it, the oftener that unlucky head of King Charles the First got into it. Seriously apprehending that his malady would increase, unless we caused him to believe that he was useful, or put him in the way of being really useful, I made up my mind to try if Traddles could help us.

We found him hard at work with his inkstand and papers. He received us cordially, and made friends with Mr. Dick in a moment.

The first subject on which I had to consult Traddles was this.—I had heard that many men distinguished in various pursuits had begun life by reporting the debates in Parliament, and I wished to know how I could qualify myself for this pursuit. Traddles now informed me that a perfect command of the mystery of shorthand was about equal in difficulty to the mastery of six languages. Traddles reasonably supposed that this would settle the business; but I said, "I'll begin to-morrow."

Traddles looked astonished, as he well might.

"I'll buy a book," said I. "I'll work at it at the Commons, where I haven't half enough to do—Traddles, my dear fellow, I'll master it!"

"Dear me," said Traddles, opening his eyes, "I had no idea you were such a determined character, Copperfield!"

I don't know how he should have had, for it was new enough to me. I passed that off, and brought Mr. Dick on the carpet.

"You see," said Mr. Dick, wistfully, "if I could exert myself, Mr. Traddles—if I could beat a drum—or blow anything!"

Traddles, who would not have smiled for the world, replied composedly: "But you are a very good penman, Sir. You told me so, Copperfield?"

"Excellent!" said I. And indeed he was.

"Don't you think," said Traddles, "you could copy writings, Sir?"

Mr. Dick looked doubtfully at me. "Eh, Trotwood?"

I shook my head. Mr. Dick shook his, and sighed. "Tell him about the Memorial," said Mr. Dick.

I explained to Traddles that there was a difficulty in keeping King Charles the First out of Mr. Dick's manuscripts.

"But these writings, you know, that I speak of, are already finished," said Traddles. "Wouldn't that make a difference?"

This gave us new hope, and Traddles and I concocted a scheme in virtue of which we got him to work next day, with triumphant success.

On a table by the window we set out the work Traddles procured for him—which was to make, I forget how many copies of a legal document—and on another table we spread the last unfinished Memorial. Our instructions to Mr. Dick were that he should copy exactly what he had before him and that when he felt it necessary to make the slightest allusion to King Charles the First, he should fly to the Memorial. My aunt reported to us, afterwards, that, at first, he was like a man playing the kettle-drums, and constantly divided his attentions between the two; but that having his copy there, plainly before his eyes, he soon sat at it in an orderly business-like manner, and postponed the

Memorial to a more convenient time. In a word, he earned by the following Saturday night ten shillings and ninepence; and never shall I forget his going about to all the shops in the neighborhood to change this treasure into sixpences, or his bringing them to my aunt arranged in the form of a heart upon a waiter.

"No starving now, Trotwood," said Mr. Dick. "I'll provide for her, Sir!" and he flourished his ten fingers in the air, as if they were ten banks.

I hardly know which was the better pleased, Traddles or I. "It really," said Traddles, suddenly, taking a letter out of his pocket, and giving it to me, "put Mr. Micawber quite out of my head!"

The letter ran thus:

"My dear Copperfield,

"You may possibly not be unprepared to receive the intimation that something has turned up.

"I am about to establish myself in one of the provincial towns in immediate connexion with one of the learned professions.

"In bidding adieu to the modern Babylon, Mrs. Micawber and myself cannot disguise from our minds that we part with an individual linked to the altar of our domestic life. If, on the eve of such a departure, you will accompany our mutual friend, Mr. Thomas Traddles, to our present abode you will confer a Boon

"On

"One

"Who

"Is

"Ever yours,

"Wilkins Micawber."

Learning from Traddles that the invitation referred to the evening then wearing away, we went off together to the lodging which Mr. Micawber occupied as Mr. Mortimer.

The resources of this lodging were so limited that we found the twins, now some eight or nine years old, reposing in a turn-up bedstead in the family sitting-room, where Mr. Micawber had prepared, in a wash-stand jug, the agreeable beverage for which he was famous.

"My dear Copperfield," said Mr. Micawber, "yourself and Mr. Traddles find us on the brink of migration, and will excuse any little discomforts incidental to that position."

I congratulated Mrs. Micawber on the approaching change.

"My dear Mr. Copperfield," said Mrs. Micawber, "of your friendly interest in all our affairs, I am well assured. My family may consider it banishment, if they please; but I am a wife and mother, and I never will desert Mr. Micawber."

"My dear," said Mr. Micawber, a little impatiently, "I am not conscious that you are expected to do anything of the sort."

"It may be a sacrifice," said Mrs. Micawber, "to immure one's self in a Cathedral town; but surely Mr. Copperfield, if it is a sacrifice in me, it is much more a sacrifice in a man of Mr. Micawber's abilities."

"Oh! You are going to a Cathedral town?" said I.

Mr. Micawber replied:

"To Canterbury. In fact, my dear Copperfield, I stand pledged and contracted to our friend Heep, to assist and serve him in the capacity of—and to be—his confidential clerk."

I stared at Mr. Micawber, who greatly enjoyed my surprise.

"I am bound to state to you," he said, "that the prudent suggestions of Mrs. Micawber have conduced to this result. The gauntlet being thrown down in the form of an advertisement, was taken up by my friend Heep, and led to a mutual recognition. My friend Heep has not fixed the positive remuneration at too high a figure, but he has made a great deal contingent on the value of my services; and on the value of those services, I pin my faith."

When we were nearly come to the last round of the punch, I addressed myself to Traddles, and reminded him that we must not separate, without wishing our friends health, happiness, and success in their new career.

Sixpences arranged in the form of a heart.

"My dear Copperfield," said Mr. Micawber, rising with one of his thumbs in each of his waistcoat pockets,—"and my esteemed friend Traddles—will allow me, on the part of Mrs. Micawber, myself, and our offspring, to thank them in the warmest terms." He then said with much solemnity:

"One thing more I have to do. My friend Mr. Thomas Traddles has, on two several occasions, 'put his name,' if I may use a common expression, to bills of exchange. To leave this metropolis, without acquitting myself of the pecuniary part of this obligation, would weigh upon my mind to an insupportable extent. I therefore beg to hand to my friend Mr. Thomas Traddles my I.O.U. for forty-one, ten, eleven, and a half."

With this introduction, Mr. Micawber placed his I.O.U. in the hands of Traddles, and I am persuaded, not only that this was quite the same to Mr. Micawber as paying the money, but that Traddles himself hardly knew the difference until he had had time to think about it.

CHAPTER XXXVII

A LITTLE COLD WATER

My new life had lasted for more than a week, and I was stronger than ever in those tremendous practical resolutions that I felt the crisis required.

As yet, little Dora was quite unconscious of my desperate firmness, but, another Saturday came, and on that Saturday evening she was to be at Miss Mills's; I was to go there to tea.

By this time, we were quite settled down in Buckingham Street, where Mr. Dick continued his copying in a state of absolute felicity.

My aunt, being uncommonly neat and ingenious, made so many little improvements in our domestic arrangements, that I seemed to be richer instead of poorer.

Peggotty had considered herself highly privileged in being allowed to participate in these labours, but the time had now come (I am speaking of the Saturday when I was to take tea at Miss Mills's) when it was necessary for her to return home. "So good bye, Barkis," said my aunt, "and take care of yourself! I am sure I never thought I could be sorry to lose you!"

I took Peggotty to the coach-office and saw her off. She cried at parting, and confided her brother to my friendship as Ham had done. We had heard nothing of him since he went away, that sunny afternoon.

"And now, my own dear Davy," said Peggotty, "if, you should want any money to spend; or if you should want any to set you up, who has such a good right to ask leave to lend it you as stupid me!"

"And, my dear!" whispered Peggotty, "tell the pretty little angel that before she marries my boy, I'll come and make your house so beautiful for you, if you'll let me!"

I declared that nobody else should touch it; and this gave Peggotty such delight, that she went away in good spirits.

At the appointed time in the evening I repaired to Mr. Mills's. Dora came to the drawing-room door to meet me; and Jip came scrambling out, tumbling over his own growls, and we all three went in, as happy and loving as could be. I soon carried desolation into the bosom of our joys—not that I meant to do it, but that I was so full of the subject—by asking Dora, without the smallest preparation, if she could love a beggar?

My pretty, little, startled Dora! Her only association with the word was a pair of crutches, or a wooden leg, or something of that kind; and she stared at me with the most delightful wonder.

"How can you ask me anything so foolish?"

"Dora, my own dearest!" said I. "*I* am a beggar!"

"I declare I'll make Jip bite you!" said Dora, shaking her curls, "if you are so ridiculous."

But I looked so serious, that Dora began to cry. That was dreadful. I fell upon my knees before the sofa, caressing her, and imploring her not to rend my heart; but, for some time, poor little Dora did nothing but exclaim Oh dear! oh dear! And oh, she was so frightened!

At last I got Dora to look at me. Then I told her how I loved her, so dearly, and so dearly; how I felt it right to offer to release her from her engagement, because now I was poor; how I was already working with a courage such as none but lovers knew; how a crust well-earned was sweeter far than a feast inherited; and much more to the same purpose.

"Is your heart mine still, dear Dora?" said I, rapturously.

"Oh, yes!" cried Dora. "Oh, yes, it's all yours. Oh, don't talk about being poor, and working hard! Oh, don't, don't!"

"My dearest love," said I, "the crust well-earned——"

"Oh, yes; but I don't want to hear any more about crusts!" said Dora. "And Jip must have a mutton-chop every day at twelve, or he'll die!"

I was charmed. I fondly explained to Dora that Jip should have his mutton-chop with his accustomed regularity. I drew a picture of our frugal home, and my aunt in her room up-stairs.

"I am not dreadful now, Dora?" said I, tenderly.

"Oh, no, no!" cried Dora. "But I hope your aunt will keep in her own room a good deal. And I hope she's not a scolding old thing!"

If it were possible for me to love Dora more than ever, I am sure I did. But I felt she was a little impracticable. It damped my newborn ardour, to find that ardour so difficult of communication to her. When she was quite herself again, and was curling Jip's ears, as he lay upon her lap, I became grave, and said:

"My own! May I mention something?"

"Oh, please don't be practical!" said Dora coaxingly. "Because it frightens me so!"

"My love, perseverance and strength of character will enable us to bear much worse things."

"But I haven't got any strength at all," said Dora, shaking her curls. "Have I, Jip? Oh, do kiss Jip, and be agreeable!"

It was impossible to resist kissing Jip, when she held him up to me. I did as she bade me—rewarding myself afterwards—and she charmed me out of my graver character for I don't know how long.

"But, Dora, my beloved!" said I, at last resuming it; "if you will sometimes think—not despondingly, you know—that you are engaged to a poor man——"

"Don't, don't! Pray don't!" cried Dora. "It's so very dreadful!"

"My soul, not at all!" said I cheerfully. "If you will sometimes think of that, and endeavour to acquire a little habit—of accounts, for instance——"

Poor little Dora received this suggestion with something that was half a sob and half a scream.

"—It would be so useful to us afterwards," I went on. "And if you would promise me to read a little Cookery Book that I would send you, it would be so excellent for both of us. For our path in life, my Dora," said I, "is stony and rugged now. We must fight our way onward."

I was going on at a great rate, but it was quite unnecessary. I had done it again. I thought I had killed her, this time. I sprinkled water on her face. I implored her forgiveness. I did every wild extravagance that could be done, and was a long way beyond the end of my wits when Miss Mills came into the room.

"Who has done this!" exclaimed Miss Mills.

I replied, "*I*, Miss Mills! *I* have done it!" and hid my face in the sofa cushion.

At first Miss Mills thought it was a quarrel, but she soon ascertained from me in a few words what it was all about, comforted Dora, and so brought us together in peace. When we were quite composed, and Dora had gone up-stairs to put some rose-water to her eyes, Miss Mills rang for tea. In the ensuing interval, I told Miss Mills that she was evermore my friend.

I then put it to Miss Mills, to say whether she considered that there was or was not any practical merit in the suggestion concerning the accounts, the housekeeping, and the Cookery Book?

Miss Mills, after some consideration, thus replied: "Mr. Copperfield, I will be plain with you. No. The suggestion is not appropriate to our Dora. Our dearest Dora is a thing of light, and airiness, and joy. I am free to confess that if it could be done, it might be well, but——" And Miss Mills shook her head.

I was encouraged by this closing admission to ask her if she would take charge of the Cookery Book; and, if she ever could insinuate it upon Dora's acceptance, without frightening her, undertake to do me that crowning service. Miss Mills accepted this trust, but was not sanguine.

And Dora returned, looking such a lovely little creature, that I really doubted whether she ought to be troubled with anything so ordinary. And she loved me so much, and was so captivating that I felt like a sort of Monster who had got into a Fairy's bower, when I thought of having frightened her, and made her cry.

After tea we had the guitar; and Dora sang those same dear old French songs about the impossibility of ever on any account leaving off dancing, La ra la, La ra la, until I felt a much greater Monster than before.

Well! I loved her, and I went on loving her, most absorbingly, entirely, and completely. But going on, too, working pretty hard, I would sit sometimes thinking how I had frightened Dora that time, until I used to fancy that my head was turning quite gray.

CHAPTER XXXVIII

A DISSOLUTION OF PARTNERSHIP

I DID not allow my resolution, with respect to the Parliamentary Debates, to cool. I bought an approved scheme of the noble art and mystery of stenography and plunged into a sea of perplexity that brought me, in a few weeks, to the confines of distraction. The changes that were rung upon dots and circles; the marks like flies' legs; the tremendous effects of a curve in a wrong place; not only troubled my waking hours, but reappeared before me in my sleep. When I had groped my way, blindly, through these difficulties, there then appeared a procession of new horrors, called arbitrary characters. When I had fixed these wretches in my mind, I found that they had driven everything else out of it; then, beginning again, I forgot them; while I was picking them up, I dropped the other fragments; in short, it was almost heart-breaking.

It might have been quite heart-breaking, but for Dora, who was the stay and anchor of my tempest-driven bark. I went on with such vigour, that in the three or four months I was in a condition to make an experiment on one of our crack speakers in the Commons. Shall I ever forget how the crack speaker left my imbecile pencil staggering about the paper as if it were in a fit!

This would not do, it was quite clear. I resorted to Traddles for advice; who suggested that he should dictate speeches to me, at a pace adapted to my weakness. Very grateful for this friendly aid, I accepted the proposal; and almost every night, for a long time, we had a sort of Private Parliament after I came home from the Doctor's.

I should like to see such a Parliament anywhere else!

My aunt and Mr. Dick represented the Government or the Opposition (as the case might be), and Traddles thundered astonishing invectives against them. My aunt would occasionally throw in an interruption or two, as "Hear!" or "No!" or "Oh!" which was always a signal to Mr. Dick (a perfect country gentleman) to follow lustily with the same cry.

The result of so much good practice was, that by-and-by I began to keep pace with Traddles pretty well, and should have been quite triumphant if I had had the least idea what my notes were about. But, as to reading them, I might as well have copied the Chinese inscriptions on an immense collection of tea-chests!

There was nothing for it, but to turn back and begin all over again. It was very hard, but I turned back and began laboriously and methodically to plod over the same tedious ground at a snail's pace; making the most desperate efforts to know these elusive characters by sight wherever I met them. I was always punctual at the office; at the Doctor's too; and I really did work, as the common expression is, like a cart-horse.

One day, when I went to the Commons as usual, I found Mr. Spenlow in the doorway looking, extremely grave. Instead of returning my "Good morning" he coldly requested me to accompany him to a certain coffee-house. I complied, in a very uncomfortable state, and my mind misgave me that he had found out about my darling Dora.

If I had not guessed this, on the way to the coffee-house, I could hardly have failed to know what was the matter when I followed him into an up-stairs room, and found Miss Murdstone there.

Miss Murdstone gave me her chilly finger-nails, and sat severely rigid. Mr. Spenlow shut the door, motioned me to a chair, and stood on the hearth-rug in front of the fire-place.

"Have the goodness to show Mr. Copperfield," said Mr. Spenlow, "what you have in your reticule, Miss Murdstone."

Miss Murdstone opened it and produced my last letter to Dora, teeming with expressions of devoted affection.

"I believe that is your writing, Mr. Copperfield?" said Mr. Spenlow.

I was very hot, and the voice I heard was very unlike mine, when I said, "It is, Sir!"

"If I am not mistaken," said Mr. Spenlow, as Miss Murdstone brought a parcel of letters out of her reticule, tied round with the dearest bit of blue ribbon, "those are also from your pen, Mr. Copperfield?"

I took them from her with a most desolate sensation; and, glancing at such phrases at the top, as "My ever dearest and own Dora," "My best beloved angel," "My blessed one for ever," and the like, blushed deeply, and inclined my head.

"Miss Murdstone, be so good as to proceed!"

That gentle creature, after a moment's thoughtful survey of the carpet, delivered herself as follows:

"I have had my suspicions of Miss Spenlow, in reference to David Copperfield, for some time, but I found no proof until last night. It appeared to me that Miss Spenlow received too many letters from her friend Miss Mills, but it was not for me to interfere. Last evening after tea," pursued Miss Murdstone, "I observed the little dog worrying something. I said to Miss Spenlow, 'Dora, what is that the dog has in his mouth? It's paper.' Miss Spenlow gave a sudden cry, and ran to the dog. I interposed, and said, 'Dora my love, you must permit me.'"

Oh Jip, miserable Spaniel, this wretchedness, then, was your work!

"Miss Spenlow endeavoured," said Miss Murdstone, "to bribe me with kisses, work-boxes and small articles of jewellery—that, of course, I pass over. The little dog retreated under the sofa and was with great difficulty dislodged by the fire-irons. He still kept the letter in his mouth; and on my endeavouring to take it from him, he kept it between his teeth so pertinaciously as to suffer himself to be held suspended in the air by means of the document. At length I obtained possession of it. After perusing it, I taxed Miss Spenlow with having many such letters in her possession; and ultimately obtained from her the packet which is now in David Copperfield's hand."

"You have heard Miss Murdstone," said Mr. Spenlow, turning to me. "I beg to ask, Mr. Copperfield, if you have anything to say in reply?"

The picture I had before me, of the beautiful little treasure of my heart, sobbing and crying all night, and all for me—very much impaired the little dignity I had been able to muster. I am afraid I was in a tremulous state for a minute or so, though I did my best to disguise it.

"There is nothing I can say, Sir," I returned, "except that all the blame is mine."

"You are very much to blame, Sir," said Mr. Spenlow, walking to and fro upon the hearth-rug. "You have done a stealthy and unbecoming action, Mr. Copperfield."

"I feel it, Sir, I assure you, I returned. "But I never thought so, before. I love Miss Spenlow to that extent——"

"Pooh! Nonsense!" said Mr. Spenlow, reddening, "Pray don't tell me to my face that you love my daughter, Mr. Copperfield!"

"Could I defend my conduct if I did not, Sir?" I returned.

"Can you defend your conduct if you do, Sir?" said Mr. Spenlow, stopping short upon the hearth-rug. "Have you considered my daughter's station in life? Have you considered anything, Mr. Copperfield?"

"Very little, Sir, I am afraid," I answered. "But I have considered my own worldly position. When I explained it to you, we were already engaged——"

"I BEG," said Mr. Spenlow, as he energetically struck one hand upon the other—"that you will NOT talk to me of engagements, Mr. Copperfield!"

"When I explained my altered position to you, Sir," I began again, "this concealment, into which I am so unhappy as to have led Miss Spenlow, had begun. Since I have been in that altered position, I have strained every nerve to improve it. I am sure I shall improve it in time. Will you grant me time—any length of time? We are both so young, Sir,——"

"You are right," interrupted Mr. Spenlow, frowning very much, "you are both very young. Let there be an end of the nonsense. Take away those letters, and throw them in the fire. Give me Miss Spenlow's letters to throw in the fire; and we will agree to make no further mention of the past."

No. I couldn't think of agreeing to it. I was very sorry. I was resolute.

"Very well, Mr. Copperfield," said Mr. Spenlow, "I must try my influence with my daughter."

A silence succeeding, I was moving quietly towards the door, when he said:

"You are probably aware, Mr. Copperfield, that I am not altogether destitute of worldly possessions, and that my daughter is my nearest and dearest relative?"

I hurriedly made him a reply to the effect, that I hoped the error into which I had been betrayed did not induce him to think me mercenary too?

"I don't allude to the matter in that light," said Mr. Spenlow. "No. I merely say you are probably aware I have some property to bequeath to my child!"

I certainly supposed so.

"And you can hardly think," said Mr. Spenlow, "having experience in the Commons of the negligent proceedings of men, in respect of their testamentary arrangements, but that mine are made?"

I inclined my head in acquiescence.

"I should not allow," said Mr. Spenlow, "my suitable provision for my child to be influenced by a piece of youthful folly. But I might guard her from the consequences of any foolish step in the way of marriage."

There was a calm-sunset air about him, which quite affected me. He was so peaceful and resigned—clearly had his affairs so systematically wound up—that he was a man to feel touched in the contemplation of.

He told me I had better take a week to consider. How could I say I wouldn't take a week, yet how could I fail to know that no amount of weeks could influence such love as mine?

"In the meantime, confer with Miss Trotwood," said Mr. Spenlow. "Take a week, Mr. Copperfield."

I submitted; and came out of the room. Miss Murdstone's heavy eyebrows followed me to the door—I say her eyebrows rather than her eyes, because they were much more important in her face—and she looked so exactly as she used to look in our parlour at Blunderstone, that I could have fancied I had been breaking down in my lessons again!

When I got to the office I fell into such a state of torment about Dora, that I wonder I did not take up my hat and rush insanely to Norwood. The idea of their frightening her was so excruciating, that it impelled me to write a wild letter to Mr. Spenlow. I implored him to spare her gentle nature and addressed him generally, as if, instead of being her father, he had been an Ogre. This letter I sealed and laid upon his desk.

Before he went away in the afternoon he told me that I need not make myself at all uneasy about his daughter's happiness. He had assured her, he said, that it was all nonsense; and he had nothing more to say to her.

"You may make it necessary, Mr. Copperfield," he observed, "for me to send my daughter abroad again, for a term; but I have a better opinion of you. As to Miss Murdstone, I respect that lady's vigilance, but she has strict charge to avoid the subject. All I desire, Mr. Copperfield, is, that it should be forgotten. All you have got to do is to forget it."

All! In the note I wrote to Miss Mills, I bitterly quoted this sentiment. At night I repaired to Miss Mills's street, and walked up and down, until I was stealthily fetched in by Miss Mills's maid.

I raved as became me. Miss Mills had received a hasty

note from Dora, telling her that all was discovered, and saying, "Oh pray come to me, Julia, do, do!" But Miss Mills, mistrusting the acceptability of her presence to the higher powers, had not yet gone. She made me much more wretched than I was before, and I felt (and told her with the deepest gratitude) that she was indeed a friend. We resolved that she should go to Dora the first thing in the morning, and find some means of assuring her of my devotion and misery.

I confided all to my aunt when I got home; and in spite of all she could say to me, went to bed despairing. I got up despairing, and went out despairing.

I was surprised, when I came within sight of our office-door to see the ticket-porters standing outside talking together. I went hurriedly in.

The clerks were there, but nobody was doing anything. Old Tiffey, for the first time in his life, I should think, was sitting on somebody else's stool, and had not hung up his hat.

"This is a dreadful calamity, Mr. Copperfield," said he, as I entered.

"What is?" I exclaimed. "What's the matter?"

"Don't you know?" cried Tiffey.

"No!" said I, looking from face to face.

"Mr. Spenlow," said Tiffey.

"What about him?"

"Dead!"

I thought it was the office reeling as one of the clerks caught hold of me. They sat me down in a chair, untied my neckcloth, and brought me some water.

"Dead?" said I.

"He dined in town yesterday, and drove down in the phaeton by himself," said Tiffey. "The horses stopped at the stable gate. Nobody in the carriage. They found him a mile off."

"More than a mile off, Mr. Tiffey," interposed a junior.

"Was it? I believe you are right," said Tiffey,—"*more*

than a mile off—lying on the road-side. Whether he fell out in a fit, or got out, feeling ill before the fit came on, no one appears to know."

I cannot describe the state of mind into which I was thrown by this intelligence. I went down to Norwood that night; and finding from one of the servants that Miss Mills was there, got my aunt to direct a letter to her, which I wrote. I deplored the untimely death of Mr. Spenlow. I entreated her to tell Dora, if Dora were in a state to hear it, that he had spoken to me with the utmost kindness, and had coupled nothing but tenderness, not a single or reproachful word, with her name.

My aunt received a few lines next day in reply. Dora was overcome by grief; and when her friend had asked her should she send her love to me, had only cried, as she was always crying, "Oh, dear papa! Oh, poor papa!"

Mr. Jorkins came to the office a few days afterwards. He and Tiffey were closeted together and then Tiffey beckoned to me.

"Oh!" said Mr. Jorkins. "Mr. Tiffey and myself, Mr. Copperfield, are about to examine the desks, the drawers, and other such repositories of the deceased, searching for a Will. There is no trace of any, elsewhere. It may be as well for you to assist us, if you please."

We began the search at once; Mr. Jorkins unlocking the drawers and desks, and we all taking out the papers.

We had sealed up several packets; and were still going on dustily, when Mr. Jorkins said to us:

"Mr. Spenlow was very difficult to move from the beaten track. I am disposed to think he had made no will."

"Oh, I know he had!" said I.

They both stopped and looked at me.

"On the very day when I last saw him," said I, "He told me that he had, and that his affairs were long since settled."

Mr. Jorkins and old Tiffey shook their heads.

"That looks unpromising," said Tiffey.

"Surely you don't doubt——" I began.

"My good Mr. Copperfield!" said Tiffey, "If you had been in the Commons as long as I have, you would know that there is no subject on which men are so inconsistent.

It appeared a wonderful thing to me, but it turned out that there *was* no will. What was scarcely less astonishing to me was, that his affairs were in a most disordered state. By little and little it came out, that he had spent more than his professional income and had reduced his private means to a very low ebb indeed; and Tiffey told me he wouldn't give a thousand pounds for all the assets remaining.

This was at the expiration of about six weeks. Miss Mills still reported that my broken-hearted little Dora would say nothing, when I was mentioned, but "Oh, poor papa! Oh, dear papa!" Also, that she had no other relations than two aunts who lived at Putney, and who had not held any other than chance communication with their brother for many years. Not that they had ever quarrelled (Miss Mills informed me), but that having been, on the occasion of Dora's christening, invited to tea, when they considered themselves privileged to be invited to dinner, they had expressed their opinion in writing, that it was "better for the happiness of all parties," that they should stay away.

These two ladies now proposed to take Dora to live at Putney. Dora, clinging to them both, and weeping, exclaimed, "O yes, aunts! Please take Julia Mills and me and Jip to Putney!" and so they went, very soon after the funeral.

How I found time to haunt Putney, I am sure I don't know; but I contrived, by some means or other, to prowl about the neighbourhood pretty often. Miss Mills kept a journal; and she used to lend it to me. How I treasured up the entries, of which I subjoin a sample!

"Monday. My sweet D. still much depressed. Headache."

"Tuesday. D. weak and nervous. Beautiful in pallor."

"Wednesday. D. comparatively cheerful. Sang to her

Evening Bells. Effect not soothing. Found sobbing afterwards, in own room."

"Thursday. D. certainly improved. Resolved to mention name of D.C. Introduced same, cautiously. D. immediately overcome. 'Oh, dear, dear Julia! Oh, I have been a naughty and undutiful child!' Soothed and caressed."

CHAPTER XXXIX

WICKFIELD AND HEEP

My aunt, beginning to be made seriously uncomfortable by my prolonged dejection, made a pretence of being anxious that I should go to Dover to see that all was working well at the cottage, which was let.

Although it required an effort to leave Miss Mills, I fell rather willingly into my aunt's pretence, as a means of enabling me to pass a few tranquil hours with Agnes. I consulted the good Doctor and he, wishing me to take that relaxation, I made up my mind to go.

As to the Commons, I had no great occasion to be particular about my duties in that quarter. To say the truth, we were rapidly sliding down to but a doubtful position. Mr. Jorkins was an easy-going, incapable sort of man, and when I saw him take his snuff and let the business go, I regretted my aunt's thousand pounds more than ever.

I found everything in a satisfactory state at the cottage; and was enabled to gratify my aunt exceedingly by reporting that the tenant waged incessant war against donkeys. Having slept there one night, I walked on to Canterbury early in the morning, and loitered through the old streets with a sober pleasure. It appeared so long, since I had been a schoolboy there, that I wondered the place was so little changed, until I reflected how little I was changed myself.

Arrived at Mr. Wickfield's house, I found, in the little lower room on the ground floor, where Uriah Heep had been of old accustomed to sit, Mr. Micawber plying his pen. He was extremely glad to see me, but a little confused too.

"How do you like the law, Mr. Micawber?" said I.

"My dear Copperfield," he replied. "The objection to legal studies is that the mind is not at liberty to soar to any exalted form of expression. Still, it is a great pursuit. A great pursuit!"

I asked him whether he had reason, so far, to be satisfied with his friend Heep's treatment of him? He got up to ascertain if the door were close shut, before he replied, in a lower voice:

"My dear Copperfield, a man who labours under the pressure of pecuniary embarrassments, is at a disadvantage. That disadvantage is not diminished, when that pressure necessitates the drawing of stipendiary emoluments, before those emoluments are strictly due and payable. All I can say is, that my friend Heep has responded to appeals in a manner calculated to redound equally to the honour of his head, and of his heart."

"Do you see much of Mr. Wickfield?" I asked.

"Not much," said Mr. Micawber, slightingly. "Mr. Wickfield is—in short, he is obsolete."

"I am afraid his partner seeks to make him so," said I.

"My dear Copperfield!" returned Mr. Micawber, "allow me to offer a remark! I am here, in a position of trust. The discussion of some topics, even with Mrs. Micawber, is incompatible with the functions now devolving on me. I would therefore take the liberty of suggesting that in our friendly intercourse we draw a line. On one side of this line," said Mr. Micawber, representing it on the desk with the office ruler, "is the whole range of the human intellect; on the other, the affairs of Messrs. Wickfield and Heep. I trust I give no offence."

I felt I had no right to be offended. My telling him so, appeared to relieve him; and he shook hands with me. As I left him I clearly perceived that there was something interposed between him and me which quite altered the character of our intercourse.

There was no one in the quaint old drawing-room. I

looked into the room still belonging to Agnes, and saw her sitting by the fire, writing.

My darkening the light made her look up. What a pleasure to be the cause of that bright change in her attentive face!

"Ah, Agnes!" said I, when we were sitting together, side by side; "I have missed you so much, lately!"

"Again! And so soon?"

"I don't know how it is, Agnes; I seem to want some faculty of mind that I ought to have. I get so miserable and worried, that I know I must want—shall I call it—reliance?"

"Call it so, if you will," said Agnes.

"Whenever I have not had you, Agnes, to advise me, I have seemed to get into all sorts of difficulty. When I have come to you, at last, I have come to peace and happiness."

With her beaming eyes; and with that sweet composure, she soon led me on to tell all that had happened since our last meeting.

"And there is not another word to tell, Agnes," said I. "Now my reliance is on you."

"But it must not be on me, Trotwood."

"On Dora?" said I.

"Assuredly."

"Why, I have not mentioned, Agnes," said I, a little embarrassed, "that Dora is rather difficult to—rather difficult to—I hardly know how to express it, really, Agnes. She is a timid little thing, and some time ago, when I thought it right to mention to her—but I'll tell you, if you will bear with me, how it was."

Accordingly, I told Agnes about the Cookery Book, the housekeeping accounts, and all the rest of it.

"Oh, Trotwood!" she remonstrated, with a smile. "Just your old headlong way! You might have been in earnest without being so very sudden! Poor Dora!"

I never heard such sweet forbearing kindness. It was

as if I had seen Dora, in all her fascinating artlessness, caressing Agnes, and thanking her.

"What ought I to do then, Agnes?" I inquired, after looking at the fire a little while.

"I think that the honourable course would be to write to those two ladies," replied Agnes, "and ask their permission to visit sometimes at their house. I would not be too vehement or propose too much. I would trust to my fidelity—and to Dora."

"But if they were to frighten Dora again, Agnes," said I. "Or if the two Miss Spenlows should not be likely persons to address in that way!"

"I don't think, Trotwood," returned Agnes, "I would consider that. Perhaps it would be better only to consider whether it is right to do this; and, if it is, to do it."

I had no longer any doubt on the subject. I devoted the whole afternoon to the draft of this letter. But first I went down-stairs to see Mr. Wickfield and Uriah Heep.

I found Uriah in a new, plaster-smelling office, built out in the garden. He received me in his usual fawning manner, and pretended not to have heard of my arrival from Mr. Micawber. He accompanied me into Mr. Wickfield's room and stood before the fire while Mr. Wickfield and I exchanged greetings.

"You stay with us, Trotwood, while you remain in Canterbury?" said Mr. Wickfield.

"Is there room for me?" said I.

"I am sure, Master Copperfield—I should say Mister, but the other comes so natural," said Uriah,—"I would turn out of your old room with pleasure."

"No, no," said Mr. Wickfield. "There's another room."

"Oh, but you know," returned Uriah, with a grin, "I should really be delighted!"

To cut the matter short, I said I would have the other room or none at all, and taking my leave of the firm until dinner, I went up-stairs again.

I had hoped to have no other companion than Agnes. But Mrs. Heep had asked permission to bring herself and her knitting near the fire, in that room.

She never left us but sat there plying her knitting needles.

"I'm umbly thankful to you, Sir," said Mrs. Heep, in acknowledgement of my inquiries concerning her health, "but I'm only pretty well. How do you think my Ury looking, Sir?"

I thought him looking as villainous as ever, and I replied that I saw no change in him.

"Oh," said Mrs. Heep. "Don't you see a thinness in him?"

"Not more than usual," I replied.

"Don't *you* see a wasting and a wearing in him, Miss Wickfield," inquired Mrs. Heep.

"No," said Agnes. "You are too solicitous about him. He is very well."

Mrs. Heep, with a prodigious sniff, resumed her knitting.

She never left off, or left us for a moment. We had still three or four hours before dinner; but she sat there, plying her knitting-needles as monotonously as an hour-glass might have poured out its sands. At dinner she maintained her watch, with the same unwinking eyes. After dinner there was the mother knitting and watching again.

Next day the knitting and watching began again, and lasted all day. Towards the twilight I went out by myself, musing on what I ought to do. I had not walked far when I was hailed. The shambling figure, and the scanty great coat, were not to be mistaken. I stopped, and Uriah Heep came up.

"Well?" said I.

"How fast you walk!" said he. "My legs are pretty long, but you've given 'em quite a job."

"Where are you going?" said I.

"I am coming with you, Master Copperfield." Saying this, with a jerk of his body, he fell into step beside me.

"To tell you the truth, I came out to walk alone, because I have had so much company."

He looked at me sideways, and said with his hardest grin: "You mean mother."

"Why yes, I do," said I.

"Ah! But all stratagems are fair in love, Sir. You

see," he said, "you're quite a dangerous rival, Master Copperfield."

"Do you set a watch upon Miss Wickfield because of *me?*" said I.

"Oh! Master Copperfield! Those are very arsh words."

"Do you suppose," said I, "that I regard Miss Wickfield otherwise than as a very dear sister?"

"Well, Master Copperfield," he replied, "You may not, you know. But then, you see, you may!"

"Come then!" said I. "For the sake of Miss Wickfield——"

"My Agnes!" he exclaimed.

"I will tell you that I am engaged to another young lady."

He caught hold of my hand and gave it a squeeze.

"Oh, Master Copperfield," he said. "I'm sure I'll take off mother directly, and only too appy."

"Before we leave the subject, you ought to understand," said I, breaking a pretty long silence, "that I believe Agnes Wickfield to be as far above *you* as that moon herself!"

"Peaceful! Ain't she!" said Uriah. "Very! Now confess, Master Copperfield, that you haven't liked me quite as I have liked you. All along you've thought me too umble now, I shouldn't wonder?"

"I am not fond of professions of humility," I returned.

"There now!" said Uriah, "Didn't I know it! But how little you think of the rightful umbleness of a person in my station, Master Copperfield! Father and me, and mother, she was likewise brought up at a sort of charitable establishment. They taught us all a deal of umbleness—not much else that I know of, from morning to night. We was to pull off our caps here, and to make bows there; and always to abase ourselves before our betters. And we had such a lot of betters! Father got the monitor-medal by being umble. So did I. 'Be umble, Uriah,' says father to me. 'Be umble,' says father, 'and you'll do!' And really it ain't done bad!"

He talked more at dinner than was usual with him, and

when we three males were left alone he got into a more adventurous state.

I had observed yesterday, that he tried to entice Mr. Wickfield to drink; and had limited myself to one glass, and then proposed that we should follow Agnes. I would have done so again to-day; but Uriah was too quick for me.

"We seldom see our present visitor, Sir," he said, addressing Mr. Wickfield, "and I should propose to give him welcome in another glass or two of wine. Mr. Copperfield, your elth and appiness!"

I was obliged to make a show of taking the hand he stretched across to me; and then, with very different emotions, I took the hand of his partner.

"Come, fellow-partner," said Uriah, "now, suppose you give us something or another appropriate to Copperfield!"

I pass over Mr. Wickfield's proposing my aunt, Mr. Dick, Doctor's Commons, Uriah, his drinking everything twice; his consciousness of his own weakness, the ineffectual effort that he made against it, and the manifest exultation with which Uriah twisted and turned.

"Come, fellow-partner!" said Uriah, at last, "I'll give you the divinest of her sex! Agnes Wickfield. To be her father is a proud distinction, but to be her usband ——"

Spare me from ever again hearing such a cry, as that with which her father rose up from the table!

I had my arms round him imploring him to calm himself. He was mad for the moment; tearing out his hair, beating his head, trying to force himself from me, not looking at or seeing any one, his face all staring and distorted—a frightful spectacle. By degrees he struggled less, and began to look at me—strangely at first, then with recognition in his eyes. At length he said, "I know, Trotwood! My darling child and you—I know! But look at him!"

He pointed to Uriah, pale and glowering in a corner.

"Look at my torturer. Before him I have step by step abandoned name and reputation, house and home."

"You had better stop him, Copperfield, if you can," cried Uriah. "He'll say something presently he'll be sorry to have said."

"Oh, Trotwood, Trotwood! What I have come down to be, since I first saw you in this house! Weak indulgence has ruined me."

Mr. Wickfield dropped into a chair, and weakly sobbed. "*I* don't know all I have done," said Mr. Wickfield. "*He* knows, for he has always been at my elbow. You find him in my house, you find him in my business. You heard him, but a little time ago. What need have I to say more!"

"You haven't need to say so much, nor half so much, nor anything at all," observed Uriah, half defiant, and half fawning. "You'll think better of it to-morrow, Sir."

The door opened, and Agnes, gliding in, put her arm round his neck, and steadily said, "Papa, you are not well. Come with me!" He laid his head upon her shoulder and went out with her. Her eyes met mine for but an instant, yet I saw how much she knew of what had passed.

"I didn't expect he'd cut up so rough, Master Copperfield," said Uriah. "I'll be friends with him to-morrow. I'm umbly anxious for his good."

I gave him no answer, and went up-stairs. I took up a book and tried to read. I heard the clocks strike twelve, and was still reading, without knowing what I read, when Agnes touched me.

"You will be going early in the morning, Trotwood! Let us say good-bye, now!"

She had been weeping, but her face then was so calm and beautiful!

"Dearest Agnes!" I returned. "Is there nothing to be done? Can *I* do nothing—*I*, who come to you with *my* poor sorrows?"

"And make mine so much lighter," she replied. "Dear Trotwood, no!"

"It is presumptuous to doubt or direct you; but you know how much I love you, and how much I owe you.

You will never sacrifice yourself to a mistaken sense of duty, Agnes?"

More agitated than I had ever seen her, she took her hand from me, and moved a step back.

"Say you have no such thought, dear Agnes! Think of the priceless gift of such a heart as yours!"

She told me she had no fear for herself—I need have none for her, and was gone!

It was dark in the morning when I got upon the coach at the inn door. The day was just breaking when we were about to start, and then came struggling up the coach side, Uriah's head.

"Copperfield!" said he, in a croaking whisper, "I thought you'd be glad to hear, before you went off, that I've been into his room already, and we've made it all smooth."

I obliged myself to say that I was glad he had made his apology.

"Oh, to be sure!" said Uriah. "When a person's umble, you know, what's an apology? I suppose, you have sometimes plucked a pear before it was ripe, Master Copperfield?"

"I suppose I have," I replied.

"*I* did that last night," said Uriah; "but it'll ripen yet! I can wait!"

CHAPTER XL

THE WANDERER

We had a very serious conversation that night, about the domestic occurrences I have detailed in the last chapter. My aunt was deeply interested in them, and walked up and down the room with her arms folded, for more than two hours afterwards.

She read my letter to the two old ladies, in the morning, and approved of it. I posted it, and had nothing to do then, but wait, as patiently as I could, for the reply. I was still in this state of expectation, and had been, for nearly a week; when I left the Doctor's one snowy night, to walk home.

My shortest way home was through Saint Martin's Lane. As I passed the steps of the church which gives its name to the lane, I encountered a woman's face. It looked in mine, passed across the narrow lane, and disappeared. I knew it. I had seen it somewhere. But I could not remember where.

On the steps of the church was the stooping figure of a man, who had put down some burden on the smooth snow, to adjust it. He rose, turned, and came down towards me. I stood face to face with Mr. Peggotty!

Then I remembered the woman. It was Martha, to whom Emily had given the money that night in the kitchen.

We shook hands heartily. At first, neither of us could speak a word.

"Mas'r Davy!" he said, "it do my art good to see you, Sir."

"Well met, my dear old friend!" said I.

"I had my thowts o' coming to make inquiration for you, Sir, to-night," he said, "but I was afeered it was too late. I should have come early in the morning, Sir, afore going away."

"Again?" said I.

"Yes, Sir," he replied, patiently shaking his head, "I'm away to-morrow."

"Where were you going now?" I asked.

"Well!" he replied, "I was a going to turn in somewheers."

There was a side-entrance to the Golden Cross Inn, nearly opposite to where we stood. I put my arm through his, and we went across.

When I saw him in the light, I observed that the lines in his face and forehead were deeper, but he looked very strong, and like a man upheld by steadfastness of purpose.

"I'll tell you, Mas'r Davy," he said, "wheer all I've been, and what-all we've heerd. I've been fur, and we've heerd little; but I'll tell you!

"When she was a child," he said, "she used to talk to me a deal about the sea, and about them coasts where the sea got to be dark blue, and to lay a shining and a shining in the sun. When she was—lost, I know'd in my mind, as he would take her to them countries, and I went across-Channel to France."

I saw the door move, and the snow drift in. I saw it move a little more, and a hand softly interpose to keep it open.

"When I come to any town," he pursued, "I found the inn, and waited about the yard till some one turned up as know'd English. Then I told how that I was on my way to seek my niece, and they told me what manner of gentlefolks was in the house, and I waited to see any as seemed like her, going in or out. When it warn't Em'ly, I went on agen."

It was Martha at the door. I saw her haggard, listening face distinctly.

"At last I come to the sea. It warn't hard, you may

suppose, for a seafaring man like me to work his way over to Italy. When I got theer, I wandered on as I had done afore. The people was just as good to me, and I should have gone from town to town, maybe the country through, but that I got news of her being seen among them Swiss mountains yonder. One as know's his sarvant see 'em there, all three, and told me where they was. I made for them mountains, Mas'r Davy, day and night, and I crossed 'em. But, Mas'r Davy, it warn't to be—not yet! I was too late, and they was gone. Some said heer, and some said theer. I travelled heer, and I travelled theer, but I found no Em'ly, and I travelled home."

"How long ago?" I asked.

"A matter o' fower days," said Mr. Peggotty.

From some pocket in his breast he took out a small paper bundle containing two or three letters or little packets.

"This fust one come," he said, "afore I had been gone a week. A fifty pound bank-note, directed to me, and put underneath the door in the night. She tried to hide her writing, but she couldn't hide it from Me!"

"This come to Missis Gummidge," he said, opening another, "two or three months ago. Be so good as read it, Sir." It read as follows:

"Oh what will you feel when you see this writing, and know it comes from my wicked hand! But try, try to let your heart soften to me, and write down on a bit of paper whether he is well, and what he said about me before you left off ever naming me among yourselves.

"Dear, if your heart is hard towards me, ask him whose wife I was to have been, before you decide against my poor prayer! Tell him when I hear the wind blowing at night, I feel as if it was going up to God against me. Tell him that if I was to die to-morrow (and oh, if I was fit, I would be so glad to die!) I would bless him and uncle with my last words!"

Some money was enclosed in this letter also. Five pounds. It was untouched like the previous sum.

"What answer was sent?" I inquired of Mr. Peggotty.

"Missis Gummidge," he returned, "not being a good

scholar, Sir, Ham drawed it out, and she made a copy on it. They told her I was gone to seek her, and what my parting words was."

"Is that another letter in your hand?" said I.

"It's money, Sir," said Mr. Peggotty, "Ten pound, you see. And wrote inside, 'From a true friend,' like the fust. But the fust was put underneath the door, and this come by the post, day afore yesterday. I'm a going to seek her at the post-mark."

He showed it to me. It was a town on the Upper Rhine. I asked him how Ham was? He shook his head.

"He works," he said, "as bold as a man can. He's never been heerd fur to complain. But my sister's belief is as it has cut him deep."

"Poor fellow, I can believe it!"

"When there's hard duty to be done with danger in it, he steps for'ard afore all his mates. And yet he's as gentle as any child."

He gathered up the letters, put them into their little bundle; and placed it tenderly in his breast again.

The face was gone from the door. I still saw the snow drifting in; but nothing else was there.

"Well!" Mr. Peggotty said, looking to his bag, "having seen you to-night, Mas'r Davy (and that does me good!), I shall away betimes to-morrow morning. All that troubles me is, to think that any harm might come to me, afore that money was give back."

He rose, and I rose too; we grasped each other by the hand again, before going out.

"I'd go ten thousand mile," he said, "I'd go till I dropped dead, to lay that money down afore him. If I do that, and find my Em'ly, I'm content. If I doen't find her, maybe she'll come to hear, sometime, as her loving uncle only ended his search for her when he ended his life; and if I know her, even that will turn her home at last!"

CHAPTER XLI

DORA'S AUNTS

At last, an answer came from the two old ladies. They presented their compliments to Mr. Copperfield, and informed him that they had given his letter their best consideration, "with a view to the happiness of both parties." If Mr. Copperfield would do them the favour to call, upon a certain day (accompanied, if he thought proper, by a confidential friend), they would be happy to hold some conversation on the subject.

To this favour, Mr. Copperfield immediately replied, that he would have the honour of waiting on the Misses Spenlow, at the time appointed; accompanied by his friend Mr. Thomas Traddles of the Inner Court.

It was a great augmentation of my uneasiness to be bereaved of the services of Miss Mills. But Mr. Mills, who was always doing something or other to annoy me—or I felt as if he were, which was the same thing—had brought his conduct to a climax, by taking it into his head that he would go to India. Why should he go to India, except to harass me? To be sure he had a good deal to do with that part of the world, being entirely in the Indian trade. But this was nothing to me. However, it was so much to him that for India he was bound, and Julia with him.

I was in several minds how to dress myself on the important day; being divided between my desire to appear to advantage, and my apprehensions of putting on anything that might impair my severely practical character in the eyes of the Misses Spenlow. I endeavoured to hit a happy medium; my aunt approved the result; and Mr. Dick threw one of his shoes after Traddles and me, for luck, as we went down-stairs.

Excellent fellow as I knew Traddles to be, I could not help wishing, on that delicate occasion, that he had never contracted the habit of brushing his hair so very upright. I took the liberty of mentioning it as we were walking to Putney; and saying that if he *would* smooth it down a little——

"My dear Copperfield," said Traddles, "nothing would give me greater pleasure. But it won't."

"Won't be smoothed down?" said I.

"No," said Traddles. "Nothing will induce it. If I was to carry a half-hundredweight upon it, all the way to Putney, it would be up again the moment the weight was taken off. You have no idea what obstinate hair mine is, Copperfield."

I was a little disappointed, I must confess, but thoroughly charmed by his good-nature too. I told him that his hair must have taken all the obstinacy out of his character, for *he* had none.

On our approaching the house where the Misses Spenlow lived I was in a state of excessive trepidation. I had a vague sensation of being, as it were, on view, when the maid opened the door; and of wavering, somehow, into a quiet little drawing-room. Also of sitting down here, on a sofa, and seeing Traddles's hair start up. Also of hearing an old-fashioned clock ticking. Also of looking round the room for any sign of Dora, and seeing none. Also of thinking that Jip once barked in the distance, and was instantly choked by somebody. Ultimately I found myself backing Traddles into the fireplace, and bowing in great confusion to two dry little elderly ladies.

"Pray," said one of the two little ladies, "be seated."

When I had done tumbling over Traddles, and had sat upon something which was not a cat—my first seat was—I so far recovered my sight, as to perceive that there was a disparity of six or eight years between the two sisters;

and that the younger had my letter in her hand and was referring to it through an eye-glass. The sister who had not my letter, had her arms crossed on her breast, and resting on each other, like an Idol.

"Mr. Copperfield, I believe," said the sister who had got my letter, addressing herself to Traddles.

This was a frightful beginning. Traddles had to indicate that I was Mr. Copperfield, and I had to lay claim to myself.

"Mr. Copperfield!" said the sister with the letter.

I did something—bowed, I suppose—and was all attention, when the other sister struck in.

"My sister Lavinia," said she, "being conversant with matters of this nature, will state what we consider most calculated to promote the happiness of both parties."

I discovered afterwards that Miss Lavinia was an authority in affairs of the heart, by reason of there having anciently existed a certain Mr. Pidger, who was supposed to have been enamoured of her. My private opinion is that Pidger was altogether innocent of any such sentiments. Both Miss Lavinia and Miss Clarissa had a superstition, however, that he would have declared his passion, if he had not been cut short in his youth, at about sixty.

"We will not," said Miss Lavinia, "enter on the past history of this matter. Our poor brother Francis's death has cancelled that."

"We had not," said Miss Clarissa, "been in the habit of frequent association with our brother Francis. Francis took his road; we took ours. We considered it conducive to the happiness of all parties that it should be so. And it was so."

"Our niece's position is much changed by our brother Francis's death," said Miss Lavinia; "and therefore we consider our brother's opinions as being changed too. We have no reason to doubt, Mr. Copperfield, that you are a young gentleman of honourable character; or that you have an affection—or are fully persuaded that you have an affection—for our niece."

I replied, as I usually did whenever I had a chance, that nobody had ever loved anybody else as I loved Dora.

Miss Lavinia was going on to make some rejoinder, when Miss Clarissa struck in again:

"If Dora's mamma," she said, "when she married our brother Francis, had at once said that there was not room for the family at the dinner-table, it would have been better for the happiness of all parties."

"Sister Clarissa," said Miss Lavinia. "Perhaps we needn't mind that now."

"Sister Lavinia," said Miss Clarissa, "it belongs to the subject. With your branch of the subject, I should not think of interfering. On this branch of the subject I have a voice and an opinion."

Miss Lavinia resumed: "You ask permission of my sister Clarissa and myself, Mr. Copperfield, to visit here, as the accepted suitor of our niece. We have no doubt that you think you like her very much."

"*Think,* ma'am," I rapturously began, "oh!——"

But Miss Clarissa giving me a look as requesting that I would not interrupt the oracle, I begged pardon.

"Affection," said Miss Lavinia, "mature affection, does not easily express itself. Its voice is low. It waits and waits. In comparison with such sentiments, the light inclinations of very young people," pursued Miss Lavinia, "are dust, compared to rocks. It is owing to the difficulty of knowing whether they are likely to endure, that my sister Clarissa and myself have been in great doubt in reference to the likings, or imaginary likings, of such very young people as Mr. Copperfield and our niece."

"Our brother Francis's' child," remarked Miss Clarissa. "If our brother Francis's wife had found it convenient to invite the family to her dinner-table, we might have known our brother Francis' child better at the present moment. Sister Lavinia, proceed."

"It seems to us," said she, "prudent, Mr. Traddles, to bring these feelings to the test of our own observation.

Therefore we are inclined so far to accede to Mr. Copperfield's proposal, as to admit his visits here."

"I shall never, dear ladies," I exclaimed, "forget your kindness!"

"But," pursued Miss Lavinia,—"but, we would prefer to regard those visits, Mr. Traddles, as made, at present, to us. We must guard ourselves from recognising any positive engagement between Mr. Copperfield and our niece, until we have had an opportunity——"

"Until *you* have had an opportunity, sister Lavinia," said Miss Clarissa.

"Be it so, Clarissa!" assented Miss Lavinia resignedly—"until I have had an opportunity of observing them. We must require from Mr. Copperfield, on his word of honour, that no communication shall take place between him and our niece without our knowledge. If you, Mr. Copperfield, feel the least scruple, in giving this promise, I beg you to take time to consider it."

I exclaimed that not a moment's consideration could be necessary.

"Stay!" said Miss Lavinia; "we resolved, before we had the pleasure of receiving you, to leave you alone for a quarter of an hour, to consider this point. You will allow us to retire."

Exactly at the expiration of the quarter of an hour they reappeared. I then bound myself once more to the prescribed conditions.

"Sister Clarissa," said Miss Lavinia, "the rest is with you."

"We shall be happy," said Miss Clarissa, "to see Mr. Copperfield to dinner, every Sunday. Our hour is three."

I bowed.

"In the course of the week," said Miss Clarissa, "we shall be happy to see Mr. Copperfield to tea. Our hour is half-past six."

I bowed again.

"Twice in the week," said Miss Clarissa, "but, as a rule, not oftener."

I bowed again.

"Miss Trotwood," said Miss Clarissa, "mentioned in Mr. Copperfield's letter, will perhaps call upon us."

I intimated that my aunt would be delighted to make their acquaintance; though I must say I was not quite sure of their getting on very satisfactorily together.

Miss Lavinia then arose, and begging Mr. Traddles to excuse us for a minute, requested me to follow her. I obeyed, all in a tremble, and was conducted into another room. There, I found my blessed darling stopping her ears behind the door, with her dear little face against the wall; and Jip in the plate-warmer with his head tied up in a towel.

Oh! How beautiful she was in her black frock, and how she sobbed and cried at first, and wouldn't come out from behind the door! How fond we were of one another, when she did come out at last; and what a state of bliss I was in! I don't know how long I should have stayed there, if Miss Lavinia had not come in to take me away.

I wanted to persuade Dora to come and see Traddles, but on my proposing it she ran off to her own room, and locked herself in; so I went to Traddles without her, and walked away with him on air.

"Nothing could be more satisfactory," said Traddles; "I shouldn't be at all surprised if you were to be married years before me, Copperfield."

"Does your Sophy play on any instrument, Traddles?" I inquired, in the pride of my heart.

"She knows enough of the piano to teach it to her little sister," said Traddles.

"Does she sing at all?" I asked.

"Why, she sings ballads, sometimes, to freshen up the others a little when they're out of spirits," said Traddles.

"She doesn't sing to the guitar?" said I.

"Oh dear no!" said Traddles.

"Paint at all?"

"Not at all," said Traddles.

I promised Traddles that he should hear Dora sing, and

see some of her flower-painting. He said he should like it very much, and we went home arm in arm in great good humour and delight.

I had my hands more full than ever, now. The proposed tea-drinkings being quite impracticable, I compounded with Miss Lavinia for permission to visit every Saturday afternoon, without detriment to my privileged Sundays. So, the close of every week was a delicious time for me; and I got through the rest of the week by looking forward to it.

My aunt made her promised visit within a few days; and within a few more days, Dora's aunts called upon her, in due state and form. I know that my aunt distressed Dora's aunts very much, by walking out to Putney at extraordinary times; likewise by wearing her bonnet in any manner that happened to be comfortable to her head; but she loved me too well not to sacrifice some of her little peculiarities to the general harmony.

The only member of our small society, who positively refused to adapt himself to circumstances, was Jip. He never saw my aunt without immediately displaying every tooth in his head, retiring under a chair, and growling incessantly. All kinds of treatment were tried with him—coaxing, scolding, slapping; but he never could prevail upon himself to bear my aunt's society. At length, Dora muffled him in a towel and shut him up whenever my aunt was reported at the door.

One thing troubled me much; it was that Dora seemed by one consent to be regarded like a pretty toy or plaything. My aunt always called her Little Blossom; and the pleasure of Miss Lavinia's life was to wait upon her, curl her hair, and treat her like a pet child. What Miss Lavinia did, her sister did as a matter of course. I made up my mind to speak to Dora about this; and one day I said to her that I wished she could get them to behave towards her differently.

"Because you know, my darling," I remonstrated, "you are not a child."

"I am sure they're very kind to me," said Dora, "and I am very happy."

"Well! But my dearest life!" said I, "you might be very happy, and yet be treated rationally."

Dora gave me a reproachful look, and then began to sob, saying, if I didn't like her, why had I ever wanted so much to be engaged to her? What could I do, but kiss away her tears, and tell her how I doted on her, after that!

I was charmed by her presently asking me, of her own accord, to give her that Cookery Book I had once spoken of, and to show her how to keep accounts. I brought the volume with me on my next visit and I showed her an old housekeeping-book of my aunt's, and gave her a set of tablets, and a pretty little pencil-case, and box of leads, to practise housekeeping with.

But the Cookery Book made Dora's head ache, and the figures made her cry. They wouldn't add up, she said. So she rubbed them out, and drew little nosegays, and likenesses of me and Jip all over the tablets.

Then I playfully tried verbal instruction: For example, I would say: "Now suppose, my pet, that we were married, and you were going to buy a shoulder of mutton for dinner, would you know how to buy it?"

Dora would think a little, and then reply, perhaps, with great triumph: "Why the butcher would know how to sell it, and what need *I* know? Oh, you silly boy!"

Consequently, the principal use to which the Cookery Book was devoted, was being put down in the corner for Jip to stand upon. But Dora was so pleased, when she had trained him to stand upon it and to hold the pencil-case in his mouth, that I was very glad I had bought it.

CHAPTER XLII

MISCHIEF

AGNES came on a visit of a fortnight to the Doctor's. Mr. Wickfield was the Doctor's old friend, and the Doctor wished to talk with him, and do him good. I was not much surprised to hear from her that she had engaged to find a lodging in the neighborhood for Mrs. Heep. Neither was I surprised when, on the very next day, Uriah, like a dutiful son, brought his worthy mother to take possession.

"You see, Master Copperfield," said he, as he forced himself upon my company for a turn in the Doctor's garden, "where a person loves, a person is a little jealous."

"Of whom are you jealous, now?" said I.

"Thanks to you, Master Copperfield," he returned, "of no one in particular just at present—no male person, at least."

"Do you mean that you are jealous of a female person?"

"Really, Master Copperfield," he said, "—I should say Mister, I'm not a lady's man in general, Sir, and I never was, with Mrs. Strong."

His eyes looked green now, as they watched mine with a rascally cunning.

"What do you mean?" said I.

He seemed very much amused, and after some scraping of his chin he went on to say: "When I was but a numble clerk, she always looked down upon me. I was too far beneath her to be noticed."

"Well?" said I; "suppose you were!"

"——And beneath him too," pursued Uriah.

"Don't you know the Doctor better," said I, "than to suppose him conscious of your existence, when you were not before him?"

"Oh dear, I am not referring to the Doctor! Oh no, poor man! I mean Mr. Maldon!"

My heart quite died within me.

"He never could come into the office, without ordering and shoving me about," said Uriah. "I was very meek and umble—and I am. But I didn't like that sort of thing—and I don't!"

"She is one of your lovely women, she is," he pursued. "She's just the person as would put my Agnes up to higher sort of game."

I endeavoured to appear unconscious but with poor success.

"Now, I'm not a going to let myself be run down, Copperfield," he continued, "and I shall do what I can to put a stop to this friendship. I can't allow people in my way. Really they must come out of the cart, Master Copperfield!"

"I don't understand you," said I.

"Don't you, though?" he returned. "I'm astonished at that, Master Copperfield.—Is that Mr. Maddon a-norseback, ringing at the gate, Sir?"

"It looks like him," I replied, as carelessly as I could.

Uriah stopped short, and doubled himself up with laughter. With perfectly silent laughter. I turned away without any ceremony; and left him doubled up in the middle of the garden, like a scarecrow in want of support.

It was on the next evening but one, which was a Saturday; that I took Agnes to see Dora. I was in a flutter of pride and anxiety; pride in my dear little betrothed, and anxiety that Agnes should like her. She was not in the drawing-room when I presented Agnes to her little aunts, but was shyly keeping out of the way.

Dora was afraid of Agnes. She had told me that she knew Agnes was "too clever." But when she saw her she gave a faint little cry of pleased surprise, and just put her affectionate arms round Agnes's neck, and laid her innocent cheek against her face.

I never was so happy!

The short evening flew away. The time was at hand when the coach was to call for us. I was standing alone before the fire, when Dora came stealing softly in.

"Don't you think, if I had had her for a friend a long time ago, Doady," said Dora, her bright eyes shining very brightly, "I might have been more clever perhaps?"

"My love!" said I, "what nonsense!"

"I wonder why you ever fell in love with me?" said Dora.

"Perhaps because I couldn't see you, and not love you, Dora!"

"Suppose you had never seen me at all."

"Suppose we had never been born!" said I, gaily.

When the coach came there was a hurried but affectionate parting between Agnes and herself; and Dora was to write to Agnes, and Agnes was to write to Dora; and they had a second parting at the coach-door, and a third when Dora would come running out once more to remind Agnes at the coach-window about writing.

Never, never, had I loved Dora so deeply and truly, as I loved her that night. When we were walking in the starlight along the quiet road that led to the Doctor's house, I told Agnes it was her doing.

"When you were sitting by her," said I, "you seemed to be no less *her* guardian angel than mine."

"A poor angel," she returned, "but faithful."

The clear tone of her voice, going straight to my heart, made it natural to me to say:

"The cheerfulness that belongs to you, Agnes, is so restored that I hope you are happier at home?"

"I am happier in myself," she said. "There has been no change at home. Have no apprehensions for me, Trotwood," she added, after a moment; "the step you dread my taking, I shall never take."

It was an unspeakable relief to me to have this assurance from her own truthful lips. I told her so, earnestly.

We were now within the little court-yard of the Doctor's cottage. It was growing late, and Agnes bade me good-night.

"Do not be troubled," she said, giving me her hand, "by our misfortunes and anxieties. If you can ever give me help, rely upon it I will ask you for it. God bless you always!"

I was going out at the gate, when, happening to turn my head, I saw a light in the Doctor's study. With the view of bidding him good-night, I turned back and gently opening the door, looked in. The first person whom I saw, to my surprise, was Uriah. He was standing with one of his skeleton hands over his mouth, and the other resting on the Doctor's table. The Doctor sat in his study chair, covering his face with his hands. Mr. Wickfield was leaning forward, irresolutely touching the Doctor's arm.

For an instant, I supposed that the Doctor was ill. I hastily advanced a step when I met Uriah's eye, and saw what was the matter. I would have withdrawn, but the Doctor made a gesture to detain me.

"I have felt it incumbent upon me, Master Copperfield," said Uriah, "to point out to Doctor Strong what you and me have already talked about. You didn't exactly understand me, though?"

I gave him a look, but no other answer; and, going to my good old master, said a few words that I meant to be words of comfort and encouragement. He put his hand upon my shoulder, but did not lift his grey head.

"As you didn't understand me, Master Copperfield," resumed Uriah in the same officious manner, "I may take the liberty of umbly mentioning that I have called Doctor Strong's attention to the goings-on of Mrs. Strong. That was what my meaning was, Sir, when you didn't understand me."

"I have mentioned to Doctor Strong," he proceeded, "that any one may see that Mr. Maldon, and the lovely and agreeable lady as is Doctor Strong's wife, are too sweet on one another. When you come in, Sir, I was just putting it to my fellow-partner to say to Doctor Strong upon his word and honour, whether he'd ever been of this opinion long ago, or not. Come, Mr. Wickfield, Sir! Would you be so good as to tell us? Yes or no, Sir?"

"For God's sake, my dear Doctor," said Mr. Wickfield, "don't attach too much weight to any suspicions I may have entertained."

"There!" cried Uriah, shaking his head. "What a melancholy confirmation: ain't it? Him! Such an old friend!"

"My dear Strong," said Mr. Wickfield in a tremulous voice, "I needn't tell you that it has been my vice to look for some one master motive in everybody. I may have fallen into such doubts as I have had, through this mistake."

"You have had doubts, Wickfield," said the Doctor, without lifting up his head."

"I had, at one time, certainly," said Mr. Wickfield. "I—God forgive me—I thought *you* had."

"No, no, no!" returned the Doctor, in a tone of most pathetic grief.

"Since we have got so far," said Uriah, "I ought to take the liberty of mentioning that Copperfield has noticed it too."

I turned upon him, and asked him how he dared refer to me!

"Oh!" returned Uriah, "we all know what an amiable character yours is; but you know that the moment I spoke to you the other night, you knew what I meant."

I saw the mild eye of the good old Doctor turned upon me and I felt that the confession was too plainly written in my face to be overlooked.

We were silent again, and remained so, until the Doctor rose and walked twice or thrice across the room. Presently he returned to where his chair stood; and, leaning on the back of it, said:

"I believe I have been very much to blame. I have exposed one whom I hold in my heart, to aspersions of which she never, but for me, could have been the object. But Gentlemen, my life—my life—upon the truth and honour of the dear lady who has been the subject of this conversation!"

"I am not prepared," he went on, "to deny that I may have unwittingly ensnared that lady into an unhappy marriage. My life with this lady has been very happy. Until to-night, I have had uninterrupted occasion to bless the day on which I did her great injustice."

His voice, more and more faltering, stopped for a few moments; then he went on:

"Once I awakened from my dream, I see how natural it is that she should have some regretful feeling towards her old companion. That she does regard him with some innocent regret is, I fear, too true. But beyond this, the dear lady's name never must be coupled with a word, a breath, of doubt.

"Gentlemen, I have shown you my heart. What we have said to-night is never to be said more. Wickfield, give me an old friend's arm upstairs!"

Without interchanging a word they went slowly out of the room together, Uriah looking after them.

"Well, Master Copperfield!" said Uriah, meekly turning to me. "The thing hasn't took quite the turn that might have been expected, but *this* family's out of the cart, I think!"

I needed but the sound of his voice to be so madly enraged as I never was before, and never have been since.

"You villain," said I, "how dare you appeal to me just now."

As we stood, front to front, I saw so plainly, in the stealthy exultation of his face that he had set a deliberate trap for me that I couldn't bear it. The whole of his lank cheek was invitingly before me, and I struck it with my open hand with that force that my fingers tingled as if I had burnt them. He caught the hand in his, and we stood looking at each other.

"Copperfield," he said at length, "have you taken leave of your senses?"

"I have taken leave of you," said I, wresting my hand away. "Why should I dread your doing your worst to all about you? What else do you ever do?"

"Copperfield," he said, "you have always gone against me. And yet I always liked you."

I deigned to make him no reply; and, taking up my hat, was going out to bed, when he came between me and the door.

"Copperfield," he said, "there must be two parties to a quarrel. I won't be one."

"You may go to the devil!" said I.

"Don't say that!" he replied. "I know you'll be sorry afterwards. How can you show such a bad spirit? But I forgive you."

"You forgive me!" I repeated disdainfully.

"To think of your going and attacking *me*," replied Uriah. "I will be a friend to you, in spite of you. So now you know what you've got to expect."

Several weeks elapsed before I saw the least change in Mrs. Strong. It came on slowly, like a cloud when there is no wind. At first, she seemed to wonder at the gentle compassion with which the Doctor spoke to her, and at his wish that she should have her mother with her. Gradually, an unhappy shadow fell upon her beauty, and deepened every day.

The Doctor became older in appearance, and more grave; but the sweetness of his temper and his benevolent solicitude for her, if they were capable of any increase, were increased. I saw him once, early on the morning of her birthday, take her forehead between his hands, kiss it, and go hurriedly away, too much moved to remain. I saw her stand where he had left her, like a statue; and then bend down her head, and clasp her hands, and weep, I cannot say how sorrowfully.

Sometimes, after that, I fancied that she tried to speak. But she never uttered word. The Doctor always had some new project for her participating in amusements away from home, with her mother; and Mrs. Markleham was loud in her commendations. But Annie only went whither she was led.

I did not know what to think. Neither did my aunt;

who must have walked, at various times, a hundred miles in her uncertainty. What was strangest of all was, that the only real relief which seemed to make its way into the secret region of this domestic unhappiness, made its way there in the person of Mr. Dick.

He had proudly resumed his privilege of walking up and down the garden with the Doctor. But matters were no sooner in this state, when he devoted all his spare time to these perambulations. When the Doctor and I were engaged, he now fell into the custom of walking up and down with Mrs. Strong, and helping her trim her favourite flowers, or weed the beds. I dare say he rarely spoke a dozen words in an hour; but his quiet interest, and his wistful face, found immediate response in both their breasts; each knew that the other liked him, and that he loved both; and he became what no one else could be—a link between them.

"Nobody but myself, Trot, knows what that man is!" my aunt would proudly remark, when we conversed about it. "Dick will distinguish himself yet!"

I must refer to one other topic before I close this chapter. While the visit at the Doctor's was still in progress, I observed that the postman brought two or three letters every morning for Uriah Heep directed by Mr. Micawber. I was glad to infer that Mr. Micawber was doing well; and consequently was much surprised to receive, about this time, the following letter from his amiable wife:—

"Canterbury, *Monday Evening.*

"You will doubtless be surprised, my dear Mr. Copperfield, to receive this communication. Still more so, by its contents. But my feelings as a wife and mother require relief; and I know no one of whom I can better ask advice than my friend and former lodger.

"You will picture to yourself, my dear Mr. Copperfield, what the poignancy of my feelings must be, when I inform you that Mr. Micawber is entirely changed. He is reserved. He is secret.

"But this is not all. Mr. Micawber is morose. He is severe. He is estranged from our eldest son and daughter, he has no pride in his twins, he looks with an eye of coldness even on the unoffending stranger who last became a member of our circle.

"This is heart-breaking. If you will advise me, you will add another friendly obligation to the many you have already rendered me. With loves from the children, and a smile from the happily-unconscious stranger, I remain, dear Mr. Copperfield,

"Your afflicted,

"EMMA MICAWBER."

I did not feel justified in giving a wife of Mrs. Micawber's experience any other recommendation, than that she should try to reclaim Mr. Micawber by patience and kindness (as I knew she would in any case); but the letter set me thinking about him very much.

CHAPTER XLIII

ANOTHER RETROSPECT

ONCE again let me pause upon a memorable period of my life, to see the phantoms of those days go by me in dim procession.

Weeks, months, seasons, pass along. I have come legally to man's estate. I have attained the dignity of twenty-one. Let me think what I have achieved.

I have tamed that savage stenographic mystery. I make a respectable income by it. I am joined with eleven others in reporting the debates in Parliament for a Morning Newspaper. Night after night, I record predictions that never come to pass, explanations that are only meant to mystify.

I have come out in another way. I wrote a little something and sent it to a magazine, and it was published. Since then, I have taken heart to write a good many trifling pieces. Now, I am regularly paid for them. Altogether, I am well off.

We have removed to a pleasant little cottage. My aunt, however, (who has sold the house at Dover, to good advantage), is not going to remain here, but intends removing herself to a still more tiny cottage close at hand. What does this portend? My marriage? Yes!

Yes! I am going to be married to Dora! Miss Lavinia and Miss Clarissa have given their consent; and if ever canary birds were in a flutter, they are.

Miss Clarissa and my aunt roam all over London, to find out articles of furniture for Dora and me to look at. It would be better for them to buy the goods at once; for when we go to see a kitchen fender and meat-screen, Dora sees a Chinese house for Jip, with little bells on the top, and prefers that.

Peggotty comes up to make herself useful, and falls to work immediately. Her department appears to be, to clean everything over and over again. And now it is, that I begin to see her solitary brother passing through the dark streets at night, and looking, as he goes, among the wandering faces.

Why does Traddles look so important when he calls upon me this afternoon? I am going to take out the license.

It is a little document to do so much; and Traddles contemplates it half in admiration, half in awe.

"I hope the next time you come here, my dear fellow," I say to Traddles, "it will be on the same errand for yourself. And I hope it will be soon."

"Thank you for your good wishes, I hope so too. It's a satisfaction to know that she'll wait and that she really is the dearest girl——"

"When are you to meet her at the coach?" I ask.

"At seven," says Traddles. "That is about Miss Wickfield's time, is it not?"

"A little earlier. Her time is half-past eight."

Sophy arrives at the house of Dora's aunts, in due course, and is one of the most unaffected, engaging creatures I have ever seen. Traddles presents her to us with great pride; and rubs his hands for ten minutes by the clock, with every individual hair upon his head standing on tiptoe, when I congratulate him on his choice.

I have brought Agnes from the Canterbury coach, and her cheerful and beautiful face is among us for the second time. We have a delightful evening, and are supremely happy; but I don't believe it yet.

Next day, too, when we all go in a flock to see the house—our house—Dora's and mine—I am quite unable to regard myself as its master. Such a beautiful little house as it is, with everything so bright and new, and Dora's garden hat with the blue ribbon, already hanging

Our going.

on its little peg; the guitar-case in a corner; and everybody tumbling over Jip's pagoda, which is much too big for the establishment.

Another happy evening, quite as unreal as all the rest of it, and I go home and get up very early in the morning to fetch my aunt.

I have never seen my aunt in such state. She is dressed in lavender-coloured silk, and has a white bonnet on, and is amazing. Janet has dressed her, and is there to look at me. Peggotty is ready. Mr. Dick has had his hair curled.

My aunt sits with my hand in hers all the way. When we stop she gives it a squeeze, and me a kiss.

"God bless you, Trot! My own boy never could be dearer."

The rest is all a more or less incoherent dream.

A dream of their coming in with Dora. Of the clergyman and clerk appearing. Of Miss Lavinia being the first to cry, and of Miss Clarissa applying a smelling-bottle; of little Dora trembling very much, and making her responses in faint whispers.

Of our kneeling down together, side by side; of Dora's trembling less and less, but always clasping Agnes by the hand; of the service being got through, quietly and gravely.

Of our signing the register all round. Of my going into the gallery for Peggotty to bring *her* to sign it; of Peggotty's hugging me in a corner, and telling me she saw my own dear mother married; of its being over, and our going away.

Of there being a breakfast, with abundance of things to eat and drink, whereof I partake without the least perception of their flavour. Of our being very sociably and simply happy; and of Jip's having wedding cake, and its not agreeing with him afterwards.

Of Dora's being ready, and of Miss Lavinia's hovering about her. Of Dora's making a long series of surprised discoveries that she had forgotten all sorts of little things; and of everybody's running everywhere to fetch them.

Of my wanting to carry Jip (who is to go along with us), and Dora's saying, No, that she must carry him, or else he'll think she don't like him any more, now she is married. Of our going, arm in arm.

Of her stopping and looking back, and hurrying to Agnes, and giving Agnes her last kisses and farewells.

We drive away together, and I awake from the dream. I believe it at last. It is my dear, dear, little wife beside me, whom I love so well!

"Are you happy now, you foolish boy?" says Dora, "and sure you don't repent?"

CHAPTER XLIV

OUR HOUSEKEEPING

It was a strange condition of things when I found myself sitting down in my own small house with Dora, and sometimes of an evening, when I looked up from my writing, and saw her seated opposite, I would lean back in my chair, and think how queer it was that there we were, alone together as a matter of course—nobody's business any more—no one to please but one another—one another to please, for life.

When there was a debate and I was kept out very late, it seemed so strange to me, as I was walking home, to think that Dora was at home! It was such a wonderful thing, at first, to have her coming softly down to talk to me as I ate my supper. It was such a stupendous thing to know for certain that she put her hair in papers. It was altogether such an astonishing event to see her do it!

I doubt whether two young birds could have known less about keeping house, than I and my pretty Dora did. We had a servant, of course. I have still a latent belief that she must have been Mrs. Crupp's daughter in disguise, we had such an awful time of it with Mary Anne. She was the cause of our first little quarrel.

"My dearest life," I said one day to Dora, "do you think Mary Anne has any idea of time?"

"Why, Doady?" inquired Dora, looking up, innocently, from her drawing.

"My love, because it's five, and we were to have dined at four."

Dora glanced wistfully at the clock, and hinted that she thought it was too fast.

"On the contrary, my love," said I, referring to my watch, "it's a few minutes too slow."

My little wife came and sat upon my knee, to coax me to be quiet.

"Don't you think, my dear," said I, "it would be better for you to remonstrate with Mary Anne?"

"Oh no, please! I couldn't, Doady!" said Dora.

"Why not, my love?" I gently asked.

"Oh, because I am such a little goose," said Dora, "and she knows I am!"

I frowned a little.

"No, no! please!" cried Dora, with a kiss, "don't be a naughty Blue Beard! Don't be serious!"

"My precious wife," said I, "we must be serious sometimes. Come! Sit down on this chair, close beside me! Now let us talk sensibly. You know, my love, it is not exactly comfortable to have to go out without one's dinner. Now, is it?"

"N—n—no!" replied Dora, faintly.

"My love, how you tremble!"

"Because I *know* you're going to scold me," exclaimed Dora, in a piteous voice.

"My sweet, I am only going to reason."

"Oh, but reasoning is worse than scolding!" exclaimed Dora, in despair.

"Dora, my darling!"

"No, I am not your darling. Because you *must* be sorry that you married me, or else you wouldn't reason with me!"

I felt so injured by the inconsequential nature of this charge that it gave me courage to be grave.

"Now, my own Dora," said I, "you are very childish, and are talking nonsense. I was obliged to go out yesterday when dinner was half over; and the day before, I was made quite unwell by being obliged to eat underdone veal in a hurry; to-day, I don't dine at all. I don't mean to reproach you, my dear, but this is not comfortable."

"Oh, you cruel, cruel boy, to say I am a disagreeable wife!" cried Dora.

"Now, my dear Dora, you must know that I never said that!"

"You said I wasn't comfortable!" said Dora.

"I said the housekeeping was not comfortable."

"It's exactly the same thing!" cried Dora. And she evidently thought so, for she wept most grievously.

I took another turn across the room, full of love for my pretty wife, and distracted by self-accusatory inclinations to knock my head against the door. I sat down again, and said:

"I am not blaming you, Dora. I am only trying to show you, my dear, that you must—you really must" (I was resolved not to give this up) "accustom yourself to look after Mary Anne, and me."

"I wonder, I do, at your making such speeches," sobbed Dora.

She was so pathetic that I felt as if I had said I don't know what to hurt her. I was obliged to hurry away; I was kept out late; and I felt such pangs of remorse as made me miserable.

It was two or three hours past midnight when I got home. I found my aunt, in our house, sitting up for me.

"Is anything the matter, aunt?" said I, alarmed.

"Nothing, Trot," she replied. "Sit down, sit down. Little Blossom has been rather out of spirits, and I have been keeping her company. That's all."

I leaned my head upon my hand; and felt more sorry and downcast than I could have supposed possible. As I sat thinking, I happened to meet my aunt's eyes. There was an anxious expression in them, but it cleared directly.

"I assure you, aunt," said I, "I have been quite unhappy myself all night, to think of Dora's being so. But I had no other intention than to speak to her tenderly and lovingly about our home-affairs."

My aunt nodded encouragement.

"You must have patience, Trot," said she.

"Of course. Heaven knows I don't mean to be unreasonable, aunt!"

"No, no," said my aunt. "But Little Blossom is a very tender little blossom, and the wind must be gentle with her."

"Don't you think, aunt," said I, "that you could advise and counsel Dora a little now and then?"

"Trot," returned my aunt, with some emotion, "No! Don't ask me such a thing."

Her tone was so very earnest that I raised my eyes in surprise.

"Division must not come between us, at this time of day."

"Division between *us!*" cried I.

"Child, child!" said my aunt, smoothing her dress, "How soon it might come between us, or how unhappy I might make our Little Blossom, if I meddled in anything, a prophet couldn't say. I want our pet to like me, and be as gay as a butterfly."

I comprehended, at once, that my aunt was right.

"But remember, my dear," she pursued, "your future is between you two. You are to work it out for yourselves. This is marriage, Trot; and Heaven bless you both, in it, for a pair of babes in the wood as you are!"

My aunt said this in a sprightly way, and gave me a kiss to ratify the blessing.

"Now," said she, "light my little lantern, and see me into my band-box by the garden path. Give Betsy Trotwood's love to Blossom, when you come back; and whatever you do, Trot, never dream of setting Betsey up as a scarecrow."

With this my aunt tied her head up in a handkerchief, and I escorted her home.

Dora came stealing down in her little slippers, to meet me, now that I was alone; and cried upon my shoulder, and we made it up, and agreed that our first little difference was to be our last, and that we were never to have another if we lived a hundred years.

One of our first feats in the housekeeping way was a little dinner to Traddles. I could not have wished for a prettier little wife at the opposite end of the table, but I certainly could have wished when we sat down, for a little more room. Though there were only two of us, we were always cramped for room, and yet had always room enough to lose everything in. On the present occasion, Traddles was so hemmed in by Jip's pagoda and the guitar-case, and Dora's flower-painting, and my writing-table, that I had serious doubts of the possibility of his using his knife and fork; but he protested, with his own good-humour, "Oceans of room, Copperfield! I assure you, Oceans!"

There was another thing I could have wished; namely, that Jip had never been encouraged to walk about the table-cloth during dinner. On this occasion he barked at my old friend, and made short runs at his plate, with such undaunted pertinacity, that he may be said to have engrossed the conversation.

However, as I knew how tender-hearted my dear Dora was, I hinted no objection. For similar reasons I made no allusion to the skirmishing plates upon the floor; or to the disreputable appearance of the castors, which were all at sixes and sevens, and looked drunk. I could not help wondering, as I contemplated the boiled leg of mutton before me, how it came to pass that our joints of meat were of such extraordinary shapes—and whether our butcher contracted for all the deformed sheep that came into the world!

"My love," said I to Dora, "what have you got in that dish?"

"Oysters, dear," said Dora, timidly.

"Was that *your* thought?" said I, delighted.

"Ye-yes, Doady," said Dora.

"There never was a happier one!" I exclaimed. "There is nothing Traddles likes so much!"

"Ye-yes, Doady," said Dora, "and so I bought a beautiful little barrel of them, and the man said they were very good. But I—I am afraid there's something the matter with them. They don't seem right."

"Do you know, Copperfield," said Traddles, cheerfully examining the dish, "they are capital oysters, but I *think* it is in consequence—of their never having been opened."

They never had been opened; and we had no oyster-knives; so we looked at the oysters and ate the mutton. At least we ate as much of it as was done, and made up with capers.

When Traddles went away, my wife planted her chair close to mine, and sat down by my side.

"I am very sorry," she said. "Will you try to teach me, Doady?"

"I must teach myself first, Dora," said I. "I am as bad as you, love."

"Ah! But you can learn," she returned; "and you are a clever, clever man!"

"Nonsense, Mouse!" said I.

"Will you call me a name I want you to call me?" inquired Dora, without moving.

"What is it?" I asked with a smile.

"It's a stupid name," she said, "Child-wife."

I laughingly asked my child-wife what her fancy was.

"I don't mean, you silly fellow, that you should use the name instead of Dora. I only mean that you should think of me that way. When you are going to be angry with me, say to yourself, 'It's only my child-wife!' When you miss what I should like to be, and I think can never be, say, 'still my foolish child-wife loves me!' For indeed I do."

I had not been serious with her; having no idea, until now, that she was serious herself. But this appeal made a strong impression on me. I look back on the time I write of; and I can still declare that this one little speech was constantly in my memory.

Dora told me, shortly afterwards, that she was going to be a wonderful housekeeper. Accordingly she bought an immense account-book, carefully stitched up with a needle and thread all the leaves of the Cookery Book which Jip had torn, and made quite a desperate little attempt "to be good," as she called it. But the figures *would not* add up.

Sometimes, of an evening, when I was at home and at work—for I wrote a good deal now—I would lay down my pen, and watch my child-wife trying to be good. She would sit down with the tablets, and a little basket of bills and other documents, which looked more like curl-papers than anything else, and endeavour to get some result out of them. After severely comparing one with another, and making entries on the tablets, and blotting them out, and counting all the fingers of her left hand over and over again, backwards and forwards, she would be so vexed and discouraged, and would look so unhappy that I would go softly to her, and say:

"What's the matter, Dora?"

Dora would look up hopelessly, and reply, "They won't come right. They make my head ache so. And they won't do anything I want!"

Then I would say, "Now let us try together. Let me show you, Dora."

Then I would commence a practical demonstration, to which Dora would pay profound attention, perhaps for five minutes; when she would begin to be dreadfully tired, and would lighten the subject by curling my hair. If I persisted, she would look so scared as she became more and more bewildered, that the remembrance of her natural gaiety, and of her being my child-wife, would come reproachfully upon me; and I would lay the pencil down, and call for the guitar.

Thus it was that I took upon myself the toils and cares of our life, and had no partner in them. We lived much as before, in reference to our scrambling household arrangements; but I had got used to those, and Dora was bright and cheerful in the old childish way, loved me dearly, and was happy with her old trifles.

When the debates were heavy and I went home late,

Dora would always come down-stairs to meet me. When I was engaged in writing at home, she would sit quietly near me, however late the hour, and be so mute, that I would often think she had dropped asleep. But generally, when I raised my head, I saw her blue eyes looking at me with quiet attention.

"Oh, what a weary boy!" said Dora one night, when I met her eyes as I was shutting up my desk.

"What a weary girl!" said I. "You must go to bed another time, my love. It's far too late for you."

"No, don't send me to bed!" pleaded Dora, coming to my side. "Pray, don't do that!"

To my amazement she was sobbing on my neck.

"Not well, my dear! not happy!"

"Yes! quite well, and very happy!" said Dora. "But say you'll let me stop, and see you write. Will you mind it if I say something very, very silly?"

"What wonderful thing is that?" said I.

"Please let me hold the pens," said Dora. "I want to have something to do with all those many hours when you are so industrious. May I hold the pens?"

The remembrance of her pretty joy when I said Yes, brings tears into my eyes. Regularly afterwards, she sat in her old place, with a spare bundle of pens at her side. Her triumph in this connexion with my work, and her delight when I wanted a new pen—which I very often feigned to do—are touching recollections to me, simple as they might appear to other men.

Her delight when I wanted a new pen—which I very often feigned to do.

CHAPTER XLV

MR. DICK FULFILS MY AUNT'S PREDICTIONS

It was some time now, since I had left the Doctor. Living in his neighbourhood, I saw him frequently; and we all went to his house on two or three occasions to dinner or tea. The Old Soldier was in permanent quarters under the Doctor's roof. She was exactly the same as ever, and the same immortal butterflies hovered over her cap.

Like some other mothers whom I have known, Mrs. Markleham was far more fond of pleasure than her daughter was.

"My dear soul," she said to the Doctor one day, "you know it would be a little pokey for Annie to be always shut up here."

The Doctor nodded his benevolent head.

"When she comes to her mother's age," said Mrs. Markleham, with a flourish of her fan, "then it'll be another thing. You might put ME into a jail, with genteel society and I should never care to come out. But I am not Annie, you know."

"Surely, surely," said the Doctor.

"You are the best of creatures, but of course you don't—now do you?—enter into the same pursuits and fancies as Annie."

"No," said the Doctor, in a sorrowful tone.

"No, of course not," retorted the Old Soldier. "Take your Dictionary, for example. What a useful work a Dictionary is! But we can't expect a Dictionary—especially when it's making—to interest Annie, can we?"

The Doctor shook his head.

"And that's why I *so* much approve of your thoughtfulness. You have studied Annie's character, and you understand it. *That's* what I find so charming!"

Even the calm and patient face of Doctor Strong expressed some little sense of pain, I thought.

"Therefore, my dear Doctor," said the Soldier, "you may command me, at all times. I am ready to go with Annie to operas, concerts, all kinds of places; and you shall never find that I am tired."

She was as good as her word. It was in vain for Annie to protest. Her mother's remonstrance always was, "Now, my dear Annie, I am sure you know better; and I must tell you, my love, that you are not making a proper return for the kindness of Doctor Strong."

One night Mr. Dick put his head into the parlour, where I was writing alone, and said, with a significant cough:

"You couldn't speak to me without inconveniencing yourself, Trotwood, I am afraid?"

"Certainly, Mr. Dick," said I; "come in!"

"Trotwood," said Mr. Dick, "before I sit down, I wish to make an observation. You know your aunt?"

"A little," I replied.

"She is the most wonderful woman in the world, Sir!"

Mr. Dick sat down with greater gravity than usual, and looked at me.

"Now, boy," said Mr. Dick, "I am going to put a question to you. What do you consider me, Sir?"

"A dear old friend," said I.

"Thank you, Trotwood," returned Mr. Dick, laughing. "But I mean, boy," resuming his gravity, "what do you consider me in this respect?" touching his forehead .

I was puzzled how to answer, but he helped me with a word.

"Weak?" said Mr. Dick.

"Well," I replied, dubiously. "Rather so."

"Exactly!" cried Mr. Dick, who seemed quite enchanted by my reply. "She pretends I am not, but I am.

I know I am. If she hadn't stood my friend, Sir, I should have been shut up, to lead a dismal life these many years. But I'll provide for her! I never spend the copying money. I put it in a box. I have made a will. I'll leave it all to her. She shall be rich—noble!"

Mr. Dick took out his pocket-handkerchief, and wiped his eyes. He then folded it up with great care, pressed it smooth between his two hands and put it in his pocket.

"Now you are a scholar, Trotwood," said Mr. Dick. "You know what a learned man the Doctor is. You know what honour he has always done me. I have sent his name up, on a scrap of paper, to the kite, along the string, when it has been in the sky, among the larks. The kite has been glad to receive it, Sir, and the sky has been brighter with it."

I delighted him by saying that the Doctor was deserving of our highest esteem.

"And his beautiful wife is a star," said Mr. Dick. "A shining star. But," bringing his chair nearer, and laying one hand upon my knee—"clouds, Sir—clouds."

Mr. Dick sat considering.

"Doctor not angry with her, Trotwood?" he said, after some time.

"No. Devoted to her."

"Then, I have got it, boy!" said Mr. Dick.

The sudden exultation with which he slapped me on the knee made me think him farther out of his wits than ever. He became as suddenly grave again, and leaning forward as before, said:

"Most wonderful woman in the world, Trotwood. Why has *she* done nothing to set things right?"

"Too delicate and difficult for such interference."

"Fine scholar," said Mr. Dick, touching me with his finger. "Why has *he* done nothing?"

"For the same reason," I returned.

"Then, I have got it, boy!" said Mr. Dick. "A poor fellow with a craze, Sir," said Mr. Dick, "present company, you know!" striking himself again, "may do what wonderful people may not do. I'll bring them together, boy. I'll try. They'll not blame *me*. I'm only Mr. Dick. Dick's nobody! Whoo!" He blew a slight, contemptuous breath, as if he blew himself away.

"Not a word, boy!" he pursued in a whisper; "leave all the blame with Dick—simple Dick. After what you have said to me, I am sure I have got it. All right!"

To my surprise, I heard no more about it for some two or three weeks, and I began to believe that he had either forgotten his intention or abandoned it.

One fair evening, when Dora was not inclined to go out, my aunt and I strolled up to the Doctor's cottage. Mrs. Strong was just coming out of the garden, where Mr. Dick yet lingered, helping point some stakes. We went into the drawing-room with Mrs. Strong and sat down by the darkening window.

We had not sat here many minutes, when Mrs. Markleham came bustling in, with her newspaper in her hand, and said, "Annie, my love, I am going to the Study with my paper, for I am a poor creature without news. Miss Trotwood, David, pray come and see the Doctor."

I was conscious of Mr. Dick's standing in the shadow of the room when we accompanied her to the Study, but who got first into the Study, or how Mrs. Markleham settled herself in a moment in her easy chair, I have forgotten if I ever knew. But this I know—that we saw the Doctor sitting at his table, resting his head calmly on his hand. That, in the same moment, we saw Mrs. Strong glide in, pale and trembling. That Mr. Dick supported her on his arm. That he laid his other hand upon the Doctor's arm. That, as the Doctor moved, his wife dropped down on one knee at his feet, and, with her hands imploringly lifted, fixed upon his face the memorable look I have never forgotten. That, at this sight Mrs. Markleham dropped the newspaper, and stared.

"Doctor!" said Mr. Dick. "What is amiss? Look here!"

"Annie!" cried the Doctor. "Not at my feet, my dear!"

"Yes!" she said. "I beg and pray that no one will leave the room! Oh my husband and father, break this long silence. Let us both know what it is that has come between us!"

Mrs. Markleham seeming to swell with family pride and motherly indignation, here exclaimed, "Annie, get up immediately."

"Mama," returned Annie, "my appeal is to my husband."

"Annie," said the Doctor, tenderly taking her in his hands, "if any change has come, you are not to blame. The fault is mine. There is no change in my affection and respect. Rise, Annie, I pray."

But she did not rise. She laid her arm across his knee, and dropping her head upon it, said:

"If I have any friend here who has anything within his knowledge that may help to mediate between us, I implore that friend to speak."

There was a profound silence. After a few moments of hesitation I said:

"Mrs. Strong, there is something which I have been earnestly entreated by Dr. Strong to conceal, and have concealed until to-night."

She turned her face toward me.

"Our future peace," she said, "may be in your hands. I trust confidently to your not suppressing anything."

Thus earnestly besought, without any other compromise of the truth than a little softening of the coarseness of Uriah Heep, I stated plainly what had passed in that same room.

When I had finished, Annie remained for some few minutes silent. Then she took the Doctor's hand and pressed it to her breast, and kissed it. Mr. Dick softly raised her and she stood leaning on him and looking down upon her husband.

"All that has ever been in my mind since I was married," she said in a low, tender voice, "I will lay bare before you. I could not live and have one reservation now."

"Nay, Annie," said the Doctor mildly. "There is no need."

"There is great need," she answered.

"Really," interrupted Mrs. Markleham, "if I have any discretion at all——"

("Which you haven't, you Marplot," observed my aunt, in an indignant whisper.)

"——I must observe that it cannot be requisite to enter into these details."

"No one but my husband can judge of that, mama," said Annie, "and he will hear me. If I say anything to give you pain, mama, forgive me. I have borne pain, often and long, myself."

"Upon my word!" gasped Mrs. Markleham.

"When I was quite a little child, my first associations with knowledge of any kind were inseparable from the friend of my dead father, who was always dear to me. I can remember nothing that I know, without remembering him."

"Makes her mother nothing!" exclaimed Mrs. Markleham.

"Not so, mama," said Annie; "but I make him what he was. As I grew up I was deeply, gratefully attached to him. I looked up to him as a father, as a guide, as one in whom I could have trusted and confided, if I had doubted all the world. You know, mama, how young and inexperienced I was, when you presented him before me, of a sudden, as a lover."

"I have mentioned the fact, fifty times at least, to everybody here!" said Mrs. Markleham.

("Then hold your tongue, for the Lord's sake, and don't mention it any more!" muttered my aunt.)

"I was but a girl; and when so great a change came, I think I was sorry. But I was proud that he should think me so worthy, and we were married."

"——At Saint Alphage, Canterbury," observed Mrs. Markleham.

("Confound the woman!" said my aunt, "she *won't* be quiet!")

"I never thought," proceeded Annie, with a heightened colour, "of any worldly gain that my husband would bring to me. Mama, forgive me when I say that it was *you* who first presented my mind the thought that any one could wrong me, and wrong him, by such a cruel suspicion."

"Me!" cried Mrs. Markleham.

("Ah! You, to be sure!" observed my aunt, "and you can't fan it away, my military friend!")

"It was the first unhappiness of my new life," said Annie, "when I saw how many importunate claims were pressed upon you, my husband, in my name; how generous you were, and how Mr. Wickfield resented it; the first sense of the mean suspicion that my tenderness was bought—and sold to you—fell upon me."

"A specimen of the thanks one gets," cried Mrs. Markleham, in tears; "I wish I was a Turk!"

("I wish you were, with all my heart—and in your native country!" said my aunt.)

"It was at that time that mama was most solicitous about my Cousin Maldon. I had liked him:" she spoke softly, but without any hesitation: "very much. We had been little lovers once. If circumstances had not happened otherwise, I might have married him, and been most wretched. If I were thankful to my husband for no more, instead of for so much, I should be thankful to him for having saved me from the first mistaken impulse of my undisciplined heart."

She spoke with an earnestness that thrilled me. Yet her voice was just as quiet as before.

"When he was waiting to be the object of your munificence, I thought it would have become him better to have worked his own way on. But I thought no worse of him, until the night of his departure for India. That night I knew he had a false and thankless heart. I saw a double meaning, then, in Mr. Wickfield's scrutiny of me. I perceived the dark suspicion that shadowed my life."

"Suspicion, Annie!" said the Doctor. "No, no, no!"

"In your mind there was none, I know, my husband!" she returned. "And when I came to you, that night, and knew that I had to tell, that, underneath your roof, one of my own kindred, to whom you had been a benefactor, for the love of me, had spoken to me words that should have found no utterance, my mind revolted from the taint. It died upon my lips."

Mrs. Markleham, with a short groan, retired behind her fan.

"I have never, but in your presence, interchanged a word with him from that time."

She sank down gently at the Doctor's feet, though he did his utmost to prevent her; and said:

"Do not speak to me yet! Let me say a little more!"

"If I shrank into myself, hiding the disrespect I had undergone, it was because I honoured you so much, and so much wished that you should honour me!"

"Annie, my pure heart!" said the Doctor, "my dear girl!"

"Another word! I do not hope that any love and duty I may render will ever make me worthy of your priceless confidence; but I can lift my eyes to this dear face and solemnly dcelare that in my lightest thought I never wronged you; never wavered in the love and the fidelity I owe you!"

She had her arms around the Doctor's neck, and he leant his head down over her.

"Oh, hold me to your heart, my husband! Do not think or speak of disparity between us, for there is none, except in all my many imperfections. Take me to your heart, for my love was founded on a rock, and it endures!"

In the silence that ensued, my aunt walked gravely up to Mr. Dick, and gave him a hug and a sounding kiss. And it was very fortunate that she did so; for I am confident that I detected him in the act of making preparations to stand on one leg, as an appropriate expression of delight.

"You are a very remarkable man, Dick!" said my aunt.

With that we three stole quietly out of the room.

"That's a settler for our military friend, at any rate," said my aunt, on the way home. "I should sleep the better for that, if there was nothing else to be glad of!"

"She was quite overcome, I am afraid," said Mr. Dick.

"What! Did you ever see a crocodile overcome?" inquired my aunt.

"I don't think I ever saw a crocodile," returned Mr. Dick, mildly.

CHAPTER XLVI

INTELLIGENCE

I MUST have been married about a year or so, when one evening, as I was returning from a solitary walk, thinking of the book I was then writing, I came past Mrs. Steerforth's house. I had often passed it before, during my residence in that neighbourhood, though never when I could choose another road, and it usually awakened a long train of meditations. Coming before me on this particular evening that I mention, it was more than commonly suggestive. I fell into a brown study as I walked on, when a voice at my side made me start.

It was a woman's voice. I was not long in recollecting Mrs. Steerforth's little parlour-maid, who had formerly worn blue ribbons in her cap. She had taken them out now and wore but one or two disconsolate bows of sober brown.

"If you please, Sir, would you have the goodness to walk in, and speak to Miss Dartle?"

"Has Miss Dartle sent you for me?" I inquired.

"She saw you pass a night or two ago; and I was to sit at work on the staircase, and when I saw you pass again, to ask you to step in and speak to her."

I turned back, and was directed to Miss Dartle in the garden. She was sitting on a seat at one end of a terrace, overlooking the great city.

Our meeting was not cordial. We had parted angrily on the last occasion; and there was an air of disdain about her, which she took no pains to conceal.

"I am told you wish to speak to me, Miss Dartle," said I, standing near her.

"If you please," said she. "Pray has this girl been found?"

"No."

"And yet she has run away!"

"Run away?" I repeated.

"Yes! From him," she said, with a laugh. "Perhaps she never will be found. She may be dead! Do you wish to know what is known of her?"

"Yes," said I.

She rose and taking a few steps towards a wall of holly, said, in a louder voice, "Come here!", and returned, followed by the respectable Mr. Littimer, who, with undiminished respectability, made me a bow, and took up his position behind her.

"Now," said she, imperiously, "tell Mr. Copperfield about the flight."

"Mr. James and myself, ma'am——"

"Don't address yourself to me!" she interrupted with a frown.

"Mr. James and myself, Sir——"

"Nor to me, if you please," said I.

Mr. Littimer, without being at all discomposed, began again:

"Mr. James and myself have been abroad with the young woman, ever since she left Yarmouth under Mr. James's protection. We have been in France, Switzerland, Italy—in fact, almost all parts.

"Mr. James took quite uncommonly to the young woman; and was more settled, for a length of time, than I have known him to be since I have been in his service. The young woman was very improvable, and spoke the languages; and wouldn't have been known for the same country-person. I noticed that she was much admired wherever we went.

He made a short pause.

"The young woman being occasionally low in her spirits, she began to weary Mr. James. Mr. James he began to be restless again. The more restless he got, the worse she got; and I must say, for myself, that I had a very difficult time of it indeed between the two."

Mr. Littimer, clearing his throat behind his hand with a respectable short cough, went on:

"At last Mr. James he set off one morning, from the neighbourhood of Naples, where he had a villa (the young woman being very partial to the sea), and left it with me to break it out, that he was"—here an interruption of the short cough—"gone. But Mr. James, I must say, certainly did behave extremely honourable; for he proposed that the young woman should marry a very respectable person, who was fully prepared to overlook the past."

I was convinced the scoundrel spoke of himself, and I saw my conviction reflected in Miss Dartle's face.

"This I also had it in charge to communicate. The young woman's violence after I broke the fact of Mr. James' departure, was beyond all expectations. She was quite mad, and had to be held by force. But when I came to the second part of what had been entrusted to me," said Mr. Littimer, rubbing his hands, uneasily, "a more outrageous person I never did see. If I hadn't been upon my guard, I am convinced she would have had my blood."

"I think the better of her for it," said I, indignantly.

Mr. Littimer bent his head, as much as to say, "Indeed, Sir? But you're young!" and resumed his narrative.

"It was necessary, in short, for a time, to take away everything that she could do herself, or anybody else, an injury with, and to shut her up close. Notwithstanding which, she got out in the night; forced the lattice of a window, that I had nailed up myself; dropped on a vine that was trailed below; and never has been seen or heard of, to my knowledge, since."

"She is dead, perhaps," said Miss Dartle, with a smile.

"She may have drowned herself, miss," returned Mr. Littimer. "It's very possible. Or, she may have had assistance from the boatmen, and the boatmen's wives and children. Being given to low company, she was very much in the habit of talking to them on the beach."

"Now," said she, imperiously, "tell Mr. Copperfield about the flight."

"When it was clear," he said, with infinite respectability, and an obedient bow; "that she was not to be found, I went to Mr. James and informed him of what had occurred. Words passed between us in consequence, and I felt it due to my character to leave him. Knowing the unfortunate difference between himself and his mother, I took the liberty of coming home to England, and relating——"

"For money which I paid him," said Miss Dartle to me.

"Just so, ma'am—and relating what I knew. I am not aware," said Mr. Littimer, after a moment's reflection, "that there is anything else. I am at present out of employment, and should be happy to meet with a respectable situation."

With that, he made a polite bow, and went away through the arch in the wall of holly by which he had come.

"He says besides," she observed, with a slow curling of her lip, "that his master, as he hears, is coasting Spain. But this is of no interest to you. Between these two proud persons, mother and son, there is a wider breach than before, and time makes each more obstinate and imperious. Neither is this of any interest to you; but it introduces what I wish to say. This devil whom you make an angel of, I mean this low girl, may be alive. If she is, you will desire to have a pearl of such price found and taken care of. We desire that, too; that he may not by any chance be made her prey again, and that is why I, who would do her any mischief that so coarse a wretch is capable of feeling, have sent for you to hear what you have heard."

I saw, by the change in her face, that some one was advancing behind me. It was Mrs. Steerforth. She was greatly altered, but she was a handsome lady still.

"Is Mr. Copperfield informed of everything, Rosa?"

"Yes."

"And has he heard Littimer himself?"

"Yes; I have told him why you wished it."

"You are a good girl. I have no other object in this, Sir, than what Rosa has mentioned."

"Madam," I said respectfully, "I understand. But I must say, even to you, having known this injured family from childhood, that if you suppose the girl would not rather die a hundred deaths than take a cup of water from your son's hand now, you cherish a terrible mistake."

"Well," said Mrs. Steerforth, "it is no matter. Let it be. You are married, Sir, I am told?"

I answered that I had been some time married.

"And are doing well? I understand you are beginning to be famous."

"I have been very fortunate," I said.

"You have no mother?"—in a softened voice.

"No."

"It is a pity," she returned. "She would have been proud of you. Good night!"

As I moved away, I could not help observing how steadily they both sat gazing on the prospect, and how it thickened and closed around them.

Reflecting on what had been thus told me, I felt it right that it should be communicated to Mr. Peggotty. On the following evening I went into London in quest of him. Often and often, now, had I seen him in the dead of night passing along the streets, searching for what he dreaded to find.

He kept a lodging over the little chandler's shop in Hungerford Market, and hither I directed my walk. He was sitting reading by a window. The room was very neat and orderly. I saw in a moment that it was always kept prepared for her reception. He had not heard my tap at the door, and only raised his eyes when I laid my hand upon his shoulder.

"Mas'r Davy! Thankee, Sir! thankee hearty, for this visit! Sit ye down. You're kindly welcome, Sir!"

"Mr. Peggotty," said I, taking the chair he handed me, "don't expect much! I have heard some news."

"Of Em'ly!"

"It gives no clue to where she is; but she is not with him."

He sat down, looking intently at me, and listened in profound silence to all I had to tell.

When I had done, he shaded his face, and continued silent.

"How do you fare to feel about it, Mas'r Davy?" he inquired at length.

"I think that she is living," I replied.

"I doen't know. Maybe the first shock was too rough, and in the wildness of her 'art——! And yet," he added, "Mas'r Davy, I have felt so sure as she was living—I have know'd, awake and sleeping, as I should find her, that I doen't believe I can have been deceived. No! Em'ly's alive!" he said, stedfastly, *"I am told* as she's alive!"

He looked almost like a man inspired. I waited for a few moments and then proceeded:

"Now, my dear friend, if she should make her way to London, I believe there is one person, here, more likely to discover her than any other in the world. Do you remember —do you remember Martha?"

"Of our town?"

I needed no other answer than his face.

"Do you know that she is in London?"

"I have seen her in the streets," he answered with a shiver.

"But you don't know," said I, "that Emily was charitable to her, with Ham's help, long before she fled from home. Nor, that, when you and I met one night, she listened at the door."

"Mas'r Davy!" he replied in astonishment. "That night when it snew so hard?"

"That night. I have never seen her since, but she is the person with whom I think we should communicate. Do you understand?"

"Too well, Sir!" he replied.

"Do you think that you could find her?"

"I think, Mas'r Davy, I know wheer to look."

"Shall we try to find her to-night?"

He assented, and prepared to accompany me. We were

not far from Blackfriars Bridge, when he pointed to a solitary female figure flitting along the opposite side of the street. I knew it, readily, to be the figure that we sought.

We crossed the road, and were pressing on towards her, when it occurred to me that she might be more disposed to feel interest in the lost girl, if we spoke to her in a quieter place, and where we should be less observed. I advised my companion, therefore, that we should not address her yet, but follow her.

She went on a long way. At length she turned into a dull, dark street, where the noise and crowd were lost; and I said, "We may speak to her now"; and, mending our pace, we went after her.

CHAPTER XLVII

MARTHA

THERE was, at the end of that low-lying street, a dilapidated little wooden building, probably an obsolete old ferry-house. Its position is just at that point where the street ceases, and the road begins to lie between a row of houses and the river. As soon as Martha came here, and saw the water, she stopped as if she had come to her destination; and presently went slowly along by the brink of the river, looking intently at it.

I think she was talking to herself. I am sure that her shawl was off her shoulders, and that she was muffling her hands in it, in a bewildered way. I know, and never can forget, that there was that in her wild manner which gave me no assurance but that she would sink before my eyes, until I had her arm within my grasp.

At the same moment I said, "Martha!"

She uttered a terrified scream, and struggled with me with such strength that I doubt if I could have held her alone. But a stronger hand than mine was laid upon her; and when she saw whose it was, she dropped down between us.

"Oh, the river!" she cried passionately. "Oh, the river!"

"Hush, hush!" said I. "Calm yourself."

"I know it's like me!" she exclaimed. "I know that I belong to it. It comes from country places, where there was once no harm in it—and it creeps through the dismal streets, defiled and miserable—and it goes away, like my life, to a great sea, that is always troubled."

I have never known what despair was, except in the tone of those words.

"I can't keep away from it. I can't forget it. Oh, the dreadful river!"

A new burst of crying came upon her now, in which she once more hid her face among the stones, and we stood by in silence until she became more tranquil.

"Martha," said I then, leaning down, and helping her to rise. "Do you know who this is, who is with me?"

She said faintly, "Yes."

"Do you know that we have followed you a long way to-night?"

She shook her head.

"Are you composed enough," said I, "to speak on the subject which so interested you that snowy night?"

Her sobs broke out afresh.

"I want to say nothing for myself," she said, after a few moments. "I am bad, I am lost. But tell him, Sir, that I never was in any way the cause of his misfortune."

"It has never been attributed to you," I returned earnestly. "You are innocent of any part in it,—we know."

"What shall I ever do!" she said. Suddenly she turned to my companion. "Stamp upon me, kill me! You can't believe—why should you?—a syllable that comes out of my lips. I don't complain. I don't say she and I are alike. I know there is a long, long way between us. I only say that I am grateful to her from my soul, and love her."

"Martha," said Mr. Peggotty, "God forbid as I should judge you. Forbid as I, of all men, should do that, my girl! You doen't understand what 'tis we has afore us. Listen now!"

His influence upon her was complete. She stood, shrinkingly, before him.

"If you heerd," said Mr. Peggotty, "owt of what passed between Mas'r Davy and me, th' night when it snew so hard, you know as I have been—wheer not—fur to seek my dear niece."

Martha put her hands before her face; but otherwise remained quiet.

"I have heerd her tell," said Mr. Peggotty, "as you was early left fatherless and motherless, with no friend fur to take, in a rough seafaring way, their place. Maybe you can guess that if you'd had such a friend, you'd have got into a way of being fond of him and that my niece was kiender daughter-like to me."

As she was silently trembling, he put her shawl carefully about her.

"According to our reckoning," he proceeded, "Mas'r Davy's here, and mine, she is like, one day, to make her own poor solitary course to London. You're thankful to her and you love her. Help us all you can to find her!"

"Will you trust me?" she asked, in a low voice of astonishment.

"Full and free!" said Mr. Peggotty.

She lifted up her eyes, and solemnly declared that she would devote herself to this task and never relinquish it while there was any chance of hope.

We judged it expedient, now, to tell her all we knew; and she listened with great attention. It seemed as if her spirits were quite altered, and she could not be too quiet.

She asked when all was told, where we were to be communicated with. Under a dull lamp in the road, I wrote our two addresses on a leaf of my pocketbook, which I tore out and gave to her, and which she put in her poor bosom. I took out my purse; but I could not prevail upon her to accept any money.

"There may be work to be got," she said. "I'll try."

"At least take some assistance," I returned, "until you have tried."

"I could not do what I have promised, for money," she replied. "To give me money would be to take away your trust, to take away the only certain thing that saves me from the river."

It was midnight when I arrived at home. I had reached my own gate, and was standing listening for the deep bell of Saint Paul's among the multitude of striking clocks, when I was surprised to see that the door of my aunt's cottage was open, and that a faint light in the entry was shining out across the road. I went to speak to her, and it was with very great surprise that I saw a man standing in her little garden.

I stopped short, among the thick foliage outside, and I recognized the man whom I had once encountered with my aunt in the streets of the City.

The light in the passage was obscured for a moment, and my aunt came out. She was agitated, and told some money into his hand. I heard it chink.

"What's the use of this?" he demanded.

"I can spare no more," returned my aunt.

"Then I can't go," said he. "Here! You may take it back!"

"You bad man," returned my aunt, with great emotion; "how can you use me so?"

He stood moodily rattling the money, and shaking his head, until at length he said: "Is this all you mean to give me, then?"

"You stripped me of the greater part of all I ever had. You treated me falsely and cruelly. Don't add new injuries to the long, long list of injuries you have done me!"

"Ay!" he returned. "It's all very fine!—Well! I must do the best I can, for the present, I suppose."

In spite of himself, he appeared abashed and came slouching out of the garden. Taking two or three quick steps I met him at the gate, and went in as he came out.

"Aunt," said I, hurriedly. "This man alarming you again! Let me speak to him. Who is he?"

"Child," returned my aunt, taking my arm, "come in, and don't speak to me for ten minutes."

We sat down in her little parlour. My aunt retired behind the round green fan for about a quarter of an hour. Then she came out, and took a seat beside me.

"Trot," said my aunt calmly, "it's my husband."

"Your husband, aunt? I thought he had been dead!"

"Dead to me," returned my aunt, "but living."

I sat in silent amazement.

"Betsey Trotwood don't look a likely subject for the tender passion," said my aunt, composedly, "but the time was, Trot, when she believed in that man most entirely. When she loved him, Trot, right well. He repaid her by breaking her fortune, and nearly breaking her heart."

"My dear, good aunt!"

"I left him," my aunt proceeded, "generously; but he soon made ducks and drakes of what I gave him, sank lower and lower, married another woman, I believe, became an adventurer, a gambler, and a cheat. What he is now, you see. But he was a fine-looking man when I married him," said my aunt, "and I believed him—I was a fool!—to be the soul of honour!"

She gave my hand a squeeze, and shook her head.

"He is nothing to me now, Trot,—less than nothing. But sooner than have him punished for his offences, I give him more money than I can afford, at intervals when he reappears, to go away.

My aunt dismissed the matter with a heavy sigh, and smoothed her dress.

"There, my dear!" she said, "Now, you know the beginning, middle, and end, and all about it. This is my grumpy, frumpy story, and we'll keep it to ourselves, Trot!"

CHAPTER XLVIII

DOMESTIC

I LABOURED hard at my book and it came out and was very successful, so that I considered myself reasonably entitled to escape from the dreary debates. One joyful night, therefore, I noted down the music of the parliamentary bagpipes for the last time, and I have never heard it since.

I now write of the time when I had been married, I suppose, about a year and a half. We had given up the housekeeping as a bad job. The house kept itself, and we kept a page. The principal function of this retainer was to quarrel with the cook.

He appears to me to have lived in a hail of saucepan-lids. He would shriek for help on the most improper occasions,—as, when we had a little dinner party, or a few friends in the evening,—and would come tumbling out of the kitchen, with iron missiles flying after him. We wanted to get rid of him, but he was very much attached to us, and wouldn't go. He was a tearful boy, and was always rubbing his eyes with the sleeve of his jacket, or stooping to blow his nose on the extreme corner of his little pocket-handkerchief, which he never *would* take completely out of his pocket.

This unlucky page was a source of continual trouble to me. One day he stole Dora's watch and spent the produce (he was always a weak-minded boy) in incessantly riding up and down between London and Uxbridge outside the coach. He was taken to Bow Street on the completion of his fifteenth journey; when four-and-sixpence, and a second-hand fife which he couldn't play, were found upon his person.

Our page.

The surprise and its consequences would have been much less disagreeable to me if he had not been penitent. But he was very penitent indeed, and in a peculiar way. For example; he made certain revelations touching a hamper in the cellar, which we believed to be full of wine, but which had nothing in it except bottles and corks. A day or two afterwards, he disclosed how the cook had a little girl, who, early every morning, took away our bread; and also how he himself had been suborned to maintain the milkman in coals. In two or three days more I was informed of his having led to the discovery of sirloins of beef among the kitchen-stuff, and sheets in the rag-bag. I got to be so ashamed of being such a victim that at last I ran away myself and lived a stealthy life until he was tried and ordered to be transported. Even then he was always writing us letters; and wanted so much to see Dora before he went away, that Dora went to visit him, and fainted when she found herself inside the iron bars. In short, I had no peace of my life until he was expatriated!

All this presented our mistakes in a new aspect; as I could not help communicating to Dora one evening.

"My love," said I, "it is very painful to me to think that our want of management, involves other people."

"Now you are going to be cross!" said Dora.

"No, my dear, indeed! Let me explain."

"I think I don't want to know," said Dora.

"But I want you to know, my love. Put Jip down."

Dora ordered him into his Pagoda, and sat looking at me, with her hands folded, and a most resigned little expression of countenance.

"It is not merely, my pet," said I, "that we lose money and comfort by not learning to be more careful; but I begin to be afraid that these people all turn out ill because we don't turn out very well ourselves."

"Oh, what an accusation," exclaimed Dora, opening her eyes wide; "to say that you ever saw me take gold watches! Oh!"

"My dearest," I remonstrated. "Who has made the least allusion to gold watches?"

"You did. You know you did. You said I hadn't turned out well, and compared me to him."

"To whom?" I asked.

"To the page," sobbed Dora. "Oh, you cruel fellow! Oh, what a dreadful opinion to have of me! Oh, my goodness!"

"Now, Dora, my love," I returned, "this is not only very ridiculous of you, but very wrong. In the first place, it's not true."

"You always said he was a story-teller," sobbed Dora. "And now you say the same of me! Oh, what shall I do! What shall I do!"

In short, Dora was so afflicted, and so afflicted me, that I felt it was of no use repeating this kind of effort. I must take some other course, and I resolved to form Dora's mind.

I began immediately. When Dora was very childish, I tried to be grave. I read Shakespeare to her—and fatigued her to the last degree. I accustomed myself to giving her little scraps of useful information—and she started from them when I let them off, as if they had been crackers.

I pressed Traddles into the service without his knowledge, whenever he came to see us. The amount of practical wisdom I bestowed upon Traddles was immense, but it had no other effect upon Dora than to depress her spirits, and make her always nervous.

At last it began to occur to me that perhaps Dora's mind was already formed. On further consideration this appeared so likely, that I abandoned my scheme, resolving henceforth to be satisfied with my child-wife, and to try to change her into nothing else. So I bought a pretty pair of ear-rings for her, and a collar for Jip, and went home one day to make myself agreeable.

Dora was delighted with the little presents, and kissed me joyfully; but, there was a shadow between us, and I had made up my mind that it should not be there. If there must be such a shadow anywhere, I would keep it for the future in my own breast.

I sat down by my wife on the sofa, and put the ear-rings in her ears; and then I told her that I feared we had not been quite as good company lately, as we used to be, and that the fault was mine.

"The truth is, Dora, my life," I said, "I have been trying to be wise."

"And to make me wise too," said Dora, timidly. "Haven't you, Doady?"

I nodded assent to the pretty inquiry of the raised eye-brows, and kissed the parted lips.

"But I shall never try any more," said I. "For I love you dearly as you are! We'll go back to our old way, and be happy."

"And be happy!" returned Dora. "Yes! All day! And you won't mind things going a tiny morsel wrong, sometimes?"

"No, no," said I. "We must do the best we can."

She turned her delighted bright eyes up to mine, kissed me, broke into a merry laugh, and sprang away to put on Jip's new collar.

So ended my last attempt to make any change in Dora. And the shadow. How did that fall? The old unhappy feeling pervaded my life, but it was as undefined as ever. I loved my wife dearly, and I was happy; but there was always something wanting. I had endeavoured to adapt Dora to myself, and found it impracticable. It remained for me to adapt myself to Dora. This made my second year much happier than my first; and, what was better still, made Dora's life all sunshine.

But, as that year wore on, Dora was not strong. I had hoped that a baby-smile upon her breast might change my child-wife to a woman. It was not to be. The little spirit fluttered for a moment, and took wing.

"When I can run about again, as I used to do, aunt," said Dora, "I shall make Jip race. He is getting quite slow and lazy."

"I suspect, my dear," said my aunt, quietly working by her side, "he has a worse disorder than that. Age, Dora."

"Do you think he is old?" said Dora, astonished.

"It's a complaint we are all liable to, Little One, as we get on in life," said my aunt, cheerfully.

"But Jip," said Dora, "even little Jip! Oh, poor fellow!"

Dora made him lie down by her, and drew one of his long ears through her hand, repeating thoughtfully, "Even little Jip! Oh, poor fellow."

My pretty Dora! When she came down to dinner on the ensuing Sunday, and was so glad to see old Traddles (who always dined with us on Sunday), we thought she would be "running about as she used to do," in a few days. But they said, wait a few days more; and then, wait a few days more; and still she neither ran nor walked.

I began to carry her down-stairs every morning, and up-stairs every night. She would clasp me round the neck and laugh, the while. Jip would bark and caper round us, and go on before, and look back on the landing, breathing short, to see that we were coming. My aunt, the best and most cheerful of nurses, would trudge after us, a moving mass of shawls and pillows. Mr. Dick would not have relinquished his post of candle-bearer to any one alive. Traddles would be often at the bottom of the staircase, looking on, and taking care of sportive messages from Dora to the dearest girl in the world. We made quite a gay procession of it, and my child-wife was the gayest there.

But, sometimes, when I took her up, and felt that she was lighter in my arms, a dead blank feeling came upon me, as if I were approaching to some frozen region yet unseen, that numbed my life.

CHAPTER XLIX

I AM INVOLVED IN MYSTERY

I RECEIVED one morning by the post, the following letter, dated Canterbury, and addressed to me at Doctors' Commons; which I read with some surprise:

"MY DEAR SIR,

"Circumstances beyond my control have, for a considerable lapse of time, effected a severance of that intimacy which has ever afforded me gratifying emotions.

"It is not for one situated as is the foundered Bark who now takes up the pen to address you, to adopt the language of compliment. That, he leaves to abler and to purer hands.

"You will naturally inquire by what object am I influenced, then, in inditing the present missive? Allow me to say that it is *not* an object of pecuniary nature.

"Without more directly referring to any latent ability of wielding the thunderbolt, I may be permitted to observe that my peace is shattered and that I no more walk erect before my fellow-man. But I will not digress.

"Placed in a mental position of peculiar painfulness, it is my intention to devote a respite of eight-and-forty hours to revisiting some metropolitan scenes of past enjoyment. Among other havens, my feet will naturally tend towards the King's Bench Prison. In stating that I shall be (D. V.) on the outside of the south wall the day after to-morrow, at seven in the evening, precisely, my object in this epistolary communication is accomplished.

"I do not feel warranted in soliciting my former friend Mr. Copperfield, or my former friend Mr. Thomas Traddles, to condescend to meet me. I confine myself to throwing out the observation, that, at the hour and place I have indicated, may be found such ruined vestiges as yet

"Remain,
"Of
"A
"Fallen Tower,
"WILKINS MICAWBER."

"P. S. It may be advisable to superadd to the above, the statement that Mrs. Micawber is *not* in confidential possession of my intentions."

I read the letter over several times. Making due allowance for Mr. Micawber's lofty style, I still believed that something important lay hidden at the bottom of this roundabout communication. I put it down, to think about it; and took it up again, to read it once more; and was still pursuing it, when Traddles found me.

"My dear fellow," said I. "I never was better pleased to see you. I have received a very singular letter, Traddles, from Mr. Micawber."

"No?" cried Traddles. "You don't say so? And I have received one from Mrs. Micawber!"

With that, Traddles produced his letter and made an exchange with me. Mrs. Micawber's epistle ran thus:

"My best regards to Mr. Thomas Traddles, and may I beg a few moments of his leisure time? I assure Mr. T. T. that I would not intrude upon his kindness, were I in any other position than on the confines of distraction.

"The alienation of Mr. Micawber from his wife and family, is the cause of my unhappy appeal. Mr. T. can form no adequate idea of the change in Mr. Micawber's conduct, of his wildness, of his violence. I have become accustomed to hear Mr. Micawber assert that he has sold himself to the D. Mystery and secrecy have long been his principal characteristic. Last night, on being childishly solicited for twopence, to buy 'lemon-stunners'—a local sweetmeat—he presented an oyster-knife at the twins!

"May I now venture to confide to Mr. T. the purport of my letter?

"The quick eye of affection is not easily blinded, when of the female sex. Mr. Micawber is going to London. Dare I fervently implore Mr. T. to see my misguided husband, and to reason with him?

"If Mr. Copperfield should yet remember one unknown to fame, will Mr. T. take charge of my unalterable regards and similar entreaties? In any case, he will have the benevolence to consider this communication strictly private, and on no account whatever to be alluded to, however distantly, in the presence of Mr. Micawber.

"Mr. Thomas Traddles's respectful friend and suppliant,

"EMMA MICAWBER."

"What do you think of that letter?" said Traddles.

"What do you think of the other?" said I.

"I think that the two together, Copperfield," replied

Traddles, "mean more than Mr. and Mrs. Micawber usually mean in their correspondence—but I don't know what. Poor thing!" he was now alluding to Mrs. Micawber. "It will be a charity to write to her, at all events, and tell her that we will not fail to see Mr. Micawber."

I acceded to this and wrote a comforting letter, and we both signed it. We took my aunt into our counsels in the afternoon; but our only decided conclusion was, that we would be very punctual in keeping Mr. Micawber's appointment.

Although we appeared a quarter of an hour before the time, we found Mr. Micawber already there. When we accosted him, his manner was something more confused, and something less genteel, than of yore.

"Gentlemen!" said Mr. Micawber, "you are friends in need, and friends indeed, and your cordiality overpowers me.

"And this," said Mr. Micawber, nodding his head sorrowfully, "is the Bench Prison. When I was an inmate of that retreat, I could look my fellow-man in the face, and punch his head if he offended me. My fellow-man and myself are no longer on those glorious terms!"

Turning from the building in a downcast manner, Mr. Micawber accepted my arm on one side, and the arm of Traddles on the other, and walked away between us.

"How is our friend Heep, Mr. Micawber?" said I, after a silence.

"My dear Copperfield," returned Mr. Micawber, "if you ask after my employer as *your* friend, I am sorry for it; if you ask after him as *my* friend, I sardonically smile at it. In whatever capacity you ask after my employer, I beg to limit my reply to this—that whatever his state of health may be, his appearance is foxy: not to say diabolical."

I expressed my regret for having innocently touched upon a theme that roused him so much. "May I ask," said I, "how my old friends Mr. and Miss Wickfield are?"

"Miss Wickfield," said Mr. Micawber, now turning red, "is, as she always is, a pattern, and a bright example. My dear Copperfield, she is the only starry spot in a miserable existence."

"It is my fate," said Mr. Micawber, sobbing, "that the finer feelings of our nature have become reproaches to me. You had better leave me, if you please, to walk the earth as a vagabond."

Without attending to this invocation, we stood by, until he put up his pocket-handkerchief, pulled up his shirt-collar, and hummed a tune with his hat very much on one side. I then mentioned that it would give me great pleasure to introduce him to my aunt, if he would ride out to Highgate.

"You shall make us a glass of your own punch, Mr. Micawber," said I.

"Gentlemen," returned Mr. Micawber, "do with me as you will! I am a straw upon the surface of the deep, and am tossed in all directions by the elephants—I beg your pardon; I should have said the elements."

My aunt welcomed Mr. Micawber with gracious cordiality. Mr. Micawber kissed her hand, returned to the window, and pulling out his pocket-handkerchief, had a mental wrestle with himself.

Mr. Dick was at home. He was by nature so exceedingly compassionate of any one who seemed to be ill at ease, and was so quick to find any such person out, that he shook hands with Mr. Micawber, at least half-a-dozen times in five minutes. To Mr. Micawber this was so extremely touching that he could only say, "My dear Sir, you overpower me!" Which gratified Mr. Dick so much, that he went at it again with greater vigour than before.

At another time I should have been amused by this; but I watched Mr. Micawber so anxiously, in his vacillations between an evident disposition to reveal something, and a counter-disposition to reveal nothing, that I was in a perfect fever. My aunt had more useful possession of her wits.

"I hope Mrs. Micawber and your family are well, Sir," said my aunt.

Mr. Micawber inclined his head. "They are as well, ma'am," he desperately observed, after a pause, "as Aliens and Outcasts can ever hope to be."

"Lord bless you, Sir!" exclaimed my aunt in her abrupt way. "What are you talking about?"

"The subsistence of my family, ma'am," returned Mr. Micawber, "Trembles in the balance. My employer——"

Here Mr. Micawber provokingly left off; and began to peel the lemons that had been set before him, together with all the other appliances he used in making punch.

"Your employer, you know," said Mr. Dick, jogging his arm as a gentle reminder.

"My good Sir," returned Mr. Micawber, "you recall me. I am obliged to you." They shook hands again. "My employer, ma'am—Mr. Heep—once did me the favour to observe to me, that if I were not in the receipt of the stipendiary emoluments appertaining to my engagement with him, I should probably be a mountebank about the country, swallowing a sword-blade."

My aunt leaned her elbow on the little round table that she usually kept beside her, and eyed him attentively. I should have taken him up at this point, but for the strange proceedings in which I saw him engaged; whereof his putting the lemon-peel into the kettle, and confidently attempting to pour boiling water out of a candle-stick, were among the most remarkable. I saw that a crisis was at hand, and it came. He clattered all his implements together, rose from his chair, pulled out his pocket-handkerchief, and burst into tears.

"My dear Copperfield," said Mr. Micawber, behind his handkerchief, "this is an occupation requiring an untroubled mind. I cannot perform it!"

"Mr. Micawber," said I, "what is the matter? Pray speak out. You are among friends."

"Among friends, Sir!" repeated Mr. Micawber; "Good Heavens, it is because I *am* among friends that my state of mind is what it is. What is the matter, gentlemen? What is *not* the matter? Villany is the matter; deception, fraud, conspiracy, are the matter; and the name of the whole atrocious mass is—HEEP!"

My aunt clapped her hands, and we all started up as if we were possessed.

"The struggle is over!" said Mr. Micawber, violently gesticulating with his pocket-handkerchief. "I will lead this life no longer. I have been under a Taboo in that infernal scoundrel's service. Give me back my wife, give me back my family, substitute Micawber for the petty wretch who walks about in the boots at present on my feet, and call upon me to swallow a sword to-morrow, and I'll do it!"

I never saw a man so hot in my life.

"I'll put my hand in no man's hand," said Mr. Micawber, gasping, puffing, and sobbing, "until I have—blown to fragments—the—a—detestable—serpent—HEEP! I—a—I'll say nothing—until I have crushed—to—a—undiscoverable atoms—the—hypocrite—HEEP!"

"No communication—a—until—Miss Wickfield—a—redress from wrongs inflicted by consummate scoundrel—HEEP! Inviolable secret—this day week—a—at breakfast time—a—everybody present—to be at the hotel at Canterbury—a—where—Mrs. Micawber and myself—Auld Lang Syne in chorus—and—a—will expose intolerable ruffian, HEEP!"

With this last repetition of the magic word Mr. Micawber rushed out of the house; leaving us in a state of excitement, hope, and wonder.

CHAPTER L

MR. PEGGOTTY'S DREAM COMES TRUE

By this time, some months had passed since our interview with Martha. I had never seen her since, but she had communicated with Mr. Peggotty on several occasions. Nothing had come of her zealous intervention; nor could I infer that any clue had ever been obtained, for a moment, to Emily's fate.

One evening he told me that he had found Martha waiting near his lodging on the preceding night and that she had asked him not to leave London on any account, until he should have seen her again.

"Did she tell you why?" I inquired.

"I asked her, Mas'r Davy," he replied, "but she on'y got my promise and so went away."

I made no other comment than that I supposed he would see her soon.

I was walking alone in the garden, one evening, about a fortnight afterwards. It was the second evening in Mr. Micawber's week of suspense. There was a little green perspective of trellis-work and ivy at the side of our cottage, through which I could see into the road. I happened to turn my eyes towards this place, and I saw a figure beyond, bending eagerly towards me, and beckoning.

"Martha!" said I, going to it.

"Can you come with me?" she inquired. "He is not at home. I wrote down where he was to come, and left it on his table. They said he would not be out long. I have tidings for him. Can you come directly?"

My answer was to pass out at the gate immediately. I stopped an empty coach, and we got into it. We alighted at one of the entrances to the square she mentioned to the driver, and she hurried me to a sombre street where the houses had long degenerated into poor lodgings. Entering at the open door of one of these, she beckoned me to follow her up the common staircase.

We proceeded to the top-story of the house. Two or three times I thought I observed a female figure going up before us. As we turned to ascend the last flight of stairs we caught a full view of this figure pausing for a moment, at a door. Then it turned the handle, and went in.

"What's this!" said Martha, in a whisper. "She has gone into my room. I don't know her!"

I knew her. I had recognized her with amazement, for Miss Dartle.

Martha, with an astonished look, led me up the stairs; and into a small empty garret. Between this, and the room she had called hers, there was a small door standing partly open. I could not see Miss Dartle, or the person whom we had heard her address.

A dead silence prevailed for some moments.

"It matters little to me her not being at home," said Rosa Dartle, haughtily. "It is you I come to see."

"Me?" replied a soft voice.

At the sound of it, a thrill went through my frame. For it was Emily's!

"Yes," returned Miss Dartle, "I have come to look at you, the bold, practised companion of James Steerforth. I want to know what such a thing is like."

There was a rustle, as if the unhappy girl ran towards the door.

When Miss Dartle spoke again, it was through her set teeth, and with a stamp upon the ground.

"Stay there!" she said, "or I'll proclaim you to the whole street!"

"Oh!" exclaimed Emily. "For Heaven's sake, spare me!"

Miss Dartle placed herself in a chair and looked downward, as if Emily were crouching on the floor before her. I could see her curled lip, and her cruel eyes.

He carried her, motionless and unconscious, down the stairs.

"Listen to what I say!" she said. "Do you ever think of the home you have laid waste?"

"Oh, is there ever night or day, when I don't think of it!" cried Emily. "Oh, home, home! Oh, dear, dear uncle!"

Rosa Dartle sat as inflexible as a figure of brass.

"The miserable vanity of these earthworms!" she said. "*Your* home! Do you imagine that I suppose you could do any harm to that low place, which money would not pay for, and handsomely?"

"Oh not that!" cried Emily. "Don't visit my disgrace on folks who are as honourable as you!"

"I speak," Miss Dartle said, "of *his* home—where I live. Here is a worthy cause of division between lady-mother and gentleman-son, this piece of pollution!"

"No! No!" cried Emily, clasping her hands together. "I had been brought up as virtuous as you or any lady. I don't defend myself, but I know well, and he knows well, that I trusted him, and loved him!"

Rosa Dartle sprang from her seat and struck at her. The blow fell upon the air.

"*You* love him? *You* tell that to *me.* If I could order it to be done, I would have this girl whipped to death."

And so she would, I have no doubt.

"I came here," she said, "to tell you that if you live here to-morrow, I'll have your story and your character proclaimed on the common stair."

"Oh me, oh my!" exclaimed the wretched Emily. "What, what shall I do?"

"Do?" returned the other. "Live happy in the recollection of James Steerforth's tenderness—he would have made you his serving-man's wife, would he not? If this will not do, die! There are doorways and dust-heaps for such deaths. Find one, and take your flight to Heaven!"

I heard a foot upon the stairs. It was his, thank God!

"But mark!" she added, opening the door to go away, "What I say, I mean to do!"

The foot upon the stairs came nearer—passed her as she went down—rushed into the room!

"Uncle!"

A fearful cry followed the word. I paused, and, looking in, saw him supporting her insensible figure in his arms.

"Mas'r Davy," he said, in a low tremulous voice, "I thank my Heav'nly Father as my dream's come true!"

With those words he took her up in his arms and carried her, motionless and unconscious, down the stairs.

CHAPTER LI

THE BEGINNING OF A LONGER JOURNEY

It was yet early in the morning of the following day, when, as I was walking in my garden with my aunt (who took little other exercise now, being so much in attendance on my dear Dora), Mr. Peggotty came into the garden. My aunt shook hands with him, and patted him on the arm. It was so expressively done, that she had no need to say a word. Mr. Peggotty understood her quite as well as if she had said a thousand.

She drew her arm through Mr. Peggotty's, and we walked to a leafy little summer-house where she sat down on a bench, and I beside her. Mr. Peggotty preferred to stand, leaning his hand on the small rustic table.

"I took my dear child away last night," Mr. Peggotty began, "to my lodging. It was hours afore she knowed me right; and when she did, she kneeled down at my feet, and kiender said to me, as if it was her prayers, how it all come to be."

He drew his sleeve across his face, without any pretence of concealing why; and then cleared his voice.

"When my Em'ly took flight," he said, "from the house wheer she was made a pris'ner by that theer spotted snake as Mas'r Davy see, she took flight in the night. She was wild. Ever so fur she run, and there was fire afore her eyes, and roarings in her ears. Of a sudden—or so she thowt, you understand—the day broke, wet and windy, and she was lying b'low a heap of stone upon the shore, and a woman was speaking to her, saying, what was it as had gone so much amiss?"

"As Em'ly's eyes—which was heavy—see this woman

better," Mr. Peggotty went on, "she know'd as she was one of them as she had often talked to. Em'ly had took notice of her and they had soon made friends. Sermuchser, that when Em'ly went that way, she always giv Em'ly flowers. This was her as now asked what it was that had gone so much amiss. Em'ly told her, and she—took her home. She did indeed. She took her home," said Mr. Peggotty, covering his face.

He was more affected by this act of kindness, than I had ever seen him affected by anything since the night she went away.

"It was a little cottage, you may suppose," he said, presently, "but she found space for Em'ly in it,—her husband was away at sea,—and she kept it secret. Em'ly was took bad with fever. The fire was afore her eyes, and the roarings in her ears; and there was no to-day nor yesterday nor yet to-morrow; but everything was crowding on her all at once. How long this lasted, I doen't know; but then there come a sleep, and she begun to mend.

"When Em'ly got strong again," said Mr. Peggotty, "the husband was come home, and the two together put her aboard a small trader bound to France. She had a little money, but it was less than a little as they would take for all they done. I'm a'most glad on it, though they was so poor. What they done, is laid up wheer neither moth nor dust doth corrupt, Mas'r Davy; it'll outlast all the treasure in the wureld.

"Em'ly got to France, and took service to wait on travelling ladies at a inn in the port. Theer, theer come, one day, that snake. Soon as she see him, all her fear returned upon her, and she fled. She come to England, and was set ashore at Dover.

"I doen't know," said Mr. Peggotty, "for sure, when her 'art begun to fail her. All the way to England she had thowt to come to her dear home, but fear turned her from it.

"She come," said Mr. Peggotty, dropping his voice to an awe-stricken whisper, "to London—without a penny—

young—so pretty—come to London. A'most the moment as she lighted heer, she found (as she believed) a friend; a decent woman as spoke to her about needlework and about a lodging for the night. When my child," he said aloud, "stood upon the brink of more than I can say or think on—Martha, trew to her promise, saved her!"

I could not repress a cry of joy.

"Mas'r Davy!" said he, "she was arnest. And the Lord was above all! She come, white and hurried, upon Em'ly in her sleep. She says to her, 'Rise up from worse than death, and come with me!' Them belonging to the house would have stopped her, but she brought her safe out from that black pit of ruin! My niece is found!

"All night long," said Mr. Peggotty, "we have been together, Em'ly and me. Her arms has been about my neck; and her head has laid heer; and we know full well, as we can put our trust in one another, ever more."

"You have quite made up your mind," said I to Mr. Peggotty, "as to the future, good friend?"

"Quite, Mas'r Davy," he returned; "and told Em'ly. Theer's mighty countries, fur from heer. No one can't reproach my darling in Australia. We will begin a new life over theer!"

I asked him if he yet proposed to himself any time for going away.

"I was down at the Docks early this morning, Sir," he returned. "In about six weeks or two months from now, there'll be a ship sailing, and we shall take our passage in her."

"Quite alone?" I asked.

"Ay, Mas'r Davy!" he returned. "My sister, you see, it wouldn't be hardly fair to let her go. Besides which, theer's one she has in charge, Mas'r Davy, as doen't ought to be forgot."

"Poor Ham!" said I. "And Mrs. Gummidge?"

"Well, I've had a mort of con-sideration, I do tell you," returned Mr. Peggotty, "concerning of Missis Gummidge. You see, wen Missis Gummidge falls a thinking of the old 'un, she ain't what you may call good company. Therefur 'tan't my intentions to moor Missis Gummidge 'long with my sister, but to find a Bein' fur her wheer she can fisherate for herself." (A Bein' signifies, in that dialect, a home, and to fisherate is to provide.) "I means to make her a 'lowance. She's the faithfullest of creeturs."

"Theer's one thing furder, Mas'r Davy," said he, gravely taking out the little paper bundle I had seen before. "Theer's these heer bank-notes—fifty pound, and ten. To them I wish to add the money as she come away with. This money, Mas'r Davy, I shall put up just afore I go, in a cover d'rected to him; and put that up in another, d'rected to his mother. I shall tell her what it's the price on; and that I'm gone.

"I said that theer was on'y one thing furder," he proceeded, "but there was two. I warn't sure as I could go and break to Ham what had so thankfully happened. So I writ a letter telling of 'em how all was as 'tis, and that I should come down to-morrow and, most-like, take my farewell leave of Yarmouth."

"And do you wish me to go with you?" said I.

"If you could do me that kind favour, Mas'r Davy," he replied.

Next morning, consequently, we were on the Yarmouth coach and again passing over the old ground.

As we passed along the familiar street at night I glanced into Omer and Joram's shop, and saw my old friend Mr. Omer there, smoking his pipe. I felt reluctant to be present, when Mr. Peggotty first met his sister and Ham; and made Mr. Omer my excuse for lingering behind.

"How is Mr. Omer after this long time?" said I, going in. He fanned away the smoke of his pipe and soon recognized me with great delight.

I congratulated him on his contented looks and saw that his easy chair went on wheels.

"It's an ingenious thing, ain't it?" he inquired. "And I tell you what—it's a most uncommon chair to smoke a pipe in. And I see more of the world, I can assure you, in this chair than ever I see out of it. You'd be surprised at the number of people that looks in of a day."

I never saw such a good old fellow to make the best of a thing as Mr. Omer.

I told him of Emily, and of her restoration to her uncle by the aid of Martha.

"I am rejoiced at it, Sir!" he said, feelingly. "It's the best news I have heard for many a day. Dear, dear, dear! And what's going to be undertook for that unfortunate young woman, Martha, now?"

"You touch a point that my thoughts have been dwelling on," said I, "but Mr. Peggotty has not alluded to it. I am sure he has not forgotten it."

"Because you know," said Mr. Omer, "whatever *is* done, I should wish to be a member of it. Put me down for anything you may consider right, and let me know. I never could think the girl all bad, and I am glad to find she's not."

After a stroll about the town, I went to Ham's house. Peggotty had now removed here for good; and had let her own house to the successor of Mr. Barkis in the carrying business. I believe the very same slow horse that Mr. Barkis drove, was still at work.

I found them in the neat kitchen, accompanied by Mrs. Gummidge. Mr. Peggotty had evidently told them all. Both Peggotty and Mrs. Gummidge had their aprons to their eyes, and Ham had just stepped out "to take a turn on the beach." He presently came home, very glad to see me, and was the serenest of the party.

But, Peggotty told me, when she lighted me to a little chamber where the Crocodile Book was lying ready for me on the table, that she believed he was broken-hearted; though he was as full of courage as of sweetness, and worked harder and better than any boat-builder in all that part.

I thought I had read in his face that he would like to speak to me alone. I therefore resolved to put myself in his way next evening, as he came home from his work.

All next day Mr. Peggotty was occupied in packing such of his possessions as he thought would be useful to him; and in parting with the rest. As I had a sorrowful wish to see the old place once more, I engaged to be there in the evening. But I so arranged it, as that I should meet Ham first.

I met him at a retired part of the sands, and turned back with him. We had walked but a little way together, when he said:

"Mas'r Davy, shall you see her, d'ye think?"

"It would be too painful to her, perhaps," said I, "but if there is anything that I could write, anything you would wish to make known to her through me; I should consider it a sacred trust."

"I thankee, Sir, most kind! I think theer is something I could wish said or wrote."

We walked a little farther in silence, and then he spoke.

" 'Tain't that I forgive her. 'Tis more as I beg of her to forgive me, for having pressed my affections upon her. Odd times, I think that if I hadn't had her promise fur to marry me, Sir, she was that trustful of me that she'd have told me what was struggling in her mind, and I might have saved her."

I pressed his hand. "Is that all?"

"Theer's yet something else," he returned, "if I can say it, Mas'r Davy.

"I loved her—and I love the mem'ry of her—too deep—to be able to lead her to believe as I'm a happy man. But if you could think of anything to say as would ease her sorrowful mind, and yet not make her think 'twas possible that any one could ever be to me what she was—I should ask of you to say that—with my prayers for her—that was so dear."

I pressed his manly hand again, and told him I would charge myself to do this as well as I could.

The door of the boat-house stood open when I approached; and, on entering, I found it emptied of all its furniture, saving one of the old lockers, on which Mrs.

Gummidge, with a basket on her knee, was seated, looking at Mr. Peggotty.

"Come, according to promise, to bid farewell to't, eh, Mas'r Davy?" he said. "Bare enough, now, an't it?"

"Dan'l," said Mrs. Gummidge, suddenly deserting her basket, and clinging to his arm, "my dear Dan'l, the parting words I speak in this house is, I mustn't be left behind. Oh, doen't ye ever do it!"

Mr. Peggotty, taken aback, looked from Mrs. Gummidge to me, and from me to Mrs. Gummidge, as if he had been awakened from a sleep.

"Doen't you, dearest Dan'l, doen't ye!" cried Mrs. Gummidge, fervently. "Take me 'long with you and Em'ly!"

"My good soul," said Mr. Peggotty, shaking his head, "you doen't know what a long voyage, and what a hard life 'tis!"

"Yes I do, Dan'l! I can guess!" cried Mrs. Gummidge. "I can work. I can live hard. I can be loving and patient now—more than you think, Dan'l, if you'll on'y try me. I ain't sat here, so long, a watching, and a thinking of your trials, without some good being done me. Mas'r Davy, speak to him for me! Dan'l, deary Dan'l, let me go 'long with you!"

And Mrs. Gummidge took his hand, and kissed it in a homely rapture of devotion and gratitude.

Next day, when we were returning to London outside the coach, Mrs. Gummidge and her basket were on the seat behind, and Mrs. Gummidge was happy.

CHAPTER LII

I ASSIST AT AN EXPLOSION

When the time Mr. Micawber had appointed so mysteriously, was within four-and-twenty hours of being come, my aunt was very unwilling to leave Dora. Ah! how easily I carried Dora up and down-stairs, now!

We were disposed to arrange that my aunt should stay at home when Dora again unsettled us by declaring that she never would forgive herself, and never would forgive her bad boy, if my aunt remained behind, on any pretence.

"Besides," said Dora, putting back her hair, and looking wonderingly at my aunt and me, "why shouldn't you both go? I am not very ill indeed. Am I?"

"Why, what a question!" cried my aunt.

"What a fancy!" said I.

"Well, then," said Dora, "you must both go, or I shall not believe you; and then I shall cry!"

I saw, in my aunt's face, that she began to give way now, and Dora brightened again, as she saw it too.

We agreed, without any more consultation, that we would both go, and that Dora was a little Impostor, who feigned to be rather unwell, because she liked to be petted. She was greatly pleased, and very merry; and we four, that is to say, my aunt, Mr. Dick, Traddles, and I, went down to Canterbury by the Dover mail that night.

At the hotel, which we got into in the middle of the night, I found a letter, importing that Mr. Micawber would appear in the morning punctually at half-past nine. After which, we went shivering to our respective beds.

Early in the morning, I sauntered through the dear old tranquil streets. Among those who were stirring in the shops, I saw my ancient enemy, the butcher, now advanced to top-boots and a baby, and in business for himself. He was nursing the baby, and appeared to be a benignant member of society.

We all became very anxious and impatient, when we sat down to breakfast. As it approached nearer and nearer to half-past nine o'clock, our restless expectation increased, and I looked out of the window to give early notice of Mr. Micawber's coming. Nor had I long to watch, for, at the first chime of the half-hour, he appeared in the street.

My aunt tied the strings of her bonnet, and put on her shawl. Traddles buttoned his coat with a determined air. Mr. Dick pulled his hat, with both hands, as firmly over his ears as he possibly could; and instantly took it off again, to welcome Mr. Micawber.

"Gentlemen, and madam," said Mr. Micawber, "good morning! My dear Sir," to Mr. Dick, who shook hands with him violently, "you are extremely good."

"Have you breakfasted?" said Mr. Dick. "Have a chop!"

"Not for the world, my good Sir!" cried Mr. Micawber, "appetite and myself, Mr. Dixon, have long been strangers."

Mr. Dixon was so well pleased with his new name that he shook hands with Mr. Micawber again, and laughed rather childishly.

"Dick," said my aunt, "attention!"

Mr. Dick recovered himself, with a blush.

"Now, Sir," said my aunt to Mr. Micawber, "we are ready for Mount Vesuvius."

"Madam," returned Mr. Micawber, "I trust you will shortly witness an eruption. Mr. Traddles, I have your permission, I believe, to mention here that we have been in communication together?"

"It is undoubtedly the fact, Copperfield," said Traddles, to whom I looked in surprise. "Mr. Micawber has consulted me, and I have advised him to the best of my judgment."

"Unless I deceive myself, what I contemplate is a disclosure of an important nature," pursued Mr. Micawber.

"Highly so," said Traddles.

"Perhaps, under such circumstances, madam and gentlemen," said Mr. Micawber, "you will do me the favour to submit yourselves to one, who, however unworthy, is still your fellow-man."

"We have perfect confidence in you, Mr. Micawber," said I, "and will do what you please."

"Mr. Copperfield," returned Mr. Micawber, "I would beg to be allowed a start of five minutes, and then to receive the present company, inquiring for Miss Wickfield, at the office of Wickfield and Heep."

We found Mr. Micawber at his desk. The large office-ruler was stuck into his waistcoat, and a foot or more protruded like a new kind of shirt-frill. As it appeared to me that I was expected to speak, I said aloud: "How do you do, Mr. Micawber? Is Miss Wickfield at home?"

"Mr. Wickfield is unwell in bed, Sir, of a rheumatic fever," he returned; "but Miss Wickfield, I have no doubt, will be happy to see old friends. Will you walk in, Sir?"

He preceded us to the dining-room, and flinging open the door of Mr. Wickfield's former office, said, in a sonorous voice:

"Miss Trotwood, Mr. David Copperfield, Mr. Thomas Traddles, and Mr. Dixon!"

I had not seen Uriah Heep since the time of the blow. Our visit astonished him, evidently. He frowned to that degree that he almost closed his small eyes, while the hurried raising of his grisly hand to his chin betrayed some trepidation. A moment afterwards, he was as fawning and as humble as ever.

"Well, I am sure," he said. "This is indeed an unexpected pleasure. Mr. Copperfield, I hope I see you well, and Mrs. Copperfield, Sir, I hope she's getting on. Things are changed this office, Miss Trotwood, since I was a numble clerk, and held your pony; ain't they? But *I* am not changed, Miss Trotwood."

"You are not busy, Mr. Heep?" said Traddles.

"No, Mr. Traddles," replied Uriah. "Not so much as I could wish. You've not been intimate with Mr. Wickfield, I think, Mr. Traddles?"

"No, I have not been intimate with Mr. Wickfield," returned Traddles; "or I might perhaps have waited on you long ago, Mr. Heep."

Agnes now entered. She had evidently undergone anxiety and fatigue, but her quiet beauty shone with the gentler lustre for it.

I saw Uriah watch her while she greeted us; and he reminded me of an ugly and rebellious genie watching a good spirit. In the meanwhile, some slight sign passed between Mr. Micawber and Traddles; and Traddles, unobserved except by me, went out.

"Don't wait, Micawber," said Uriah.

Mr. Micawber, with his hand upon the ruler in his breast, stood erect before the door.

"What are you waiting for?" said Uriah. "Micawber! did you hear me tell you not to wait?"

"Yes!" replied the immovable Mr. Micawber.

"Then why *do* you wait?" said Uriah.

"Because I—in short—choose," replied Mr. Micawber.

Uriah's cheeks lost colour, and he looked at Mr. Micawber attentively.

"You are a dissipated fellow," he said, "and I am afraid you'll oblige me to get rid of you. Go along! I'll talk to you presently."

"If there is a scoundrel on this earth," said Mr. Micawber, "with whom I have already talked too much, that scoundrel's name is—HEEP!

Uriah fell back, as if he had been struck or stung. Looking slowly round upon us he said, in a lower voice:

"Oho! This is a conspiracy! You have met here, by appointment. None of your plots against me; I'll counterplot you! Micawber, you be off. Miss Trotwood, you had better stop this; or I'll stop your husband shorter than will be pleasant to you. I won't know your story professionally, for nothing, old lady! Miss Wickfield, if you have any love for your father, you had better not join that gang. Think twice! Where's mother?" he said, suddenly appearing to notice, with alarm, the absence of Traddles.

"Mrs. Heep is here, Sir," said Traddles, returning. "I have taken the liberty of making myself known to her."

"Who are you to make yourself known?" retorted Uriah. "And what do you want here?"

"I am the agent and friend of Mr. Wickfield, Sir," said Traddles. "And I have a power of attorney from him to act for him in all matters."

"It has been got from him by fraud!" said Uriah.

"Something has been got from him by fraud, I know," returned Traddles quietly; "and so do you, Mr. Heep."

"Ury——!" Mrs. Heep began, with an anxious gesture.

"You hold your tongue, mother," he returned.

Mr. Micawber, whose impetuosity I had restrained thus far with the greatest difficulty, and who had repeatedly interposed with the first syllable of SCOUN-drel! without getting to the second, now burst forward, drew the ruler from his breast (apparently as a defensive weapon), and produced from his pocket a foolscap document, folded in the form of a large letter. Opening this packet, with his old flourish, he began to read as follows:

"'Dear Miss Trotwood and gentlemen——'"

"Bless and save the man!" exclaimed my aunt in a low voice. "He'd write letters by the ream, if it was a capital offence!"

Mr. Micawber, without hearing her, went on.

"'In appearing before you to denounce probably the most consummate Villain that has ever existed,'" Mr. Micawber, without looking off the letter, pointed the ruler, like a ghostly truncheon at Uriah Heep, "'I ask no consideration for myself. In an accumulation of Ignominy, Want, Despair, and Madness, I entered the office conducted under the appellation of Wickfield and—HEEP, but, in reality, wielded by—HEEP alone. HEEP, and only HEEP, is the Forger and the Cheat.'"

Uriah, more blue than white at these words, made a dart at the letter. Mr. Micawber, with a perfect miracle of dexterity or luck, caught his advancing knuckles with the ruler, and disabled his right hand.

"The Devil take you!" said Uriah, writhing in a new way with pain. "I'll be even with you."

"Approach me again, you—you—you HEEP of infamy," gasped Mr. Micawber, "and if your head is human, I'll break it. Come on, come on!"

His enemy slowly drew off his neck-kerchief and bound up his wounded hand; then sat with his sullen face looking down.

Mr. Micawber proceeded, " 'The stipendiary emoluments in consideration of which I entered into the service of—HEEP,' " always pausing before that word and uttering it with astonishing vigour, " 'were not defined, beyond the pittance of twenty-two shillings and six per week. The rest was left contingent on the value of my professional exertions; in other words, on the poverty of my family and the general moral (or rather immoral) resemblance between myself and—HEEP. Need I say, that it soon became necessary for me to solicit from—HEEP—pecuniary advances, and that I thus became immeshed in the web he had spun for my reception?

" 'Then it was that I found that my services were constantly called into requisition for the falsification of business, and the mystification of an individual whom I will designate as Mr. W.

" 'My object, when the contest within myself between stipend and no stipend ceased, was to take advantage of my opportunity to discover and expose the malpractices committed. I therefore entered on a not unlaborious task of clandestine investigation, protracted now, to the best of my knowledge, information, and belief, over a period exceeding twelve calendar months.' "

He read this passage, as if it were from an Act of Parliament; and appeared majestically refreshed by the sound of the words.

" 'My charges against—HEEP,' " he read on, drawing the ruler into a convenient position under his left arm, in case of need, " 'are as follows.' "

We all held our breath, I think. I am sure Uriah held his.

" 'First,' " said Mr. Micawber. " 'When Mr. W.'s faculties and memories for business became weakened and confused,—HEEP—induced Mr. W. to empower him to draw out one particular sum of trust-money, and employed it to meet pretended business deficiencies. He gave this proceeding the appearance of having been accomplished by Mr. W.'s own dishonest act; and he has used it, ever since, to torture and constrain him.' "

"You shall prove this," said Uriah, with a threatening shake of the head.

"Ask—HEEP—Mr. Traddles, who lived in Heep's house after him," said Mr. Micawber.

"The fool himself—and lives there now," answered Uriah.

"Ask—HEEP—if he ever kept a pocket-book in that house," said Mr. Micawber; "will you? or ask if he ever burnt one there. If he says Yes, and asks you where the ashes are, refer him to Wilkins Micawber."

Mr. Micawber then proceeded with his composition.

" 'Second. HEEP has, on several occasions, to the best of my knowledge, information, and belief——' "

"But *that* won't do," muttered Uriah, relieved.

"We will endeavour to provide something that *will* do, very shortly," replied Mr. Micawber.

" 'Second. HEEP has, on several occasions, to the best of my knowledge, information, and belief, forged the signature of Mr. W.; and has distinctly done so in one instance, capable of proof by me. To wit, in manner following, that is to say:' "

He read on, almost smacking his lips:

" 'To wit, in manner following, that is to say. Mr. W. being infirm, it was within the bounds of probability that his decease might lead to the downfall of—HEEP'S—power, unless the filial affection of his daughter could be influenced from allowing any investigation of the partnership affairs. Therefore the said—HEEP—deemed it expedient to have a bond ready for the before-mentioned sum, stated to have been advanced by—HEEP—to Mr. W., though really the sum was never advanced to him, and has long been replaced. The signatures to this instrument, purporting to be executed by Mr. W. and attested by Wilkins Micawber, are forgeries by—HEEP. I have, in my possession, several similar imitations of Mr. W.'s signature. And I have the document itself, in my possession.' That is to say, I had, early this morning, but have since relinquished it to Mr. Traddles."

"It is quite true," assented Traddles.

Uriah remained for a little, biting his handkerchief, and then said to me with a scowl:

"What more have you got to bring forward?"

Mr. Micawber promptly resumed his letter.

" 'Third. And last. I am now in a position to show, by —HEEP'S—false books, and—HEEP'S—real memoranda, that the engrossing object of—HEEP—was, next to gain, to subdue Mr. W. and Miss W. entirely to himself. That his last act was to induce Mr. W. to execute a relinquishment of his share in the partnership, and even a bill of sale on the very furniture of his house, in consideration of a certain annuity, to be well and truly paid by—HEEP. That these meshes gradually thickened, until the unhappy Mr. W. could see no world beyond. Bankrupt, as he believed, alike in circumstances, in all other hope, and in honour, his sole reliance was upon the monster in the garb of man, who had achieved his destruction. All this I undertake to show. Probably much more!' "

There was a movement among us, as if Mr. Micawber had finished. He said, with exceeding gravity, "Pardon me," and proceeded.

" 'I have now concluded. It merely remains for me to substantiate these accusations; and then, with my ill-starred family, to disappear from the landscape. I trust that the labour and hazard of an investigation slowly pieced together under the watchful eye of one whom it were superfluous to call Demon, may be as the sprinkling of a few drops of sweet water on my funeral pyre. I ask no more.

"'Remaining always, &c., WILKINS MICAWBER.'"

Much affected, but still intensely enjoying himself, Mr. Micawber folded up his letter, and handed it with a bow to my aunt.

There was an iron safe in the room. The key was in it. A hasty suspicion seemed to strike Uriah; and he went to it, and threw the doors clanking open. It was empty.

"Where are the books?" he cried.

"Don't be uneasy," said Traddles. "They have come into my possession."

What was my astonishment when I beheld my aunt, who had been profoundly quiet and attentive, make a dart at Uriah Heep, and seize him by the collar with both hands!

"You know what *I* want?" said my aunt.

"A strait-waistcoat," said he.

"No. My property!" returned my aunt. "Agnes, my dear, as long as I believed it had been really made away with by your father, I wouldn't breathe a syllable of its having been placed here for investment. But, now I know this fellow's answerable for it, and I'll have it!"

Whether my aunt supposed that he kept her property in his neck-kerchief, I am sure I don't know; but she certainly pulled at it as if she thought so. I hastened to put myself between them, and to assure her that he should make the utmost restitution.

During the last few minutes, Mrs. Heep had been clamouring to her son to be "umble"; and had been going down on her knees to all of us in succession. Her son sat her down in his chair; and, standing sulkily by her, said, with a ferocious look:

"What do you want done?"

"I will tell you what must be done," said Traddles. "First, the deed of relinquishment must be given over to me now—here. Then you must prepare to disgorge all that your rapacity has become possessed of, and to make restoration to the last farthing. Everything here must remain in our possession."

"Must it? I don't know that," said Uriah. "I must have time to think about that."

"Certainly," replied Traddles; "but, in the meanwhile, we shall maintain possession, and beg you—in short—compel you—to keep your own room."

"I won't do it!" said Uriah, with an oath.

"Maidstone Jail is a safer place of detention," observed Traddles; "and though the law may be longer in righting us there is no doubt of its punishing *you*. Dear me, you know that quite as well as I! Copperfield, will you go round to the Guildhall, and bring a couple of officers?"

Here, Mrs. Heep broke out again, crying on her knees to Agnes to interfere.

"Stop!" he growled to me. "Mother, hold your noise. Well! Let 'em have that deed. Go and fetch it!"

"Do you help her, Mr. Dick," said Traddles, "if you please."

Proud of his commission, Mr. Dick accompanied her. But Mrs. Hep gave him little trouble; for she not only returned with the deed, but with the box in which it was, where we found other papers that were afterwards serviceable.

"Good!" said Traddles. "Now, Mr. Heep, you can retire to think."

Uriah shuffled across the room, and pausing at the door said: "Copperfield, I have always hated you. Micawber you old bully, I'll pay *you!*"

Mr. Micawber, supremely defiant, then proffered me the satisfaction of "witnessing the re-establishment of mutual confidence between himself and Mrs. Micawber." After which, he invited the company generally to the contemplation of that affecting spectacle.

I dare say we should all have gone, but that it was necessary for Agnes to return to her father; and for some one else to hold Uriah in safe keeping. So Traddles remained, and Mr. Dick, my aunt, and I, went home with Mr. Micawber.

His house was not far off. He bolted in with a precipitation quite his own, and exclaiming, "Emma! my life!" rushed into Mrs. Micawber's arms. Mrs. Micawber shrieked, and folded Mr. Micawber in her embrace. Miss Micawber was sensibly affected. The twins testified their joy by several inconvenient but innocent demonstrations. Master Micawber blubbered.

"Emma!" said Mr. Micawber. "The cloud is past from my mind. Mutual confidence is restored. Now, welcome poverty!" cried Mr. Micawber, shedding tears. "Welcome misery, welcome houselessness, welcome hunger, rags, tempest, and beggary! Mutual confidence will sustain us to the end!"

With these expressions, Mr. Micawber placed Mrs. Micawber in a chair, and embraced the family all round, and then my aunt was introduced.

"Is this all your family, ma'am?" said my aunt.

"There are no more at present," returned Mrs. Micawber.

"Good gracious, I didn't mean that, ma'am," said my aunt. "I mean are all these yours?"

"Madam," replied Mr. Micawber, "it is a true bill."

My aunt mused a little while, and then said:

"Mr. Micawber, I wonder you have never turned your thoughts to emigration."

"Madam," returned Mr. Micawber, "it was the dream of my youth, and the fallacious aspiration of my riper years." I am thoroughly persuaded, by the bye, that he had never thought of it in his life.

"Ay?" said my aunt. "Why, what a thing it would be if you were to emigrate now."

"Capital, madam, capital," urged Mr. Micawber, gloomily.

"Capital?" cried my aunt. "But you are doing us a great service, and what could we do for you, that would be half so good as to find the capital?"

"I could not receive it as a gift," said Mr. Micawber,

full of fire and animation, "but if a sufficient sum could be advanced, say at five per cent. interest, per annum, upon my personal liability——"

"Could be? Can be and shall be, on your own terms," returned my aunt, "if you say the word. Here are some people David knows, going out to Australia shortly. If you decide to go, why shouldn't you go in the same ship."

"There is but one question, my dear ma'am, I could wish to ask," said Mrs. Micawber. "Are the circumstances of the country such, that a man of Mr. Micawber's abilities should have a fair chance of rising in the social scale?"

"No better opening anywhere," said my aunt, "for a man who conducts himself well, and is industrious."

"For a man who conducts himself well," repeated Mrs. Micawber, with her clearest business manner, "and is industrious. Precisely. It is evident to me that Australia is the legitimate sphere of action for Mr. Micawber!"

Shall I ever forget how, in a moment, he was the most sanguine of men, looking on to fortune; or how Mrs. Micawber presently discoursed about the habits of the kangaroo!

CHAPTER LIII

ANOTHER RETROSPECT

I MUST pause yet once again. Oh, my child-wife, there is a figure in the moving crowd before my memory, quiet and still, saying, Stop to think of me—turn to look upon the Little Blossom as it flutters to the ground!

I am again with Dora in our cottage. I do not know how long she has been ill. I am so used to it in feeling, that I cannot count the time. It is not really long, in weeks or months; but, in my usage and experience, it is a weary while.

Jip is, as it were suddenly, grown very old. He mopes, and his sight is weak, and his limbs are feeble.

Dora lies smiling on us, and is beautiful, and utters no hasty or complaining word. She says that her dear old careful boy is tiring himself out; that my aunt has no sleep, yet is always wakeful, active, and kind. Sometimes, the little bird-like ladies come to see her; and then we talk about our wedding-day, and all that happy time.

It is evening; and I sit by the bed, with the same face turned towards me. We have been silent, and there is a smile upon her face. I have ceased to carry my light burden up and down stairs now. She lies here all the day.

"Doady!"

"My dear Dora!"

"You won't think what I am going to say, unreasonable. I want to see Agnes. Very much I want to see her."

"I will write to her, my dear."

"Will you?"

"Directly."

"What a good, kind boy!"

It is night; and I am with her again. Agnes has been among us for a whole day and an evening. We have not talked much, but Dora has been perfectly contented and cheerful. We are now alone.

"I am going to say something I have often thought of saying, lately. You won't mind?" with a gentle look.

"Mind, my darling?"

"Because I don't know what you will think. Perhaps you have often thought the same. Doady, dear, I am afraid I was too young."

She looks into my eyes, and speaks very softly

"I am afraid, dear, I was too young. I don't mean in years only, but in experience, and thoughts, and everything. I have begun to think I was not fit to be a wife."

I try to stay my tears, and to reply, "Oh, Dora, love, as fit as I to be a husband!"

"I don't know," with the old shake of her curls. "Perhaps! But you are very clever, and I never was."

"We have been very happy, my sweet Dora."

"I was very happy, very. But, as years went on, my dear boy would have wearied of his child-wife. She wouldn't have improved. It is better as it is. Is it lonely, down-stairs, Doady?"

"Very! Very!"

"Don't cry! Is my chair there?"

"In its old place."

"Oh, how my poor boy cries! Hush, hush! Now, make me one promise. I want to speak to Agnes quite alone."

I promise that she shall, immediately; but I cannot leave her, for my grief.

"I said that it was better as it is!" she whispers, as she holds me in her arms. "Oh, Doady, after more years, you never could have loved your child-wife better than you do; and, after more years, she would so have tried and disappointed you, that you might not have been able to love her half so well! It is much better as it is!"

Agnes is down-stairs, and I give her the massage. She disappears, leaving me alone with Jip.

How the time wears, I know not; I am recalled by my child-wife's old companion who looks at me, and wanders to the door, and whines to go up-stairs.

"Not to-night, Jip! Not to-night!"

He comes very slowly back to me, lies down at my feet, and with a plaintive cry, is dead.

"Oh, Agnes! Look, look, here!"

——That face, so full of pity, and of grief!

"Agnes?"

It is over. Darkness comes before my eyes; and, for a time, all things are blotted out of my remembrance.

CHAPTER LIV

MR. MICAWBER'S TRANSACTIONS

THIS is not the time at which I am to enter on the state of my mind beneath its load of sorrow. How it came to be agreed among us that I was to seek peace in change and travel, I do not know. The spirit of Agnes so pervaded all, that I assume I may refer the project to her influence. But her influence was so quiet that I know no more. She was like a sacred presence in my lonely house. Let me go on.

I was to go abroad. That seemed to have been determined among us from the first. I waited only for what Mr. Micawber called the "final pulverisation of Heep," and for the departure of the emigrants.

At the request of Traddles, most affectionate and devoted of friends in my trouble, we returned to Canterbury: I mean my aunt, Agnes, and I, where my friend had been labouring ever since our explosive meeting.

"Well, Mr. and Mrs. Micawber," was my aunt's first salutation after we were seated. "Pray, have you thought about that emigration proposal of mine?"

"My dear madam," returned Mr. Micawber, "perhaps I cannot better express the conclusion at which Mrs. Micawber, your humble servant, and I may add our children, have arrived, than to reply that our Boat is on the shore, and our Bark is on the sea."

"That's right," said my aunt. "I augur all sorts of good from your sensible decision."

"Madam," he replied, "Mrs. Micawber and myself are deeply sensible of the very considerate kindness of our friends. What I wish is, to be perfectly businesslike.

Turning over, as we are about to turn over, an entirely new leaf; and falling back, as we are now in the act of falling back, for a Spring of no common magnitude; it is important that these arrangements should be concluded as between man and man."

My aunt observed, that in a case where both parties were willing to agree to anything, she took it for granted there would be no difficulty in settling this point. Mr. Micawber was of her opinion.

"In reference to our domestic preparations, madam," said Mr. Micawber, with some pride, "my eldest daughter attends at five every morning in a neighbouring establishment, to acquire the process of milking cows. My younger children are instructed to observe the habits of the pigs and poultry maintained in the poorer parts of this city, and my son Wilkins has issued forth with a walking-stick and driven cattle, when permitted, by the rugged hirelings who had them in charge.

"All very right indeed," said my aunt, encouragingly.

Mr. Micawber then gave Mrs. Micawber his arm, and glancing at the heap of books and papers lying before Traddles on the table, said they would leave us to ourselves; which they ceremoniously did.

"My dear Copperfield," said Traddles, looking at me with an affection that made his eyes red, and his hair all kinds of shapes, "My dear boy, I hope you are not worn out?"

"I am quite myself," said I, after a pause. "We have more cause to think of my aunt than of any one. You know how much she has done."

"Surely, surely," answered Traddles. "Who can forget it!"

"But even that is not all," said I. "During the last fortnight, some new trouble has vexed her; and she has been in and out of London every day. Last night, Traddles, it was almost midnight before she came home. You know what her consideration for others is. She will not tell me what has happened to distress her."

My aunt, very pale, sat immovable until I had finished; when some stray tears found their way to her cheeks, and she put her hand on mine.

"It's nothing, Trot. You shall know by-and-by. Now, Agnes my dear, let us attend to these affairs."

"I must do Mr. Micawber the justice to say," Traddles began, "that although he would appear not to have worked to any good account for himself, he is a most untiring man when he works for other people. I never saw such a fellow. The manner in which he has been diving, day and night, among papers and books; to say nothing of the immense number of letters he has written me when he might much more easily have spoken; is quite extraordinary."

"Letters!" cried my aunt. "I believe he dreams in letters!"

"There's Mr. Dick, too," said Traddles, "has been doing wonders! As soon as he was released from overlooking Uriah Heep he began to devote himself to Mr. Wickfield. His usefulness in copying, and fetching, and carrying, have been quite stimulating to us."

"Dick is a very remarkable man," exclaimed my aunt; "and I always said he was. Trot, you know it."

"I am happy to say, Miss Wickfield," pursued Traddles, at once with great delicacy and with great earnestness, "that in your absence Mr. Wickfield has considerably improved. At times, even his impaired power of concentrating has recovered itself very much; and he has been able to assist us in making some things clear, that we should have found very difficult without him."

"Now, let me see," said Traddles, looking among the papers on the table. "Having reduced to order a great mass of unintentional confusion in the first place, and of wilful confusion and falsification in the second, we take it to be clear that Mr. Wickfield might now wind up his business, and his agency-trust, and exhibit no deficiency of defalcation whatever."

"Oh, thank Heaven!" cried Agnes, fervently. "Papa free

with honour, what could I wish for! To take our future on myself, will be the next great happiness that I can know."

"Have you thought how, Agnes?"

"Often! If I rent the dear old house, and keep a school, I shall be useful and happy."

"Next, Miss Trotwood," said Traddles, "that property of yours."

"Well, Sir," sighed my aunt. "All I have got to say about it, is, that if it's gone, I can bear it; and if it's not gone, I shall be glad to get it back."

"It was originally, I think, eight thousand pounds, Consols?" said Traddles.

"Right!" replied my aunt.

"I can't account for more than five," said Traddles, with an air of perplexity.

"——thousand, do you mean?" inquired my aunt, with uncommon composure, "or pounds?"

"Five thousand pounds," said Traddles.

"It was all there was," returned my aunt. "I sold three, myself. One, I paid for your articles, Trot, my dear; and the other two I have by me. When I lost the rest, I thought it wise to keep that sum secretly for a rainy day. I wanted to see how you would come out of the trial, Trot; and you came out nobly—persevering, self-reliant, self-denying! So did Dick."

"Then I am delighted to say," cried Traddles, beaming with joy, "that we have recovered the whole money!"

"Don't congratulate me, anybody!" exclaimed my aunt. "If anybody speaks to me, I'll leave the house!"

We all remained quiet; Agnes covering her face.

"Well, my dear friend," said my aunt, after a pause, "what's become of Uriah?"

"I don't know. He left here," said Traddles, "with his mother, who had been clamouring, and beseeching, and disclosing, the whole time. They went away by one of the London night coaches, and I know no more about him."

"He's a monster of meanness!" said my aunt.

"Really I don't know about that," observed Traddles thoughtfully. "Many people can be very mean, when they give their minds to it."

"And now, touching Mr. Micawber," said my aunt.

"Well, really," said Traddles, cheerfully, "I must, once more, give Mr. Micawber high praise. And I think we ought to consider that Mr. Micawber did right, for right's sake, when we reflect what terms he might have made with Uriah Heep himself, for his silence."

"I think so too," said I.

"Now, what would you give him?" inquired my aunt.

"Oh! Before you come to that," said Traddles, a little disconcerted, "I am afraid I thought it discreet to omit two points, in making this adjustment. Those I. O. U.'s and so forth, which Mr. Micawber gave him——"

"Well! They must be paid," said my aunt.

"Yes, but I don't know when they may be proceeded on," rejoined Traddles, opening his eyes; "and I anticipate, that, between this time and his departure, Mr. Micawber will be constantly arrested."

"Then he must be constantly set free again," said my aunt. "What's the amount altogether?"

"Why, Mr. Micawber has entered the transactions with great form in a book, and he makes the amount a hundred and three pounds, five."

"Now, what shall we give him, that sum included?" said my aunt. "Five hundred pounds?"

Upon this, Traddles and I both struck in at once. We both recommended a small sum in money, and the payment of the Uriah claims as they came in. We proposed that the family should have their passage and their outfit, and a hundred pounds; and that Mr. Micawber's arrangement for repayment should be gravely entered into. To this, I added the suggestion, that I should give some explanation of his character and history to Mr. Peggotty and that to Mr. Peggotty should be quietly entrusted the discretion of advancing another hundred. I further proposed to interest Mr. Micawber in Mr. Peggotty and to endeavour to bring each of them to bear upon the other, for the common advantage.

Seeing that Traddles now glanced anxiously at my aunt again, I reminded him of the second point.

"You and your aunt will excuse me, Copperfield, if I touch upon a painful theme," said Traddles, hesitating; "but I think it necessary. On the day of Mr. Micawber's memorable denunciation, a threatening allusion was made by Uriah Heep to your aunt's—husband."

My aunt assented with a nod.

"There was—pardon me—really such a person, and at all in his power?" hinted Traddles.

"Yes, my good friend," said my aunt.

Traddles, with a perceptible lengthening of his face, explained that this subject had shared the fate of Mr. Micawber's liabilities in not being comprehended in the terms he had made, and that if Uriah could do us, or any of us, any injury or annoyance, no doubt he would.

My aunt remained quiet; until again some stray tears found their way to her cheeks.

"You are quite right," she said. "It was very thoughtful to mention it."

"Can I—or Copperfield—do anything?" asked Traddles, gently.

"Nothing," said my aunt. "I thank you many times. Trot, my dear, a vain threat! Let us have Mr. and Mrs. Micawber back. And don't any of you speak to me!"

"Well, Mr. and Mrs. Micawber!" said my aunt, when they entered. "We have been discussing your emigration and I'll tell you what arrangements we propose."

These she explained, to the unbounded satisfaction of the family,—children and all being then present. Mr. Micawber could not be dissuaded from immediately rushing out to bring the stamps for his notes of hand. But, his joy received a sudden check; for within five minutes, he returned in the custody of the sheriff's officer, informing us, in a flood of tears, that all was lost. We, being quite prepared for this event, soon paid the money; and in five minutes more Mr. Micawber was seated at the table with an expression of perfect joy.

This closed the proceedings of the evening. We passed the night at the old house, which, freed from the presence of the Heeps, seemed purged of a disease; and I lay in my old room, like a shipwrecked wanderer come home.

We went back next day to my aunt's house—not to mine; and when she and I sat alone, as of old, before going to bed, she said:

"Trot, do you really wish to know what I have had upon my mind lately?"

"Indeed I do, aunt."

"Would you ride with me a little way to-morrow morning at nine?" asked my aunt. "I'll tell you then, my dear."

At nine, accordingly, we drove to London. We drove a long way through the streets until we came to one of the large hospitals. Standing hard by the building was a plain hearse. The driver recognized my aunt, and drove slowly off; we following.

"You understand it now, Trot," said my aunt. "He is gone!"

"Did he die in the hospital?"

"Yes."

Again I saw the stray tears on her face.

"He was ailing a long time—a shattered, broken man, these many years. When he knew his state in this last illness, he asked them to send for me. He was sorry then. Very sorry."

"You went, I know, aunt."

"I went. I was with him a good deal afterwards. No one can harm him now. It was a vain threat."

We drove to the churchyard at Hornsey; we alighted; and followed the plain coffin to a corner I remember well, where the service was read consigning it to the dust.

"Six-and-thirty years ago, this day, my dear," said my aunt, as we walked back to the chariot, "I was married. God forgive us all!"

We took our seats in silence; and so she sat beside me for a long time, holding my hand. At length she suddenly burst into tears, and said:

"He was a fine-looking man when I married him, Trot—and he was sadly changed!"

CHAPTER LV

TEMPEST

I NOW approach an event in my life, so indelible, so awful, so bound to all that has preceded it that, from the beginning of my narrative, I have seen it growing larger and larger as I advanced, like a great tower in a plain.

For years after it occurred, I dreamed of it often. I dream of it sometimes to this hour. As plainly as I behold what happened, I will try to write it down. I do not recall it, but see it done; for it happens again before me.

The time drawing on rapidly for the sailing of the emigrant-ship, my good old nurse came up to London. I was constantly with her, and her brother, and the Micawbers, but Emily I never saw.

One evening I was alone with Peggotty and her brother. Our conversation turned on Ham. She described to us how tenderly he had taken leave of her, and how manfully and quietly he had borne himself. Most of all, of late, when she believed he was most tried.

I wavered in the original purpose I had formed, of leaving a letter for Emily when I should take leave of her uncle on board the ship, and thought it would be better to write to her now. She might desire, I thought, to send some parting word by me to her unhappy lover.

I therefore sat down in my room, before going to bed, and wrote to her. I told her that I had seen him, and that he had requested me to tell her what I have already written in its place in these sheets. I left it out, to be sent round in the morning; with a line to Mr. Peggotty, and went to bed at day-break.

Not falling asleep until the sun was up, I lay late, and

was roused by the silent presence of my aunt at my bedside.

"Trot, my dear," she said, when I opened my eyes, "I couldn't make up my mind to disturb you. Mr. Peggotty is here; shall he come up?"

I replied yes, and he soon appeared.

"Mas'r Davy," he said, when we had shaken hands, "I giv Em'ly your letter, Sir, and she writ this heer; and begged of me fur to ask you to read it, and if you see no hurt in't, to be so kind as take charge on't."

"Have you read it?" said I.

He nodded sorrowfully. I opened it, and read as follows:

"Oh, what can I write, to thank you for your good and blessed kindness to me!

"I have put the words close to my heart. They are sharp thorns, but they are such comfort. When I find what you are, and what uncle is, I think what God must be, and can cry to Him.

"Now, my dear; my friend, good-bye for ever in this world. In another world, if I am forgiven, I may wake a child and come to you. All thanks and blessings. Farewell, evermore!"

"May I tell her as you doen't see no hurt in't, and as you'll be so kind as take charge on't, Mas'r Davy?" said Mr. Peggotty, when I had read it.

"Unquestionably," said I—"but I am thinking that I'll go down again to Yarmouth. To put this letter in his hand and to enable you to tell her that he has got it, will be kindness to both of them. The journey is nothing to me. I'll go down to-night."

I saw that he was of my mind and in the evening I started.

"Don't you think that," I asked the coachman, "a very remarkable sky?"

"That's wind, Sir," he replied. "There's be mischief done at sea, I expect, before long."

It was a murky confusion—here and there blotted with a colour like the colour of the smoke from damp fuel—of flying clouds tossed up into most remarkable heaps through which the wild moon seemed to plunge headlong. There had been a wind all day; and it was rising then, with an extraordinary great sound.

As the night advanced it came on to blow, harder and harder. It still increased, until our horses could scarcely face the wind. Many times the leaders turned about, or came to a dead stop; and we were often in serious apprehension that the coach would be blown over.

When the day broke, it blew harder and harder. I had been in Yarmouth when the seamen said it blew great guns, but I had never known the like of this, or anything approaching to it.

As we struggled on, nearer and nearer to the sea, from which this mighty wind was blowing dead on shore, its force became more and more terrific. Long before we saw the sea, its spray was on our lips, and showered salt rain upon us. When at last we got into the town, the people came out to their doors, making a wonder of the mail that had come through such a night.

I put up at the old inn, and went down to look at the sea; staggered along the street, afraid of falling slates and tiles; and holding by people I met, at angry corners. Coming near the beach, I saw half the people of the town, lurking behind buildings; some, now and then braving the fury of the storm to look away to sea, and blown sheer out of their course in trying to get zigzag back.

Joining these groups, I found bewailing women whose husbands were away in herring or oyster boats; grizzled old sailors shaking their heads; ship-owners, excited and uneasy; children, huddling together; even stout mariners, disturbed and anxious.

The tremendous sea itself confounded me. As the high watery walls came rolling in, they looked as if the least would engulf the town. As the receding wave swept back with a hoarse roar, it seemed as if its purpose were to undermine the earth.

Not finding Ham among the people whom this memorable wind—for it is still remembered down there, as the greatest ever known to blow upon that coast—had brought together, I made my way to the yard where he worked. I learned, there, that he had gone to Lowestoft but would be back to-morrow morning.

I went back to the inn; and had not sat five minutes by the coffee-room fire, when the waiter coming to stir it, as an excuse for talking, told me that two colliers had gone down, with all hands, a few miles away; and that some other ships had been seen trying, in great distress, to keep off shore. Mercy on them, and on all poor sailors, said he, if we had another night like the last!

It was reassuring, on such a night, to be told that some of the inn-servants had agreed together to sit up until morning. I went to bed, exceedingly weary and heavy; but, on my lying down, all such sensations vanished, and I was broad awake.

For hours I lay there, listening to the wind and water; imagining, now, that I heard shrieks out at sea; now, the firing of signal guns; and now, the fall of houses in the town. I got up, several times, and looked out; but could see nothing, except the reflection of the faint candle and of my own haggard face.

At length I went down-stairs. In the large kitchen the watchers were clustered together about a table, purposely moved away from the great chimney, and brought near the door.

I remained there, I dare say, two hours. Once, I opened the yard-gate, and looked into the empty street. The sand, the seaweed, and the flakes of foam, were driving by; and I was obliged to call for assistance before I could shut the gate again, and make it fast against the wind.

There was a dark gloom in my solitary chamber, when I at length returned to it; but I was tired now, and, getting into bed, again, fell—off a tower and down a precipice—into the depths of sleep.

It was broad day when I awoke, the storm raging, and some one knocking and calling at my door.

"What is the matter?" I cried.

"A wreck! Close by! A schooner, from Spain or Portugal!" The excited voice went clamouring along the staircase; and I wrapped myself in my clothes as quickly as I could and soon came facing the wild sea.

The wind might by this time have lulled a little, but the sea was infinitely more terrific than when I had seen it last, and the height to which the breakers rose, and bore one another down, and rolled in, was most appalling.

In the unspeakable confusion, and my first breathless efforts to stand against the weather, I looked for the wreck, and saw nothing but the foaming heads of the great waves. A half-dressed boatman pointed to the left. Then, O great Heaven, I saw it, close in upon us!

One mast was broken short off and lay over the side, entangled in a maze of sail and rigging; and all that ruin beat the side as if it would stave it in. Some efforts were even then being made to cut this portion of the wreck away; for I plainly descried her people at work with axes, especially one active figure with long curling hair. But at this moment the sea, sweeping over the rolling planks, made a clean breach, and carried men, spars, casks, planks, bulwarks, heaps of such toys, into the boiling surge.

The second mast was yet standing, with the rags of a rent sail, and a wild confusion of broken cordage flapping to and fro. The ship had struck once, the same boatman hoarsely said in my ear, and then lifted in and struck again. As he spoke, four men arose with the wreck out of the deep, clinging to the rigging of the remaining mast; uppermost, the active figure with the curling hair.

Again we lost her, and again she rose. Two men were gone. The agony on shore increased. Men groaned; women shrieked, and turned away their faces. Some ran wildly up and down along the beach, crying for help where no help could be. I found myself one of these, frantically imploring a knot of sailors whom I knew, not to let these two lost creatures perish before our eyes.

They were making out to me, in an agitated way, that the lifeboat had been bravely manned an hour ago, and could do nothing; and no man would be so desperate as to attempt to wade off with a rope, when I saw Ham come breaking through them to the front.

Distracted though I was, the determination in his face awoke me to a knowledge of his danger. I held him back with both arms; and implored the men not to let him stir from off that sand!

Another cry arose on shore; and looking to the wreck, we saw the cruel sail, with blow on blow, beat off the lower of the two men, and fly up in triumph round the active figure left alone upon the mast.

Against such a sight I might as hopefully have entreated the wind. "Mas'r Davy," he said cheerily, grasping me by both hands, "if my time is come, 'tis come. It 'tan't, I'll bide it. Lord above bless you, and bless all! Mates, make me ready! I'm a going off!"

Then, I saw him standing alone, a rope slung to his wrist; another round his body; and several men holding to the latter, slack upon the shore, at his feet.

The wreck, even to my unpractised eye, was breaking up. I saw that she was parting in the middle, and that the life of the solitary man upon the mast hung by a thread. He had a singular red cap on,—not like a sailor's cap, but of a finer colour; and he was seen by all of us to wave it. I saw him do it now, and his action brought an old remembrance to my mind of a once dear friend.

Ham watched the sea, until there was a great retiring wave, when, with a backward glance at those who held the rope, he dashed in and in a moment was buffeting with the water; rising with the hills, falling with the valleys, lost beneath the foam; then drawn again to land.

He was hurt. I saw blood on his face; but he took no thought of that. He seemed hurriedly to give them some directions and was gone as before.

And now he made for the wreck, rising with the hills, falling with the valleys, lost beneath the rugged foam, borne in towards the shore, borne on towards the ship, striving hard and valiantly. At length he neared the wreck. He was so near, that with one more of his vigorous

Then, O great Heaven, I saw it, close in upon us!

strokes he would be clinging to it,—when, a high, green vast hill-side of water, moving shoreward from beyond the ship, he seemed to leap up into it with a mighty bound, and the ship was gone! They drew him to my very feet —insensible—dead. He was carried to the nearest house; and every means of restoration were tried; but he had been beaten to death by the great wave, and his generous heart was stilled for ever.

As I sat beside the bed, a fisherman whispered my name at the door.

"Sir," said he, with tears starting to his weather-beaten face, "will you come over yonder?"

The old remembrance that had been recalled to me, was in his look. I asked him, terror-stricken:

"Has a body come ashore?"

He said, "Yes."

"Do I know it?" I asked then.

He answered nothing.

But he led me to the shore. And on that part of it where some lighter fragments of the old boat, blown down last night, had been scattered by the wind—among the ruins of the home he had wronged—I saw him lying with his head upon his arm, as I had often seen him lie at school.

CHAPTER LVI

THE NEW WOUND, AND THE OLD

No need, O Steerforth, to have said, when we last spoke together, "Think of me at my best!" I had done that ever; and could I change now, looking on this sight!

They brought a hand-bier, and laid him on it, and covered him with a flag, and took him up and bore him on towards the houses. All the men who carried him had known him, and gone sailing with him, and seen him merry and bold.

We went into the town, and took our burden to the inn. I knew that the care of it, and the hard duty of preparing his mother to receive it, could only rest with me.

I chose the night for the journey, and about noon I arrived at Highgate. I had not, at first, the courage to ring at the gate; and when I did ring, my errand seemed to me to be expressed in the very sound of the bell. The little parlour-maid came out, and looking earnestly at me said:

"I beg your pardon, Sir. Are you ill?"

"I have been much agitated, and am fatigued."

"Is anything the matter, Sir?—Mr. James——?"

"Hush!" said I. "Yes, something has happened, that I have to break to Mrs. Steerforth. She is at home?"

The girl anxiously replied that her mistress kept her room; and in a few minutes I stood before her.

At her chair, as usual, was Rosa Dartle. From the first moment of her dark eyes resting on me, I saw she knew I was the bearer of evil tidings.

"I am sorry to observe you are in mourning, Sir," said Mrs. Steerforth.

"I am unhappily a widower," said I.

"I am grieved to hear it," she returned. "I hope Time will be good to you."

"I hope Time," said I, looking at her, "will be good to all of us. Dear Mrs. Steerforth, we must all trust to that."

The earnestness of my manner, and the tears in my eyes, alarmed her.

I tried to command my voice in gently saying his name, but it trembled. She repeated it to herself, two or three times, in a low tone. Then, addressing me, she said, with enforced calmness:

"My son is ill."

"Very ill."

"You have seen him?"

"I have."

"Are you reconciled?"

I could not say Yes, I could not say No. She slightly turned her head and in that moment I said, by the motion of my lips, to Rosa, "Dead!"

"The night before last was a dreadful one at sea," I faltered. "If he were at sea that night, and near a dangerous coast——"

"Rosa!" said Mrs. Steerforth, "come to me!"

She came, but with no sympathy or gentleness. Her eyes gleamed like fire as she confronted his mother.

"Now," she said, "is your pride appeased, you madwoman? *Now* has he made atonement to you—with his life! Do you hear?—His life!"

Mrs. Steerforth, fallen back stiffly in her chair, and making no sound but a moan, cast her eyes upon her with a wide stare.

"Ay!" cried Rosa, "Moan, and groan, and look at me! Look here!" striking the scar, "at your dead child's handiwork!"

The moan the mother uttered, from time to time, went to my heart.

Rosa proceeded. "Do you remember when he did this, and disfigured me for life?"

"Miss Dartle," I entreated her. "For Heaven's sake——"

"I tell you," she returned, "I *will* speak to her. No power on earth should stop me. I loved him better than you ever loved him!" turning on her fiercely. "You were exacting, proud, punctilious, selfish. My love would have been devoted—would have trod your paltry whimpering under foot!"

With flashing eyes, she stamped upon the ground as if she actually did it.

"Look here!" she said, striking the scar again, "Many a time, when you were put off with a slight word, he has taken Me to his heart!"

She said it with a taunting pride in the midst of her frenzy—yet with an eager remembrance.

"Miss Dartle," said I, "if you can be so obdurate as not to feel for this afflicted mother——"

"Who feels for me?" she sharply retorted.

"And if his faults——" I began.

"Faults!" she cried, bursting into passionate tears. "Who dares malign him? He had a soul worth millions of the friends to whom he stooped."

"——if his faults cannot," I went on, "be banished from your remembrance, in such an hour; look at that figure and render it some help!"

All this time, the figure was unchanged. Motionless, rigid, staring; moaning in the same dumb way, but giving no other sign of life. Miss Dartle suddenly kneeled down before it, and began to loosen the dress.

"A curse upon you!" she said, looking round at me, with a mingled expression of rage and grief. "It was in an evil hour that you ever came here! A curse upon you! Go!"

CHAPTER LVII

THE EMIGRANTS

One thing more, I had to do, before yielding myself to the shock of these emotions. It was, to conceal what had occurred, from those who were going away; and to dismiss them on their voyage in happy ignorance.

I took Mr. Micawber aside that same night, and confided to him the task of standing between Mr. Peggotty and intelligence of the late catastrophe. He zealously undertook to do so.

"If it penetrates to him, Sir," said Mr. Micawber, striking himself on the breast, "it shall first pass through this body!"

Mr. Micawber, I must observe, in his adaptation of himself to a new state of society, had acquired a bold buccaneering air, not absolutely lawless, but defensive and prompt. He had provided himself, among other things, with a complete suit of oil-skin, and a straw hat with a very low crown, pitched or caulked on the outside. In this rough clothing, with a common mariner's telescope under his arm, and a shrewd trick of casting up his eye at the sky as looking out for dirty weather, he was far more nautical, after his manner, than Mr. Peggotty.

The Micawber family were lodged in a little, dirty, tumble-down public-house whose protruding wooden rooms overhung the river. My aunt and Agnes were there, busily making some little extra comforts, in the way of dress, for the children. Peggotty was quietly assisting, and it was not easy to answer her inquiries; still less to whisper Mr. Peggotty, when Mr. Micawber brought him in, that I had given the letter, and all was well. But I did both, and made them happy. If I showed any trace of what I felt, my own sorrows were sufficient to account for it.

"And when does the ship sail, Mr. Micawber?" asked my aunt.

"Madam," he replied, "I am informed that we must positively be on board before seven to-morrow morning."

"Heyday!" said my aunt, "That's soon. Is it a seagoing fact, Mr. Peggotty?"

" 'Tis so, ma'am. She'll drop down the river with that theer tide. If Mas'r Davy and my sister comes aboard at Gravesen', arternoon o' next day, they'll see the last on us."

"And that we shall do," said I, "be sure!"

"If you have any opportunity of sending letters home, on your passage, Mrs. Micawber," said my aunt, "you must let us hear from you, you know."

"My dear Miss Trotwood," she replied, "I shall only be too happy to think that any one expects to hear from us."

"Please Heaven, there will be many such opportunities," said Mr. Micawber. "The ocean, in these times, is a perfect fleet of ships; and we can hardly fail to encounter many, in running over. It is merely crossing," said Mr. Micawber, trifling with his eyeglass, "merely crossing. The distance is quite imaginary."

I think now, how odd it is, but how wonderfully like Mr. Micawber, that, when he went from London to Canterbury, he should have talked as if he were going to the farthest limits of the earth; and, when he went from England to Australia, as if he were going for a little trip across the Channel.

In the afternoon of the next day, my old nurse and I went down to Gravesend. We found the ship in the river, surrounded by a crowd of boats. I hired a boat directly, and we went on board.

Mr. Peggotty was waiting for us on deck. He told me that Mr. Micawber had just now been arrested again (and for the last time) at the suit of Heep, and that he had paid the money. He then took us down between decks; and there, any lingering fears I had of his having heard any rumours of what had happened, were dispelled by Mr. Micawber's taking his arm with an air of friendship and protection, and telling me that they had scarcely been asunder for a moment.

At first I could make out hardly anything; but, by degrees, my eyes became more accustomed to the gloom. Among the great beams, bulks, and ringbolts of the ship, and the emigrant-berths, and chests, and bundles, and barrels—lighted up, here and there, by dangling lanterns; and elsewhere by the yellow daylight straying down a hatchway—were crowded groups of people, talking, laughing, crying, eating and drinking; some, already settled down into the possession of their few feet of space, others wandering disconsolately. From babies who had but a week or two of life behind them, to crooked old men and women who seemed to have but a week or two of life before them, every age and occupation appeared to be crammed into the narrow compass of the 'tween decks.

As my eye glanced round this place, I thought I saw a figure like Emily's and another figure parting from it with a kiss, reminding me of Agnes! But in the confusion I only knew that all visitors were being warned to leave the ship; that my nurse was crying and that Mrs. Gummidge, assisted by some younger stooping woman in black, was busily arranging Mr. Peggotty's goods.

"Is there any last wured, Mas'r Davy?" said he.

"One thing!" said I. "Martha!"

He touched the younger woman and Martha stood before me.

"Heaven bless you, you good man!" cried I. "You take her with you!"

She answered for him, with a burst of tears, and if ever I have loved and honoured any man, I loved and honoured that man in my soul.

We went over the side into our boat, and lay at a little distance to see the ship wafted on her course. It was then calm, radiant sunset. She lay between us and the red light; and every spar was visible against the glow. A sight at once so beautiful, so mournful, and so hopeful, as the glorious ship with all the life on board her crowded at the bulwarks, and there clustering, for a moment, bare-headed and silent, I never saw.

Silent, only for a moment. As the sails rose to the wind, and the ship began to move, there broke from all the boats three resounding cheers, which those on board took up, and echoed back, and which were echoed and re-echoed.

Then I saw Emily at her uncle's side. He pointed to us with an eager hand; and she saw us, and waved her last good-bye to me. Surrounded by the rosy light, and standing high upon the deck, apart together, she clinging to him, and he holding her, they solemnly passed away.

CHAPTER LVIII

ABSENCE

It was a long and gloomy night that gathered on me. I went away from England; not knowing, even then, how great the shock was, that I had to bear. The knowledge came upon me, not quickly, but little by little. The desolate feeling with which I went abroad deepened and widened hourly.

For many months I travelled with this ever-darkening cloud upon my mind. Sometimes I proceeded restlessly from place to place, stopping nowhere; sometimes, I lingered long in one spot. I had no purpose, no sustaining soul within me, anywhere.

I was in Switzerland. I had come out of Italy, over one of the great passes of the Alps, and had since wandered with a guide among the by-ways of the mountains but as yet they had taught me nothing.

I came, one evening before sunset, down into a valley as the sun was shining on the remote heights of snow, that closed it in, like eternal clouds. Dotted here and there on the mountain's side, each tiny dot a home, were lonely wooden cottages, so dwarfed by the towering heights that they appeared too small for toys. In the quiet air, there was a sound of distant singing—shepherd voices. All at once, in this serenity, great Nature spoke to me; and soothed me to lay down my weary head upon the grass, and weep as I had not wept yet, since Dora died!

I had found a packet of letters awaiting me but a few minutes before, and had strolled out of the village to read them. Other packets had missed me, and I had received none for a long time.

The packet was in my hand. I opened it, and read the writing of Agnes.

She was happy and useful, was prospering as she had hoped. That was all she told me of herself. The rest referred to me.

She gave me no advice; she only told me in her own fervent manner what her trust in me was. She knew (she said) how such a nature as mine would turn affliction to good. She, who so gloried in my fame, well knew that I would labour on. She knew that in me, sorrow must be strength. She commended me to God, who had taken my innocent darling to His rest; and in her sisterly affection cherished me always, proud of what I had done, but infinitely prouder yet of what I was reserved to do.

I read her letter, many times. I wrote to her before I slept. I told her that I had been in sore need of her help; that without her I was not, and never had been, what she thought me; but, that she inspired me to be that, and I would try.

I did try. I worked early and late, patiently and hard. I wrote a story and sent it to Traddles, and he arranged for its publication very advantageously for me; and the tidings of my growing reputation began to reach me. After some rest and change, I fell to work, in my old ardent way, on a new fancy. This was my third work of fiction. It was not half written, when, in an interval of rest, I thought of returning home. My health was quite restored. I had seen much. I had been in many countries, and I hope I had improved my store of knowledge.

I have now recalled all that I think needful of this term of absence—with one reservation. I enter on it now.

I do not know when I began to think that I had thrown away the treasure of Agnes' love. I could not forget that the feeling with which she now regarded me had grown up in my own free choice. That if she had ever loved me with another love—and I sometimes thought the time was when she might have done so—I had cast it away. I had bestowed my passionate tenderness upon another object;

and what Agnes was to me, I and her own noble heart had made her. I made no effort to conceal from myself that I loved her, but I brought the assurance home to myself, that it was too late, and that our relation must be undisturbed.

Three years had elapsed since the sailing of the emigrant ship. Three years. Long in the aggregate, though short as they went by. And home was very dear to me, and Agnes too—but she was not mine—she was never to be mine. She might have been, but that was past!

CHAPTER LIX

RETURN

I LANDED in London on a wintry autumn evening. It was dark and raining, and I saw more fog and mud in a minute than I had seen in a year.

For some changes in the fortunes of my friends, I was prepared. My aunt had long been re-established at Dover, and Traddles had chambers in Gray's Inn, now; and had told me, in his last letters, that he was not without hopes of being soon united to the dearest girl in the world.

They expected me home before Christmas; but had no idea of my returning so soon. I had purposely misled them, that I might have the pleasure of taking them by surprise. And yet, I was perverse enough to feel a chill and disappointment in receiving no welcome, and rattling, alone and silent, through the misty streets.

The well-known shops, however, with their cheerful lights, did something for me; and when I alighted at the door of the Gray's Inn Coffee-house, I had recovered my spirits.

"Do you know where Mr. Traddles lives in the Inn?" I asked the waiter.

"Holborn Court, Sir. Number two."

"Mr. Traddles has a rising reputation among the lawyers, I believe?" said I.

"Well, Sir," returned the waiter, "probably he has, Sir; but I am not aware of it myself."

I really was quite cast down on Traddles's account. I meekly ordered a bit of fish and a steak, and stood before the fire musing on his obscurity.

Being very anxious to see the dear old fellow, nevertheless, I despatched my dinner and hurried out by the back way. Number two in the Court was soon reached; and an inscription on the door-post informing me that Mr. Traddles occupied a set of chambers on the top story, I ascended the staircase. A crazy old staircase I found it to be, feebly lighted on each landing by a club-headed little oil wick.

In the course of my stumbling up-stairs, I fancied I heard a pleasant sound of laughter; and not the laughter of an attorney or barrister, but of two or three merry girls. Happening, however, as I stopped to listen, to put my foot in a hole, I fell with some noise, and when I recovered my footing all was silent.

Groping my way more carefully, I found the outer door, which had MR. TRADDLES painted on it. I knocked. A considerable scuffling within ensued, but nothing else. I therefore knocked again.

A small sharp-looking lad, very much out of breath, presented himself.

"Is Mr. Traddles within?" I said.

"Yes, Sir, but he's engaged."

"I want to see him."

After a moment's survey of me, the sharp-looking lad admitted me, first, into a little closet of a hall, and next into a little sitting-room; where I came into the presence of my old friend (also out of breath), seated at a table, and bending over papers.

"Good God!" cried Traddles, looking up. "It's Copperfield!" and rushed into my arms, where I held him tight.

"All well, my dear Traddles?"

"All well, my dear, dear Copperfield, and nothing but good news!"

We cried with pleasure, both of us.

"My dear fellow!" said Traddles. "And grown so famous! My glorious Copperfield! Good gracious me, *when* did you come, *where* have you come from, *what* have you been doing?"

Never pausing for an answer, Traddles clapped me into an easy chair by the fire and pulled at my neck-kerchief under some wild delusion that it was a great-coat.

"To think," said Traddles, "that you should have been so nearly coming home as you must have been, my dear old boy, and not at the ceremony!"

"What ceremony, my dear Traddles?"

"Good gracious me!" cried Traddles, opening his eyes in his old way. "Didn't you get my last letter?"

"Certainly not, if it referred to any ceremony."

"Why, my dear Copperfield," said Traddles, "I am married!"

"Married!" I cried joyfully.

"Lord bless me, yes!" said Traddles—"by the Rev. Horace—to Sophy. Why, my dear boy, she's behind the window curtain! Look here!"

To my amazement, the dearest girl in the world came out at that same instant, laughing and blushing, from her place of concealment. And a more amiable, honest, happy, bright-looking bride, I believe the world never saw. I kissed her as an old acquaintance should, and wished them joy with all my might of heart.

"Dear me," said Traddles, "what a delightful re-union this is! How happy I am!"

"And so am I," said I.

"And I am sure I am!" said the blushing and laughing Sophy.

"We are all as happy as possible!" said Traddles. "Even the girls are happy. Dear me, I declare I forgot them!"

"Forgot?" said I.

"The girls," said Traddles. "Sophy's sisters. They have come to have a peep at London. The fact is, when—was it you that tumbled up-stairs, Copperfield?"

"It was," said I, laughing.

"Well then, when you tumbled up-stairs," said Traddles, "we were playing Puss in the Corner. But as it wouldn't look quite professional, they decamped. And they are now listening, I have no doubt. My love, will you fetch them?"

Sophy tripped away, and we heard her received in the adjoining room with a peal of laughter.

"Really musical, isn't it, my dear Copperfield?" said Traddles. "It's very agreeable to hear. The society of girls is not professional, but it's very delightful. But then," said Traddles, "even Sophy's being here, is unprofessional."

"And you are happily married at last, my dear Traddles!" said I. "How rejoiced I am!"

"Thank you, my dear Copperfield. Yes, I am as happy as it's possible to be. There's your old friend, you see," said Traddles, nodding triumphantly at the flower-pot and stand; "and there's the table with the marble top! All the other furniture is plain and serviceable, you perceive. And as to plate, Lord bless you, we haven't so much as a tea-spoon."

"All to be earned?" said I, cheerfully.

"Exactly so. Of course we have something in the shape of tea spoons, because we stir our tea. But they're Britannia metal."

"And in short, my dear friend," said I, "you feel as blest as you deserve to feel!"

"Oh! That's your partiality!" laughed Traddles. "But, indeed, I am in a most enviable state. I work hard, and read Law insatiably. I hide the girls in the day-time, and make merry with them in the evening. And I assure you I am quite sorry that they are going home on Tuesday. But here," said Traddles, "*are* the girls! Mr. Copperfield, Miss Crewler—Miss Sarah—Miss Louisa—Margaret and Lucy!"

They were a perfect nest of roses; they looked so wholesome and fresh. They were all pretty, and Miss Caroline was very handsome; but there was a loving, cheerful, fireside quality in Sophy's bright looks which assured me that my friend had chosen well. We all sat round the fire; while the sharp boy produced the tea-things. After that, Mrs. Traddles, with perfect pleasure and composure beaming from her household eyes, having made the tea, quietly made the toast as she sat in a corner by the fire.

Altogether, it was a scene I could not help dwelling on with pleasure, for a long time after I got back to the coffee-house. Drawing a chair before one of the fires I gradually fell from the consideration of Traddles's happiness to thinking of the principal vicissitudes and separations that had marked my life.

I could think of the past now, gravely, but not bitterly; and could contemplate the future in a brave spirit. Home, in its best sense, was for me no more. She in whom I might have inspired a dearer love, I had taught to be my sister. It was right that I should pay the forfeit of my headlong passion. What I reaped, I had sown.

I was thus thinking, when I found my eyes resting on a countenance that might have arisen out of the fire, in its association with my early remembrances.

Little Mr. Chillip the Doctor sat reading a newspaper in the shadow of an opposite corner. He had left Blunderstone six or seven years ago, and I had never seen him since. He sat placidly perusing the newspaper, with his little head on one side, and a glass of warm sherry negus at his elbow. He was so extremely conciliatory in his manner that he seemed to apologise to the very newspaper for taking the liberty of reading it.

I walked up to where he was sitting, and said, "How do you do, Mr. Chillip?"

He was greatly fluttered, and replied, in his slow way, "I thank you, Sir, you are very good. Thank you, Sir. I hope *you* are well."

"You don't remember me?" said I.

"Well, Sir," returned Mr. Chillip, smiling very meekly, "I couldn't lay my hand upon your name, really."

"And yet you knew it, long before I knew it myself," I returned.

"Did I indeed, Sir?" said Mr. Chillip. "Is it possible that I had the honour, Sir, of officiating when——"

"Yes," said I.

"Dear me!" cried Mr. Chillip. "But no doubt you are a good deal changed since then, Sir?"

"Probably," said I.

On my telling him my name, he was really moved. "Dear me, Sir!" he said, surveying me with his head on one side. "And it's Mr. Copperfield, is it? We are not ignorant, Sir, down in our part of the country of your fame."

"What is your part of the country now?" I asked, seating myself near him.

"I am established within a few miles of Bury St. Edmund's, Sir," said Mr. Chillip. Are you aware, Sir, that your father-in-law is again a neighbour of mine?"

"No," said I.

"He is indeed, Sir!" said Mr. Chillip. "Married a young lady of that part, with a very good little property, poor thing. She was a charming woman, Sir!"

"The present Mrs. Murdstone?"

"A charming woman indeed, Sir," said Mr. Chillip. "Mrs. Chillip's opinion is that she is all but melancholy mad. And the ladies," observed Mr. Chillip, timorously, "are great observers, Sir."

"I suppose she was to be subdued and broken to their detestable mould, Heaven help her!" said I.

"Well, Sir, there were violent quarrels at first, I assure you," said Mr. Chillip; "but she is quite a shadow now."

I told him I could easily believe it.

"I have no hesitation in saying," said Mr. Chillip, "between you and me, Sir, that tyranny, gloom, and worry have made Mrs. Murdstone nearly imbecile. They go about with her, now, more like her keepers than her husband and sister-in-law. That was Mrs. Chillip's remark to me only last week. And I assure you, Sir, the ladies are great observers."

"Intuitively," said I, to his extreme delight.

I told him that I was going down to my aunt; and that she was one of the most tender-hearted and excellent of women, as he would know if he knew her better. The mere notion of his ever seeing her again, appeared to terrify him. He replied with a small, pale smile, "Is she so, indeed, Sir? Really?" and almost immediately called for a candle and went to bed.

Thoroughly tired, I went to bed at midnight; passed the next day on the Dover coach; burst safe and sound into my aunt's old parlour while she was at tea, and was received by her, and Mr. Dick, and dear old Peggotty, who acted as housekeeper, with open arms and tears of joy.

CHAPTER LX

AGNES

My aunt and I, when we were left alone, talked far into the night.

"And when, Trot," said my aunt, patting the back of my hand, as we sat in our old way before the fire, "when are you going over to Canterbury?"

"I shall get a horse, and ride over to-morrow morning, aunt, unless you will go with me?"

"No!" said my aunt, in her short abrupt way. "I mean to stay where I am."

We both kept silent for some minutes. When I raised my eyes, I found that she was steadily observant of me.

"Has Agnes any——"

"Well? Hey? Any what?" said my aunt, sharply.

"Any lover," said I.

"A score," cried my aunt. "She might have married twenty times, my dear, since you have been gone!"

"No doubt," said I. "But has she any lover who is worthy of her? Agnes could care for no other."

My aunt sat musing for a little while. Slowly raising her eyes to mine, she said gravely:

"I suspect she has an attachment, Trot. She has never confided it to me, but I suspect it."

"If it should be so," I said, "Agnes will tell me at her own good time. A sister to whom I have confided so much, aunt, will not be reluctant to confide in me."

My aunt withdrew her eyes from mine, and covered them thoughtfully with her hand. By-and-by she put her other hand on my shoulder; and so we both sat, looking into the past, without saying another word, until we parted for the night.

I rode away, early in the morning, for the scene of my old school days. The well-remembered ground was soon traversed, and I came into the quiet streets, where every stone was a boy's book to me. I went on foot to the old house, and looking through the low window of the turret-room where first Uriah Heep, and afterwards Mr. Micawber, had been wont to sit, saw that it was a little parlour now, and that there was no office. Otherwise the staid old house was just as it had been when I first saw it.

I was shown up the grave old staircase into the unchanged drawing-room. The books that Agnes and I had read together, were on their shelves; and the desk where I had laboured at my lessons, many a night, stood yet at the same old corner of the table. Everything was as it used to be, in the happy time.

The opening of the little door in the panelled wall made me start and turn. Her beautiful serene eyes met mine as she came towards me. She stopped and laid her hand upon her bosom, and I caught her in my arms.

"Agnes! My dear girl!"

I folded her to my heart, and, for a little while, we were both silent. Presently we sat down, side by side; and her angel-face was turned upon me with the welcome I had dreamed of, waking and sleeping, for whole years. I tried to bless her, tried to tell her what an influence she had upon me; but all my efforts were in vain. My love and joy were dumb. With her own sweet tranquillity, she calmed my agitation; spoke to me tenderly of Dora's grave; spoke to me of Emily, whom she had visited, in secret, many times.

"And you, Agnes," I said, by and by. "Tell me of yourself."

"What should I tell?" she answered, with her radiant smile. "Papa is well. You see us here, quiet in our own home; our anxieties set at rest, and knowing that, dear Trotwood, you know all."

"All, Agnes?" said I. "Is there nothing else, Sister?"

She smiled; with a quiet sadness, I thought; and shook her head.

"You have much to do, dear Agnes?"

"With my school?"

"Yes. It is laborious, is it not?"

"The labour is so pleasant," she returned, "that it is scarcely grateful in me to call it by that name."

"Nothing good is difficult to you," said I.

"You will wait and see papa," said Agnes cheerfully, "and pass the day with us? I must be a prisoner for a little while, but here are the old books, Trotwood, and the old music."

"Even the old flowers are here," said I, looking round; "or the old kinds."

"I have found a pleasure," returned Agnes, smiling, "in keeping everything as it used to be when we were children. Even this," showing me the basket-trifle, full of keys, still hanging at her side, "seems to jingle a kind of old tune!"

I walked through the streets; and, once more seeing my old adversary the butcher—now a constable—went down to look at the place where I had fought him; and there meditated on Miss Shepherd and the eldest Miss Larkins, and all the idle loves and likings, and dislikings, of that time.

When I returned, Mr. Wickfield had come home. When dinner was done, Mr. Wickfield taking no wine, and I desiring none, Agnes and her little charges sang and played, and worked. After tea the children left us; and we three sat together, talking of the bygone days.

"My part in them," said Mr. Wickfield, shaking his white head, "has much matter for deep regret, and deep contrition, Trotwood. But I would not cancel it, if it were in my power."

I could readily believe that, looking at the face beside him.

"I understand you, Sir," I softly said.

"But no one knows, not even you," he returned, "how much she has undergone, how hard she has striven. Dear Agnes!"

She had put her hand entreatingly on his arm, to stop him; and was very, very pale. She rose up from her father's side, before long; and going softly to her piano, played some of the old airs.

"Have you any intention of going away again?" Agnes asked me.

"What does my sister say to that?"

"I think you ought not, Trotwood, since you ask me," she said, mildly. "If *I* could spare my brother, perhaps the time could not."

"What I am, you have made me, Agnes. You should know best."

"*I* made you, Trotwood?"

"Yes! Agnes my dear girl. I tried to tell you, when we met to-day, something that has been in my thoughts since Dora died. You remember, when you came down to me—pointing upward, Agnes?"

"Oh, Trotwood!" she returned, her eyes filled with tears. "Can I ever forget?"

"As you were then, my sister, you have ever been to me. Ever pointing upward, Agnes; ever leading me to something better."

She only shook her head; through her tears I saw the same sad, quiet smile.

CHAPTER LXI

I AM SHOWN TWO INTERESTING PENITENTS

For a time—at all events until my book should be completed, I took up my abode in my aunt's house at Dover; and there quietly pursued my task.

Occasionally I went to London; to lose myself in the swarm of life there, or to consult with Traddles on some business point. He had managed for me, in my absence, with the soundest judgment; and my worldly affairs were prospering. As my notoriety began to bring upon me an enormous quantity of letters, I agreed with Traddles to have my name painted upon his door. There, the devoted postman delivered bushels of letters for me; and there, at intervals, I laboured through them.

The girls had gone home, when my name burst into bloom on Traddles's door; and the sharp boy looked, all day, as if he had never heard of Sophy. But, there I always found her, the same bright housewife.

"What a thoroughly good and charming wife she is, my dear Traddles," said I one day, when he had just come home through the drizzling sleet.

"My dear Copperfield," returned Traddles, "she is without any exception, the dearest girl! Bless my soul, when I see her getting up by candle-light on these dark mornings, busying herself in the day's arrangements, devising the most capital little dinners out of the plainest materials, always so neat and ornamental herself, sweet-tempered and encouraging always, and all for me, I positively sometimes can't believe it, Copperfield!"

He was tender of the very slippers she had been warming, as he put them on, and stretched his feet enjoyingly upon the fender.

"I positively sometimes can't believe it," said Traddles. "Then, our pleasures! Dear me, they are inexpensive, but they are quite wonderful! When we are at home here, of an evening, where could we be more snug? When we go out for a walk we look into the glittering windows of the jewellers' shops; and I show Sophy which of the diamond-eyed serpents I would give her if I could afford it; and Sophy shows me which of the gold watches she would buy for me if *she* could afford it; and really we go away as if we had got them! In walking home, perhaps we buy a little bit of something, and bring it here, and make a splendid supper. Now, you know, Copperfield, if I was Lord Chancellor, we couldn't do this!"

"You would do something, whatever you were, my dear Traddles," thought I, "that would be pleasant and amiable! And by the way," I said aloud, "I suppose you never draw any skeletons now?"

"Really," replied Traddles, laughing, and reddening, "I can't wholly deny that I do, my dear Copperfield. For, being in one of the back rows of the King's Bench the other day, the fancy came into my head to try. And I am afraid there's a skeleton—in a wig—on the ledge of the desk."

After we had both laughed heartily, Traddles wound up by saying, in his forgiving way, "Old Creakle!"

"I have a letter from that old—Rascal here," said I.

"From Creakle the schoolmaster?" exclaimed Traddles.

"Among the persons who discover that they were always much attached to me, is the self-same Creakle. He is not a schoolmaster now, Traddles. He is a magistrate, and he writes to me here, that he will be glad to show me, in operation, the only true system of prison discipline—solitary confinement. What do you say?"

"To the system?" inquired Traddles, looking grave.

"No. To my accepting the offer, and your going with me?"

"I don't object," said Traddles.

"Then I'll write to say so."

On the appointed day Traddles and I repaired to the prison where Mr. Creakle was powerful, and were presented to our old schoolmaster; who was one of a group of two or three magistrates, and some visitors. He received me, like a man who had formed my mind, and had always loved me tenderly. On my introducing Traddles, Mr. Creakle expressed, in like manner, that he had always been Traddles's guide, philosopher, and friend. Our venerable instructor was a great deal older, and not improved in appearance. His face was as fiery as ever; his eyes were as small; and the thick veins in his bald head were none the more agreeable to look at.

After some conversation I inquired of Mr. Creakle what were the main advantages of this system? I found them to be the perfect isolation of prisoners—so that no one man knew anything about another; and the reduction of prisoners to a wholesome state of mind, leading to sincere repentance.

I heard repeatedly of Number Twenty Seven, who appeared to be a Model Prisoner. Twenty Eight was also a bright particular star; but it was his misfortune to have his glory a little dimmed by the extraordinary lustre of Twenty Seven.

At last we came to the door of his cell; and Mr. Creakle, looking through a little hole in it, reported to us, in a state of greatest admiration, that he was reading a Hymn Book.

There was such a rush of heads to see Number Twenty Seven reading his Hymn Book, that the little hole was blocked up, six or seven heads deep. To give us an opportunity of conversing with Twenty Seven, Mr. Creakle directed the door of the cell to be unlocked, and Twenty Seven to be invited out into the passage. This was done; and whom should Traddles and I then behold but Uriah Heep!

He knew us directly; and said, as he came out—with

the old writhe—"How do you do, Mr. Copperfield? How do you do, Mr. Traddles?"

This recognition caused a general admiration in the party. I rather thought that every one was struck by his not being proud, and taking notice of us.

"Well, Twenty Seven," said Mr. Creakle, "How do you find yourself to-day?"

"I am very umble, Sir!" replied Uriah Heep.

"You are always so, Twenty Seven," said Mr. Creakle.

Here another gentleman asked, with extreme anxiety: "Are you quite comfortable?"

"Yes, I thank you, Sir!" said Uriah. "I see my follies now, Sir."

Several gentlemen were much affected; and a third inquired, "How do you find the beef?"

"Thank you, Sir," replied Uriah, "it was tougher yesterday than I could wish; but it's my duty to bear."

A murmur, partly of gratification at Twenty Seven's celestial state of mind, and partly of indignation against the Contractor who had given him any cause of complaint, having subsided, Twenty Seven stood in the midst of us, as if he felt himself the principal object of merit in a highly meritorious museum. That we might have an excess of light shining upon us all at once, orders were given to let out Twenty Eight.

I had been so much astonished already, that I only felt a kind of resigned wonder when Mr. Littimer walked forth, reading a good book!

"Twenty Eight," said a gentleman in spectacles, "you complained last week, my good fellow, of the cocoa. How has it been since?"

"I thank you, Sir," said Mr. Littimer, "it has been better made. If I might take the liberty of saying so, Sir, I don't think the milk which is boiled with it is quite genuine."

"What is your state of mind, Twenty Eight?"

"I thank you, Sir, I see my follies now, Sir. I am a good deal troubled when I think of the sins of my former companions, Sir; but I trust they may find forgiveness."

"Is there anything at all on your mind, now?" said the questioner. "If so, mention it, Twenty Eight."

"Sir," said Mr. Littimer, without looking up, "there is a gentleman present who was acquainted with me in my former life. It may be profitable to that gentleman to know, Sir, that I attribute my past follies, entirely to having lived a thoughtless life in the service of young men."

With this Number Twenty Eight retired, after a glance between him and Uriah; as if they were not altogether unknown to each other; and a murmur went round the group, as his door shut upon him, that he was a most respectable man, and a beautiful case.

"Do you know," said I, as we walked along the passage, with one of the wardens, "what felony was Number Twenty Seven's last 'folly'?"

The answer was that it was a Bank case.

"A fraud on the Bank of England?"

"Yes, Sir. Fraud, forgery, and conspiracy. It was a deep plot for a large sum."

"Do you know Twenty Eight's offence?"

"Twenty Eight," returned my informant in a low tone, "robbed a young master. I particularly recollect his case, from his being took by a dwarf."

"A what?"

"A little woman. I have forgot her name."

"Not Mowcher?"

"That's it! He was going to America in such a complete disguise as never you see when the little woman ran betwixt his legs to upset him—and held on to him like grim Death."

"Excellent Miss Mowcher!" cried I.

"You'd have said so, if you had seen her, standing on a chair in the witness-box at the trial, as I did," said my friend. "He cut her face right open, and pounded her in the most brutal manner, when she took him; but she never loosed her hold till he was locked up."

We had now seen all there was to see. We left them

to their system and themselves, and went home wondering.

"Perhaps it's a good thing, Traddles," said I, "to have an unsound Hobby ridden hard; for it's the sooner ridden to death."

"I hope so," replied Traddles.

CHAPTER LXII

A LIGHT SHINES ON MY WAY

I HAD been at home about two months and I had seen Agnes frequently. Christmas-time being come, and Agnes having reposed no new confidence in me, a doubt whether she could have that perception of the true state of my breast, which restrained her with the apprehension of giving me pain—began to oppress me heavily. I resolved to set this right beyond all doubt;—if such a barrier were between us, to break it down at once with a determined hand.

It was a cold, harsh, winter day. There had been snow some hours before; and it lay, not deep, but hard-frozen on the ground. Out at sea, beyond my window, the wind blew ruggedly from the north.

"Riding to-day, Trot?" said my aunt, putting her head in at the door.

"Yes," said I, "I am going over to Canterbury. It's a good day for a ride."

"I hope your horse may think so, too," said my aunt. "Well: go along with you!"

"Do you know anything more," said I, "of that attachment of Agnes?"

She looked up in my face a little while, before replying; "I think I do, Trot."

"Are you confirmed in your impression?" I inquired.

"I think I am, Trot."

She looked so steadfastly at me that I summoned the stronger determination to show her a perfectly cheerful face.

"And what is more, Trot—" said my aunt, "I think Agnes is going to be married."

"God bless her!" said I, cheerfully.

"God bless her!" said my aunt, "and her husband too!"

I echoed it and rode away. How well I recollect the wintry ride! The frozen particles of ice borne across my face; the hard clatter of the horse's hoofs, beating a tune upon the ground; the smoking team with the waggon of old hay, stopping to breathe on the hill-top, and shaking their bells musically; the whitened slopes and sweeps of Down-land lying against the dark sky.

I found Agnes alone. The little girls had gone to their own homes now, and she was alone by the fire, reading. She put down her book on seeing me come in; and I sat beside her on the window-seat.

As I looked at her beautiful face, she raised her mild clear eyes, and saw that I was looking at her.

"You are thoughtful to-day, Trotwood!"

"Agnes, shall I tell you what about? I came to tell you. Do you remember that I tried to tell you, when I came home, what a debt of gratitude I owed you, dearest Agnes, and how fervently I felt towards you?"

"I remember it," she said, gently, "very well."

"You have a secret," said I. "Let me share it, Agnes."

She cast down her eyes, and trembled.

"I could hardly fail to know, even if I had not heard that there is some one upon whom you have bestowed the treasure of your love. If you can trust me as you say you can, let me be your friend, your brother, in this matter, of all others!"

With an appealing, almost a reproachful, glance, she rose, put her hands before her face, and burst into such tears as smote me tc the heart.

"Agnes! Sister! Dearest! What have I done?"

"Let me go away, Trotwood. I will write to you. Don't speak to me now. Don't! don't!"

"Agnes, I cannot bear to see you so! If you have indeed a burden on your heart, let me try to lighten it."

We both leaned over her.

She was quiet now. In a little time, she said in a low voice:

"I owe it to your pure friendship for me, Trotwood, to tell you, you are mistaken. If I have any secret, it is—no new one. I cannot reveal it, or divide it. It has long been mine, and must remain mine."

"Agnes! Stay! A moment!"

She was going away, but I detained her. I clasped my arm about her waist. New thoughts and hopes were whirling through my mind.

"Dearest Agnes! Whom I so devotedly love! When I came here to-day, I thought that nothing could have wrested this confession from me. But, Agnes, if I may ever call you something more than Sister, widely different from Sister!——"

Her tears fell fast; but they were not like those she had lately shed, and I saw my hope brighten in them.

"Agnes! Ever my guide, and best support! When I loved Dora—fondly, Agnes, as you know——"

"Yes!" she cried, earnestly. "I am glad to know it!"

"When I loved her—even then, my love would have been incomplete without your sympathy. And when I lost her, Agnes, what should I have been without you, still!"

Closer in my arms, nearer to my heart, her sweet eyes shining through her tears, on mine!

"I went away, dear Agnes, loving you. I stayed away, loving you. I return home, loving you!"

"I am so blest, Trotwood, but there is one thing I must say."

"Dearest, what?"

She laid her gentle hands upon my shoulders, and looked calmly into my face. "I have loved you all my life."

It was nearly dinner-time next day when we appeared before my aunt. "Goodness me!" said she, "who's this you're bringing home?"

"Agnes," said I.

As we had arranged to say nothing at first, my aunt was not a little discomfited. She darted a hopeful glance at me, but seeing that I looked as usual, she took off her spectacles in despair, and rubbed her nose with them. She greeted Agnes heartily, nevertheless; and we were soon in the lighted parlour at dinner.

"By-the-by, aunt," said I, after dinner; "I have been speaking to Agnes about what you told me."

"Then, Trot," said my aunt, turning scarlet, "you did wrong, and broke your promise."

"You are not angry, aunt, I trust? I am sure you won't be, when you learn that Agnes is not unhappy."

"Stuff and nonsense!" said my aunt.

As my aunt appeared to be annoyed, I thought the best way was to cut her annoyance short. I took Agnes in my arm to the back of her chair, and we both leaned over her. My aunt with one clap of her hands, and one look through her spectacles, immediately went into hysterics, for the first and only time in all my knowledge of her!

We were married within a fortnight. Traddles and Sophy, and Doctor and Mrs. Strong, were the only guests. We left them full of joy; and drove away together.

"Dearest husband!" said Agnes. "Now that I may call you by that name, I have one thing more to tell you."

"Let me hear it, love."

"It grows out of the night when Dora died. She sent you for me."

"She did."

"She told me that she made a last request to me, and left me a last charge."

"And it was——"

"That only I would occupy this vacant place."

CHAPTER LXIII

A VISITOR

I HAD advanced in fame and fortune. I had been married ten happy years. Agnes and I were sitting by the fire, in our house in London, one night, and three of our children were playing in the room, when I was told that a stranger wished to see me. He was an old man, my servant said, and looked like a farmer.

"Let him come in here!" said I.

There soon appeared, pausing in the dark doorway as he entered, a hale, grey-haired old man. I had not yet clearly seen his face, when my wife cried out that it was Mr. Peggotty!

It *was* Mr. Peggotty. An old man now, but in a ruddy, hearty, strong old age. When our first emotion was over, and he sat before the fire with the children on his knees, and the blaze shining on his face, he looked, to me, as vigorous and robust, withal as handsome, an old man, as ever I had seen.

"Mas'r Davy," said he. "Mas'r Davy, 'tis a joyful hour as I see you, once more, 'long with your own trew wife!"

"A joyful hour indeed, old friend!" cried I.

"And these heer pretty ones," said Mr. Peggoty. "Why, Mas'r Davy, you was but the heighth of the littlest of these, when I first see you! When Em'ly warn't no bigger, and our poor lad were *but* a lad!"

We sat him between us, not knowing how to give him welcome enough.

"It's a mort of water," said Mr. Peggotty, "fur to come across, and on'y stay a matter of fower weeks. But water ('specially when 'tis salt) comes nat'ral to me; and friends is dear, and I am heer.—Which is verse," said Mr. Peggotty, surprised to find it out, "though I hadn't such intentions."

"Are you going back those many thousand miles, so soon?" asked Agnes.

"Yes, ma'am," he returned. "I giv the promise to Em'ly. You see, it's allus been on my mind, as I must *come* and see Mas'r Davy and your own sweet blooming self, in your wedded happiness, afore I got to be too old."

He looked at us, as if he could never feast his eyes on us sufficiently.

"And now tell us," said I, "everything relating to your fortunes."

"Our fortuns, Mas'r Davy," he rejoined, "is soon told. We haven't fared nohows, but fared to thrive. What with sheep-farming and what with stock-farming, and what with one thing and what with t'other, we are as well to do, as well could be. Theer's been kiender a blessing fell upon us," said Mr. Peggotty, reverentially inclining his head, "and we've done nowt but prosper. That is, in the long run. If not yesterday, why then to-day. If not to-day, why then to-morrow."

"And Emily?" said Agnes and I, both together.

"Em'ly," said he, "arter you left her, ma'am, was that low, at first, that, if she had know'd then what Mas'r Davy kep from us so kind and thowtful, 'tis my opinion she'd have drooped away. But theer was some poor folks aboard as had illness among 'em, and she took care of *them;* and theer was the children in our company, and she took care of *them;* and then she got to be busy, and to be doing good, and that helped her. I wonder," he said thoughtfully, "if you could see my Em'ly now, Mas'r Davy, whether you'd know her!"

"Is she so altered?" I inquired.

"I doen't know, but, odd-times, I have thowt so. A slight figure," said Mr. Peggotty, looking at the fire, "kiender worn; soft, sorrowful, blue eyes; a delicate face; a pretty head, leaning a little down; a quiet voice and way—timid a'most. That's Em'ly!"

We silently observed him as he sat, still looking at the fire.

"She might have married well a mort of times, 'But uncle,' she says to me, 'that's gone for ever.' Cheerful along with me; retired when others is by; fond of going any distance fur to do some kindness; fondly loving her uncle; sowt out by all that has any trouble. That's Em'ly!"

He drew his hand across his face, and with a half-suppressed sigh looked up from the fire.

"Is Martha with you yet?" I asked.

"Martha," he replied, "got married, Mas'r Davy, in the second year. A young man, a farm-labourer, made offers fur to take her fur his wife (wives are very scarce theer). She spoke to me fur to tell him her trew story. I did. They was married, and they live fower hundred mile away from any voices but their own and the singing birds."

"Mrs. Gummidge?" I suggested.

Mr. Peggotty burst into a roar of laughter. "Would you believe it!" he said. "Why, someun even made offers fur to marry *her!* If a ship's cook that was turning settler, Mas'r Davy, didn't make offers fur to marry Missis Gummidge, I'm Gormed!"

"And what did Mrs. Gummidge say?" I asked, when I was grave enough.

"If you'll believe me," returned Mr. Peggotty, "Missis Gummidge up'd with a bucket as was standing by, and laid it over that theer ship's cook's head 'till he sung out fur help, an I went in and reskied of him."

Mr. Peggotty burst into a great roar of laughter, and Agnes and I both kept him company.

"But I must say this for the good creetur," he resumed, "she's the willingest, the trewest, the honestest-helping woman, Mas'r Davy, as ever draw'd breath of life. And thinking of the old 'un is a thing she never done, I do assure you, since she left England!"

"Now, last not least, Mr. Micawber," said I. "He has paid off every obligation he incurred here—even to Traddles's bill, you remember, my dear Agnes. But what is the latest news of him?"

Mr. Peggotty, with a smile, produced a flat-folded paper parcel, from which he took out, with much care, a little odd-looking newspaper.

"You are to understan', Mas'r Davy," said he, "as we have left the Bush now, being so well to do; and have gone right away round to Port Middlebay Harbour, wheer theer's what *we* call a town."

"Mr. Micawber was in the Bush near you?" said I.

"Bless you, yes," said Mr. Peggotty, "and turned to with a will. I've seen that theer bald head of his, a perspiring in the sun, Mas'r Davy, 'till I a'most thowt it would have melted away. And now he's a Magistrate."

Mr. Peggotty pointed to a certain paragraph in the newspaper, where I read aloud as follows:

"The public dinner to our distinguished fellow-colonist and townsman, Wilkins Micawber, Esquire, Port Middlebay District Magistrate, came off yesterday in the large room of the Hotel. The beauty, fashion, and exclusiveness of Port Middlebay, flocked to do honour to one so highly talented, and so widely popular. Doctor Mell (of Colonial Salem-House Grammer School, Port Middlebay) presided, and on his right sat the distinguished guest. After the removal of the cloth, Dr. Mell proposed 'Our distinguished Guest, the ornament of our town. May he never leave us but to better himself, and may his success among us be such as to render his bettering himself impossible!' The cheering with which the toast was received defies description. At length all was hushed, and Wilkins Micawber, Esquire, presented himself to return thanks. Far be it from us to endeavour to follow our distinguished townsman through the smoothly-flowing periods of his address! Suffice it to observe, that it was a masterpiece of eloquence. At the conclusion of the proceedings the tables were cleared as if by art-magic for dancing. Among the votaries of Terpsichore Wilkins Micawber, Esquire, Junior, and the lovely and accomplished Miss Helena, fourth daughter of Doctor Mell, were particularly remarkable."

I was looking back to the name of Doctor Mell, pleased to have discovered, in these happier circumstances, Mr. Mell, when Mr. Peggotty pointing to another part of the paper, my eyes rested on my own name, and I read thus:

"TO DAVID COPPERFIELD, ESQUIRE.
"The Eminent Author.

"My Dear Sir,

"Years have elapsed, since I had an opportunity of ocularly perusing the lineaments, now familiar to the imaginations of a considerable portion of the civilised world.

"But, my dear sir, though estranged from the personal society of the friend and companion of my youth, I have not been unmindful of his soaring flight.

"Go on, my dear Sir! You are not unknown here, you are not unappreciated. Go on, my dear Sir, in your Eagle course!

"Among the eyes elevated towards you from this portion of the globe, will ever be found, while it has light and life,

"The
"Eye
"Appertaining to
"Wilkins Micawber,
"Magistrate."

We talked much of Mr. Micawber, on many other evenings while Mr. Peggotty remained with us. He lived with us during the whole term of his stay, and his sister and my aunt came to London to see him.

Before he left, he went with me to Yarmouth, to see a little tablet I had put up in the churchyard to the memory of Ham. While I was copying the plain inscription for him at his request, I saw him stoop, and gather a tuft of grass from the grave, and a little earth.

"For Em'ly," he said, as he put it in his breast. "I promised, Mas'r Davy."

CHAPTER LXIV

A LAST RETROSPECT

And now my written story ends. I look back, once more—for the last time—before I close these leaves.

I see myself, with Agnes at my side, our children and our friends around us; and I hear the roar of many voices.

What faces are the most distinct to me in the fleeting crowd? Lo, these; all turning to me as I ask my thoughts the question!

Here is my aunt, an old woman of fourscore years and more, but upright yet, and a steady walker of six miles at a stretch in winter weather.

Always with her, here comes Peggotty, my good old nurse. Her cheeks and arms so hard and red in my childish days, when I wondered why the birds didn't peck her in preference to apples, are shrivelled now; but her rough forefinger is just the same, and when I see my least child catching at it as it totters from my aunt to her, I think of our little parlour at home, when I could scarcely walk. My aunt's old disappointment is set right, now. She is godmother to a real living Betsey Trotwood; and Dora (the next in order) says she spoils her.

Among my boys, this summer holiday time, I see an old man making giant kites, and gazing at them in the air, with a delight for which there are no words. He greets me rapturously, and whispers, with many nods and winks, "Trotwood, you will be glad to hear that I shall finish the Memorial when I have nothing else to do, and that your aunt's the most extraordinary woman in the world, Sir!"

Who is this bent lady showing me a countenance in which are some traces of old pride and beauty? She is in a garden; and near her stands a sharp, dark, withered woman, with a white scar on her lip. Let me hear what they say.

"Rosa, I have forgotten this gentleman's name."

Rosa, bends over her, and calls to her, "Mr. Copperfield."

"You have seen my son, Sir," says the elder lady. "Are you reconciled?"

Looking fixedly at me, she cries, in a terrible voice, "Rosa, come to me. He is dead!" Rosa kneeling at her feet, by turns caresses her, and quarrels with her; now fiercely telling her, "I loved him better than you ever did!"—now soothing her to sleep on her breast, like a sick child. Thus I leave them; thus I always find them; thus they wear their time away, from year to year.

And lo, the Doctor, always our good friend, labouring at his Dictionary (somewhere about the letter D), and happy in his home and wife. Also the Old Soldier, on a considerably reduced footing, and by no means so influential as in days of yore!

Working at his chambers in the Temple, with a busy aspect, and his hair (where he is not bald) made more rebellious than ever by the constant friction of his lawyer's wig, I come, in a later time, upon my dear old Traddles.

I am going to have a family dinner with Traddles. It is Sophy's birthday; and, on our road, Traddles discourses to me of the good fortune he has enjoyed.

"I really have been able, my dear Copperfield, to do all that I had most at heart. There's the Reverend Horace promoted; there are our two boys receiving the very best education; there are three of the girls married very comfortably; there are three more living with us; there are three more keeping house for the Reverend Horace since Mrs. Crewler's decease; and all of them happy."

"Except——" I suggest.

"Except the Beauty," says Traddles. "Yes. It was very unfortunate that she should marry such a vagabond. However, now we have got her safe at our house, and got rid of him, we must cheer her up again."

Traddles's house is large, but he keep his papers in his dressing-room, and his boots with his papers; and he and Sophy squeeze themselves into upper rooms; for more of "the girls" are here, and always are here, by some accident or other, than I know how to count. Traddles, exactly the same simple, unaffected fellow as he ever was, sits at the foot of the large table like a Patriarch; and Sophy beams upon him, from the head, across a cheerful space that is certainly not glittering with Britannia metal.

And now, as I close my task, these faces fade away. But, one face, shining on me like a heavenly light, remains.

O Agnes, O my soul, so may thy face be by me when I close my life indeed; so may I still find thee near me, pointing upward!

THE END